Dilly's Hope

Dilly's Hope

Rosie Goodwin

corsair

CORSAIR

First published in Great Britain in 2016 by Corsair

13 5 7 9 10 8 6 4 2

ISBN: 978-1-4721-1785-4 (eBook)
ISBN: 978-1-4721-1756-4 (Hardback)

Typeset in Palatino by SX Composing DTP, Rayleigh, Essex
Printed and bound by CPI Group (UK) Ltd, Croydon, CR0 4YY

Papers used by Corsair are from well-managed forests
and other responsible sources

MIX
Paper from
responsible sources
FSC
www.fsc.org   FSC® C104740

Corsair
An imprint of
Little, Brown Book Group
Carmelite House
50 Victoria Embankment
London EC4Y 0DZ

An Hachette UK Company
www.hachette.co.uk

www.littlebrown.co.uk

For Nikki, Daniel, Charlotte, Jack, Layla and Tyler.
'You are my sunshine'
x x x x x x

Chapter One

Changing Times
Nuneaton, May 1926

'Whatever are you doing, Dilly?'

Glancing up from the basket she was in the process of filling, Dilly saw Max Farthing standing in the open kitchen doorway.

'I'm just putting a basket of food together for the people of the courtyard where Nell and I used to live,' she explained as she placed a cabbage in the basket. 'Nell visited them the other day and with the miners' strike some of them can't afford to eat, let alone pay the rent.'

'Hmm, it must be very grim for them,' Max agreed. 'And it will only get worse if the strike goes on for any length of time. What you're doing is a very kind gesture but I fear it won't sustain them for long.'

'Well, as they say, "every little helps",' Dilly replied.

Some years before, Dilly had lived side by side with the people she was trying to help but now she was a successful

businesswoman who owned a string of dress shops –
Dilly's Designs – that were doing very well indeed. Max
found it endearing that she could still concern herself with
those who were not so well-off as herself. Not that it
surprised him. Dilly had a heart of pure gold and always
went out of her way to help people, which was just one of
the things he loved about her.

Nell, her one-time neighbour who now shared the fine
house Dilly had purchased in St Edward's Road, entered
the kitchen then and she smiled a greeting at Max. He was
a regular visitor and they were all at ease with each other.

'Bad do, ain't it, this strike?' Nell remarked with a sigh.
'An' there but fer the grace o' God would go I, if it weren't
for our Dilly 'ere.'

'Rubbish,' Dilly chided. 'I don't know what I'd do
without you, pet.' Nell flushed at the praise as Dilly then
commented, 'And you're looking very smart today.'

Nell self-consciously ran her hands down the sides of
the black skirt Dilly's seamstresses had made for her. With
it she was wearing a crisp white cotton blouse; she liked to
look neat when she was going to work in Dilly's Nuneaton
dress shop, but it hadn't always been that way. Once upon
a time Nell could only have been described as slatternly –
but Dilly had changed all that. She'd changed Nell's whole
life, in fact, and the woman would have walked through
fire for her if need be. Their friendship stretched back
many years, and at one time it had been Nell who had
helped Dilly through the most difficult period of her whole
life.

When Dilly's family were young, her husband Fergal
had been crippled in a terrible accident at work on the
railways, and for a while, Dilly had feared that she would
have to place her children in the workhouse. But Nell had
helped in any way she could until a terrible solution was

found. In 1900, Dilly had given her newborn daughter to Max's wife, Camilla, following the death of Camilla's own little daughter, Violet, in exchange for a sum of money, which she had used to get her remaining children safely over to their grandparents in Ireland. In addition Dilly had been given a permanent full-time position as a maid in Max's home, Mill House, which had enabled her to earn enough money to get the family back on their feet and eventually fetch the children home again. Dilly had worked tirelessly to keep her family together, and she had made a grand job of it.

Max had marvelled at the way Dilly had coped with seeing another woman bring up little Olivia, with never a word of complaint, and over the years his esteem of her had grown. Sadly, Dilly's decision to give up her baby daughter had had disastrous consequences. Both Dilly and Max had suffered because of their deception to Olivia, but neither felt that they could admit to her true parentage because of the oath Dilly had made to Camilla. Even now, when Camilla was incarcerated in Hatter's Hall, the local mental asylum on the outskirts of the town, Dilly couldn't bring herself to break her promise – and Max doubted that she ever would. Dilly Carey was a woman of her word.

'Right then, if you're goin' to take those round to the courtyard I'll go an' open the shop, shall I?' Nell said, after checking her hair in the mirror. She'd been helping Dilly in the shop for some time now and it seemed to have given her a new lease of life and made her take pride in her appearance again.

'I'd be very grateful if you would,' Dilly answered, lifting and testing the weight of the basket.

Nell took the shop keys from the hook above the sink and with a smile at them both she left, as Max told Dilly, 'Here, I'll carry that for you. I walked this morning so I'm

3

going back that way anyway. It'll give us a chance to talk.'

'What about?' Dilly enquired curiously as she shrugged her slim arms into the sleeves of her coat.

'Well, I was wondering if you'd reached a decision about taking on the lease of that shop in London.' Max hoisted the heavy basket and followed Dilly outside, waiting patiently while she locked the door before falling into step with him.

She shrugged. 'I'm not sure what to do, to be honest, what with the current situation. The sales in my other shops are down already and if the Strike goes on I can only imagine things will get worse – although Philip assures me that my designs are continuing to sell well in his shops.'

'Ah, but Philip Maddison caters to a different clientele in London,' Max pointed out. 'Most of his customers are wealthy and the strike won't really affect them.'

'You could be right, which is why I've been toying with an idea,' Dilly told him. 'As you know, I already sell a broad range of clothes varying in price, and the bridal shops are still doing good business, but I wondered if I shouldn't introduce a new budget range of clothing. What do you think?'

Max pursed his lips as they strode along, deep in thought, but finally answered, 'It does sound plausible, but how would you afford to do it? You still have to pay the seamstresses and the shops' overheads.'

'I know that, but if I bought slightly cheaper material, that would reduce the cost of the clothes at a stroke. I'd be aiming the range at the working classes.'

'Then I suppose it's worth a try.'

Dilly changed the subject then. 'And how is my favourite little girl this morning?' she asked with a grin. 'Was she up when you left the house?'

'She certainly was.' Max knew exactly who Dilly was

4

referring to: Olivia's four-year-old daughter, Jessica, who was their mutual granddaughter. 'And as usual she had everyone running around after her. I'm telling you, that little minx has the entire household wrapped around her little finger.'

Dilly chuckled, thankful that Max had accepted the child despite the fact that she was illegitimate.

Soon they were at the entrance to the courtyard and Max handed Dilly the basket asking, 'What on earth have you got in there – house bricks?'

'Just some slices of pork and some vegetables, but it's hardly going to be enough to fill all their bellies, is it?'

'Here.' Max opened her hand and dropped some silver coins into it. 'Share them out as well for me, would you?'

She smiled at him, remembering a time when she had been hungry and thinking how grateful she would have been.

'Thanks, Max, that should get them all another meal each at least. I've had a word with the Salvation Army. They're thinking of setting up a soup kitchen if the Strike goes on, so at least then everyone will get at least one hot meal a day. But let's hope it won't come to that, eh?'

'I'm rather afraid it will,' Max replied solemnly. 'The General Council of the Trades Union Congress has voted to back the miners after the breakdown of their negotiations so this could be a long and bitter battle. But you go ahead and deliver those things now and I must get off to work. Lawrence will think I've disappeared. Will you be coming around to the house later?'

'Of course I will – it's Thursday, isn't it? Oscar will be bringing George to play with Jessica and you know I love to see them together. I think Patty might be bringing William too. Goodbye for now, Max.' With that she swung about and headed for the entrance to the courtyard.

5

Max watched her go. With the sun shining on her copper hair, which was showing only the slightest hints of grey, Dilly looked nothing like a woman who was fast approaching her fiftieth birthday. But then she had always been attractive as far as he was concerned. When she finally disappeared from view, Max turned and headed towards his mill in Attleborough. His son, Lawrence, and the father to his three-year-old grandson, William, was also his right-hand man and had teased him the day before saying that he was developing a middle-age spread . . . so Max had decided that a walk would do him good.

Chapter Two

'They're as close as two peas in a pod those two, ain't they?' Mrs Pegs, Max's cook, commented to Dilly. The kindly woman had just taken Jessica and George some home-made jam tarts and a glass of milk each for their mid-afternoon snack and now she and Dilly had settled down in the kitchen to enjoy a cup of tea while Gwen, the young maid, prepared the vegetables for the evening meal.

'I'm rather afraid they are.' Dilly and Mrs Pegs exchanged a look and without a word being said they each knew what the other was thinking. It was like watching Olivia and Max's son Oscar at that age all over again, and both women hoped that there wasn't more heartache ahead. Olivia and Max had fallen in love – a love that was taboo, since they believed they were blood-related, brother and sister. But because of Dilly's oath to Camilla, no one would tell them the truth.

'Have you heard from the family in Ireland lately?' Mrs

Pegs asked then, keen to change the subject as she took a noisy slurp of her tea.

'Yes, I have. As a matter of fact, a letter came this morning. I'm afraid Daniel still isn't too well. He can't seem to shake off the cold he caught in the winter, by all accounts. Still, on the bright side, Roisin tells me that they're all taking very good care of him. I intend to go over for a short visit as soon as I can spare the time. Between you and me he's never been the same since Maeve died. Those two were inseparable and I think he still misses her terribly, bless him. Roisin also told me that Roddy is growing like a weed. I wonder what Bessie will think when she next sees him?'

'I had a letter from Bessie only last week,' Mrs Pegs told her. 'She's almost completed her nurse's trainin' now, an' then she's comin' back to Nuneaton and hopes to get a job at the Weddington Hall Hospital. I reckon she'll use some o' the money her husband left her to buy herself a little place then.'

'Hmm, I wonder if she'll want Roddy back when she does return?' Dilly mused worriedly. 'I think it would break Declan and Roisin's hearts to part with the little chap now. Roisin had another miscarriage recently – that's six in all, poor soul – and she and Declan look on Roddy as their own now.'

'Huh! I reckon there's little chance o' Bessie wantin' him back,' Mrs Pegs snorted. 'You an' I both know she never took to the poor little chap. He's a million times better off where he is than wi' his real mother, but then I don't want to be too harsh on the girl. She didn't ask to be raped an' end up pregnant, did she? Talkin' o' which . . .' She lowered her voice at that point and glanced towards the door. 'Do yer happen to know if the master's heard from that no-good son o' his?'

8

'Not a dickey bird as far as I'm aware – and we can only hope that it stays that way. Life around these parts has been so much more peaceful without Master Samuel Farthing about. He has a lot to answer for.'

Dilly remembered the terrible shame he had brought down on her own daughter, Niamh, after he had raped her as well as Bessie, also leaving her with child. Admittedly, Max had forced him to do the right thing by marrying her, and the result of the rape had been Constance – a beautiful little girl who had sadly died when she was two years old. From then on, the farce of a marriage had gone from bad to worse and when Bessie, Max's former maid, had reappeared and disclosed that Roddy, her young son, was also the result of her being raped by Samuel, Niamh had refused to have anything more to do with him. Now she was happily living in New York with Ben, the love of her life, but it hurt Dilly to think that she was still legally tied to Samuel. Niamh and Ben had been meant for each other and it seemed a shame that they were forced to live in sin.

'As well as going to Ireland, I'd also like to go and see Niamh and Ben in New York,' she confided to Mrs Pegs. 'I've never even set eyes on James, my grandson, and he's almost two years old now. And I've also got to find time to visit Kian's grave in France.'

'So why don't yer just do it instead o' keep harpin' on about it?' Mrs Pegs said bluntly.

'Because now I have the other three shops I never seem to find the time.' Dilly sipped at her tea as she gazed from the window. Primroses were peeping from beneath the hedge and tender green leaves were just beginning to sprout on the trees.

'Six shops, eh?' Mrs Pegs whistled out a breath. 'Who'd ever have thought it, eh, lass? It don't seem so long ago since you were workin' here as a maid wi' not two pennies

9

to rub together. You've worked damned hard to get where you are. The only thing I'd say is, don't go puttin' the businesses afore things you'd like to do. Life is passin' by an' one day you might regret it if you do. Your Seamus is more than capable o' keepin' things goin' while you're away – so think on it.'

Dilly knew that Mrs Pegs was right and a stab of guilt pierced through her. But if and when she decided to go, where would she go first? She knew that she would never forgive herself if anything happened to her father-in-law before she'd seen him for one last time. Daniel and Maeve his late wife had been very good to her over the years. Then there was Niamh and little James. It hurt to have a grandson she had never even met, although Niamh always sounded happy in the letters she wrote. She now had her own small art gallery in Manhattan and appeared to be doing very well. It came as no surprise to Dilly. Niamh had always had a talent for painting and now it appeared she was actually making a living from the pictures she sold.

Finally, Dilly's thoughts turned to the lonely grave in France where her beloved son Kian was buried after being killed in the war. Every year she promised herself she would visit it to say her last goodbyes, but somehow she had never seemed to spare the time. Perhaps Mrs Pegs was right? On top of everything else, Philip Maddison was badgering her to visit him in London. She'd long thought of opening a shop there too, since the designs she did for Philip were selling like hot cakes in the capital, but again she never seemed to get around to it . . .

Just then, the door leading into the hallway burst open and Jessica and George raced in, closely followed by Olivia and Oscar.

'I'm afraid they've come to try and con you out of some

more of your delicious jam tarts,' Oscar warned the cook with a grin. 'There'll be hell to pay from his mother though, if he doesn't eat all his dinner tonight.'

'Huh, a bit o' spoilin' never hurt anyone,' Mrs Pegs responded indulgently as she loaded some more jam tarts into the two tiny pairs of waiting hands. 'An' what his ma don't see won't hurt her, will it, George?' She winked at him conspiratorially and he giggled with delight as she affectionately ruffled his fair curls. 'He looks so like you did at his age,' Mrs Pegs said to Oscar, sighing nostalgically. 'It make me wonder where all the years have gone.'

Jessica meanwhile had clambered up on to Dilly's lap and Dilly promptly planted a kiss on her springy copper curls. Jessica had jam smeared all around her mouth and on the end of her nose, and Dilly thought she looked delightful.

'Mrs Pegs here was just saying that she thinks it's time I got round to paying a visit to Ireland,' Dilly told Olivia and Oscar. 'And I also think I should make plans to get to New York and France.'

'I thoroughly agree,' Olivia said instantly. 'Seamus and Mary are more than capable of holding the fort while you're away and a break would do you good. You're always working.'

'They're more than capable of keeping the shops supplied,' Dilly readily admitted, 'but what about my designs for Philip in London?'

'Now don't get looking for problems,' Olivia scolded gently. 'I'm sure Philip has enough to keep him going for a while. You're always sketching, and anyway, he'd be the first to say you work too hard.'

'Hmm . . .' The thought of a break was very tempting, Dilly had to admit.

'Why don't you telephone Declan in Ireland right now and tell him that you're coming while you're in the mood?' Olivia encouraged. 'I know what you're like. You'll go home, get sketching again and postpone it once more. Go on – ring him. Daddy won't mind you using his telephone.'

Dilly lifted Jessica on to the floor and headed for the telephone on the hall table before she could change her mind. Luckily she knew the number off by heart and Roisin answered it almost immediately.

'I've decided it's time I paid you all a visit,' Dilly told her and Roisin was delighted.

'Wonderful! When will you be coming? It'll do Daniel a power of good to see you, so it will.'

'I'm going to try and book the ferry for tomorrow,' Dilly promised and after chatting for a few more minutes she went back to the kitchen with a spring in her step.

When she got home later and told Nell of her plans, her friend was pleased too. 'You've been lookin' tired lately an' a break away will breathe new life into yer. Just stay as long as yer like, luvvie. Me, Seamus an' Mary are more than able to keep things runnin' smoothly 'ere.'

And so after ringing Philip Maddison, the designer who sold her designs in London and telling him of her plans she hastily packed a small case and prepared for leaving the very next day. There was no time like the present, and Dilly knew that if she didn't go now she'd only find an excuse to postpone the visit – yet again.

Max ran her to the station the next morning and insisted on carrying her case on to the platform for her although it wasn't heavy and contained only the basic essentials.

'I feel almost envious,' he told her as they stood together

12

waiting for the train to arrive. 'I could do with a little break myself.'

As Dilly glanced at him she saw that he looked tired, and a little shiver of fear ran through her. Max was an important part of her life and she didn't like to think what she would do without him. For years he had been her friend, her confidant and her rock.

'So why don't you arrange to take a little time off and have a short holiday, then?' she said. 'If I can do it, so can you.'

He laughed. 'Oh? And where would I go? It's different for you. You're going to visit family but I don't think it would be much fun on my own.'

'So take Olivia and Jessica away with you. I'm sure Jessica would love a few days at the seaside.'

He chewed thoughtfully on his lip for a moment before saying, 'You could be right there. I might ask Olivia how she feels about the idea this evening. It's been a few years now since I've wielded a bucket and spade but I suppose it's a bit like riding a bicycle. Once you've learned you never forget.'

'Oh, get away with you,' Dilly grinned but then their attention was distracted by the sound of the train approaching. 'Here we are then,' she said, trying to ignore the look of sadness that had settled on his face.

'Any idea how long you might be staying?'

'Not long,' she assured him. 'I've only packed enough clothes for a few days.' She was missing him already although her journey hadn't even begun and she could see that he felt the same.

He lifted the case into the carriage for her and she pulled on the brown leather strap to let down the window.

'Ring me and tell me when you're coming back,' he said, 'and I'll be here to meet you.'

13

She nodded, but then there was a hiss of steam and the train began to move, so after a hasty wave she closed the window. By the time she had placed her case on the overhead luggage rack and settled herself, Nuneaton station was already far behind her.

Chapter Three

As the ferry pulled into the dock in Dublin later that evening, Dilly hung on to her hat and peered across the rail for a sight of someone familiar. She spotted Declan and her heart did a little skip. Her son was so tall and handsome – a strapping man now – and she wondered where all the years had gone. It seemed only yesterday he had been a little boy.

'*Mammy!*'

As Dilly reached the end of the gangplank, Declan picked her up and whirled her around, his face alight with pleasure.

Dilly laughed and scolded playfully, 'Will you please put me down! People are looking.'

'Let them look.' Declan planted her back on her feet and grasping her case with one hand he then hustled her through the crowd on the quayside to the waiting pony and trap.

'Up we go then!' And after throwing her case into the

back, again lifted her effortlessly and plonked her up on the wooden bench-seat of the cart. 'Right – we're off then,' he said when he'd climbed up beside her and taken up the reins. 'Giddy up there, boy.' The horse instantly obeyed him and Declan steered him expertly towards the road that would take them out of Dublin.

'So how is everyone?' Dilly enquired, still hanging on to her hat. A wind had blown up and the sky looked full of rain if she wasn't very much mistaken.

'All well, apart from Granda.' Declan was suddenly serious. 'If anything, that bad chest cold he had has gotten worse. Roisin had the doctor out to him again yesterday but apart from a tonic, which Granda refuses to take as it tastes vile, there doesn't seem to be much he can do for him. We're keeping him warm and getting lots of drinks down him, but he isn't himself – but then he hasn't been since we lost Gran'ma. We're all hoping your visit will perk him up a little, Mammy.'

At that moment, the first spots of rain began to fall and reaching into the back of the cart with one hand and expertly steering the horse with the other, Declan pulled a tarpaulin over the seat, telling his mother, 'Put that over your head. It'll go some way towards keeping you dry. It would be a shame to get that smart outfit you're wearing wet, so it would.'

Dilly did as she was told and was soon glad that she had, for suddenly the heavens seemed to open and the rain began to come down in torrents.

Declan was soaked through in seconds, but seeing the worried look on his mother's face he laughed, 'Don't be frettin' about me now. I'm used to workin' out in all weathers an' a little bit o' rain never hurt no one.'

Giving up all attempts at conversation, Dilly huddled under the tarpaulin as best she could, and somewhere along the way the clip-clop of the horse's hooves soothed her and she drifted off to sleep with her head resting on Declan's shoulder.

'Here we are then.' Her son's voice jolted Dilly awake and she blinked in surprise when she found that they were in the farmyard.

'You go in now,' he urged. 'I'll bring your case in when I've got the horse stabled and rubbed down.'

Only too glad to get out of the rain, Dilly did as she was told, and after a dash through the madly squawking chickens she opened the kitchen door.

'Dilly!' Roisin raced towards her, closely followed by Roddy as Dilly looked guiltily down at the puddle of water that was forming on the quarry tiles beneath her feet.

'Aw, don't be worryin' about that now.' Roisin flapped her hand airily. 'Just kick those wet shoes off an' come over by the fire for a warm. I'll away an' get you a nice hot cup of tea. The kettle's singing so it shouldn't take more than a minute or two.'

Dilly gratefully did as she was told, glancing towards the bed by the far wall. Daniel was tucked up in it but he appeared to be fast asleep.

She was warming her hands by the fire when the door burst open and Roddy erupted into the room, closely followed by Patrick.

'Hello, Dilly.'

Dilly stared at Roddy in amazement as he skidded to a halt in front of her.

'Why, look at you!' she gasped as she opened her arms. It was only just over a year since she'd last seen him but he appeared to have had a growth-spurt. He went into her arms willingly and she gave him a loving cuddle. He seemed to grow more like his father, Samuel Farthing,

17

each day, in looks at least, she thought. The resemblance had given her a shock. Thankfully he was completely different in nature. There was no sign now of the skinny, nervous little boy called Roderick whom Bessie had once presented to the Farthing family. Roddy was now nine years old and a sturdy little chap with rosy cheeks from the many hours he spent outside. He was tall for his age too – almost as tall as Patrick, who was smiling at Dilly shyly.

'How you've grown,' she said admiringly when she eventually held Roddy at arm's length. 'And how handsome you are. I think you're going to break a few young girls' hearts, my lad.'

Roddy screwed his face up in disgust. He was coming to the age when he found girls to be a pain, apart from Bridie that was, whom he absolutely worshipped. According to Roisin's letters, Bridie loved him too and followed him about like a little puppy dog.

'And you've shot up too,' Dilly said, addressing Patrick, who instantly blushed to the roots of his hair. She hugged him and ruffled his hair.

Roisin chuckled as she carried a hot mug of tea over to Dilly. 'Patrick is a bit shy nowadays,' she told her with a grin as she placed a loving arm about his shoulders.

'Roisin . . . is that you, lass?'

The conversation was interrupted by the voice that came from the bed, and Dilly saw her father-in-law emerge from beneath the blankets. Instantly she placed her cup down and advanced on him, a wide smile on her face. But then as she neared the bed and she got a better look at him, it was all she could do to keep the smile in place.

'What's this I've been hearing then about you not being well?' she asked gently as she leaned over to kiss him.

'Why, if it ain't our Dilly!' Daniel's wrinkled old face lit up at the sight of her. 'Roisin told me you were coming, so she did, but I wasn't sure you'd make it, knowing how busy you are.'

'Wild horses wouldn't have kept me away. It's been far too long and I apologise for that. I should have come sooner.'

'Get away with you, woman. But now come and sit by me and tell me all that's going on back in Nuneaton. You've six shops in all now – is that right?'

'It is that.' Dilly nodded. 'And I've also got a small factory in Coton now where I employ a number of seamstresses to keep the shops supplied with garments that I've designed.'

'You've done well, lass, an' you deserve to; you've certainly worked hard enough. My Maeve would have been right proud of you, so she would.'

Hearing the catch in his voice, Dilly patted his hand. He was clearly still missing his wife dreadfully, but then they all were. The farm just didn't feel the same without her.

'And have you heard from Niamh lately?' he asked then.

'Oh yes, she writes regularly. Little James is two now and a right handful according to what she says in her letters. But then they do call it the "terrible twos", don't they? They seem to be into everything at that age. Between you and me, I think she and Ben would love a little brother or sister for him but it just hasn't happened for them yet – although I've no doubt it will. They're both young and healthy.' Suddenly realising what she had said in front of Roisin she wished she could bite her tongue off. After all the miscarriages the poor girl had suffered she must think she was heartless – but thankfully, sensing her discomfort, Roisin immediately reassured her.

'It's all right,' she said. 'Me an' Declan haven't given up

19

hope yet, not by a long shot. The doctor reckons it will happen in time so we've just to be patient.' As she spoke, she beamed affectionately at Roddy, and Dilly saw just how much she loved him – far more than his natural mother Bessie ever had. The boy seemed to be filling the hole that all the lost babies had left – and he looked so content.

'Now,' Roisin said, 'I've kept you some cottage pie warm in the oven. Come and have it before it all dries up. You must be hungry after your long journey and tired too, no doubt. There'll be time to catch up on all the gossip tomorrow when you've had a good night's sleep.'

'Is there enough left for me too?' Roddy asked hopefully and Roisin gently cuffed his ear, telling him firmly, 'No, there is not, me laddo. You ate enough for two at dinner and it's way past your bedtime. I only let you stay up to say hello to Dilly, but you can take yourself off home now and have a wash. And that means behind your ears as well, so don't try getting away with it because I shall check them when I come to tuck you in, so I shall.'

'Aw!' Roddy pugged but his eyes were smiling as he turned and headed for the door.

'He looks so well,' Dilly commented when the boys had left.

'I can't imagine our life without him now,' Roisin said quietly as she carried Dilly's meal to the table. 'But have you heard from his mother lately?' She lived in dread that Bessie would have a change of heart and want Roddy to go home to her, but on that score Dilly was able to put her mind at ease – for now at least.

'There was no mention of it in her last letter, although she did say that she's almost completed her nurse's training now.' Dilly settled herself at the table and lifted her knife and fork, suddenly realising how hungry she was. It had been a long time since breakfast. 'She's planning on coming back to Nuneaton by all accounts and hoping to get a job with Olivia at Weddington Hall Hospital.'

'I see. And how is Olivia and the baby?'

'Oh wonderful – although Jessica isn't a baby now. She's four years old and looking forward to going to school next year.'

'And is everything all right between Olivia and Mr Farthing?'

Dilly swallowed a mouthful of the tasty cottage pie before answering, 'Yes, fine. I think Max felt it initially – the fact that Jessica was illegitimate, I mean – but he accepted it eventually and he adores her now. George is making a lovely little boy too. He and Jessica are inseparable – when Penelope lets him out of her sight, that is.'

'Oh dear. Still a sourpuss, is she?'

Dilly nodded. 'I'm afraid so. She makes poor Oscar's life hell, but then I don't suppose it's all one-sided. I think she genuinely loved him when they got married, but once she realised that her love wasn't reciprocated, she turned bitter. If it wasn't for George I think Oscar would leave her, but he's such a good father and he and Lawrence are invaluable to Max now. They're both so efficient and keep Max's businesses running like clockwork.'

'Has he retired then?'

'Oh no, but I think he's letting his sons play more of a role lately to prepare for the time when he does. He's decided to leave the businesses to them jointly rather than to the eldest. It's a more modern approach, don't you think?'

'I suppose it is,' Roisin agreed. 'But what about Olivia and Samuel?'

'I've no doubt Max will make sure that Olivia is very well provided for. As for Samuel . . . well, we don't even

21

know where he is, and between you and me I hope it stays that way. He's caused his father nothing but grief, and were he to inherit anything I'm sure he'd gamble it away in no time.'

Shelagh arrived then, bearing an apple pie fresh from the oven, and after they had greeted each other Dilly finished her meal before joining the women for another welcome cup of tea. Liam was out in the fields checking on the newborn lambs and helping the ewes that were about to give birth, and Declan had gone to join him so Dilly doubted very much whether she would see either of them that evening.

'You must all miss Ben helping about the place,' she said after a time and Shelagh and Roisin nodded in unison.

'We do that, but then he deserved to be happy, so he did, an' if his letters are anything to go by he and Niamh are very happy. He informs me that she's making quite a name for herself as an artist now,' Shelagh answered.

'She certainly is.' Dilly's chest swelled with pride. 'Ben's mother leased her a small studio in Manhattan somewhere apparently and as word has spread about her work she's always busy with commissions for portraits now, although I do know she prefers to do landscapes.'

She looked at the small painting that Niamh had once done of the farmhouse for her Gran'ma. Maeve had loved it and it still hung in pride of place on the wall above Daniel's bed. He was fast asleep again and Dilly lowered her voice to ask, 'Does he sleep a lot nowadays?'

Roisin sighed with worry as she looked towards him. 'Yes, he does, God bless his soul. Me and Shelagh both spend as much of our time as we possibly can in here with him, but I fear he must get lonely. We've both asked him to move into our places with us. It would make things so much easier, to be sure, but he's a stubborn old devil. He says this is the home he shared with his Maeve an' he'll not leave it till they carry him out feet first in a box!'

'I think I can understand that,' Dilly replied, stifling a yawn, and seeing how tired she was Shelagh rose and began to clear away the teacups.

'I think it's time you turned in,' she told her, much as she would one of the children. 'Get yourself up to bed now. Me an' Shelagh will see to things down here an' make sure that Daddy has all he needs.'

'I think I will, if you're sure you don't mind.' Dilly was having trouble keeping her eyes open now, so after kissing both of the women soundly on their cheeks she made her way upstairs to the room that had become hers over the years. There were clean crisp sheets on the bed and after washing in the bowl on the nightstand and changing into her nightgown she tumbled gratefully under the covers. All that could be heard was the sound of the cattle lowing and the pigs snuffling about their styes and she sighed with contentment. It was so peaceful here and she could well understand why Daniel loved his home so very much. She thought briefly of Max and Jessica who she was missing already, but then sleep claimed her . . . and soon she was snoring gently.

Chapter Four

'You're telling me this is all you have to show after being on the streets all night?' Samuel Farthing threw the coins the young woman held out to him against the wall in disgust. 'The docks are *teeming* with sailors – surely you've earned more than that?'

'I ain't, 'onestly, Samuel,' the girl whimpered, cowering away from him. Sometimes she hardly recognised him any more. When they'd first met, Samuel had owned his own tattoo parlour in Plymouth and she'd thought him rich and charming. He'd certainly known how to show a girl a good time and she'd been sure that she'd fallen on her feet – but it hadn't lasted for long. Within no time the parlour had been closed down. The tattooist, a man named Ted Fellows, had been rather lax with his hygiene standards and after numerous complaints from clients who had suffered severe infections from unsterilised needles, Samuel had been forced to close the shop. It was either that or risk being beaten to a pulp.

Even then, Kitty had still been smitten with her Sammy. Brought up in the back streets of Plymouth, she had known nothing but cruelty from her drunken father. Samuel had appeared like her knight in shining armour, promising her a better life and saying that he was going to take her away from all that. However, after his regular income from the shop had dried up they had been forced to do a moonlight flit from the smart house he'd been renting, and now they were stuck here in a filthy little tenement where they lived in just one room and shared an outside privy with seven other families.

It had been one evening when they didn't even have the price of a meal between them that Samuel had suggested she might *'be nice'* to one of his friends. Kitty knew all too well what being nice meant. She had often walked the streets for her father, turning up the money she had earned to him at the end of each evening, receiving a beating if he didn't consider she had been 'nice' enough. But things would be different with Samuel, she told herself. This would only go on until they had enough money saved to start again. And so Samuel would show one of his so-called friends into the room, leaving Kitty to entertain them. Then the weather had turned cold and he expected her to walk the streets and find her own 'friends'. She did it because she loved him and because he was the only man who had ever been kind to her, but all that was changing now and it worried her. On a few occasions lately she had returned to their room, cold, hungry and completely demoralised to find Samuel roaring drunk and she'd known that he'd used the money she'd earned to buy it. Worse still, when she'd tackled him about it he'd become aggressive – and one night he'd beaten her so badly that she'd been unable to go out for days. Yet still she loved him, for each time he'd be full of regrets when he sobered up. *Of course he'll change*, she tried to convince herself. Kitty was just eighteen years old – and where would she go if she left him?

'Where are you going?' she asked in a panic as she saw him putting his coat on.

'Out!' he told her abruptly, gathering up the coins he'd recently flung away in disgust. He supposed anything was better than nothing.

'H-how long will you be?'

'As long as it takes.' He glared at her before leaving the room, slamming the door so loudly behind him that it danced on its hinges.

'Keep that bleedin' racket down, can't yer?' a voice screeched through the thin wall. 'You've woke the bleedin' baby up now, yer noisy buggers!'

Kitty sank on to the edge of the thin mattress as tears pricked at the back of her eyes. Samuel had gone out a few times lately at night and she was worried that he might be seeing another woman. After all, he was devastatingly handsome and she knew that she was lucky he gave her the time of day. Curling herself into a tight ball, she willed sleep to claim her. At least while she was asleep she didn't feel hungry.

Once outside, Samuel shoved his hands deep into his pockets and hurried through the maze of back streets. Unknown to Kitty there were another two girls working for him and it was time for them to cough up what they had earned. They always seemed to do better than Kitty, but that was probably because they knew that the more they earned, the more opium he would supply them with. Silly cows! he thought. If they had half a brain between them they'd be able to source it for themselves, it wasn't that difficult – but they were reliant on him now and what they handed over always far outweighed what the drugs cost him.

The further he ventured into the back streets the closer together the houses became until he felt as if he was walking through a narrow tunnel. Some of the houses had rags pinned across the windows; the glass was long gone but those who lived there couldn't afford to replace it. Most people shunned this area at night. It was a den of thieves, but Samuel was well-known thereabouts now and most allowed him to pass without a second glance.

Eventually he came to a tall terraced house and stepped into the hallway through the opening where a door had once hung. The smell of stale urine was overpowering here but Samuel was used to it and he took the narrow staircase two steps at a time. At the top of the house he paused outside a door before pushing it open. The whole room was in darkness but he could see a shape lying on the metal bed shoved against one wall.

'Is that you, Samuel?' A strained voice reached him through the darkness, and feeling in the gloom for the table in the middle of the room, he approached it, struck a match and lit the oil lamp that stood on it. Electricity had not reached this slum area yet.

As the flickering glow chased the shadows away, the young woman lying on the bed held her hand out imploringly. ''Ave yer got me stuff?' she whimpered.

He saw at a glance that she was in a cold sweat and her lips and fingernails had a bluish tinge to them. A pile of rags on the box that passed as a bedside table were thick with pink frothy sputum. His lips curled in contempt. She was having withdrawals from her opium addiction and he knew that she would have sold her very soul to the devil at that moment for what he had in his pocket. Carol Wallis was just twenty-one years old but with her sunken eyes and lank hair she could have been taken for at least double that age.

'I've got it,' he growled. 'But first of all, how much have you got for *me*?'

'I had a good couple o' nights but couldn't go out tonight 'cos I've got the shakes. It puts the punters off, see?' She fumbled beneath her pillow as the sweat stood out on her brow, and when she placed some money in his hand he shrank away from the cold clammy feel of her skin. After hastily counting it he slid the cash into his pocket and withdrew a small packet of white powder which he tossed on to the filthy bed.

She pounced on it as a child might pounce upon sweeties, and he averted his eyes as he asked, 'And where's Katie?'

'Out workin',' she answered, clutching the little bag to her. 'She got a hidin' off a sailor that turned nasty the other night an' she couldn't go out fer a couple o' nights after that. I reckon he broke one of 'er ribs.'

'Well, she knows the rules,' he answered coldly. 'No money, no chillum.'

At that moment they heard the sound of someone coming up the wooden stairs above the sound of babies crying and people rowing. Eventually a hollow-eyed skinny girl appeared in the doorway clutching her chest. She looked so ill that she appeared in danger of collapsing at any moment, but Samuel wasn't concerned.

'I . . . I ain't done so well this week,' she wheezed. 'Did Carol tell you I got beat up?'

'That's no concern of mine,' Samuel said scornfully. 'No money, no drugs – that's the rules.' He could smell the ripe sickly scent of her from where he was standing and wondered how anyone could bear to touch her, let alone have sex with her. But thankfully the sailors who

28

came off the boats after long sea trips weren't that fussy.

'I've got some,' she told him eagerly, leaning one hand on the back of a chair for support as she fumbled in the pocket of her thin coat with the other.

When she tentatively held the coins out to him, his lip curled with disdain. 'Is this some sort of a joke?' he rasped.

'We 'ad to pay the rent on the room else the landlord was goin' to kick us out. We ain't even kept any back for food. But I'll go out again in a while, I promise. Just give us a little bit to be goin' on wi', eh?' she begged.

Samuel paused – but then, relenting, he threw another small bag of powder at her. 'I shall be round for what you owe me for that tomorrow and you'd better have it,' he threatened her.

She clutched the powder to her, her head nodding vigorously. 'It'll be 'ere.'

Samuel strode from the room without a backward glance, in an even worse ill-humour. Carol and Katie had let him down, but at least there was enough here for a few jugs of ale, he consoled himself, and headed for the Angel near the docks. It never occurred to him that he was now as addicted to alcohol as the girls were to drugs. If he went too long without a drink now he broke out in a cold sweat and got the shakes – but that didn't bother him. If all else failed he could always go home and play his trump card. His father must have been lulled into a false sense of security after all this time, but Samuel wasn't done with him yet – or the Carey woman, not by a long shot. He sniggered into the darkness as he imagined telling Dilly Carey that he knew Olivia was really her child. Both she and his father had kept the fact from Olivia for years, and he'd no doubt they would do anything to prevent her learning of her true parentage.

With a grin on his face, Samuel moved on, the mist that

had rolled in from the sea swirling about him. Once or twice he thought he heard footsteps behind him and glanced over his shoulder, only to see someone step back into the shadows . . . but he wasn't afraid. He'd never had problems walking the streets at night before, even in the dock area, so why should tonight be any different? When the blow to the back of his head came it took him completely by surprise and he stumbled, shinning his knees on the cobbles.

'What th—' His words were cut off by a kick in the ribs and he rolled on to his side, staring up at his attacker. All he saw were two dark shapes looming over him.

'I've hardly any money on me if that's what you're after,' he gasped, curling into a ball to try and protect himself. His words were greeted by guttural grunts from the darkness, and kicks and blows began to rain down on him.

'Take my Carol off me, would yer?' one of them growled. 'Well, we'll show yer what 'appens to blokes who come 'ere and ponce off our girls. She was a good little earner, my Carol was. We pimps stick to our own patches round 'ere, an' this is just a fuckin' taste of what you're gonna get you stuck-up bastard.'

'Please – I didn't—'Another kick silenced him and all he could do then was shield his face with his arms as they went to town on him. At one point, one of the kicks landed on his arm and he heard a crack as agony coursed through him. Then a darkness greater than the night was rushing towards him and Samuel sank into it gratefully.

Samuel awoke in an eerie grey light. He was lying in the gutter and as his good hand went instinctively to his pocket, he found it empty. The drugs and what small amount of money he had had were gone. He had no idea how long he had been lying there but it must have been for some hours because dawn was trying to break through the fog.

When he tried to sit up, the pain in his arm was excruciating and he cried out.

'What's goin' on 'ere then, shipmate?'

Samuel peered through swollen eyes to see a large docker who had been on his way to work staring down at him with his hands on his hips.

'I . . . I was attacked.' The effort of speaking made his cracked lips bleed and he felt blood trickling down his chin.

'Yer certainly were,' the man agreed. Bending he helped Samuel to his feet. 'They've done you over good an' proper, my lad. But tell me where yer live an' I'll 'elp yer 'ome. I reckon yer gonna need a doctor to check you over. That arm looks broken to me.'

Samuel managed to mumble his address then leaning heavily on his rescuer he limped his way home.

'Will yer be all right from 'ere?' The man asked eventually when they arrived at the tenement where Samuel was staying.

'Y-yes, th-thank you,' Samuel gasped out, and the docker nodded and went on his way, considering he had done his good deed for the day.

Once the world had stopped swimming in front of his eyes, Samuel tackled the stairs. It seemed to take for ever to reach the top, and by the time he got there, he was in so much pain he was dizzy. Every single bone in his body ached and his mouth kept filling with blood, making him retch.

'K-Kitty,' he called weakly, hanging on to the top of the banister rail, but the sounds of babies crying and people screeching at each other drowned out his voice.

31

Holding his broken arm tightly to him, he took a step towards the door but the agony was so intense that he was forced to stop. 'Kitty . . .' he mumbled again as for the second time in hours he mercifully slipped away in a dead faint.

Chapter Five

'Hello, sweetheart, have you been a good girl for Gwen?'
Olivia asked as she entered the kitchen, slipping her
nurse's cape from her shoulders.

'Good as gold, miss. We went to feed the ducks in the
park this afternoon, didn't we?' Gwen smiled as Jessica
flew into her mother's arms.

Mrs Pegs, who was rolling out the pastry she would use
to make an apple pie for their pudding that night, mused
fondly, *How things have changed*. In years gone by, it would
have been unheard of for Olivia or any of the other Farthing
offspring to enter by the kitchen door, although most of
them had regularly sneaked in there for a treat when their
mother wasn't aware of it. Camilla had believed that the
family and the servants should know their places, but how
different things were these days. She and Gwen now
looked after Jessica while her mother was at work. Olivia
was a modern-thinking young woman and wouldn't hear
of employing a nanny even though her father would

gladly have paid for one. Of course, the child would be at school soon and then everything would return to some sort of normality, with Gwen seeing to the majority of the cleaning and herself cooking.

They'd miss the little girl though for sure, Mrs Pegs thought. She'd stolen their hearts from the day she had turned up at Mill House with her mother. Oh, there'd been plenty of gossip to start with. After all, it was evident that Jessica was illegitimate, even though Olivia had told people that she had been married and widowed in London. No one believed it, but then there were so many other little ones like Jessica in the town since the war. Sweethearts had given themselves to each other while the young men were on leave because they didn't know when or if they might see each other again . . . and sadly, many of the lads had never come home, so Jessica's presence had been nothing more than a nine days' wonder. Mrs Pegs couldn't help but wonder what Camilla would have made of it though. The mistress had been a stickler for things being done correctly before her illness. So had Mr Farthing if it came to that, but he'd mellowed with the years thank goodness and now they all lived very comfortably together.

Gwen had rushed off to put the kettle on and now as Olivia sat with Jessica on her lap, Mrs Pegs asked, 'So how has your day at the hospital been, lass?'

'Much the same as usual.' Olivia yawned. She'd been on an early shift after working late the night before and the lack of sleep was beginning to catch up on her. However, Mrs Pegs knew better than to suggest she went for a lie-down. Olivia wouldn't settle now until Jessica was tucked in and she couldn't fault the girl for that. She was a good little mother.

'I had a word with Matron today to see what the possibility was of Bessie getting a job at the hospital when

34

she comes home, and Matron was all for it,' Olivia informed the cook and the woman beamed.

'Why, that's wonderful, I'll tell her in me next letter.' Mrs Pegs paused in the middle of rolling the pastry. 'Though she ain't said exactly when she'll be home as yet.'

'Well, whenever it is, Matron will be happy to interview her. But what do you think Bessie will do about Roddy? Dilly says he's really happy living with Roisin and Declan in Ireland, and it would break the poor little chap's heart if she suddenly decides she wants him back.'

'We'll just have to bide us time an' see,' Mrs Pegs said sagely. She then expertly flipped the pastry into a pie dish and proceeded to fill it with sliced apples from the orchard as Gwen poured out a welcome cup of tea for Olivia.

'Thank you, that's just what the doctor ordered.' Taking it from her, Olivia kicked her shoes off, wriggled her aching toes and sighed with contentment as Jessica started to chase her kitten around the kitchen. Dilly had turned up with her as a surprise for the child a few weeks ago and Jessica was totally enchanted with her. She was a sweet little thing, admittedly. Ginger with a long bushy tail but Mrs Pegs could well have done without the extra work if she'd been honest. Even so, she wouldn't have dreamed of upsetting Jessica by sending 'Foxy' as the child had named it to live in the outhouse so every morning now it fell on her to clean up after it and feed it. Unless Olivia was there, and then she would happily do it – unlike her mother, she wasn't afraid to turn her hand to anything on her days off, which went a long way towards making it a happy household.

'So have you heard when Dilly is coming home?' Olivia asked then as Mrs Pegs put the top on the pie and deftly began to trim round it.

'Matter o' fact, she rang earlier this afternoon to speak

to Mr Farthing but he weren't in so I had a quick chat wi' her. Seems she might stay a bit longer than she intended as Daniel still ain't too grand, God bless him. I reckon Dilly looks on him as her dad after all these years. I dread to think how she'll take it when owt happens to 'im.'

'Well, he has been very good to her and her family over the years,' Olivia agreed. 'And from things Dilly has said, he's gone steadily downhill since he lost his wife.' Then, with a grin at Mrs Pegs: 'I bet you're looking forward to Bessie coming home, aren't you?'

'I am that,' Mrs Pegs confessed. 'It ain't the same here since she left – not that I blamed her. She's young enough to make somethin' of her life an' nursin' is a fine career to go into. She did a wonderful job o' carin' for the missus. Between you an' me, I always hoped that I'd be able to train her up to take my place here when I retire. I ain't gettin' no younger as me old bones tell me every mornin'. Still, there's always Gwen. She's turnin' into a fine little cook so happen when I do finish she'll step into me shoes nicely.'

'You're not planning to go just yet, are you?' Olivia asked worriedly. Mrs Pegs had been a part of her life and she couldn't imagine the house without her in it.

'Oh, I reckon I've got a few years left in me yet,' Mrs Pegs assured her airily. 'Then I'll go an' live wi' me brother in Yorkshire. He's got a lovely little cottage there an' he's lonely since he lost his wife last year. But now I'd best get this pie in the oven else the master will be home fer his dinner an' it won't be ready.'

'Yes, and I'd better go and get changed.' Olivia drained her cup and taking Jessica's hand she headed upstairs feeling slightly unnerved by Mrs Pegs' admission that in the not too distant future she might be leaving them. Still, she told herself, nothing stays the same. She'd learned that the hard way when Oscar married Penelope – and the scars went deep.

'Ah, what time is it?' Samuel groaned as he slowly opened his eyes and tried to focus.

'Shush an' lie still,' Kitty said softly. She was sitting in a chair at the side of the bed in their room, but although he recognised her voice his eyes were so swollen that he could scarcely see through them. 'It's over a day since I found yer out on the landin',' she told him. 'The doctor's been out an' set yer arm. It's broken, I'm afraid – that's why it's strapped up, but apart from that you've just got cuts an' bruises an' a cracked rib. The doctor says yer were lucky.'

'*Lucky!*' Samuel snapped – then winced as pain shot through him. Just to move was extremely painful and he felt as if he'd been run over by a tractor.

Kitty lifted a damp cloth she had in a bowl by the bed and ran it across his chapped lips. He licked at the moisture eagerly although he'd have liked it to be something stronger.

'Have we got any whisky or brandy . . . for the pain?'

Kitty shook her head. 'No, I sold the bottle you 'ad under the bed to the Trents along the landin' so I could pay the doctor.'

'*Damn!*' Samuel ground his teeth together, only to find that one was dangerously loose. 'So how are we supposed to eat?' he choked out.

'Now yer awake I'll go back out on the streets again,' Kitty answered. 'In fact, I'll go now an' hopefully I'll be back in a few hours with something to cook fer us.'

Samuel was too weak to argue and watched helplessly as Kitty crossed to a bowl and had a hasty wash. She then dragged a brush through her limp greasy hair and smiled at him. 'Right, there's a glass o' water on the table next to

37

yer and the guzunder is close an' all if yer can manage to get out o' bed to use it. Bye fer now.' With that she swung about and left the room, closing the door behind her and leaving Samuel to wallow in self-pity. The beating he'd taken the night before had been just a taster, according to the thugs who'd attacked him; it wouldn't be safe to stay here now, but then there was no chance of him making his escape just yet. He didn't think he'd even be able to walk as far as the door at present.

As usual, Samuel thought only of himself. He'd pulled some terrible stunts across his father in his time and yet he still believed that Max would help him if he could only let him know what had happened. He smirked as he thought back to how he had sold the house his father had bought for him and Niamh to live in right from under his nose. It had been easy once he'd had one of his shady acquaintances have false deeds drawn up. He wondered briefly where Niamh was living now. It must have come as a shock to his wife to know that she was suddenly homeless, not that it bothered him; she'd deserved all she got after forcing him into marriage as she had – and all for the sake of an illegitimate kid! He shuddered as he did each time he pictured Constance. It had been easy to stab Snowy White – he'd got no more than he deserved – but the kid was another matter altogether. He'd only got rid of her so that Niamh would give him his freedom but it had all backfired because of her Catholic religion, so little Constance, his daughter, had died for nothing. He forced himself to concentrate on thinking about his father again. How to get word to him of his dilemma was the problem. And then it came to Samuel: he could ring him – when he was able to get to a telephone, that was – but only as a last resort. It would go against the grain, having to eat humble pie and throw himself on his father's mercy, but anything was

38

better than having to lie here. He'd sunk just about as low as he could get. Even so, he decided he'd wait for a while before he made a final decision. He was in no state to do anything else anyway at the minute, and he might come up with another, better option.

Kitty came in later that night clutching a steaming parcel to her chest.

'I got us some faggots an' peas,' she told Samuel. 'I'm afraid I couldn't afford a pie but these'll fill a hole, no doubt. An' I've got enough money left to get some coal tomorrer so we'll be able to 'ave a fire an' all.'

He grunted. It hurt too much to talk but his stomach was grumbling with hunger so he supposed he should try and eat something to build his strength back up.

'Come on then, let's get you a bit more comfy.' Kitty winced as she tried to haul him up on to the pillows. Her own cracked rib wasn't healed yet but Samuel howled in agony. 'Sorry, but it's gotta be done,' she panted as she managed to raise him another few inches. 'There, now. That's better, ain't it?' She smiled cheerfully as she placed a newspaper full of hot food on his chest. 'Get some o' that down yer. You'll feel much better with a full belly.'

Samuel lifted a faggot with his free hand; the doctor had bound the other tightly to his chest. The effort of chewing made him break out in a cold sweat and it didn't help when halfway through the meal, his loose tooth fell out.

'*Damn* the bastards who did this to me,' he snarled as he spat it out in disgust, but he supposed it could have been worse. At least it was one of his back teeth rather than one of the front ones. Eventually he finished the meal. His lips had cracked open again and were painful but he did feel slightly better with something inside him.

Kitty kept up a constant stream of chatter, no doubt trying to cheer him up, and had he been able to, he knew he would have swiped her one. As it was he kept his mouth shut. He was completely at her mercy at the moment and didn't want to do anything to upset her. At last she turned off the light and settled beside him – and soon her exhausted snores echoed around the room. But there was no sleep for him; his mind was too busy working as he tried to figure out where he might go from here.

Chapter Six

'I'll be sorry to see you go so I will, lass,' Daniel said regretfully the night before Dilly was due to go home.

She gave him a gentle hug. 'I've already stayed longer than I'd planned to,' she pointed out. 'But you do seem a little better now so I really ought to get back and see what's happening with all the shops.'

'I dare say you should,' he acknowledged, before going on, 'Remember, me darlin', there is more to life than work. You should make a little more time for yourself. Go and see Niamh and Ben in New York, why don't you? They'd love to have you, I'm sure. You're still young enough to enjoy yourself so do it while you can.'

'You must be joking,' she grinned. 'I'm racing towards fifty. I'd hardly call that young!'

'It is when you get to my age. You're just a wean compared to me. But seriously, I want you to cut down on your work a bit.'

'I'll try,' she said, although she could see by the

41

expression on his face that he didn't believe a word of it. 'But now I want to go and say goodbye to the others if you're all right on your own for a while? There won't be much time in the morning if I'm to catch the early ferry.'

'You do that, lass, I'm fine.'

Dilly tucked the blankets more closely about him then let herself out of the back door into the farmyard where she stood taking deep breaths of the clean fresh air. Had it not been for leaving Olivia she knew that she and the children would have come to live here years ago after losing Fergal; however, she hadn't been able to leave the girl even though the Farthings were bringing her up. Now Olivia had Jessica, and the tiny child was yet another tie to the Midlands. Jessica, Olivia, Max and the shops. Perhaps I'll take Philip Maddison up on his offer of going to stay with him while I look round at the London shops, after all, Dilly thought, then grinned. So much for her taking Daniel's advice.

It was harder than usual to say her goodbyes to Daniel when it came time to leave the next morning and Dilly was tearful.

'You take your time now and once you're up and about again don't get trying to run before you can walk,' she warned him as she gripped his hand.

'Hark at the pot calling the kettle black,' he joked. 'You just remember what I said to you too – there's more to life than just work, my girl. Do yourself a favour and take a little time out to enjoy yourself. The work'll still be there when you're pushing up daisies, though I hope that won't be for some long time yet.'

She planted a gentle kiss on his cheek but then Declan was at the door waiting for her and with a final wave she was off.

'I heard what Grandpa said to you, Mammy,' her son

told her as the horse clip-clopped along the lane, 'an' he's right, you know. You *do* work too hard. There's only our Seamus left in Nuneaton now an' he's happily wed – so what's to stop you coming out here to live? Seamus would take care o' the runnin' o' the shops for you. From what you've said, he'd be more than capable.'

'I dare say he would be,' Dilly said somewhat primly. How could she tell him about Olivia and Jessica? 'But in actual fact I enjoy working and being busy. Idle hands make work for the devil, isn't that what your gran'ma always used to say?'

Declan chuckled. 'Aye, I dare say she did – but in your case I reckon she'd agree with Granda.'

A fat pheasant darted in front of them then, making the horse shy – and thankfully by the time Declan had the horse under control again he had forgotten all about scolding his mother and they went peacefully on their way.

'Why, it's grand to see yer, luvvie,' Nell declared when Dilly arrived home tired and hungry that evening. The ferry crossing had been choppy and she'd developed a headache that was now throbbing away behind her eyes. 'Max called in a while since to see if you were back. I wouldn't be at all surprised if he didn't call again later on.'

'If he does, I'm afraid he'll be disappointed because all I want is a nice hot cup of tea, a quick sandwich and my bed,' Dilly answered as she slipped her coat off and threw it carelessly across the back of a chair.

Nell raised an eyebrow as she filled the kettle at the sink. It wasn't like Dilly to miss out on an opportunity to see Max, especially when they'd been apart for a while.

'Good visit, was it?' she questioned casually.

Dilly nodded then admitted, 'Daniel has aged so much

43

since the last time I saw him, and for some reason when I left I had the awful feeling that I might never see him again.' She brushed her fingers across her eyes. 'Oh, take no notice of me, Nell. I'm just being morbid because I'm tired, I suppose. How are things here?'

'All shipshape.' Nell was busily spooning tea into the brown teapot, adding an extra spoonful for luck. Dilly looked like she could do with it. 'Philip Maddison rang the shop the day before yesterday hoping to speak to you. He's found premises that might be suitable for you to rent in London and he's asked if you'll ring him back as soon as you get home. The rental properties get snapped up very quickly by all accounts.'

'Hmm, well, I'm not ringing him tonight,' Dilly said firmly. 'He can wait until tomorrow.'

Again, Nell was surprised. She'd expected Dilly to jump at the chance of owning a shop in London. Could it be that everything was finally getting too much for her? Sensing that Dilly was in rather a strange mood she finished making the tea in silence and once it was poured and whilst Dilly was drinking it she then cut her a cheese sandwich and settled down with the newspaper.

'She's in bed,' Nell informed Max when he called round later that evening.

'Oh!' Max looked mildly taken aback. It wasn't like Dilly to retire early. 'She's not ill, is she?'

Nell shook her head as she continued knitting. She was making a little cardigan for Jessica. 'Just a bit of an 'eadache an' tired, I think, but I'll tell her yer called when she wakes up in the mornin'. Would yer like me to make yer a drink afore yer go?'

'No, thanks, Nell. I'll get on. I'm hoping to pop by and see Lawrence and Patty before I turn in. I dare say William

44

will be in bed by now, but they might let me take a peek at him. He's three years old already! Where does the time go?'

Once Max had left, Nell settled back down to her knitting, her needles clicking furiously.

Philip Maddison rang early again the next morning and Dilly answered the call as she was on her way to join Nell for breakfast in the kitchen. The smell of bacon was making her stomach grumble with anticipation and so her voice was somewhat clipped as she lifted the receiver and said, 'Yes!'

'Oh dear, it sounds as if someone's got out of bed the wrong side this morning.'

'Oh, I'm so sorry, Philip.' Dilly recognised his voice instantly. 'Nell did say you'd called and you wanted to speak to me. Something about finding a shop that might suit me?'

'That's right.' He quickly went on to tell her about the empty premises he had found. 'I think it would be ideal for you. It has a huge window which would be just perfect to show off your bridal collection. But if you're interested, you'll have to act fast. The shops don't stay empty around here for long.'

'How fast?' Dilly asked warily. 'I only got back from Ireland last night. I'm not sure it would be right to clear off again and leave all my staff to it so quickly.'

'Rubbish!' Philip scoffed. 'You've got them all so well trained they could run the shops with their eyes shut now, and this is an opportunity not to be missed.'

'Then in that case I suppose I could come tomorrow. Could you book me into a hotel somewhere?'

'There'll be absolutely no need for that. You're welcome to stay at my apartment.'

45

Dilly chuckled. 'And what will your housekeeper make of that?'

'Nothing whatsoever. She's used to me having guests to stay. It's not as if we're going to be sleeping in the same room, is it? Unless you'd like to, of course?' he said teasingly. Philip Maddison was one of the most eligible bachelors in London and took full advantage of the fact. He was handsome, charming and rich and his face regularly appeared in the newspapers as he left the theatre or a dance hall with some young model or actress hanging on his arm.

'Behave yourself,' Dilly laughed. 'I think we'll keep things just as they are. I'm too old for you now anyway. Everyone knows you tend to go for the younger models.'

'Perhaps it's time to settle down and I'm looking for someone suitable now?' he suggested and Dilly chortled with laughter.

'There's about as much chance of that happening as hell freezing over. But I will take you up on your offer if you're sure it won't be putting you to any bother. I'll get the first train into Euston tomorrow so should be with you by lunchtime and we'll have plenty of time to go and look at the shop.'

'Just let me know what time your train should be in and I'll be at Euston to meet you,' he promised – and so it was decided.

'You're goin' where?' Nell asked in amazement when Dilly told her of the plans over breakfast.

'To London,' Dilly answered calmly. 'I know it's a bit soon after my trip to Ireland but it can't be helped. If I don't go now, Philip reckons the shop will be snapped up by someone else.'

'But you ain't even seen Olivia or Jessica since you got back – and are yer quite sure that yer want to take on the responsibility of another shop?' Nell said, flabbergasted.

Dilly shrugged. 'I shall call in and see the girls sometime today. And as for taking on another shop – why shouldn't I?'

Nell tipped another spoonful of sugar into her tea looking slightly uncomfortable. 'Well, no offence intended, luvvie, but you ain't gettin' any younger, are yer? An' the shops yer already have keep yer runnin' around like a blue-arsed fly as it is. To be honest I'm surprised Philip wants yer to open a shop there when he sells yer designs in his. I wouldn't have thought he'd want the competition.'

'But we wouldn't be in competition. My shop would be a bridalwear shop. He sells evening gowns and day clothes,' Dilly explained.

'Well, I still think yer might be over-reachin' yerself,' Nell muttered as she slathered butter on to a slice of toast. 'Yer should be startin' to slow down now an' spend more time wi' yer family.'

Slightly affronted, Dilly pursed her lips, and worried that she might have said too much, Nell wisely fell silent and put the wireless on for the eight o'clock news.

Max's reaction to her proposed trip was much as Nell's had been.

'But you've only just come home and I've missed you,' he objected. 'So has Jessica, if it comes to that. I've lost count of the number of times she's asked me when Dilly is coming.'

'Look, Max, you're a businessman. You of all people should understand that this opportunity is too good to miss.'

They were in the library at Mill House and they could both hear Gwen humming as she mopped the tiled floor in the hallway. Olivia was at work at the hospital and Jessica was outside in the yard helping Mrs Pegs to hang the washing on the line, although she was being more of a hindrance than a help if truth be told.

'Surely you're happy with *six* shops?' Max said then and Dilly became annoyed.

'How many businesses do *you* own, Max?' she asked with a hint of sarcasm in her voice. 'Or is it all right for you to go on expanding because you're a man?'

Max was saved from having to answer when a little whirling dervish ran into the room and launched herself at Dilly, her copper curls glinting in the sun that shone through the window.

'Oh, Dilly, I *missed* you,' the child gurgled as she wrapped her solid little arms about Dilly's neck. Then both adults were laughing when Jessica asked brazenly, 'Have you brought me a present?'

'I have, as it happens,' Dilly said, drinking in the smell of the little body in her arms. 'If you go and get my bag from over there I'll see if I can find it for you.'

Jessica scurried away and was back wide-eyed with anticipation seconds later. Dilly made a great show of fumbling about in the bag before extracting a little box. Jessica took it from her and crowed with delight when she lifted the lid. It was a tiny silver chain bracelet from which dangled a silver cat.

'I saw it in a jeweller's window in Dublin while I was waiting for the ferry and it reminded me of your new pet, Foxy,' Dilly told the child fondly. 'But you must take it off when you go to bed.' She fastened it on her wrist for her and Jessica jiggled her arm about delightedly, setting the bracelet jangling. Then she was on Dilly's lap again.

'I don't want you to go away again for a long time,' she said firmly and Dilly flinched.

'As it happens, darling, I do have to go away again tomorrow, but just for a short time.'

Jessica's lovely blue eyes welled with tears. 'But *why?*' she demanded. 'You've only just come home.'

'I know, but I won't be gone for long,' Dilly apologised as Jessica slithered off her lap with a resigned sigh.

'I'll go and show Gwennie an' Mrs Pegs an' Foxy my bracelet then,' she said, and as she scurried away Dilly suffered a terrible pang of guilt.

Chapter Seven

As Dilly was making her way to the railway station the next morning, Samuel was staring down into the bowl that Kitty had just balanced on a tray in front of him.

'What the hell do you call *this*?' he asked in disgust.

'It's porridge, but we ain't got no milk so I 'ad to make it with water,' Kitty explained nervously. Her lover had never been the easiest of men to live with, but since he'd become bedridden he was even more intolerant.

'*Porridge!*' Samuel lifted the bowl with his one good hand and slammed it against the wall. The cheap pottery dish instantly shattered and the porridge began to run down the peeling wallpaper in dollops. 'How is a bloke supposed to get his strength back on *that* mess?' he stormed.

Kitty wrung her hands as tears filled her eyes. 'I'm doin' me best,' she whimpered. 'I'll try an' afford us a bit o' meat fer our dinner, eh? You'll enjoy that. An' I'll get an' onion an' some potatoes to go with it.'

'As long as it's not that awful scrag-end stuff you tried to get me to eat the other day,' he growled ungratefully. 'That wasn't fit to feed to a dog.'

Kitty didn't bother to argue with him. When he was in this mood there was no point. He was like a bear with a sore head and had been ever since he'd been confined to bed. His bruises had now faded to dull yellows and purples and his eyes weren't quite so swollen but his broken rib was still making it painful for him to move, and with his injured arm strapped to his chest he was virtually helpless. Kitty was even having to help him to get out of bed to use the chamber pot, not that she ever got a word of thanks. Yet still she cared for him although she never got so much as one kind word in return. Now she headed for the door saying, 'I'll pop out and get us some food then. Will you be all right while I'm gone?'

'Do I *look* all right?' he scowled and Kitty made a hasty exit, actually relieved to be getting out of his way for a time.

As the train rattled along the track, Dilly stared unseeingly from the window. She'd suffered all manner of guilt since Jessica had become upset about her going away again so soon the night before. Max had been none too pleased either but Dilly was determined to continue to build her little empire.

By the time the train chugged into Euston, she was in a thoroughly bad humour but the sight of Philip waiting on the platform for her softened her a little. They had become good friends over the years and she enjoyed his company.

'Dilly, looking as beautiful as ever,' he said gallantly as she stepped from the train on to the platform.

'Hello, Philip. You've lost none of your charm, I see,'

Dilly said with a grin as he kissed her hand and lifted her small case.

'I thought we might go to lunch before we go to look at the shop in Marylebone,' Philip said. 'And then we'll drop your luggage off at my apartment. Then how about a trip to the theatre this evening?'

'But I don't think I've brought anything suitable to wear for the theatre,' she said worriedly.

'Oh, don't get worrying about inconsequential details like that. We can sort that out later,' he said, airily waving aside her concerns with a flick of the wrist.

So Dilly nodded agreement. Now that she was here she might as well make the most of it.

The streets were teeming as they left the station but Philip hailed a cab and in no time they were heading along the main Euston Road towards the chic area of Marylebone.

'Do you like Italian food?' he asked once the cab had dropped them off in a rather smart street.

Dilly had no idea at all where she was, nor did she know if she liked Italian food, never having tried it before. Even so, she had no wish to show her ignorance so she nodded as Philip took her elbow and led her into a very swish restaurant where a waiter instantly showed them to a window table. It appeared that Philip was known there.

'The man who owns this place is Italian and he's always happy to cook Italian food for those who enjoy it,' he confided. 'So . . . what do you fancy?'

They studied their menus, which were mainly English dishes.

'I er . . .'

Seeing her hesitation, Philip asked kindly, 'Shall I order for us?'

'Oh yes – yes, please,' Dilly gulped, feeling totally out of her depth, then stifled a giggle as a picture of her and

Nell sitting at their kitchen table eating home-made stew flashed in front of her eyes. This was like another world and she couldn't imagine what Nell would have thought of it.

'Right.' Philip closed the menu with a snap and beckoned to the waiter. 'We'll have bruschetta to start with, and then we'll try some of your magnificent spaghetti bolognese, please. Oh, and we'll also have a bottle of the Chianti.'

'*Sí, signor*.' The waiter, who Philip later informed her was the restaurant-owner's son Silvio, dashed away and was back in seconds with the wine. After pouring them both a glass he disappeared again.

'Cheers then, Dilly. Here's to a good long partnership,' Philip said, raising his glass. They drank a toast and as Dilly peeped at him over the rim of her glass she thought how handsome he looked. He was getting more than a few admiring glances from some of the female customers but he seemed oblivious to the fact and kept his attention firmly fixed on Dilly.

'The latest batch of designs you sent me are selling really well,' he told her as he unfolded a crisp white napkin across his lap. 'Particularly that backless evening dress with the drape front. Women have become a lot more daring since the war and I can't get that style made up quickly enough. I would really like us to call into one of my shops so you can see them. You don't have to rush back do you?'

'Well, I don't want to be away for too long. I only got back from Ireland two days ago,' Dilly explained. 'So perhaps a couple of days – three at the latest? That should give me time to appoint some tradesmen to do the work that will need doing in the shop if it proves to be suitable.'

Philip looked vaguely disappointed but then the waiter appeared with their starters and the conversation was

53

halted for now. The bruschetta proved to be a concoction of bread, garlic, tomatoes, fresh cut basil and olive oil, and Dilly wasn't too enthralled with it although she ate it to be polite. The spaghetti bolognese was slightly more to her taste, but given the choice, Dilly realised she would prefer good old English cooking anytime.

'Is the food all right?' Philip asked halfway through the meal and she flashed a brilliant smile.

'Wonderful,' she answered diplomatically as she took another long swallow from her water glass.

Philip insisted on paying for the meal once they were done, although Dilly strongly objected. She had become a very independent woman over the years and she didn't want Philip to think that she was taking advantage of him. Soon they were in yet another cab racing towards the empty premises Philip was keen to show her – and once they drew up outside, Dilly had to admit that the shop was indeed very impressive. There was a huge window space, ideal for displaying wedding gowns, and although both the window and the entrance door were sorely in need of a coat of paint they looked solid enough. Philip had the keys, which the landlord had entrusted to him, and once they were inside Dilly walked about trying to picture where everything would go.

'I think the fitting rooms would be best over here,' she thought aloud. 'The counter could go there and the rails that would hold the dresses on that wall there.' There was also another room at the back of the shop that led into a small yard which housed a toilet – and all in all, Dilly couldn't fault it.

'My biggest problem if I took a shop on here would be finding the right person to run it,' she said. 'Also, I'd have to employ a seamstress here to make up the designs. It's too far to transport new gowns from the Midlands.'

'I've already thought of that,' Philip told her. 'And I just happen to know a very trustworthy woman who would make a perfect manageress and who would jump at the opportunity. I could keep an eye on the books for you in between your visits. As regards a seamstress, some of my ladies would be more than happy to oblige.'

'It seems you've thought of everything,' Dilly answered with a twinkle in her eye. 'And I have to admit I'm very impressed with the shop. There actually isn't all that much to do. Perhaps a coat of paint and a new sign outside, then a tidy-up in here. And the rent is more than reasonable for the size of the premises.'

'Good, but before you make a final decision I want you to come with me to one of my establishments now and see how my staff do it.'

Dilly took a last long look around then followed him outside and waited while he locked the door, then in no time they were in a cab and on their way to one of his shops, which was just off Bond Street.

Dilly couldn't fail but feel overawed when they pulled up outside. The window display was colour co-ordinated and looked quite breathtaking, and the shop window sparkled in the sunlight. Above the window was a blue striped canopy that gave shelter to anyone wanting to peruse the clothes in the window, and on either side of the door was a large bay tree in an enormous pot, giving the place an air of opulence.

'When women come to buy a new dress they want to feel pampered – and that's just what my staff aim to do,' he told her.

Dilly was eyeing a day dress in a lovely shade of pale green piped with cream; she recognised it as one of her designs and felt a little tingle of pure pleasure. Max held the shop door open for her and she stepped inside to another world. The room was gigantic but a floor-to-ceiling curtain divided it. In this side was a counter on which stood a huge vase of fresh lilies, and mannequins were dotted here and there displaying the dresses. The walls were draped in a soft cream chiffon material giving it an exclusive feel, and her feet sank into a thick green carpet. The mannequins were so exquisite that they appeared almost life-like, and Dilly guessed that each one must have cost a small fortune. The smell of the lilies and the soft green carpet made her feel as if she was walking in a meadow.

'It's quite beautiful,' she breathed.

At that moment, a young woman appeared from behind the curtain. She was tall, slim and extremely pretty, and from the look of adoration she gave Philip, Dilly guessed that she must be one of his conquests. Dilly judged her to be in her late twenties to early thirties and felt almost sorry for her as she saw the way her eyes followed Philip about. Her blonde hair was twisted into a neat chignon on the back of her head and she was dressed in a smart black fitted suit that, coupled with her high-heeled court shoes, showed off her slim figure to perfection.

'Ah, Miss March. Would you kindly show this lady a selection of evening dresses, please?' Philip asked.

'Certainly, sir.' Then, addressing Dilly: 'Would you like to come this way, madam?'

Dilly was speechless as she followed the young woman through the curtain to find herself in yet another room which had a raised dais running down the centre of it. To one side of this were a number of gilt-legged chairs and small tables, and the girl ushered her towards them, saying, 'Do take a seat. I'll arrange for a drink to be brought to you while the model prepares a selection of gowns for you to look at. Would you prefer tea or coffee, or perhaps something a little stronger?'

'Oh, just tea would be fine,' Dilly replied hastily. It appeared that nothing was too much trouble for Philip's clients.

He came in and sat down next to her, grinning as she gazed about astounded.

'It's all so . . . *so luxurious*,' she whispered.

'I'm pleased you think so. We aim to make our clients feel important. If they are happy with our service they are far more likely to come back again – and recommend us to their friends, of course.'

Minutes later, Miss March appeared with a gleaming silver tray on which was set delicate china cups and saucers as well as what looked like a very expensive selection of chocolate biscuits.

'Do help yourselves,' she told them when she had served them with their tea but Dilly politely declined. So soon after lunch she couldn't find room for another crumb.

With perfect timing, a young model appeared from behind a screen at the far end of the raised platform. She was wearing one of the evening dresses that Dilly had designed in a dark maroon satin and once again, Dilly felt a quiver of pure pleasure ripple through her. It was the backless one that Philip had mentioned earlier and it suited the model's fluid figure beautifully. She sashayed along the dais, turning this way and that until eventually she disappeared through the screen only to return a little later in another, equally beautiful dress.

'We show our customers a selection once we know what they're looking for,' Philip explained. 'Then when they've made their choice we will have the dress altered to fit them perfectly, if necessary.'

The model paraded in a number of gowns and finally Philip asked, 'Which was your favourite, Dilly?'

'Well, I think the first one,' she told him. 'You were right, it does look beautiful when it's made up.'

'Then you must try it on now,' he said, snapping his fingers at Miss March who was standing discreetly behind him.

'Oh no, I—' Dilly was deeply embarrassed but Philip would brook no argument.

'Oh yes,' he insisted. He could be a force to be reckoned with when the mood took him. 'You'll need something to wear tonight to the theatre, won't you? And it shall be my treat. We can easily get it altered in time if need be.'

But the dress when Dilly tried it on fitted perfectly and she felt like a queen in it.

'Wrap it up, would you, Miss March?' Philip instructed and meek as a lamb the young woman did as she was told. Dilly got the impression that the woman was slightly jealous of her. Perhaps she thinks I'm one of Philip's ladyfriends? Dilly thought, and would have loved to enlighten her that they were no more than business partners – but of course she didn't.

When they left shortly afterwards with Dilly swinging the dress, wrapped in silver tissue paper inside a flat box in one of the shop's beautiful bags, she was in heaven.

'I thought we might try the Vaudeville Theatre on the Strand this evening,' Philip told her in the cab on the way to his apartment. 'There's a musical on at the moment called *RSVP* which is getting very good reviews.'

'It sounds wonderful,' Dilly answered. The day had got off to a bad start but it had certainly improved.

Chapter Eight

Philip's apartment left Dilly speechless. It was situated in Mayfair and after getting into the lift he took her right to the top floor.

'This is it,' he said jovially as he inserted a key in the door. He then led her into a spacious hallway with a cream carpet that reached almost from one wall to the other. Gilt-framed pictures hung on the walls and in the centre of it was an Art Deco light that danced rainbow colours all over the walls.

'Is that you, Mr Maddison?' A plump, smartly dressed lady with steel-grey hair knotted neatly into a bun on the back of her head emerged from what Dilly was to discover was the kitchen and smiled a welcome at Dilly. 'Ah, so you've arrived then. You must be Mrs Carey. Mr Maddison has told me all about you and I'm under orders to take very good care of you.'

'Oh please, just call me Dilly,' Dilly said, extending her hand, which the woman shook warmly.

'This is Mrs Packer, she's been with me for years and I really don't know what I'd do without her,' Philip introduced her.

The woman flushed at the praise before asking Dilly, 'Would you like to see your room, dear? I have it all ready for you.'

'Thank you, that would be lovely but I hope you haven't gone to too much trouble on my account,' Dilly responded.

'It's no trouble at all,' Mrs Packer told her and then led her along the hallway to a door which she threw open.

Dilly gasped with pleasure at sight of it. All the furniture was cream with a French rococo influence, and heavy cream velvet drapes hung at the window – which she noted led out on to a little balcony. The carpet and the bedding were cream too, but the pictures on the walls dotted about the room added colour and warmth to the overall effect. It was clear that a lot of thought had gone into the colour scheme and Dilly wondered if Philip had employed an interior designer.

'There's a bathroom through here,' Mrs Packer said, gesturing towards another door. Dilly gaped at the enormous bathtub, gold taps and marble floor. She'd never seen anything quite like it.

'It's quite stunning,' she breathed. 'And you keep it so beautifully. I'm sure I could eat my dinner off the floor.'

Mrs Packer smiled broadly. She'd taken a shine to Dilly, unlike most of the flibberty-gibbets Philip usually brought home. She'd been telling him for ages that it was time he settled down and she hoped she'd see more of this woman. Vera Packer had worked for Philip for so long now that she looked upon him almost as a son and she would have walked through fire for him.

'Now, is there anything I can get for you?' she asked kindly. 'Something to eat or drink?'

'Oh no, thank you, we've just eaten,' Dilly told her hastily, then feeling she could trust this woman she lowered her voice and confessed, 'Philip took me to a restaurant and between you and me the food was like nothing I'd ever tasted before. It was Italian.'

'Pah! You can't beat a good old-fashioned English roast,' Mrs Packer agreed. 'But London has changed since the end of the war. But now if you're sure there's nothing you want I'll leave you to freshen up. Just call, dear, should you think of anything. Oh, and the telephone is on your bedside table should you need to ring anyone.'

'Thank you, Mrs Packer.'

The woman left the room, closing the door softly behind her and Dilly crossed to the full-length door that gave access to the balcony. The view gave her a panoramic glimpse of London. Dilly felt as if she had stepped into another world . . . but after a while her thoughts returned to the empty shop she had viewed and with her business head firmly back in place she went and sat down and began to calculate the costs of the rental and the refurbishments it would need.

When she rejoined Philip in his luxurious lounge an hour or so later, again she couldn't help but be impressed. The main colour scheme in there was a very soft dove grey with blue contrasts.

'Did you design all this yourself?' she asked, wondering how Mrs Packer managed to keep the carpets looking so spotlessly clean. She dreaded to think what they'd look like if they had Jessica there.

'No, I can't take credit for any of it,' he said truthfully. 'I just came up with ideas for the colours, and the interior designer did the rest. Do you approve?'

'Absolutely – it's wonderful – but now back to business.

I've been doing my sums and I think if your offer of help still stands, I'd like to go ahead with leasing the shop.' Dilly laid out the paper containing the figures she'd estimated and they went over them together.

'So shall I ring the landlord and arrange a meeting for first thing in the morning?' Philip asked.

'Yes, please, and if I could meet the tradesmen who will carry out the refurbishments, I can get all the arrangements done and dusted, and perhaps catch the train home tomorrow evening.'

She was surprised when Philip's face fell. 'Surely not so soon. You've only just arrived,' he pointed out.

'Well, let's wait and see how we get on tomorrow,' she told him, feeling a little ripple of unease. She and Philip had always been purely business partners. Surely he wasn't hoping to introduce romance into the equation? Then she realised how ridiculous she was being! Philip preferred women half her age; she was fast approaching fifty, after all.

That evening, Dilly enjoyed a luxurious soak in the splendid marble bathroom before getting ready for her evening out. She washed her hair and brushed it till it shone, then slid into the exquisite dress Philip had so kindly treated her to.

'Why, Mrs . . . Dilly,' Vera Packer gasped when she stepped out of the bedroom. 'You look absolutely beautiful. Now go through to the lounge and Mr Maddison will get you a drink before you leave.'

'Thank you, Mrs Packer.' Dilly found Philip standing on the balcony with a glass of brandy in his hand. He was dressed in a formal black evening suit and looked very handsome, and when he turned and saw her, his stare was openly admiring.

'You might have designed that dress just for yourself – it's perfect on you,' he told her, hurrying to get her a drink. 'Although I have just the thing to finish it off.' He poured her a small sherry, then went over to a mahogany sideboard and fetched a small velvet box.

'Would you turn around for me?' he asked, and wondering what he was up to, Dilly obliged. She felt him fasten something about her neck and then he led her towards a mirror. 'There! What do you think?' he asked, looking very pleased with himself.

Awed, Dilly lifted her hand to touch the magnificent necklace. The chain was gold with a small ruby heart at the centre of it, surrounded by a cluster of smaller rubies. She stared at Philip in confusion. 'But whose is it?'

'It's yours, of course,' he grinned. 'I slipped out to get it while you were resting earlier on. I have to say the rubies are perfect with the colour of that dress.'

Deeply embarrassed, Dilly placed her drink down and began to fumble clumsily with the clasp. 'It's a very kind thought,' she muttered as colour burned into her cheeks. 'But I really can't accept it, Philip. It must have been dreadfully expensive.'

He looked so crestfallen that her hands became still. 'And do you think I can't afford it?' He turned away and she knew that she'd offended him. 'I think you've earned that at least after all the trade you've brought into my shops with your designs. It was just my way of saying thank you – but if you don't like it, of course . . .'

'Oh, but I *do* like it,' she assured him hastily. 'I love it, in fact, but I feel guilty about you spending your money on me.'

'Then please take it in the spirit it was given and enjoy wearing it.' Lifting her glass again, he handed it back to her.

'Then thank you very much, I will.' Dilly smiled into his eyes – and they were friends again.

They had a wonderful evening and on the way home in the cab Dilly stared at London by night. With the lights twinkling in the darkness it looked magical, a contrast to its daytime madness.

'Everything looks so different here at night,' Dilly commented.

'London is just getting back on its feet,' Philip agreed.

A businessman through and through he gave her a rundown of everything that was occurring in the capital to do with economic growth.

'Since the opening of the King George V Docks in 1921 the volume of imports and exports here has risen again. A whole new generation of British corporations and banks has created new office jobs for people too. ICI and British Petroleum have both built large Head Offices in Central London and even more factories are being set up at Park Royal and along the new arterial roads which will create even more jobs. There's the Firestone tyre factory on the Great West Road, the Wrigley factory at Wembley and the Lyons food processing works at Hammersmith – all examples of the new generation of London's light Industry. I know fashion doesn't seem to come into it, Dilly, but it's all good news for people who own shops here. More prosperity means more customers – although I have to admit the General Strike did slow down spending a little.'

'It's much worse in the Midlands,' Dilly told him but then, not wishing to end the evening on a depressing note, she said, 'I've had a wonderful time. Thank you so much for taking me to the theatre and for all your help in securing the shop.'

'It was my pleasure,' Philip answered, then taking her hand he squeezed it gently. Again she felt the little wriggle of unease as she subtly disentangled her fingers and self-consciously stared from the window.

Once back at Philip's home they took the lift to his apartment. Mrs Packer was waiting up for them. She lived in, and her bedroom was next to the kitchen.

'Ah here you are,' she said pleasantly. 'I've just left you both a cold light supper in the kitchen. I thought you might be peckish. Do help yourselves and if there's anything else you want, just give me a shout.'

'Thank you, Mrs P.' Philip led Dilly into the kitchen. The 'light meal' Mrs Packer had referred to was more like a feast. There were sandwiches, a large pork pie, pickles and all manner of goodies, and Philip instantly loaded two plates as Dilly set about making them both a cup of cocoa.

'Isn't this cosy,' he said happily as they sat at the kitchen table looking out at the lights of London. 'Anyone seeing us could take us for an old married couple.'

'I hardly think so,' Dilly answered with a wry grin. 'I can't see you ever settling down.'

'And why not?'

His question took Dilly by surprise and not wishing to upset him she chose her words carefully when she answered.

'Well, you make no secret of the fact that you like a good social life and from what I've gathered that usually includes taking attractive young ladies out and about.'

'Perhaps I'm tired of the bachelor life and feel it's time to settle down.'

Dilly took a long sip of her cocoa.

'And the thing is, Dilly . . . well, I've become very fond of you and I admire you enormously so I was thinking perhaps that you and I—'

'Don't say any more, Philip, please.' Dilly stopped him. 'I'm enormously flattered that you might even begin to look at me in that way, but what you haven't taken into the equation is that you and I are from totally different walks of life. I'm a self-made woman but my little empire is nowhere near as big as yours. I live in a relatively small town in the Midlands and I have a grown-up family as well as a little . . .' She had been about to say 'a little granddaughter' but managed to stop herself just in time. 'What I'm trying to say,' she went on gently, 'is that although I've enjoyed visiting London I could never live here and I'm quite sure that you wouldn't want to relocate to Nuneaton. All your businesses and your social life are here, and added to that I'm far too old for you. I shall be fifty in the blink of an eye. I'm also very independent and set in my ways – boring, some might say. I've been on my own for a long time now and I don't feel that I want another relationship. If you're serious about wishing to settle down though, I think I might know just the right person for you.'

'Oh yes – and who would that be then?' Philip sounded slightly peeved. He was used to women dropping at his feet and a stranger to rejection.

'The lovely young woman who served us in your shop earlier on. Surely you know the girl is in love with you? A blind man on a galloping donkey could see it.'

'Deborah March?' Philip looked astounded before admitting, 'Well . . . I have taken her out on a few occasions. Deborah is always obliging, and willing to attend some of the functions I have to go to if I need someone to accompany me.'

'And why do you think that is?' Dilly asked with a twinkle in her eye. 'I have no wish to play Cupid but the girl is perfect for you. She's beautiful into the bargain.'

'I suppose she is,' Philip said thoughtfully. Then, with a rueful grin, 'So you're turning me down, are you, Dilly?'

'I'm afraid so,' she said lightly. 'I think you and I are just right the way we are. We're good business partners and I've come to regard you as a very dear friend. It would be such a shame to change that.'

'I suppose you're right,' he answered reluctantly. 'But I do think we could have been good together. We're both ambitious and almost the same age.'

'There is that, but I couldn't give you children,' Dilly pointed out practically. 'My childbearing years are behind me and now that you do want to settle down perhaps you might decide you want a family too.'

'Hey, steady on,' Philip said in a panic. 'I'm not quite ready to become that domesticated just yet!'

'No, but you could if you were with the right person. Think about what I've said,' Dilly urged, then she rose from the table, telling him, 'I'm going to turn in now. It's been quite a day and we have another busy one ahead of us. Thank you again for a lovely evening.'

She dropped a kiss on his cheek but Philip scarcely noticed. He was staring through the window deep in thought. Deborah March in love with him? He could hardly take it in – although now he came to think about it, he realised with a jolt that she was always the one he turned to when he needed a companion. And as Dilly had said, she *was* very beautiful and very easy to talk to. Suddenly he didn't mind so much that Dilly had turned him down. He had a lot to think about.

Chapter Nine

'Goodbye, Philip!' Dilly shouted as the train juddered into life. She watched him, waving until he was lost to sight, then settled down in the empty carriage so she could think about the momentous events of the day.

She and Philip had begun with a visit to the landlord who owned the shop. After a fair bit of bartering they had agreed on a rent that was acceptable to both of them and Dilly had signed a twelve-month contract. Philip had then taken her to call on the various tradesmen who specialised in shopfitting. Once she was quite sure that they knew exactly what she wanted, she had then negotiated the cost with them too. Next was the visit to Mrs Bishop, the lady whom Philip had approached about managing the shop, and Dilly had been very taken with her. Philip had also suggested that, for the time being, the manageress would pay the shop takings to him each evening, and he would then be responsible for banking them. Once things were established, Mrs Bishop could do the banking herself

– her references were impeccable and Dilly instinctively trusted her. It seemed that he had thought of everything. Finally she had a meeting with some of Philip's seamstresses, the ones who would be making the gowns for her shop. They had been very obliging and she and Philip had negotiated the price she would pay for their work. All in all, it had gone so smoothly that Dilly or Seamus would only need to visit London about once a month to check the shop's books and see that all was well. Any emergencies that might arise in between would be dealt with by Philip.

In a happy frame of mind, Dilly relaxed back in her seat. She was aching to be home now so that she could see Jessica, her little lass.

'So that's seven shops in all now then,' Nell said the next morning as she and Dilly sat at the kitchen table enjoying the first cup of tea of the day.

Dilly nodded. Had she noticed a slight hint of disapproval in Nell's voice?

'So you'll be harin' off to London all the time as well as workin' on yer designs an' buzzin' about between the other shops?'

'Not at all.' Dilly placed her cup down and asked pointedly, 'Aren't you happy about the London shop, Nell?'

'It ain't that I'm not happy about it. I'm just concerned that you're doin' too much,' Nell answered forthrightly. Dilly could always trust her old friend to speak her mind. 'We barely get to see you as it is. I just think it's time fer you to start thinkin' about slowin' down a bit. There's more to life than workin' yerself into an early grave.' It wasn't the first time she'd spoken on the subject.

'I wasn't thinking of doing that,' Dilly answered,

annoyed. 'And in case you'd forgotten – Seamus and Mary do most of the running about supplying the shops now.'

'I'm well aware of that. But you're still shut away workin' on yer designs half the time,' Nell nagged. 'When are yer goin' to start makin' a bit more time for yerself? With the workforce you've got you could afford to retire now and leave the young 'uns to run the businesses.'

'Oh, you sound just like my father-in-law!' Dilly could have bitten her tongue out as Nell smiled smugly.

'There you are then. I ain't the only one who thinks yer doin' too much, am I?' Glancing at the clock she hastily drained her cup before heading for the door, saying, 'Best be off or I'll be late opening up. Bye fer now!'

Left alone, Dilly quickly cleared the dirty pots from the table then hurried into the bedroom to get the present she had bought for Jessica in London. Before she started work she intended to go and see her. On the way to Mill House, the comments Nell had made lay heavy on her mind. Why was everyone telling her to slow down all of a sudden? Fifty wasn't that old, after all. Admittedly, she did need to make time to go and see Niamh in New York, and she fully intended to, but that plan would have to be put on hold for a little longer now – just till she was sure that the London shop was operating properly, she promised herself. Then when she'd been to New York, she'd visit Kian's grave in France.

'She's potterin' about somewhere wi' Gwen,' Mrs Pegs informed her when Dilly arrived at the Farthings'. 'Olivia's at work an' Mr Farthing's gone to Hatter's Hall. Camilla ain't too well, apparently.'

'Oh dear, I hope it isn't anything serious,' Dilly answered as she passed through the kitchen.

Mrs Pegs raised an eyebrow. From where she was

standing it would be a blessed relief when the poor woman went to meet her Maker now. From the bits she'd heard the master say, Camilla was unrecognisable, poor soul. But she didn't voice her opinion, of course. It wasn't her place.

Dilly heard Jessica before she saw her. The little girl was in the drawing room furiously rubbing wax polish on to the front of the sideboard, chattering away fifteen to the dozen.

'I'm making it look nice for when George comes to see me on Thursday,' she told Dilly importantly, then abandoning her duster she asked, 'Did you bring me a present? And are you going away again?'

'Yes, I did bring you a present and no, I'm not going away again. Not for a while at least,' Dilly promised as Jessica hurtled into her arms.

Gwen groaned as she stared at the sideboard doors. 'I reckon she's put at least half a tin o' wax on there. It'll take ages fer me to polish that lot off.'

'She was only trying to help, weren't you, pet,' Dilly answered indulgently as she fumbled in her bag for Jessica's present. 'I've bought you a new book – look, about a little bear called Winnie the Pooh. He lives in Half Acre Wood with his friends, Piglet and Eeyore the donkey. Look at the lovely pictures. Mummy will be able to read it to you at bedtime.'

'Read some of it to me *now*,' Jessica demanded, clambering on to her lap and so she and Dilly spent the next half an hour looking at the book, giving the long-suffering Gwen a little time to get on with her work in peace.

They were still sitting there when Max walked in looking solemn-faced – but he perked up when he saw Dilly.

'I didn't know you were back. This is a nice surprise,' he said as Jessica raced towards him clutching her new book.

'Look what Dilly bought me,' she said excitedly.

'Why, how lovely.' Max patted her curls affectionately. 'But now why don't you run along to the kitchen for me and tell Mrs Pegs that Dilly and I would love a cup of tea. Are you a big enough girl to do that?'

'Of course I am!' Jessica declared, her chest swelling with importance, and she scampered off on her mission.

Once on their own, Max became sombre again. 'I've just been to Hatter's Hall,' he said grimly. 'And Camilla is very poorly indeed.'

'What's the problem?'

'They don't seem to know. It's as if she's just lost the will to live – and who could blame her, shut up in that godforsaken place? It might be quite luxurious but it's no more than a prison really, is it? She's just lying in bed staring off into space.'

'Poor soul, but you mustn't start whipping yourself again. She's in the best place,' Dilly told him quietly.

Max shrugged before asking, 'How did your trip go?'

'Very well.' Dilly went on to tell him all about the new shop and the arrangements she had come to with Philip.

'Well, it all sounds grand. Let's just hope the miners get back to work soon though. The strike may be officially over but there are thousands still standing their ground and refusing to go back down until their terms are met. It's already affecting what people have to spend here in the Midlands, but if it goes on it could affect the shops in London too.'

'I doubt it. As you once pointed out, the sort of shops Philip owns and the sort I've just taken on cater to a wealthy clientele,' she told him.

'I hope you're right,' he said quietly but then Jessica was back and they centred all their attention on her again.

'Here are the books from the shops for you to look over, Mammy,' Seamus told her that evening. 'I've been through them and everything seems to tally.'

'I really don't know what I'd do without you,' Dilly praised him. 'But is Mary here?'

'Yes, she's in the kitchen chatting to Nell.'

'I'll come through then.' Dilly laid aside the design she'd been working on and followed her son into the kitchen.

His wife, Mary, was sitting at the kitchen table and she smiled when she saw her mother-in-law. Seamus then gave his wife a meaningful glance.

'We've err . . . come to share a little news with you all,' Mary told Dilly and Nell.

Dilly's heart did a leap of anticipation as she guessed what the news might be. Mary and Seamus had been trying for a baby for some time.

'Then tell me – don't keep us in suspense!'

Mary blushed. 'We're going to have a baby,' she said. 'It will be due round about Christmastime.'

Dilly rushed across the room and hugged Mary fiercely as Seamus looked proudly on. Mary had been the making of her son and now Dilly loved her like a daughter.

'That's wonderful news,' she told them both, meaning every word, and Nell echoed her congratulations.

'And don't worry, I shall still be helping Seamus to cover the shops if anyone is off sick,' Mary assured her. 'I shall just take the little 'un along with me.'

'I wasn't worried,' Dilly answered, then turning to Nell she asked, 'Have we still got any of that sherry left over from Christmas? I think this calls for a toast.'

'I reckon it's in the sideboard.' Nell hurried off to look as the happy couple babbled away about the forthcoming baby.

'I'm hoping it will be a lad for Seamus,' Mary confided. 'Though he says he don't care what it is, as long as it's healthy.'

'That's right,' Seamus agreed, staring at his wife adoringly. 'Lass or laddie it'll be loved.'

Nell came back then with half a bottle of sherry which she proceeded to share out into glasses.

'I'll just have a sip. It might not be good for the baby,' Mary decided.

The girl looked to be in rude health, Dilly noted. Her hair was shining and her skin had a rosy glow to it – but then she'd looked that way ever since the day she and Seamus had got wed. They were a match made in heaven and Dilly had no doubt this baby would cement their relationship even more. Hopefully, the child would be the first of many.

'You must slow down and look after yourself now,' Dilly fussed, and Mary gurgled with laughter.

'You don't need to go frettin' about me. I'm strong as a horse an' me mam says I'll fly through childbirth 'cos I've got childbearin' hips.'

'All the same I don't want you overdoing it,' Dilly warned.

'I'll make sure that she doesn't, Mammy,' Seamus promised and they then all drank a toast to the new Carey baby that would soon be joining the family.

It was only when they had gone and Dilly and Nell were alone again that Dilly told her, 'I was thinking of going over to see Niamh and Ben round about Christmastime, but I feel I ought to be here for the birth of the new baby now.'

'So go now then,' Nell said sensibly.

'I can't disappear just yet, not until I know the shop in London is up and running properly.'

Nell cocked her head to the side and said quietly, 'Shouldn't it be opening in the next couple of weeks?'

'Yes – why?'

'Then if everything goes to plan you could sail to New York in September. It's the end of June already so that allows plenty of time for the shop to get going. And you know, you have another grandchild in New York that you haven't even clapped eyes on yet who is just as important as the one that's comin'. It only takes five or six days or so on the ship to get to New York, so if you went when I suggested you could be there an' back in plenty o' time for when Mary an' Seamus's baby arrives. You could treat it as a little holiday – God knows yer deserve one! An' there's plenty of us 'ere to run things till yer got back.'

'Hmm, I suppose you're right.' Dilly chewed on her lip for a moment and then, making a decision, she told Nell with an edge of excitement in her voice, 'I'll do it! I've neglected Niamh for far too long and I do want to meet my little grandson.'

Nell smiled her approval as Dilly began to plan.

Chapter Ten

Dilly went to London for the opening of her shop at the end of July and from day one it was apparent that it was going to be a success. Mrs Bishop, the new manageress, had everything well under control and Dilly was thankful to Philip for recommending her. She stayed in London for three days, choosing to put up in a small hotel in Marylebone that was conveniently close to the shop and just a short taxi ride from Euston. Philip didn't press her to stay with him in his apartment this time, and on the second day Dilly found out why.

'I'm taking Deborah to the Electric Cinema this evening,' he said casually. 'We're going to see a showing of the Rudolph Valentino film, *The Sheikh*. Would you care to join us? It's only a short trip over to Portobello Road.'

'Thank you, but what's the saying? Two is company, three is a crowd,' she said teasingly and had the satisfaction of seeing a slight flush rise up his neck as she went on innocently, 'Should I be looking around for a new hat yet?'

'Well, you never know,' he mumbled, and Dilly couldn't have been more thrilled for him. Deborah was a lovely young woman, and she and Philip would be perfect for each other.

'I have you to thank for making me realise that I had feelings for her, Dilly,' he said then. 'It wasn't until I thought about it that I began to wonder why I always asked her out time after time, even if there were a few conquests in between.' He had the good grace to look slightly guilty. 'I'm afraid I've been a bit of a lad in my time, haven't I?'

'Not at all,' Dilly assured him. 'You were footloose and fancy free so you weren't hurting anyone.' She linked her arm through his as he walked her back to the hotel. She felt at ease with him again now that she knew he had no romantic inclinations towards her.

'But what will you do with yourself tonight?' he asked worriedly at the entrance to the hotel.

'Guess,' Dilly laughed and he sighed.

'You'll work on your designs.'

'Yes, I will – and don't get moaning. They're making us a lot of money.'

'I agree, but you know, Dilly, you showed me the error of my ways – perhaps you need someone to show you yours? There's more to life than work.'

'As it happens I'm going on holiday to New York at the beginning of September to see my daughter so what do you think of that?'

'I think it's about time.' He patted her hand. 'Good night, my dear. I'll see you in the morning.'

Dilly was feeling contented as she went up to her room. The new shop was in safe hands, and with Philip keeping his eye on the ordering, she or Seamus would not need to visit more than once a month at least.

August passed in a blur as Dilly got ready for her trip. The seamstresses had made her a good selection of clothes to take with her. Never having been on a cruise-liner before, Dilly had no idea what she should take so she was prepared for every eventuality. She had packed the beautiful evening dress that Philip had treated her to, as well as a selection of day clothes.

'I almost wish I was coming with you,' Olivia said enviously one Thursday afternoon as she and Dilly sat together in the garden at Mill House watching George and Jessica happily playing together. Max had had a swing and a slide installed and the children spent hours on them when the weather permitted.

'So why don't you? There's still time to book you a ticket and Niamh would be thrilled to see you.'

Olivia grinned. 'I was only joking. What about my job – and who'd look after Jessica?'

'I'm sure the hospital would give you some time off, and Jessica could come with us,' Dilly answered hopefully. It would be wonderful to have the two of them all to herself for a time on the ship.

'No, it's not practical. But it was a nice thought – and it's not as if we aren't having a holiday, is it? Daddy is taking us to Cornwall for two weeks while you're away. Jessica is going to love it. He's really wonderful with her,' she confided then. 'I know it was a shock to him when he discovered that she was mine, but he's handled everything really well. So has Oscar, although I don't think he or anyone believed the story Daddy put around for a minute about me being married and widowed in London.'

'I'm sure he only did that to ease things for you and Jessica,' Dilly pointed out. 'He didn't want the lass to bear the stigma of being illegitimate.'

'I suppose so. Now I'll go and get us all a nice cold drink, shall I?' With that Olivia moved away, leaving Dilly to watch the children.

The following Sunday afternoon, as Olivia was walking Jessica through the park, a couple strolling along the riverbank ahead of her caught her attention. There was something vaguely familiar about the man . . . and when he turned his head to say something to the attractive woman on his arm, Olivia's heart sank into her shoes. It was Roger Bannerman – Jessica's father!

'Jessica!' Olivia hissed. The child was throwing bread to the swans on the river and Olivia hoped that if she could distract her daughter and go the other way, Roger wouldn't spot them. She felt sick with terror. What could he be doing back here? She'd heard that he and his wife had left Nuneaton long ago, and she'd hoped never to have to see him again.

Jessica looked sulkily at her mother. She still had a fair amount of the dried bread Mrs Pegs had saved for her to throw to the ducks and swans, and seeing as it was one of the favourite things she loved to do she didn't want to waste a crumb.

'Come along, darling. I've just thought of something I need to do at home. We'll come back and feed the swans and ducks another day when I have more time.'

'But I don't *want* to go home yet,' Jessica objected loudly, which made the woman on Roger's arm look back at them and smile.

The couple then turned and began to walk towards them and Olivia had to stop herself from groaning aloud as she saw the guilt and recognition on Roger's face.

'Such a pretty little girl,' the woman remarked enviously as they drew abreast of them.

Roger nodded before saying politely, 'Hello, Olivia. How are you?' Then to his wife, 'This is Olivia Farthing, darling. We used to briefly be in the same Amateur Dramatics Society.' He then glanced towards Jessica and asked, 'Babysitting, are you?'

Olivia nodded, as colour flooded into her cheeks. 'Something like that,' she muttered, noting that at least he had the good grace to look uncomfortable.

Jessica meantime had turned her attention back to the swans so Olivia said, 'I heard that you'd moved away, Roger – with your job.'

'Yes, we did for a time but Miranda missed her folks so when a vacancy came up back in this area we relocated again.'

'I was lonely,' the woman explained with an apologetic smile at her husband. 'There was nothing to do while Roger was at work, you see, and I didn't know anyone there. We haven't been fortunate enough to have any children yet but we haven't given up hope, have we, darling?'

It was then that Jessica finally threw the rest of the crumbs to the swans, and brushing her hands together she raced back to Olivia, saying, 'I'm ready now, Mummy.' Then spotting the people her mother was talking to, she skidded to a halt and surveyed them solemnly.

Today, she was dressed in a little red and white gingham dress with a red sash about the waist. A matching red ribbon was tied in her hair and beneath the full skirt peeped a pretty white broderie anglaise petticoat. Her feet were clad in tiny black-patent shoes, and with the late-afternoon sunshine glinting off her unruly copper curls she looked adorable.

'How do you do?' she said politely, extending her hand as she had been taught to do, and it was instantly clear that Roger's wife was totally entranced with her.

'I'm very well, thank you.' Miranda bent and shook the chubby hand as Olivia's own hands began to shake. Jessica's eyes were exactly the same colour as Roger's. Would he notice? Would his wife?

'Mummy, can we go to the playground now? Just for a little while, *please*?'

Roger looked shocked. 'I didn't hear that you'd got married, Olivia,' he said.

Thankfully she was saved from having to reply when Jessica caught her hand and began to drag her towards the playground.

'I'm so sorry, I really must go but it was nice to see you both.' She then allowed Jessica to tug her away with a sigh of relief – although long after Roger and his wife had disappeared from sight a terrible fear wormed its way around her stomach.

What if Roger were to put two and two together?

'Mummy, come and push me!' Jessica's voice brought her thoughts sharply back to the present as she approached the swings to do as she was asked.

He might suspect it but he can't prove it, she told herself and began to feel a little easier as she concentrated on her little daughter again. She had never told anyone, not even her father or Dilly who Jessica's father was – and that was the way it would stay.

It was the last week of August as Olivia was walking home from the hospital late one afternoon when she bumped into Roger again. She was just about to turn the corner into Manor Court Road when he strode around it and stopped abruptly at the sight of her. Olivia had no choice but to stop too without appearing very rude.

Now that she had met his wife she couldn't understand why he had ever entered into an affair with her. Miranda

81

was beautiful and seemed a thoroughly nice person – so why on earth had he strayed?

'Hello, Olivia.'

She inclined her head, keen to get away from him at the earliest opportunity.

'And how is that delightful little girl of yours? Jessica, isn't it? Miranda was quite taken with her. How old did you say she was?'

Olivia's anger turned to ice-cold fear but she kept her voice steady as she answered, 'I don't think I did – and why would you be interested?'

He looked slightly taken aback and taking full advantage of the fact she went on, 'You'll have to excuse me. I'm in a tearing rush – things to do you know.' And with that she took off as if Old Nick himself were snapping at her heels.

She didn't slow her steps until she had turned into Earls Road, where she paused to glance anxiously over her shoulder to make sure that he wasn't following her. Satisfied that he was nowhere in sight she leaned heavily against a wall to get her breath back and calm herself before she continued on her way, but she was badly shaken. Roger obviously had suspicions that Jessica might be his. What was she to do?

I'll do nothing, she told herself firmly. *If he asks outright I shall just refuse to answer him.*

When she entered the kitchen shortly afterwards, Jessica hurtled towards her and wrapped her chubby arms about her mother's legs. Olivia's heart melted as it always did – and there and then she vowed that Roger must never discover the truth. Jessica was the most important person in her life and she had no intentions whatsoever of sharing her with anyone.

After tea, Olivia took Jessica to see Dilly and Nell.

The little girl adored Dilly, and Nell always spoiled her with treats despite Olivia's protests.

'When are you going on the big ship?' Jessica asked sadly.

Dilly stroked the child's curls. 'Next week, pet, but don't worry, I shall soon be coming home to you, and meantime you're going to the seaside with Grandfather and Mummy. Won't that be lovely?'

'Yes,' Jessica said slowly, 'but I wish you and Nell were coming too. I shall miss you both, and Mummy says the big ship is going to take you right across the sea. That's a *very* long way away, isn't it?'

'Yes, it is,' Dilly answered, touched to see that tears were trembling on the little girl's long eyelashes. 'But Nell will still be here, and when you get back from your holiday, Mummy can bring you to see her and you can tell her all about it, can't you? Then when I get home we can tell each other all about our holidays. And of course I shall bring you something very nice back. What would you like?'

'I think I would like another dolly,' Jessica answered thoughtfully. 'One with long hair. George poked one of my dollies in the eye, you know, and broke it. That's very naughty, isn't it? George says dolls are cissy but they aren't, are they, Dilly? Uncle Oscar told him off an' he says he'll buy me a new one too.'

'Well, there you are then. You'll end up with two new dollies, won't you? And I shall be back before you know it. Meantime I want you to be a very good girl for Mummy and Grandfather and Gwen and Nell and Mrs Pegs. Will you do that for me?'

'Yes,' Jessica promised solemnly, and as Dilly hugged her, her heart swelled. She adored the child and the thought of not seeing her for a time was unbearable.

Chapter Eleven

The house was a hive of activity. Nell was in a fluster and opened one of the two trunks Dilly was taking with her to New York for the third time in an hour as she'd remembered something else she insisted Dilly must take with her.

'Nell, will you please *calm* down,' Dilly implored. 'You're making me nervous now.'

'Ah, but you're goin' to be away for a whole month,' Nell fretted. 'An' once you're on board the ship yer can't pop home for anything you've forgotten, can yer?'

Dilly sighed. Nell was on a mission and Dilly knew that she wouldn't relax now until after she had left.

'New York, eh?' Nell shook her head. 'Who'd ever 'ave believed it! All that way.'

'Yes, it is strange,' Dilly agreed with her old friend. 'But with modern travel it's not so bad. Once I embark in the morning, it only takes five days to get there.'

'Ah! Now have yer got yer reservation for the hotel in Liverpool this evenin'?'

'I have all my documents safely tucked into my bag here,' Dilly said.

'Well, just treat it as a complete rest,' Nell advised. 'Enjoy spending your time wi' your daughter an' that lovely little grandson o' yours.'

'I shall. I must admit, I'm really excited to be meeting James at last.' Dilly finished doing her hair in the mirror above the mantelpiece. She secretly had no intention of lazing around while she was away. In fact, her sketchpads and pens were safely packed away in one of the trunks so that she could work on her designs during the journey. But she wouldn't tell Nell that, of course.

Max strode into the kitchen then. He was going to drive Dilly to the railway station and he plastered a smile on his face although he dreaded having to go a whole month without her. Dilly had been to Mill House the evening before and said goodbye to Olivia and Jessica, who had both become quite tearful.

'I shall be back in the blink of an eye,' Dilly had whispered to Jessica as the child clung to her. 'And remember – I shall be sure to bring you back the loveliest dolly I can find. Now won't that be grand?' Dilly had felt as if her heart was breaking. She hated to leave her, even for a little while, but across the sea was another grandchild she had never even met yet and the trip was long overdue.

'So, are we almost ready?' Max glanced at his fine gold Hunter watch.

Dolly nodded. 'Yes, I was ready half an hour ago but Nell keeps adding things to the trunks. We won't be able to lift them at this rate.'

Max laughed good-humouredly as he manoeuvred the first one outside to the trunk of his Ford motor car, leaving Nell and Dilly to say their goodbyes.

'Now you mind what you get eatin' over there,' Nell warned and Dilly laughed.

'I'm not going to Outer Mongolia,' she teased. 'I'm sure the food there will be much the same as it is here.'

'Yes, well, you just be careful an' make sure you only drink water that's been boiled,' her old friend cautioned. 'An' don't get frettin' about anythin' here. Me, Seamus an' Mary are a good team an' more than capable of keepin' everythin' goin' like clockwork while you're away.'

Dilly drew Nell into her arms and hugged her before planting a warm kiss on her cheek. 'I know you are. What would I ever do without you? Goodbye, Nell.'

Max had returned and was in the process of lugging the second trunk out to the car now – and Dilly was amused to see that he had broken out in a sweat. He helped Dilly into the front of the car, then they were off as Nell stood waving in the doorway until they turned the corner and were lost to sight.

'I shall miss her,' Dilly sighed. 'In fact, I shall miss all of you – but a month isn't so very long in the greater scheme of things, is it?'

Max remained silent. A month sounded like a lifetime to him at present but he understood why Dilly needed to go and he didn't want to spoil the trip for her, although he wished he were going with her.

When they arrived at the station Max summoned a porter to take the trunks to the van at the back of the train and then it was time to say goodbye. He desperately wanted to take Dilly into his arms and kiss her, but there were people milling about the station and he knew that she wouldn't thank him for showing her up.

Instead he took her hand and said, 'Take care now, and have a wonderful time. Oh, and do give Niamh my regards.'

'I will,' she promised as he led her towards her compartment. Most of the passengers were already aboard and she could see that the guard was ready to blow his whistle and wave his flag. She climbed aboard hurriedly, not wishing to prolong their goodbyes, and as the train pulled away she sat down with a huge lump in her throat. She had never travelled further than Ireland before, and the thought of going so far away from all that was familiar and the people she loved was daunting.

It was early evening before the train pulled into Liverpool Lime Street station and after hailing a porter to help her with her luggage, the trunks were loaded into a cab and she was driven to her hotel. The one she had chosen, the Mermaid, was quite close to the docks, much to Max's horror. He would have preferred her to stay in a better-class place further into the city, but Dilly had insisted that she would be more than comfortable for just one night; also, she preferred to be closer to the ship ready for departure the next morning. In addition, he had objected to her travelling budget class on the liner, but old habits died hard. Dilly could still clearly remember back to the days when she hadn't two pennies to rub together. Even now she would rarely spend tuppence on herself when a penny would do and so she was quite happy with just a small cabin, although she had allowed Max to choose the ship she would sail on. The RMS *Mauretania* had been built for the British Cunard Line and regularly transported up to 2,300 passengers at a time. The ship had been designed for speed, comfort and safety, and regularly did the trip between Liverpool and New York in five days, which sounded good to Dilly.

In the hotel, she unpacked the small overnight bag she had brought with her and rang room service for a meal. She was too tired to venture down to the dining room and decided she would get a good night's sleep in preparation for the journey ahead of her the next day. The meal, much like the room, was basic but adequate and despite her nerves, soon after eating it she fell into a deep sleep.

She was up bright and early the next morning and after breakfast her trunks were loaded into yet another cab and she was driven the short distance to the docks.

'Which ship were you lookin' for, missus?' the kindly driver asked.

'The *Mauretania*,' Dilly answered, gazing at the huge liners bobbing in the harbour. She had never seen anything like them in her life; they made the ferry on which she had travelled to Ireland look tiny, and she wondered aloud how they managed to stay afloat.

'You'll be safe as 'ouses's on the *Mauretania*,' the cab-driver assured her. 'I'll get you as close as I can to her then I'll find a sailor to take your trunks aboard for you.'

Dilly thanked him profusely and when the cab drew to a halt in front of the largest ship in the dock, she stared at it in awe. There were two gangplanks leading up on to it. Passengers were boarding on one and burly seamen were manoeuvring the luggage up the other. The whole place was teeming with activity and there seemed to be people of all colours and sizes everywhere she looked.

In no time at all the driver was back with a seaman who began to manhandle her trunks out of the trunk and on to a sturdy hand-trolley.

Dilly paid the driver, giving him a generous tip that had him doffing his cap, and then she was following the seaman towards the gangplank as butterflies fluttered to life in her stomach. It looked an awfully long way up to the deck, where a man in a smart white uniform whom she presumed was the Captain stood greeting the passengers as other officers checked their tickets.

'Good morning, ma'am,' he greeted her politely when she finally reached the deck. 'I do hope you will enjoy your journey with us.' He shook her hand warmly, thinking what a fine-looking woman she was. 'Would you hand your reservations to my officer there?'

Dilly quickly did as she was asked and the young officer consulted the clipboard in his hand before saying, 'Ah, Mrs Carey. There has been a change to your reservation. You've been upgraded to a suite of rooms. If you would follow the steward here, he will show you the way.'

Dilly looked confused. 'There must be some mistake. I haven't changed anything. You no doubt have the wrong person.'

'No, it's quite clear if you would care to look.' He thrust the clipboard towards her and as Dilly peered down at her name, she frowned. And then it came to her in a flash. This was just the sort of thing Max would do. 'Would you care to follow me, ma'am? Your luggage will be delivered to your suite shortly.'

'Yes – thank you.' Dilly followed him along the deck, picking her way past throngs of people who were all keen to stand at the rails and wave goodbye to loved ones who had come to see them off on their voyage. She suddenly wished that she'd allowed Max to accompany her this far, but it was too late to do anything about it now. An early-morning mist was swirling along the deck but already the sun was trying to break through, and it looked set to be a fine September morning.

Eventually the young man led her into the first-class main salon and Dilly's eyes nearly popped out of her head. This was nothing like she had expected to find on a ship: it was so luxurious that it almost took her breath away. Elevators stood against one wall and a sweeping staircase in the centre of the room led up to the next level. Through tall, etched-glass doors she glimpsed what she presumed would be the first-class dining room lit by a huge glass sky-dome. They seemed to walk for miles and again Dilly wondered at the size of the ship, but at last he paused in a long corridor and opening a door he told her, 'This is your suite, ma'am. A maid will be along shortly to check that you have everything you need, but please don't hesitate to ask if there is anything you require. We like our first-class passengers to be happy with the service they receive. Good day.'

Dilly hastily fumbled in her bag for a tip and once he had thanked her, the young man left, leaving Dilly to inspect what would be her home for the next few days. She was standing in what she assumed was a small lounge. There was a porthole in one wall and from it she could see the people swarming along the dockside. Ornate gilt chairs were placed in front of a low table, and against another wall was a small writing desk and matching chair. A larger table held a huge bouquet of flowers. Their perfume filled the room, and crossing to them Dilly plucked a small card from amongst the blooms.

Have a wonderful journey and take care, with love, Max

Dilly sniffed back tears at his thoughtfulness before spotting the bottle of champagne in an ice bucket next to the flowers. It seemed that Max had thought of everything, bless him. After opening another door she found herself in a beautiful bathroom with a huge roll-top bathtub in the centre. The walls were mirrored, the floor marble and she sighed with pleasure as she anticipated relaxing there. The next door led to the bedroom which was dominated by a large carved four-poster bed in satinwood. Matching drawers, a wardrobe and a dressing table were dotted about the room, which was decorated in shades of pale mauve and purple. Double doors led out on to a small balcony and Dilly could picture herself relaxing there watching the sun sink into the sea. She didn't dare to think what accommodation like this must have cost. She would try and sort that with Max when she got home, although she doubted he would allow her to. He could be quite as stubborn as she was when he had a mind to be.

A tap on the lounge door heralded the arrival of her luggage then and also a young maid who bobbed her knee respectfully.

'I'm Emily, madam,' she introduced herself. 'I shall be your personal maid for the duration of the journey. May I begin by unpacking your trunks for you?'

'Oh no – really, there's no need!' Dilly was quite flustered but the maid was not going to take no for an answer.

'It's all part of the service for our first-class passengers,' she explained pleasantly. 'And if any of your clothes have got creased during your journey I shall be happy to take them away and get them ironed for you. Would you like some tea or coffee perhaps, before I begin?'

'Err . . . tea would be lovely,' Dilly mumbled, feeling rather out of her depth. It had always been her waiting on other people and the sudden reversal of roles was going to take some getting used to.

'Certainly, madam. I shan't be long.' Emily bobbed her knee again and hurried away, leaving Dilly to try and get her thoughts together. It looked as if this voyage was going to be quite unforgettable.

Chapter Twelve

'Will she be on the ship by now, sir?' Gwen asked as she placed Max Farthing's breakfast in front of him on the dining table.

Glancing at the clock on the mantelpiece, he nodded. 'Yes, she should be, Gwen. The *Mauretania* should be setting sail in an hour or so.' He chuckled then as he lifted his knife and fork. 'And I don't mind betting I'll be in the doghouse. You know how independent Dilly is. She'll be mad as hell when she knows I upgraded her accommodation without telling her.'

Gwen grinned. 'I don't reckon she'll be mad at you for long. The suite you told me an' Mrs Pegs about sounds right grand.' She sighed enviously. 'I doubt I'll ever get to travel on a ship like that.'

'Who knows what life has in store for you, Gwen? Dilly must have thought the same thing once – and look at her now. A string of successful shops to her name and sailing off to see her daughter in New York – all through hard work and determination.'

'Yes, she does work hard,' Gwen agreed. 'But now I'll just pop back to the kitchen fer the coffee pot. Enjoy your meal.' As she scuttled away, Max thought moodily that Dilly wouldn't even have sailed out of port yet, and here he was, missing her already. The next four weeks stretched emptily ahead of him but then Jessica scampered into the room to join him for breakfast and his gloomy mood instantly dissipated.

'How many sleeps is it now, Granpa, till we go to the seaside?' she asked eagerly.

'Three more,' he answered kindly. 'But first you have to come here and sit by me and show me what a big girl you are by eating all of your breakfast.'

Only too happy to oblige, the child scrambled up on to the seat at the side of him.

Gwen had just delivered the coffee pot to the dining room and was on her way back to the kitchen when a knock at the front door halted her progress. Thinking it would be the postman, she hurried to answer it then gasped with delight when she saw who was standing on the step.

'Why, Bessie! Mrs Pegs'll be right thrilled to see yer! Drop yer bag down there an' come straight through to the kitchen. We've just made a fresh pot o' tea so yer timin' couldn't 'ave been better.'

Bessie did as she was told, and when Mrs Pegs clapped eyes on her she too exclaimed with delight as she hurried over to give her a hug.

'Yer lookin' well,' she commented. Bessie had lost weight and it suited her. 'But why didn't yer let us know exactly when you'd be comin? An' have yer anywhere to stay yet?'

'No,' Bessie said as she took a seat at the table. 'But I was hopin' that Dilly might let me stay with her for a while till I can find a place of my own.'

'Dilly's on board a ship on her way to New York right at this very minute. She's off to see Niamh,' Mrs Pegs informed her. 'But I'm sure Nell would 'ave no objections to yer stayin' at St Edward's Road. She'll be at the shop in town this mornin' if yer want to go an' see her. But not till yer've had sommat to eat an' drink an' brought us all up to date wi' what you've been doing. Lordy, there's so much been goin' on here since yer left that I barely know where to start.'

For the next hour the two women sat catching up on all the gossip as Gwen flitted between the kitchen and dining room, then when Mr Farthing left to visit one of his factories she brought Jessica into the kitchen to join them.

'My goodness, how you've grown!' Bessie said, as Jessica snuggled shyly into Gwen's side. Then: 'I was thinking I perhaps ought to pay a visit to Ireland to see Roddy before I start work at the hospital. He's shot up too, according to Roisin's letters.'

'So Dilly was saying,' Mrs Pegs agreed, eyeing Bessie keenly. 'But you weren't thinkin' o' fetchin' him back, were you? He's very happy an' settled there from what I can make of it, an' Roisin an' Declan adore him by all accounts.'

'So I believe.' Bessie chewed on her lip. 'An' I'm very grateful to them for steppin' in as they did. But he is *my* son at the end of the day, and having time apart from him has made me realise that I 'aven't really been fair to the poor little mite. He couldn't help who his father were, could he? Speakin' o' which, how's his father doin'? Behavin' himself fer a change, is he?'

Mrs Pegs shrugged. 'Who knows? Samuel cleared off ages ago an' we ain't seen hide nor hair of him since. He tried to sell his house right from under his dad's nose so it ain't likely he'll show his face around these parts again. He'd have to have skin as thick as a rhino's!'

'Nothing he did would surprise me,' Bessie said bitterly. 'But now I'd best be off an' see if Nell will offer me a bed. I'll leave me bags here fer now if you don't mind. Thanks for the food an' the tea. I'll see you later.' With that she gave a cheery wave and went on her way, leaving Mrs Pegs with a smile on her face.

Nell was delighted to see her when she arrived at the shop and plied her with yet more tea after agreeing that yes of course she could stay with her.

'I shall be glad o' the company,' she admitted. 'Wi' Dilly away I'm goin' to rattle around that big house like a pea in a pod an' it can be spooky on yer own at night.'

'Well, seeing as I've nothing else to do and no one else I want to see, I may as well stay here and help you,' Bessie decided and soon the two women were working together side by side.

When the shop closed that evening they went back to the Mill House to collect Bessie's bags before returning to Dilly's place together, but first Mrs Pegs insisted that they must stay for dinner and the get-together took on a party atmosphere.

On the ship, Dilly was also in a happy mood as she dressed for dinner at the Captain's table. She had decided to wear the evening dress and necklace that Philip had bought her in London, and she took especial care when doing her hair and applied only a minimum amount of make-up. When she finally left her suite to make for the dining room she drew more than a few admiring glances from male passengers and staff alike, but Dilly didn't even notice. She had never been a vain woman.

Deciding to go on deck first, she made for the rails and leaned on them, gazing out at the huge expanse of sea that stretched as far as her eyes could see. The sun was beginning to set and the sky was a blaze of reds, promising another fine day to follow. There was a nip in the early-September night air but thankfully she had thought to wear a thin shawl about her slim shoulders. It had been strange earlier in the day watching the shores of her home country blur into the distance, but now she was just looking forward to seeing her daughter and meeting her grandson. Meantime, she would spend the majority of her time working on her designs. Dilly couldn't think of anything worse than lounging about all day and saw no reason why she couldn't combine work with pleasure. She wondered what Max would be doing now. He'd probably be reading Jessica a bedtime story. The thought made her miss them both but she forced herself to remain focused. This visit to Niamh was long overdue and she'd be back home before she knew it, so she might as well make the most of it.

'Forgive me for being so forward, but would you like someone to accompany you in to dinner?'

Dilly glanced to her left to see a tall distinguished-looking man in a dinner suit standing next to her. His hair was streaked with grey but his eyes were a startling shade of blue and he was very handsome. He also had an American accent.

'Thank you very much for the kind offer but I'm perfectly all right on my own.'

'Sorry, I didn't mean to offend.'

A smile softened Dilly's face. He looked harmless enough and she didn't wish to sound standoffish. 'You didn't. I'm just not ready to go in yet. It's very peaceful out here, isn't it?'

He nodded as he leaned on the rail next to her. 'It certainly is. Are you going to New York on business?'

'No, I'm actually going to visit my daughter and her family. What about you?'

'It's been a business trip for me, I'm afraid, and I'm just on my way home.' He peeped at her appreciatively out of the corner of his eye. 'I own oilfields in America so I'm always toing and froing to the UK,' he explained.

'I see – and are you travelling alone?' Dilly hoped that he wouldn't think she was being forward by asking but he was very easy to talk to.

He gazed out across the sea and then she saw the bleakness in his eyes as he answered, 'Yes, I am. I lost my wife eight months ago.'

'Oh, I'm so sorry.' Dilly fervently wished she hadn't asked now.

'It's quite all right, you weren't to know. To be honest, death was a blessed release for her in the end. It was terrible to see her suffering, although she rarely complained. She was quite a remarkable woman. We'd been married for twenty-five years so being alone again takes some getting used to. But how about you? Are you travelling alone too?'

'Yes. I was widowed many years ago.' Then suddenly making a decision, Dilly held her hand out and smiled. 'If that offer of taking me in to dinner still stands I'd like to accept it if I may. I've never been on a ship like this before and I'm feeling a little vulnerable.'

'It would be my pleasure. I'm Hayden Crosby, by the way.'

'Dilly Carey.' They shook hands then he tucked her arm into his and they headed for the dining room.

Huge crystal chandeliers were suspended above tables covered in crisp white tablecloths and more silver cutlery than Dilly had ever seen in her life before.

They took a seat, and as her companion saw her looking bemused, he leaned towards her and whispered, 'Just start at the outside for the first course and work your way in.'

The Captain joined his guests shortly afterwards and waiters appeared as if by magic to serve one delicious course after another. In no time at all, Dilly found she was enjoying herself. Hayden was a perfect gentleman and remarkably good company, and the evening passed quickly.

When the meal was over, he led her towards the cocktail lounge but Dilly shook her head. 'I won't have any more to drink, if you don't mind. I've already had far more wine than I usually drink during dinner.'

'Then perhaps you would like to dance? I hear they have a very good band on this evening.'

Again she shook her head. 'Actually, I think I may return to my suite. It's been quite a long day and it's catching up with me now. But thank you for your company. It was lovely to meet you.'

'In that case you must allow me to escort you back to your cabin. And perhaps tomorrow we could meet up for coffee? They have a wonderful veranda café on deck.'

'That would be lovely.' For some reason Dilly felt at ease with him. He had shown no romantic inclination towards her whatsoever; she sensed that he was merely lonely and still grieving for his late wife and so she gladly allowed him to accompany her back to her rooms where they wished each other a polite good night.

On entering her bedroom she found the bed had been turned back, ready for her, and her nightdress was laid across it. Emily was still tidying in the small lounge and she smiled a welcome. 'Did you enjoy your meal and have a nice evening, madam?' she asked cheerfully.

'I had a wonderful evening, thank you,' Dilly told her, and it was the truth.

'Would you like me to fetch you some hot chocolate or cocoa?'

'Oh goodness me, no thanks. I couldn't eat or drink another single thing.' Dilly laughed as she rubbed her stomach.

'Then is there anything else I can do for you?'

'Not a thing,' Dilly told her. 'Now you get off and have some rest.'

'Very well. Good night, madam.'

'Good night, Emily.'

As the girl left the room, Dilly kicked off her shoes and sprawled across the elegant little chaise longue feeling like a queen. *This is the life*, she told herself with a cheeky grin.

The next morning, as arranged, Dilly met Hayden mid-morning for coffee. She'd chosen to have breakfast in her rooms. It was quite nice to be waited on, she'd discovered, and so she was feeling refreshed when she strolled along the deck. The sea was as calm as a millpond and the dress she was wearing was exactly the same colour as her eyes, as Hayden pointed out.

'Actually it's one of my own designs,' Dilly told him with a modest blush. 'I own some dress shops and I design most of the clothes that are sold in them.'

'Really?' He looked impressed. 'Then you and my oldest daughter would get on well. Rosalie is twenty-three and I recently bought her a little fashion house in Manhattan. She's always looking for smart designs. Perhaps I should introduce the two of you?'

'Oh, I'm sure she wouldn't be interested in my designs,' Dilly said quickly but he disagreed.

'On the contrary, I think she would be very interested to

see some of them. The one you are wearing is classic and chic, and I know at the moment she's looking around for winter designs as the fall season has of course begun. Do tell me more about what you do, I'm quite intrigued. Did you also design the evening dress you were wearing last night?'

Dilly nodded and went on to tell him about her shops and about the agreement she had with Philip Maddison in London. Hayden listened earnestly.

'I don't see why you couldn't come to a similar arrangement with Rosalie in New York if you were inclined to. We could always get a lawyer to draw up a contract.'

Dilly's heart began to race with excitement as she tried to imagine how it would feel to know that her designs were selling in New York. The arrangement she had with Philip had worked very well, and as Hayden pointed out, there was no reason why the same couldn't happen in New York – if his daughter was interested, that was.

'Very well, I'd love to meet her. As it happens I have some of my designs with me and I've been working on the new winter and spring lines.'

He nodded and so it was agreed. It was beginning to appear that Dilly's trip would combine business with pleasure, after all.

Chapter Thirteen

'Right, *that is it*!' Seamus told Mary sternly a week after Dilly had sailed. 'Just look at your ankles – they're puffy and you can hardly get your breath, woman! You're staying home today and putting your feet up and that's an end to it. Nell and I can manage perfectly well and Bessie can step in to give a hand if need be. She doesn't start her new job at the hospital until next week.'

Mary snuggled down into the chair. She quite liked it when Seamus was masterful, although she couldn't for the life of her see what all the fuss was about. It was quite normal for pregnant women to have swollen ankles and get breathless, surely?

'Look, I'm bound to get a little out of breath, aren't I? I've always been plump and now I'm carting all this extra weight about I must weigh the same as a beached whale! I've forgotten what my feet look like. Now will you *please* stop worrying?' When Seamus sighed she went on, 'I tell you what I'll do. I'll put my feet up today but I want to get back to work tomorrow. The shop in Coventry is quite busy at the moment. Is it a deal?'

'I suppose so,' he answered reluctantly. 'But you're going to have to stop working soon. The baby is due in four months and I don't want you working till the last minute.'

Mary had every intention of doing just that, but not wanting to upset Seamus she merely smiled sweetly.

'We'll see,' she said. 'And now pass me those magazines, would you? If I've got to sit here all day I may as well make the most of it.'

Seamus did as he was told then bent to kiss his wife on the lips. His life had changed hugely for the better since he'd married Mary and he sometimes wished that he could wrap her in cotton wool because he couldn't bear to think of being without her.

'I'll be back as soon as I can,' he promised, snatching up his hat. 'I've not got too many deliveries to make today so I shouldn't be too long.'

Mary waved him off then settled down to enjoy her magazines.

In the small room that he shared with Kitty, Samuel was in a foul mood. He was still experiencing a great deal of pain in his arm, although that didn't surprise him. The doctor that Kitty had fetched to set it was a well-known alcoholic and Samuel doubted if the chap would have been sober enough to make a good job of it. He hadn't ventured from the room since the night he'd been attacked and if what Kitty had heard was anything to go by, it was just as well. His attackers were still out for revenge and Samuel had been forced to acknowledge that he had no choice but to get away from Plymouth now. How to do it was the problem. They were just about managing on the little that Kitty earned walking the streets but it was barely enough to pay the rent and put food on the table. He daren't even go to see what Carol and Katie were earning for fear of being seen. *No*, he told himself, *I've got to get away from here somehow* – but he couldn't let Kitty know that, of course.

His pacing of the small confined room continued as his mind worked overtime. He would have to leave one evening under cover of darkness while Kitty was still out. There was no danger of her trying to follow him because he had never told her exactly where he'd come from, apart from to say that it was in the Midlands, which covered a large area. But what would he use for money? Everything he owned had gone to the pawnshop long ago. And then suddenly it occurred to him . . . Kitty's grandmother's wedding ring. It was the only thing of any worth she owned and she valued it above everything, not only for its monetary worth but because of the sentiment attached to it. He knew she would have died of starvation rather than ever part with it – but the way he saw it, desperate situations called for desperate measures. Pushing his guilt aside, and crossing to the empty fireplace, he dropped to his knees and thrust his good arm up the chimney until his fingers came into contact with a loose brick. The effort made his bad arm throb and beads of sweat stand out on his forehead but he continued to wiggle the brick backwards and forwards until it came loose in his hand. Behind it was a tiny piece of cloth containing the ring and after hastily pocketing it, he replaced the brick as best he could.

Once he had cleaned himself up he resumed his pacing and a plan began to form in his head. There was a chap he knew called Jake who owed him a few favours and who lived along the coast in Exeter. They'd kept in touch spasmodically ever since their schooldays. Perhaps Jake would put him up for a time? But first he would need to pawn the ring to raise enough money for the fare to get him there. It would be no good waiting until it was dark; the shop would be shut by then so he had no alternative but to venture out. Deciding that there was no time like the present, Samuel tidied himself up to the best of his ability and set off. It was the first time he'd left the house in weeks and he felt as if everyone was staring at him. *Pull yourself together, man*, he told himself sternly. Even if he came upon his attackers face to face he reasoned they were hardly likely to set upon him in broad daylight. Even so, he kept to the back streets as much as he was able to and breathed a sigh of relief when the pawnshop came into view. He waited across the street in an empty shop doorway for a time until he was sure that the place was empty, then he slipped across the road and entered.

An hour later he let himself back into the room he shared with Kitty, feeling a sense of achievement. Thankfully he'd encountered no one and now all he had to do was wait until Kitty went out again that evening to make his escape.

'Had a good day then?' he asked innocently when Kitty returned early that evening. He noticed that her lip was split and one of her eyes was swollen but he didn't comment on it. She'd lost so much weight that she looked almost skeletal, but she still raised a smile as she held a parcel wrapped in newspaper out to him.

'Have these while they're still hot. I got you some chips on the way home. I got a loaf too if you want me to cut you a slice.'

'Just the chips will do,' Samuel answered, taking them from her. 'Aren't you having any?'

'Oh, I don't really fancy them. I'll just 'ave a bit of bread.'

He knew she was lying. She would always put him before herself and again he felt a fleeting pang of guilt. *Get a grip on yourself, man. You're going soft*, he silently scolded himself. Kitty would actually be better off without him. At least then she'd only have to worry about feeding herself. With his conscience eased he began to eat his meal while Kitty made them both a cup of weak tea.

It was dark by the time she ventured out on to the streets again and a mist had rolled in from the sea. This, added to the drizzle that was steadily falling, made everywhere look and feel wet and miserable.

'I've made a small fire up in the grate. You only have to put a match to it when yer ready. There's enough coal to burn fer a couple of hours at least if yer get cold,' she told him as she pulled a shawl over her head.

'Yes, I will – and Kitty . . . thanks!'

She stared at him, bewildered. Why was he being so nice? All he normally did was shout at her – not that she was complaining; it made a pleasant change. Now that she came to think about it, he'd been nice to her ever since she got in, and long may it last. She flashed a rare smile and just for an instant Samuel saw the pretty girl she might have been if she hadn't had such a hard life.

'Bye for now, my lover. See you later.' She left the room, preparing to face whatever lay before her.

'Oh no you won't,' Samuel said to the empty room as he crossed to the window to watch her progress across the litter-strewn courtyard below. When she was gone from sight he struggled into his coat and dragged the small bag containing his few possessions from under the bed where he had hidden it. He had packed it earlier that afternoon after returning from the pawnbrokers. Lastly he patted his pocket where the money he'd been given for Kitty's ring lay. Finally he took one last look around the room then lifting his bag with his good arm he set off for the station – and he didn't once look back.

It was late when Kitty arrived home. She was soaked to the skin but even so she was in a good mood. She jangled the coins in her pocket as she climbed the stairs, thinking how pleased Samuel would be when he saw how much she had earned. A ship had docked that day and the sailors had been in a generous mood. She'd make them both a nice mug of cocoa and then dry off by the fire, she decided, before going to bed. Perhaps they could even make love.

As she opened the door to her room she frowned to find it in darkness. The fire was almost out and the place felt strangely empty.

'Samuel – are you there?' Fumbling for the spills, she put one in the dying fire and hastily lit the oil lamp. As its orange glow slowly chased the shadows from the room, the first thing she saw was the door of the rickety wardrobe hanging open. Samuel's clothes were gone and her heart sank. She somehow knew that he had left, probably for good. And then suddenly a terrible thought occurred to her and after wrapping her arm in an old towel to stop herself getting burned she reached up the chimney and awkwardly removed the loose brick. She then frantically felt around, but her grandmother's wedding ring was missing, as she'd suspected it would be. No one else knew where she had hidden it so it could only have been Samuel who had taken it. Feeling utterly betrayed, she sat back on her heels as tears spilled down her cheeks – and she didn't know if she was crying for the loss of Samuel or her grandmother's precious ring. But then Kitty was a survivor. Deep down she'd always known Samuel wasn't to be trusted and she was used to fending for herself. She would do so again.

'So how have you been today?' Seamus asked anxiously as he entered his home on Abbey Green. There was an appetising smell hanging in the air and the table was set for two.

'I've been as right as ninepence,' Mary told him cheerily as she lifted a steak and kidney pie from the oven. His stomach groaned with anticipation. There was no one could make a pie quite as good as his Mary could.

'Hmm, but I see you've been cooking. I thought I told you to keep your feet up.'

'I have,' she answered indignantly. 'Well, for most of the day anyway. I only got up to make us a bit of dinner and me ankles have gone down no end – look!' She waggled one of them at him and he grinned.

'I'm pleased to hear it. I think from now on you should just help out a couple of days a week in the shop.'

'I'll tell you when I'm ready to slow down,' she informed him, waving the potato-masher at him mock-threateningly. 'Now will you please sit down for your dinner? Honestly, the way you go on, anyone would think I was ill rather than pregnant!'

'Sorry,' he said meekly. 'But I can't help but worry about you.'

She placed the pie in the middle of the table and planted a big kiss on his cheek. 'Well, there's no need to,' she said kindly. 'Childbirth is the most natural thing in the world an' I shall sail through it. I've got the constitution of an ox.' She placed the vegetables and the potatoes next to the pie then joining him she told him, 'Bessie came round to see me earlier. She's on about going to see Roddy in Enniskerry.'

Seamus frowned. 'What – after all this time? She's not having second thoughts about letting him go, is she? It would fair break our Declan and Roisin's hearts if she did.'

'I'm not sure,' Mary admitted as she placed a generous slice of pie on his plate. 'But she certainly spoke about him with a lot more affection than she ever has before. Still, let's not fret about it. Things will pan out for the best, they usually do.'

Seamus nodded in agreement as he heaped mashed potatoes next to his pie. 'I dare say you're right,' he agreed. His Mary was very wise. 'Now please excuse me while I do justice to this delicious meal.'

Mary smiled at him affectionately before filling her own plate. This was the time of day she loved best. After the meal she would make them a pot of tea, then Seamus would help her to clear the table and wash and dry the pots before they sat down in front of the fire together to chat about their day. Their lives together had fallen into a happy routine that would be made even better with the arrival of their first child. As if it knew she was thinking of it, the baby suddenly gave her a hefty kick and smiling, the young woman stroked her swollen stomach. Life could surely not get much better than this?

Chapter Fourteen

'Is the storm over, Emily?' Dilly asked weakly from her bed on the ship.

The young maid nodded and straightened the covers on the bed. 'Almost, madam. But now let me help you sit up so you can have a sip of this tea and a dry biscuit. It will help to settle your stomach if you can keep it down.'

Two days previously, the ship had travelled through a storm that had tossed it about like a cork. Green with nausea, Dilly had taken to her bed, convinced that they were all going to die. Hayden had insisted on the ship's doctor taking a look at her, but as he had predicted, it was nothing worse than a severe case of seasickness.

'She'll rally round just as soon as the storm subsides,' the doctor had assured him. 'Meantime she's best to stay in bed and try to drink plenty of fluids to stop her dehydrating. Must be off now,' he said, snapping his black bag shut. 'Half the passenger list is down with the same thing.'

Now as Emily helped her to sit up on her pillows, Dilly noted with relief that the ship wasn't swaying about anywhere near as much as it had been. In fact, she realised with a jolt of relief that she felt much better, still wobbly but she didn't feel sick any more.

'I think I might get up when I've had this tea,' Dilly decided and Emily looked relieved.

'Shall I get some clothes out for you?' she offered.

Dilly sipped at the tea and shook her head. She just couldn't get used to being waited on.

'No, really, I shall be fine now but thank you for taking such good care of me. I thought I was dying for a time back there. Actually, I hoped I would. I really don't know how you manage to go about normally.'

Emily laughed as she headed for the door, content that her patient was on the mend. 'Oh, you get used to it – but do ring the bell if you need anything.'

Dilly nibbled on the biscuit and drained her cup, and found that she did indeed feel so much better with something inside her. She then swung her legs out of bed, waited for the slight dizziness to pass, and crossed to her wardrobe. Half an hour later, after a thorough wash, she brushed her hair and got dressed, reasoning that a bit of fresh air would do her good. She chose a cream and blue two-piece suit – one of her own designs – and with it she wore cream shoes and gloves and a large straw hat that was lavishly embellished with silk flowers.

I look almost human again, she told herself as she studied the finished effect in the mirror, although her cheeks were pale.

There were quite a few people taking the air up on deck, some of them still looking weak and pallid. Couples strolled arm-in-arm and Dilly headed for the outdoor veranda where she found Hayden reading an old newspaper.

'Ah, you're back in the land of the living again,' he said when he spotted her. 'Come and sit down and let me get you a drink, my dear.'

Dilly gratefully did as she was told, and with every minute that passed she did feel better.

'I can't believe I've spent almost half of the cruise in bed,' she grumbled when he rejoined her with a tray of tea.

He laughed. 'You weren't the only one, believe me. It's been like a ghost ship for the last couple of days. I suppose I must be used to it and thankfully it doesn't affect me. Anyway, we'll be docking the day after tomorrow, so not much longer now. So . . . shall I be mother?'

'Yes, and thank you so much for checking on me. My maid told me you'd been coming to my rooms to see if there was anything I needed.'

He shrugged. 'It was the least I could do, but your Emily seemed to have everything in hand so my services were not required.'

They went on to chat about Dilly's shops and he listened with interest. More than ever he was convinced that his daughter would like to meet her and by the time lunchtime rolled around Dilly felt as if she had known him for years.

They also talked about their families, and somewhere along the way Max's name cropped up.

'Do I take it that this Mr Farthing and you have an agreement?' Hayden questioned with a smile.

Dilly flushed. 'Oh no, Max and I are merely friends. He still has a wife, although sadly she is now in an asylum. She has a mental disorder. It's awful for her. She doesn't even recognise Max or her own children any more.'

He nodded. 'It certainly must be. At least my wife was aware of everything going on around her until the very end.'

111

Dilly saw the pain that flared in his eyes and felt sorry for him. He had clearly loved his wife very much indeed.

'Do you think you might ever marry again?' he asked her then.

Dilly raised an eyebrow. 'I think it's highly unlikely. I did come close to it a few years ago, and he was a lovely man – but I realised in time that I wasn't right for him.' She was shocked to find that she was telling Hayden things she had never shared with anyone before but he was so easy to confide in, and she found it cathartic to unburden herself.

'And how did you meet this Max Farthing?'

Dilly blinked before saying cautiously, 'When my children were young I used to work for him and his wife part-time, then Fergal had his accident and I found out that I was having another child.' She swallowed and went on, 'The Farthings had recently lost their baby daughter and Camilla, that's Mrs Farthing, approached me and offered to take my baby when it was born.' She couldn't believe that she was sharing such close secrets with a man she had only recently met, but now that she'd started she forced herself to go on and before she knew it, she'd told him the whole sorry tale.

'So that's the thing that binds your two families together?' he said quietly.

She nodded. 'Yes. It seemed the right thing to do at the time but the trouble is that as Oscar, who is one of the Farthings' sons, and Olivia grew up they formed an attachment to each other. It ended disastrously for both of them. They think they are brother and sister, you see, so Oscar married a woman he didn't love and Olivia had an affair that resulted in her having an illegitimate baby. Jessica, that's the baby, is my little lass and I adore her – but of course she has no idea that I am her grandmother.'

Hayden looked horrified as Dilly dabbed at tears. 'But surely now that they are both adults, they deserve to know the truth?'

'*No!*' Dilly shook her head. 'I vowed to Camilla that I would never tell them, and while she's still alive I would never go back on my word although I feel so guilty and it breaks my heart to see them both so unhappy.'

'Yes, I can understand that,' he answered musingly. 'It's quite a story. Like something you would read in a book.'

'I suppose it is,' she sighed. 'But sometimes life can be stranger than fiction.' She didn't regret sharing her secrets with Hayden. He was a very good listener, non-judgemental, and she suspected that they would remain good friends.

'Mrs Carey, wake up, we're almost there. If you go to the window you'll see we're sailing past the Statue of Liberty.'

Emily's voice sliced into Dilly's deep sleep and blinking she almost tumbled out of bed and crossed to the porthole.

'My goodness you're right,' she breathed. 'I must have overslept. Now I really must get dressed. My daughter will be waiting to meet me when the ship docks.'

'There's no panic,' Emily reassured her. 'The ship will wait here for the tide now before it goes into harbour. It will be mid-afternoon before we dock.'

Dilly was in a fever of excitement as she took a tray of tea from Emily. It wouldn't be too long now before she would see Niamh and Ben again, not to mention meeting her little grandson at long last. Meanwhile Emily was intent on packing Dilly's trunks for her, so after getting washed and changed, Dilly left her to it and went to join Hayden for breakfast in the dining room.

'Oh my goodness, how are we *ever* supposed to spot

113

anyone amongst that mass of people?' Dilly groaned as the ship finally sailed into the harbour later that day.

Hayden chuckled. 'Don't forget, they'll have a much better view of you as you go down the gangplank and I've no doubt they'll be waiting for you when you get to the bottom of it.'

'Yes, I hadn't thought of that,' Dilly answered as she scanned the sea of faces far below them. 'Now, have you got my address tucked away safely?'

'Yes, I have, and once you've had a few days to settle in with your family I shall be in touch to arrange a meeting with Rosalie,' he promised.

She stared up at him and smiled. 'Thank you – and thank you also for making this trip so pleasant for me.'

'It was my pleasure.' Hayden dropped a gallant little kiss on the back of her hand. 'But now if you will excuse me I must go and check that my steward has all my luggage packed. Goodbye for now, Dilly.'

She was so intent on trying to spot Niamh that she barely noticed him go – and then the ship touched the side of the dock and the seamen were manhandling the gangplanks into place as others secured the enormous ship to the dock with huge ropes and steel hawsers.

Almost instantly, seamen began to haul luggage down the furthest gangplank whilst the Captain and his officers stood at the top of the other one, saying their goodbyes to the passengers who were already queuing to get back on to dry land.

At last Dilly was descending, her eyes searching the teeming crowds below for a sight of her family. Then suddenly an upturned face swam into focus and her heart leaped.

'*Niamh!*' Almost stumbling in her haste to reach her daughter, Dilly was soon at the bottom of the gangplank

114

and Niamh was struggling through the crowds to get to her.

'*Mammy! Oh, Mammy, I've missed you so much!*' The two women were laughing and crying all at the same time as they fell into each other's arms whilst Ben stood to one side, a broad smile on his face, carrying a little boy who was the image of himself, clasped in his arms.

'I've missed you too,' Dilly said chokily, holding Niamh at arm's length so that she could look at her. The girl looked well and happy. Her hair, which had grown considerably, was like a shimmering copper curtain down her back, and her slim figure in a casual summer dress of sprigged cotton made her look even younger than she was.

Eventually, still clutching Niamh's hand as if she might never let it go, Dilly turned to Ben and he too gave her a warm hug.

'Sure it's good to see you,' he said heartily and Dilly noted he had lost none of his broad Irish accent. 'And this here is James, so it is. James, this is your grandma, the one we told you about who lives all the way over in England.'

The child stared at her blankly and Dilly's heart was lost. With his thick black wavy hair and eyes exactly the same colour as his father's he was a handsome little chap, but he was clearly very shy.

'How do you do, James,' she said, holding out her hand. 'It's very nice to meet you at last and I have an idea you and I are going to be great friends.' Again she was met with a blank stare and the first flutters of foreboding sprang to life deep within her. But already Niamh was reaching out for him so that Ben could go in search of Dilly's luggage.

'Did you have a good journey?' Niamh asked brightly to cover the awkward moment.

115

'Well, for part of the way,' Dilly said wryly. 'But I'll tell you all about that later.'

Ben was back in no time with a big black seaman who pushed a trolley containing her trunks through the crowd. Dilly and Niamh stayed close on his heels. Once the trunks were safely stored aboard Ben's car, Ben tipped the chap and he went back the way he had come after doffing his cap.

'Now, let's take you home and get something to eat inside you,' Niamh said as they all piled into the car. 'We have so much we want to do and so much we want to show you while you're here. Are you quite sure that you can only stay for three weeks?'

'Quite sure,' Dilly answered regretfully.

'I suppose you have to get back to work?' Niamh asked and when Dilly nodded she sighed. 'Oh, Mammy, when are you *ever* going to slow down and make some time to enjoy yourself?'

'Don't *you* start,' Dilly implored. 'I've had more than a few people say that to me lately. I'm beginning to feel old. But now do you think James might sit on my lap or is he a little shy?'

James cuddled further into his mother but Niamh said blithely, 'He'll be fine when he gets to know you a little. I'll explain about it later. But now tell me all the gossip about what's going on at home . . .'

So Dilly told Niamh what everyone was up to and the young woman listened intently. She loved living in New York with Ben, but then she would have lived in a cave with him if need be, although she did still get homesick from time to time.

'And Samuel?' she asked finally, lowering her voice.

'No one's seen hide nor hair of him for a good while now.'

116

'He'll turn up again when it suits him, he always does.' Niamh's voice was bitter.

'Let's not waste the time we have together talking about him,' Dilly said sensibly. 'It's your turn to tell me what's going on here.'

So Niamh told her all about her little art studio, about Ben's work on the docks in the blacksmith's he had bought, which he loved, and the time passed all too quickly as James sat there looking to neither left nor right.

The couple's ground-floor apartment was beautiful and so much bigger than it looked from the outside.

'Why, it's so deceptive from the road!' Dilly exclaimed as Niamh led her from one sunny room to another. A large door in the lounge led directly into a fair-sized walled garden which was laid to lawn with flowerbeds and a vegetable patch. It was like a little haven and Dilly found it very hard to take in that they were in the middle of a big city.

On arrival they had been met at the door by a young fair-haired woman whom Niamh introduced as Thelma: she was James' nanny as well as a general maid and a cook, Niamh explained.

'She's worth her weight in gold,' Niamh whispered as Thelma bore James off in the general direction of the kitchen. 'She looks after him for us while Ben and I are at work.' Ben was busy transferring Dilly's trunks to the room that was to be hers for the duration of her stay and now Niamh led Dilly to a bench in the shade of a large apple tree.

'While we have a moment alone I ought to explain about James,' she began with an anxious glance at her mother. 'You probably noticed that he's very quiet.'

'Well, yes I did,' Dilly admitted. 'But I thought it was perhaps because he's shy?'

Niamh avoided her eyes as she said quietly, 'I had quite a difficult birth with James. He was in a breech position and at one time during the delivery he stopped breathing. Thankfully the nursing staff managed to start his heart again, but then as he began to grow, Ben and I noticed that he seemed very behind in his development. Elizabeth, my mother-in-law, has spent a fortune on different consultations with different doctors for him, but they all say the same. They think his brain may have suffered through lack of oxygen, but no one can say what he might be capable of doing in the future. Physically he's like any normal little boy his age. He can walk and he can feed himself, but he doesn't laugh or cry and we've never heard him speak.'

'Oh, darling, whyever didn't you tell me?' Dilly said as her eyes welled with tears and she gripped Niamh's hand.

Her daughter shrugged. 'What would have been the point? You were in England, there was nothing you could have done and it would only have worried you. But we *do* love him just as he is. Most of the doctors have said that one day something might just unlock this little world he's trapped in and he may start to show signs of improvement. We just have to find that elusive something somehow.'

Dilly could have wept for her. First Niamh had lost her darling young daughter Constance, and been forced to live in sin with Ben, and now she had James, a dear boy who was locked in his own private world.

'I used to think that this was God's way of punishing me for living outside marriage with Ben,' Niamh whispered brokenly. 'But then I had to pull myself together or I would have gone mad.'

Dilly gathered her into an embrace and buried her face

in her hair. 'God would never be so unkind. It's just one of those things,' she told her daughter, but her heart ached for her. Niamh was such a loving, kind person and didn't deserve any of the blows that life had dealt her.

Chapter Fifteen

As Samuel passed the door of the lounge he heard his friend's wife say, 'How much longer is Samuel going to be here, darling? I don't wish to sound unreasonable but it would be nice to have the house to ourselves again. When he arrived he did say it would only be for a couple of nights, but the time is running on.'

'I know, sweetheart.' Jake Fullerton sighed as he looked across at his wife who was embroidering. 'But to be honest I don't quite know how to get rid of him. When he arrived he said he'd just called in to see me for old times' sake but I have a feeling there's more to it than that. He's down on his luck obviously despite the brave face he puts on things. He didn't even have much luggage with him, which is why I've lent him some of my clothes. None of what he said about his impromptu visit rings true but we go back a long way to our schooldays and I don't like to kick a man when he's down.'

'I can understand that,' Beryl replied patiently. 'But he's

hardly tried to help himself since he's been here, has he? And if it was just supposed to be a flying visit, why hasn't he gone back home? We're not a charity you know, darling.'

'I am aware of that. But it must be difficult for him with his arm in the state it's in. It's obviously still causing him a great deal of pain.'

'Then why doesn't he go home to his family? Didn't you tell me his father was a rather well-off businessman in the Midlands?'

Jake nodded. 'Yes, he is, and I don't know why Sam doesn't want to go home. Perhaps they've had a row or something? But don't worry. I'll give it another couple of days then I'll have a discreet word in his ear and explain that we're rather overcrowded. Hopefully he'll take the hint then and move on.'

He didn't enlighten his wife to the fact that he'd given Samuel a number of financial handouts since his arrival. Things were bad enough as they were without him adding fuel to the fire, so as far as Jake was concerned, the less she knew about that, the better. Not that he didn't agree with her up to a point. Jake had done rather well for himself and now had his own accountancy firm, but he had worked hard for what he had and it went against the grain to hand his hard-earned cash over to Farthing just because they'd been to school together.

With a muttered curse, Samuel crept on along the hallway and up the stairs to his room where he stood gazing thoughtfully from the window. It seemed he'd rather outstayed his welcome so it was time to put his thinking cap on and decide where he was going to go from here before he got chucked out on his arse. It was a shame because Jake's wife kept a good table, and after the rubbish he'd been forced to live on while bunking up with Kitty, he'd dined like a king. His bedroom was very comfortable too and the feather mattress was bliss after the grubby rags he'd become accustomed to . . . but then he supposed that all good things must come to an end. And then as he stared across the magnificent view of the cliffs and the sea from his window, it came to him. Felix Hargreaves! The last he'd heard of him, Felix had been making a good living for himself. Samuel had spent a couple of school holidays with Felix and his family in Llandudno. His father had been a well-known barrister, if he remembered correctly. Perhaps the Hargreaves could be his next port of call? No doubt he could wangle the fare to get there from Jake. He was clearly ready to get rid of him to keep his wife happy, so he'd probably cough up no trouble. Samuel would ask him tonight after the evening meal and leave the next day after one more night in that delightful bed. He glanced at it with regret, but then smiled optimistically. Where there was good there was always better.

As the maid was clearing the dinner table that evening, Samuel said casually, 'I can't thank you both enough for your hospitality. I've really enjoyed catching up with you again, Jake, but I really ought to be getting home now. My father will wonder where I've got to so I thought I'd leave in the morning.'

Samuel was amused to see husband and wife exchange a relieved glance.

'Well, if you're quite sure,' Jake said affably. 'It's been very nice catching up with you too and we've enjoyed your visit, haven't we, darling?'

'Of course.' Beryl dabbed at her lips to hide her relief.

Samuel sat back and patted his full stomach feeling that he'd handled that situation rather well.

*

In Cornwall, Jessica was having the time of her life with her grandfather and her mother, although she was missing Dilly.

The hotel they were staying at in Perranporth looked right out across the sea from a small balcony, although Jessica was only allowed to walk out on it when her grandfather or her mother were present. They'd spent idyllic days building sandcastles on the beach and paddling in the sea. Her grandfather had bought her a small fishing net on a long pole and they'd passed countless hours searching for crabs and starfish in the rock pools. They'd collected shells and eaten ice cream, and Jessica didn't want to go home.

'Can't we stay here for always?' she asked one evening as she sat contentedly on her mother's lap watching the setting sun sink into the sea from the balcony. 'Then George an' Dilly could come an' live with us too an' everything would be perfect.'

Olivia kissed the top of her daughter's head. 'Unfortunately, Grandpa and I have to go home so that we can go back to work,' she explained and Jessica pouted.

'But *why* do you have to go to work? If we lived here you wouldn't have to.'

'And what would we live on? Everyone has to work, sweetheart, to buy food and pay their bills. And anyway, you'll be starting school soon. That will be lovely, won't it?'

'Y . . . es,' the little girl answered cautiously. 'But only if George can come to my school too. Uncle Oscar says Aunt Penelope wants him to have a home t . . . teter or something like that.'

'Tutor,' Olivia corrected her gently. 'That's like a teacher who goes to the house to teach children at home.'

'Well, *I* don't want one of them,' Jessica declared firmly.

'It wouldn't be any fun. I want to go to school with other children so that I can make some new friends. Mrs Pegs says I can invite them home for tea sometimes if I do. But I shall only invite girls. I don't like boys, only George.'

Olivia grinned above the child's head. She'd felt much the same at Jessica's age – apart from Oscar and her other brothers, that was.

Max joined them on the balcony then and tussling Jessica's hair he asked, 'And what would my favourite girl like to do tomorrow then?'

'I'd like to go on the donkeys again and have a ride in a boat,' Jessica answered instantly as she stifled a yawn. There were blonde streaks in her bronze hair and her chubby little arms and legs were sunkissed, as were her cheeks, which had broken out in freckles despite Olivia insisting she kept her sunhat on.

'Then I suggest a certain little lady gets to bed or she might be too tired to do anything tomorrow,' Max told her with an affectionate smile.

'All right then. But will you read me a story, Grandpa – the *Winnie the Pooh* one that Dilly bought for me? It's my favourite.'

Max chuckled. He knew the book off by heart now but he could never deny his granddaughter anything.

'Very well.'

Hopping off her mother's lap, Jessica went into the bedroom and clambered into bed. Max tucked the blankets about her then started to read, but he'd gone no more than two pages into the book when her eyelids began to droop and by the time he'd finished page three she was snoring softly.

'I think that's the last we'll see of this little madam for tonight,' he whispered to Olivia. 'Will you come down and join me for a drink in the bar? I can get the maid to come and sit in here to keep her eye on Jessica.'

'No I won't, if you don't mind. All this fresh air has made me rather tired too so I think I might turn in for an early night as well. Good night, Daddy.'

'Good night, darling, sweet dreams.' As Max left the girl's room the smile slid from his face and a worried expression took its place. They'd all enjoyed their holiday enormously but he wished sometimes that Olivia would get out more. Apart from going to work she hardly ever left the house without Jessica and he felt that she was too young to sacrifice so much. She should have a social life with young people her own age, but each time he suggested it she told him that she was quite happy with her lot, thank you very much.

When Max reached the door of the bar he had a sudden change of heart and headed for the foyer instead, thinking he might sleep better if he went for a good stiff walk before turning in. He was missing Dilly greatly although he was enjoying his holiday. It was strange not to see her each day or talk to her on the telephone. But then the time would soon pass and she would be home again. On that comforting thought he tucked his hands into his pockets and set off for the seafront.

Chapter Sixteen

'Oh, Mammy, I can't believe it's less than a week until you have to go home again,' Niamh groaned at breakfast one day during the third week in September. The time seemed to have slipped by in the blink of an eye. She and Ben had taken Dilly on various sightseeing tours and Dilly had loved every second of it. They'd visited Battery Park and gazed across at the Statue of Liberty. They'd taken her to the Empire State Building and Madison Square and Dilly had spent time at Niamh's art studio watching her work. She'd been very impressed with Niamh's commissioned portraits and wasn't at all surprised that her daughter was kept so busy.

Dilly had also gone to see Hayden's daughter's fashion house with him, and she and Rosalie had hit it off straight away. Rosalie had loved Dilly's designs and they had come to an agreement much like the one she had in London with Philip Maddison. A lawyer had drawn up contracts which he had assured Dilly would be ready to sign before she sailed back to England – so all in all it had turned into a very profitable trip. They'd also dined on a number of occasions with Elizabeth McFarren, Ben's mother, and it had warmed Dilly's heart to see the close relationship that now existed between mother and son. Elizabeth had been delighted to see her and had made her feel very welcome. But the best part of all for Dilly was being able to spend time with her grandson. James never acknowledged her, but even so Dilly had fallen in love with the little chap.

'So what do you want to do today?' Niamh asked over a leisurely cup of coffee. 'I'm afraid I have to go into the studio for a few hours but you're very welcome to come with me. Or perhaps you'd rather go on a shopping trip? The big stores here are quite amazing, especially Macy's. I guarantee you'll spend a fortune if you visit that.'

'Actually I thought I'd just like to have a quiet day and spend a little time here with James. I don't feel as if my feet have touched the ground since I arrived,' Dilly answered, glancing at the child who was sitting quietly next to her. She had never once see him laugh, cry or heard him utter a sound – and it was quite heartbreaking.

Niamh smiled. 'That's fine. Thelma is here to help if you need it. But now I really must dash off and get ready or I'll be late for my client's sitting.'

Once alone with her grandson Dilly lifted him on to the floor and began to build up a stack of his brightly coloured wooden bricks, but he simply stared at them – and the same thing happened when she tried to read to him. He appeared to be totally oblivious to everyone and everything that was going on around him. And then at eleven o'clock Thelma came to take him for a nap and Dilly wandered into the garden feeling thoroughly frustrated.

There has to be *something* that would make him react, she told herself. There was an idea niggling at the back of her mind but she couldn't put her finger on it. And then suddenly it came to her in a blinding flash. It was an article she had read once in a magazine about a little girl who had been much as James was. Just like Niamh and Ben, her parents had tried everything until one day they came across the solution purely by chance.

Should I risk it? she asked herself. Niamh might well be furious if it didn't work, but then surely anything was worth a try? Making a sudden decision, Dilly strode purposefully back into the house and began to get ready. Thelma was in the kitchen when Dilly emerged from her room shortly afterwards.

'Do you mind if I go out for a while?' Dilly asked.

The girl smiled. 'Not at all, Mrs Carey. Take as long as you like. James will be fine with me and I don't think your daughter is due back until mid-afternoon.'

Returning her smile, Dilly set off for the shops. She just hoped she would be able to find what she was looking for. By day, Dilly found New York to be quite dusty and dismal but the first time she had seen it by night had left her speechless. The towering skyscrapers when lit up looked majestic – and she had been awestruck.

Now, however, her mind was completely focused on her errand so she strode along the main street looking this way and that for the type of shop she needed. She had Niamh's address safely tucked away in her bag. New York was such an enormous place that she knew it would be easy to get lost but she wasn't overly concerned. If she did she could simply hop in a cab – there were so many of them here – and they would see her safely home.

At last, after meandering up and down streets for seemingly hours she spotted the sort of shop she wanted and paused to stare into the window, almost instantly seeing what she was looking for.

The bell on the shop door tinkled when she opened it, and as she stepped inside a thousand different smells and noises met her – sawdust, kittens miaowing, the purr of the filters in the fish tanks lined up all along one wall.

A short, elderly, bald-headed man in a brown overall with the largest moustache Dilly had ever seen immediately appeared from a door behind the counter and smiled at her pleasantly.

'Good afternoon, ma'am. How may I help you?'

Dilly crossed to the large cage in the window. 'I'm interested in one of these for my grandson.'

'*Grandson?* Why, bless me, you don't look old enough to have a grandson,' he laughed. 'But I can see why you're taken with them. They're lovely little critters, ain't they? And fit as fiddles, every last one of them. You'll have no problems with these. Golden cocker spaniels, that's what they are.'

'How big will they grow?' Dilly asked as she dipped her hand into the cage, suddenly wondering if she was doing the right thing. What if James didn't like it? Worse still, what if Niamh and Ben were against having a dog? The puppies all clambered over each other to lick her.

'Oh, only so high – medium-sized, I'd say.' He held his hand a certain distance from the ground. 'What were you looking for – a dog or a bitch?'

'Er . . . a boy, I suppose,' Dilly answered bemused. She hadn't really thought about it.

'Then what about this little chap here? He's a lovely colouring and sweet as apple pie.' The man scooped one of the pups up and unceremoniously dumped it into Dilly's arms where it instantly began to squirm and lick her chin.

Dilly's heart melted. The pup was beautiful, she had to admit.

'I'll take him,' she said on a whim. 'And I'll also need a

bed for him, a collar and lead, dishes, food and anything else you can think of.'

The shopkeeper rubbed his hands together as he mentally began to add everything up.

'Right you are, ma'am. Just leave it to me.' He rushed away and in minutes the pile of things that the dog would require was beginning to mount up on the counter.

'Oh dear.' Dilly eyed the items with dismay. 'I never realised a dog would need all this. I shall have to get a cab home.'

'No problem at all,' he assured her. 'I shall go out and hail one for you just as soon as we've settled up. Oh, and I'll find a nice big box to put him in as well so that he doesn't get leaping all over you on your way home. Now I hope you don't mind me asking but that isn't an American accent I hear, is it?'

'No, I'm English, but my daughter lives in New York. I'm visiting.'

'I see. Welcome to America, ma'am.' He grabbed a stubby pencil then and swiftly added up what she owed him. It came to considerably more than Dilly had expected – but then if James liked the pup and it got a response from him – any sort of a response – then it would be worth every cent.

A little later, she was safely stowed in the back of a cab on her way home to Niamh's with the pup and all his new belongings piled around her. She realised with a little start that it was now fast approaching late afternoon. She'd been out for much longer than she'd anticipated. Niamh would be home by now and possibly Ben too, and she quaked, hoping that they wouldn't be cross with her.

When they drew up outside the apartment, Dilly paid the cabbie and while she carried the box containing the puppy, he carried the rest of her purchases and placed

130

them on the doorstep before going away with a nice tip in his pocket.

When Dilly rang the bell, Thelma came to open it and stared in amazement at the heaps of packages on the step.

'Would you help me get all these through to the kitchen?' Dilly squeaked over the lid of the box. 'And then tell Niamh that I want to see her, if you would.'

Thelma grinned as she quickly did as she was told. It didn't take much to guess what was in the box Dilly was carrying after seeing the things she'd bought.

Dilly had just put the box on the floor when Niamh appeared, scratching her head.

'Whatever have you been up to, Mammy?' she asked, her beautiful dark eyes twinkling.

'Well, today I suddenly remembered reading an article in a magazine about a little girl like James who didn't respond to anything or anyone. Then one day her parents brought a puppy home, and for the first time in her life she showed feelings and began to get better. I know it's a long shot – and I do so hope you and Ben won't be annoyed with me – but I thought it was worth a try.'

Niamh chuckled. 'Well, even if James doesn't respond to it, you know I've always wanted a dog but we could never afford one when I was little. Let's have a look at him now he's here.'

So Dilly carefully undid the lid on the box and a little bundle of golden fur spilled on to the floor and began to shake its tiny tail madly.

'Oh, he's adorable,' Niamh breathed in delight as she scooped him up. 'I shall love him even if James doesn't.'

'Hmm, and who's going to clean up after him – that's what I want to know,' Ben commented as he walked into the room to join them but his face was beaming.

131

'We'll have to think of a name for him,' Niamh said. It was obvious that she'd fallen in love with him.

'Shall I fetch James in to meet him?' Ben asked then and Niamh nodded.

James was sitting in the lounge staring off into space as usual but he let his father take him by the hand and followed him meekly into the kitchen.

The puppy bounded up to him, his little tail wagging furiously, but nothing he did elicited any response from James whatsoever. The child just stood staring blankly ahead.

Disappointment flared in Dilly's eyes. 'I'm so sorry,' she muttered. 'Now I've gone and landed you with a puppy that will need training on top of everything else.'

Ben put his arm about her and gave her a quick squeeze. 'According to the look on Thelma and Niamh's faces, I don't think they'll mind that one little bit. In fact, I might quite enjoy taking him for a walk myself when he's a little bigger. It was a really kind, generous thought and we appreciate it. But now let's feed the little fellow, eh? To be sure he must be starving and I am too come to think of it.'

By bedtime the women had agreed that the puppy should be called Charlie – after Charlie Chaplin. The name seemed to suit him somehow. He had been settled into his basket in the kitchen and was sleeping the sleep that only the very young enjoy as Ben and Niamh enjoyed a glass of wine with Dilly in the spacious lounge.

'It's been a long day.' Dilly stifled a yawn. 'Would you two mind very much if I turned in for an early night?'

'Not at all – and do take a peek at James as you go to your room if you want to.' Niamh had often found her mother standing at the side of the child's bed staring down at him and hoped that he hadn't been too much of a disappointment to her. She and Ben adored him and would have loved to have more children, but Niamh felt it wasn't right because they weren't married. Thankfully, the fact that she and Ben shared the same surname had made things slightly easier but she still regretted that they couldn't be married in the eyes of God. Still, she never gave up hope that one day they might be able to do so, and for now she was content.

The next morning, Dilly took James for a leisurely stroll as she often did to a park just down the road from the apartment. James always seemed happy to go with her, placidly plodding along at the side of her, his hand in hers, but nothing he saw evoked any reaction in him and it tore at Dilly's heart. Today she'd decided that they'd also take Charlie and introduce him to his collar and lead, but within minutes of setting off she began to wonder who was taking whom for a walk as the pup yanked on his lead ahead of her. When they reached the park, Dilly steered her charges in the direction of the pond. She'd scrounged some bread from Thelma and intended to feed the ducks.

'Here we are then, James,' she said when they reached the grassy banks of the pond. She always talked to him even though he never answered back. 'Would you like to give the ducks some bread?'

He merely stared straight ahead, giving no sign that he had heard her as Dilly threw some crumbs to the ducks. At that moment Charlie spotted another dog coming towards them with its owner and before Dilly could stop him he began to leap about in excitement and run around in circles. His lead became entangled around James's legs and before she could stop it, the little boy fell heavily on to his backside.

'Oh pet, I'm so sorry, are you all right?' Dilly squeaked as she tried to hold on to Charlie and dropped to her knees beside her grandson. Thinking that this was some new sort of game, Charlie began to leap all over the child, licking his face with glee. And then the most amazing thing happened. James looked at the dog, really focused on him, and began to laugh, a deep rumbling sound that came right from the pit of his stomach. At the same time his arms came out and wrapped around his new pet as Dilly sat back on her heels and stared with shock and delight at the scene that was being enacted in front of her.

For the very first time in his life James had laughed – and somehow Dilly knew that this would be the start of better things to come.

Chapter Seventeen

'I can't believe it,' Niamh gasped tearfully that afternoon as she watched James shuffling after Charlie around the garden. He had still as yet not spoken but now they had hope and truly believed that one day he might.

'It's incredible! Just look at him – his face is animated, so it is,' Ben breathed with a catch in his voice. 'And it's all down to you, Dilly. I don't know how we'll ever be able to thank you. I just wish we'd thought of getting him a pet ourselves.'

'And I'm just glad I read that article,' Dilly answered as she watched her little grandson with a fond expression on her face. It was as if Charlie had finally freed him from the prison of silence in which he'd been locked away. 'But now I really must go and get ready. Hayden and Rosalie are taking me out for a meal this evening then on to a jazz club.' She grinned. 'I hope they won't expect me to do the Charleston!'

'Just go and enjoy yourself, Mammy. I'm going to ring

Elizabeth and tell her about what's happened with James. She'll be over the moon as we are.'

Dilly pottered away to enjoy a leisurely soak in the bath. What had happened with James was the perfect end to her stay, and at least she could go home knowing that from now on, things would get better still. Tomorrow she would be going to sign the contracts with the lawyer Hayden had recommended to oversee her agreement with Rosalie, who was convinced that Dilly's designs would sell well. Dilly was thrilled at the thought of her outfits being sold in New York as well as London.

She had thoroughly enjoyed her stay but now she was looking forward to seeing all the people she loved back at home again.

'So this is it then,' Niamh said tearfully a few days later as they all stood on the docks. It was late afternoon and already passengers were streaming up the gangways to board the *Mauretania* for her return trip to England. It was time for Dilly to go home but she was finding it painful to leave her daughter.

'You could always come and see me?' Dilly suggested hopefully but Niamh shook her head.

'No, Mammy. I'll not be coming back to England again until Ben and I are legally wed. Here everyone accepts that we're a married couple but there we'd live in shame.'

Dilly didn't argue. She could understand how her daughter felt. 'Then I shall come back to you again just as soon as I can,' she promised as she wrapped her in her arms for one last time. She then bent to James's level and planted a kiss on his springing black curls before hugging Ben.

'Right – I'd better get aboard before I change my mind, but don't wait about too long. It's turning chilly and the ship won't sail till tomorrow with the tide,' she whispered as she choked back tears. This time, once she reached the deck she leaned across the rails and waved until she felt as if her arm would drop off before allowing the steward, who was patiently waiting for her, to show her to her suite of rooms.

When next she went on deck later that evening the docks were deserted apart from latecomers who were still boarding and an assortment of sailors. Sighing, she returned to her rooms. It looked set to be a lonely return voyage without Hayden to keep her company, but she sensed that in him she had found a friend for life and knew that she would see him again in the not too distant future. He regularly travelled to England and had promised that he would look her up the next time he did.

The next morning Dilly rose bright and early in time to see the skyline of New York fading into the distance as the ship reached the open sea and picked up speed. She was going home.

Thankfully the passage was a smooth one. Dilly spent most of her days in her rooms working, although there were numerous activities she could have joined in with, had she been so minded. There was dancing each night in the ballroom to a live band, tennis on deck during the day and countless other things going on, but Dilly just wanted to wish the time away until she was home again.

At last as she was strolling along the deck five days after they had sailed, land was sighted. Her maid was already in her rooms packing her trunks and Dilly hurried downstairs to see if she could assist her in any way. She was thrilled to be back in England but not looking forward to the final long train journey which would involve two changes. Still, she decided there was no use in moaning about it. She could stay in a hotel for the night and set off again first thing in the morning, but she just wanted to get home now. It wasn't much fun staying in a hotel alone and hopefully there would be a late train running that would get her at least part of the way home.

Once the ship had berthed at Liverpool and Dilly was on dry land again, a sailor trundled her trunks towards her on a large trolley. They were considerably heavier than they had been on the outward journey because she had bought everyone a small gift each.

'Shall I be hailin' you a cab, ma'am?' he offered.

'Er . . . yes, that would be very kind.'

'That won't be necessary, thank you.' A voice at her elbow made her whirl about to come face to face with Max, who was smiling broadly.

'Max! *Whatever* are *you* doing here?' Dilly was so delighted to see him that it was all she could do to stop herself from leaping into his arms.

'I rang the shipping company to see what time the ship would be expected and thought I'd drive here and take you home. I'm sure you'll be more comfortable in the car than you would be on a train.'

'Oh, how *wonderful*!' She couldn't seem to stop smiling but then, remembering the matelot, she fumbled in her purse and handed him a generous tip, telling him, 'Thank you so much but we can manage from here.'

'Actually,' Max told him, 'if you'll bring this luggage to my car I'll double the tip this lady just gave you.'

'Right y'are, sir.' The seaman followed Dilly and Max through the throngs of people to where Max had parked his car as close to the docks as he could get. In no time at all the man had packed the trunks into Max's boot and gone off whistling a merry tune with his pocket considerably heavier.

'Right then, now that's done we'll go and have dinner.

The nights are drawing in so rapidly I don't fancy driving home in the dark so I've booked us into a hotel for the night – in separate rooms, of course,' he added hastily seeing Dilly's raised eyebrow.

He helped her into the car then drove through the crowded streets until they came to a very swanky-looking hotel where a doorman in full uniform stood on the steps.

'The Adelphis! Isn't this rather expensive?' Dilly asked as he drew the car to a halt at the bottom of the steps.

'It's my treat,' Max told her firmly as he came round to help her out of the car then throwing the keys to the doorman he told him, 'See that my car is safely parked up for the evening, would you, my man?'

'Certainly, sir.'

Dilly linked her arm through Max's and allowed him to lead her inside to a very luxurious foyer. He then left her to go to the desk and came back minutes later with a porter who would show them the way.

'We're next door to each other on the second floor,' he told her, as they headed towards the lift. 'I didn't think to ask, do you need your trunks brought in?'

'No. I have everything I need here in my overnight bag,' Dilly whispered nervously. She believed Max when he told her that he had booked separate rooms for them – but what would everyone at home think if they were to discover that they'd stayed overnight in a hotel together? They'd be bound to jump to conclusions. Not that there was anything she could do about it now unless she went to stand and wait on a cold railway platform. The thought of that did not appeal at all.

The whole place was decorated in subtle shades of green which made Dilly feel as if she was walking through a lush forest. It was very restful and as they followed the porter she felt herself beginning to relax.

'Ah, here we are. Number forty-two. This is your room, ma'am,' the porter told her, inserting a key in the lock.

'It's lovely,' she told Max, when the porter had gone. 'But you really should stop spoiling me, Max. I still have to talk to you about upgrading my accommodation on the ship.'

He grinned. 'I'm off to get changed then. I'll call here for you in an hour to go down to dinner, if that's all right?'

He went off to his own room leaving Dilly tutting to herself. Sometimes she thought her words went in one ear and out of another but she would reimburse him – she was determined to do so somehow.

Dilly only had one outfit in her small bag so her choice of what to wear was limited that evening. Even so, when Max called for her he looked her up and down appreciatively.

'You're a damned fine-looking woman, Dilly Carey,' he told her with a cheeky grin as he held his arm out to her.

'And you don't scrub up so bad yourself, Max Farthing,' she responded, returning his smile as she looped her arm through his. Tonight she was dressed in a simple cream dress that enhanced the colour of her hair and complimented her still-slim figure.

'I don't know how you manage to stay so damn svelte,' he complained, patting his stomach ruefully. 'Well, I suppose it could have something to do with the fact that you rarely sit down for more than a minute at a time. You're not getting any younger though, my dear. You'll have to start slowing down a bit.'

'Thanks for reminding me,' she said, thinking that perhaps this wasn't the best time to tell him that she now had yet another string to her bow in New York. She'd do it later, when he'd downed a few glasses of red wine and was feeling mellower. She'd tell him all about James too, but that would be a pleasure.

140

The meal in the restaurant was delicious – parsnip soup and crusty rolls followed by roast beef cooked to perfection, served with horseradish sauce, fluffy creamed potatoes, vegetables and Yorkshire puddings. The waiter came round then with a selection of mouth-watering desserts on a trolley for them to choose from, but Dilly waved him away.

However, Max was tempted and opted for the cheese board. It was over coffee when he finally said, 'So tell me all about your trip then. Did you have a complete rest?'

'Yes I did. Well, I did do a *little* business while I was there as well,' she said cautiously, and then went on to tell him all about Hayden and Rosalie.

Max shook his head in amazement. 'So your designs will be selling in London *and* New York now? You'll be heading off for Paris next.' When a spark of interest flared in her eyes he quickly held his hand up. 'Only joking! Surely you are satisfied with your not so little empire now?'

'As a businessman you should know that there's always room for expansion,' she answered teasingly.

He sighed but his eyes were smiling. Dilly was a force to be reckoned with when she got an idea into her head so he cleverly steered the conversation into different channels.

'And now tell me all about Niamh and Ben, and little James of course.' He still suffered all manner of guilt when he thought of what his son had done to Dilly's daughter, and his heart still ached when he thought of little Constance. She had been such a beautiful child. For much of the time he tried not to think about the manner of it that hadn't felt quite right to his mind. Constance had seemed to have turned a corner – even the doctor had thought so – and yet she had died so suddenly when left alone for a few minutes with her father. Yet he daren't allow his thoughts to go down that route hence he tried not to dwell on it. What was done was done and nothing could bring her beloved Connie back now. Anyway, he told himself, Samuel might be heartless – but surely he would never contemplate harming his own child?

For the next hour Dilly told him all about Niamh and Ben and the wonderful places they had taken her to. She also told him about little James and the puppy she had bought him, and Max was saddened to think that after the heartache of losing Constance, Niamh had then given birth to a child with a disability, although Dilly quickly assured him that both her daughter and Ben adored the child.

'Do you think they'll ever come back to England?'

'Not unless they can come back as a married couple. Over there everyone thinks they're wed, but there are too many people here who know otherwise.' Dilly suddenly stifled a yawn and Max grinned.

'It looks like someone is ready for their bed.'

'I am, to be honest.' The long journey had suddenly caught up with Dilly and she felt as if she could sleep for a month at least.

'In that case I'll see you up to your room.' Max signed for their meal, then courteously pulled her chair out for her and led her towards the elevator, saying 'It's so lovely to see you again and you know I always enjoy your company.' Squeezing her hand affectionately, he added, 'We can chat all the way home tomorrow.'

Once they arrived at the door of her room he gave her a quick peck on the cheek. 'It's good to have you back, Dilly. It hasn't been the same without you,' he whispered sincerely, then turning about he strode on to his own room as Dilly let herself into hers, feeling suddenly bereft.

Chapter Eighteen

'Aw, lass, it's so good to have yer back!' Nell exclaimed late the following afternoon when Dilly arrived home. She and Max had stopped for a leisurely lunch in a country inn to break their journey and now Nell enveloped Dilly in a bear hug that almost winded her.

'I've missed you too,' Dilly responded with a laugh. 'In fact, I've missed everyone! I didn't realise just how much until Max pulled up outside. It was lovely seeing Niamh and her family but it's wonderful to be home.'

'Well, I've cooked you some dinner. It'll only need popping in the oven to heat up. There's some for Bessie too. Oh – did I mention she was back from her trainin' in London? She came back shortly after you left fer New York. I said you wouldn't mind her stayin' here temporarily. She's on the late shift at the hospital an' I've been glad of her company while you've been gone, I don't mind tellin' yer. I'd have rattled round this place all on me own, wouldn't I?' Nell prattled on but Dilly was eager to see

Olivia and Jessica now, Seamus and Mary too if they were home yet.

'Can I have my dinner later?' She gave Nell an apologetic smile as Max carried one of her trunks into the kitchen. 'We stopped to eat on the way home and I'm not really hungry again just yet. Besides, I'm so eager to see Jessica before she settles down for the night. But I won't be gone for too long and then we'll have a lovely long catch-up,' she promised.

'It'll keep,' Nell assured her good-naturedly.

Dilly was already struggling with the lock on the trunk, keen to find the presents she had bought for everyone. 'Ah, here they are,' she said eventually, handing Nell a bottle of very expensive perfume from Macy's.

Nell beamed with delight as she sprayed it liberally all over herself, almost choking herself in the process. She'd expected that Dilly would be bursting to see the family and wasn't offended in the slightest at her shooting off again so quickly.

Max had manhandled the second heavy trunk in by then and Dilly smiled at him gratefully.

'So may I have a lift back to your house with you to see Olivia and Jessica?' she asked. 'That is, if you were planning on going straight home,' she ended hastily. Max had been so kind coming all that way to Liverpool to meet her from the ship, she didn't want to put him to any more trouble.

'Of course, but don't you want to have a bit of a rest first?'

'Not at all,' she told him, collecting the presents together and handing one to him. 'And this is for you.'

When he opened a bag to find a very fine brown leather wallet his face creased into a delighted smile.

'Why thank you, this is lovely – almost too good to use,'

144

he told her. Then seeing that she was impatient to be off, he grinned at Nell and headed for the door.

As they stepped outside, the cold made Dilly shiver. The weather had changed drastically in the month she had been away and now the leaves were fluttering from the trees in the wind like confetti.

'Brr, it's certainly autumn now, isn't it?' She quickly hopped back into the car and seconds later they were on their way.

Jessica was fresh out of the bath when Max and Dilly arrived at Mill House and at sight of Dilly and her grandpa she flew towards them, her small face wreathed in smiles.

'I missed you so much,' she told Dilly, then almost in the same breath, added 'Have you brought me a present?'

'Of course. I said I would, didn't I?' Dilly winked at Olivia who hadn't managed to get a word in up to now.

When she handed Jessica a doll with a ceramic face, bright blue glass eyes and long blonde hair the child's own eyes grew round with delight.

'I shall call her Molly,' she declared, and suddenly forgetting how much she had missed Dilly she shot off to show Mrs Pegs and Gwen her new treasure.

Dilly chuckled as she handed Olivia her present. It was a silk blouse with a lace ruffle all down the front of it and she and Niamh had spent hours choosing it.

'Oh my goodness!' Olivia gasped. It looked very expensive. 'You really shouldn't have,' she said self-consciously, then grinned. 'But I'm glad you did. It's really beautiful. I shall keep it for special occasions.'

'I'll just pop along to the kitchen and give Mrs Pegs and Gwen their presents,' Dilly told her. 'Then if I can get the little madam back here I'll tuck her in and tell her a story – if you don't mind, that is?'

145

'Of course I don't mind.' Olivia was still admiring the blouse so Dilly trotted off thinking how wonderful it was to be home.

Mrs Pegs and Gwen were equally delighted with their presents. Dilly had chosen a pair of smart, soft leather gloves for Mrs Pegs and a very pretty silk headscarf in autumn colours for Gwen.

'Eeh, I ain't never owned nothin' like it,' Gwen declared as she fingered the fine material. 'I shall save it to wear to church on Sundays.'

'Well, that won't get to see the light o' day very often then, will it?' Mrs Pegs chuckled.

Gwen sniffed, unamused. 'Per'aps I'll go more often now I've this to wear,' she retorted.

Dilly grinned to herself as she shooed Jessica back to the drawing room where a cheery fire was burning. The light outside was fast fading now that the nights were rapidly drawing in and Dilly settled the child on to her lap and read her a story, enjoying the feel of the little girl's body curled against her.

'I'll run you back home,' Max offered an hour later when Olivia took Jessica off to bed, but Dilly shook her head as she put her warm coat and hat back on.

'Thank you, but I'll walk. I want to call in and see Seamus and Mary on my way home to check that all is well with the shops, and they're only a stone's throw away. You stay here in the warm. You must be tired after all the driving you've done.'

'I'm fine,' he argued, but Dilly wouldn't hear of it and soon after she set off along Earls Road. In no time at all the little house on Abbey Green was in sight and she rapped on the front door.

Seamus answered it and his face broke into a smile when he saw his mother standing there. 'I was just wondering if you were back yet.' He ushered her inside. 'I was going to pop round later on to see you.'

'Then I've saved you the trouble,' Dilly answered as she slid her coat off again and handed it to him. 'Now you go and put the kettle on while I go through to Mary then you can tell me all about what's been going on here.'

Seamus hurried off to do as he was told and Dilly found Mary sitting beside the fire in the lounge with her feet resting on a stool.

'Hello, Dilly. Seamus has made me rest,' she told Dilly, and her mother-in-law glanced at the young woman's swollen ankles.

'And quite right too, looking at the state of your feet.' Dilly looked concerned. 'Perhaps it's time you thought of finishing work now until after the baby is born? It's only weeks away now and we don't want you overdoing it.'

'Oh, don't *you* start fussing too,' Mary groaned. 'Seamus is bad enough. Anyone would think I was the only woman in the world who has ever carried a baby. I keep telling him I'm absolutely fine! Having this baby will be like shelling peas if I take after me mam.'

'Hmm.' Dilly wasn't convinced. Mary was invaluable, always ready to step in and take over if any of the shop staff were off sick, but she truly felt that the young woman should be taking it a little easier now.

Seamus arrived then with a loaded tea tray and as Dilly set out the cups and saucers the couple told her all about how the various shops had been doing. It appeared that they'd both done an admirable job of keeping everything going like clockwork in her absence, and so she then went on to tell them all about her trip, for Seamus sorely missed his sister Niamh and was keen to hear all the news. Finally she gave them a beautiful white shawl that she had bought in New York for the baby, and the couple were delighted with it.

Dilly was in a contented mood when she returned to her home later that evening. Bessie was back by then and she was clearly pleased to see her, although Dilly had a feeling that something was troubling her.

Her feeling was confirmed when Bessie confided, 'The Sister at the hospital told me that I'm going to be out of work for a while after Christmas.'

'But why?' Dilly was shocked. 'I thought Nell told me they were happy with your work.'

'Oh, they are,' Bessie said. 'But I only got set on really because one of the nurses was going off to have a baby. It appears that she's had it now and her mother has agreed to mind it so that she can come back to work after Christmas. The Sister has promised that just as soon as another position comes up they'll have me back, but that could be some time away.' She sighed. 'The thing is, now that most of the soldiers who were admitted there during and after the war have been allowed home, they don't need such a large staff, so I suppose I'll have to think of something else to do.'

'I could always find you work in the shops,' Dilly offered. 'I've just come from Mary and Seamus's house and I told Mary I think she should be resting more now.'

Bessie nodded. 'Well, that would keep me busy, I suppose, until I can return to the hospital. Thanks, Dilly.'

It was then that the harsh ringing of the telephone interrupted the conversation and Dilly wondered who it could possibly be, ringing so late at night. 'I'll get it, pet,' she told Nell who was rising from her chair and so saying she slid out of the cosy kitchen into the chilly hallway to answer it.

'Declan!' she said with delight when she heard his

voice. 'I was going to ring you in the morning. I just got back today. How are you all? Is everything all right?'

'Well . . .' he answered hesitantly and Dilly clutched the receiver as a terrible feeling of dread came over her. 'Not really, Mammy. I'm sorry to have to tell you this so soon after you got home but it's Granda – he died earlier this evenin', I'm afraid.'

Dilly felt as if she'd been douched in cold water as tears sprang to her eyes.

'It was very peaceful, Mammy,' her son went on with a catch in his voice. 'Liam was holdin' his hand an' Granda gave him the sweetest smile afore he passed.'

Dilly struggled to get her own feelings under control. Declan sounded heartbroken, which was understandable. Daniel had brought him up since he'd been a wean and she knew how close they'd been, yet try as she might she couldn't think of a single thing to say.

'Dilly, are you all right? You look as if you've seen a ghost.'

Dilly started. She hadn't noticed Bessie come into the hallway.

'It – its Daniel,' she croaked. 'He's passed away.' Then suddenly remembering that Declan was still on the other end of the line she told him, 'I'll be there as soon as I can, pet.'

'There's nothin' you can do, Mammy.'

'Even so I shall be there, tomorrow if possible. I couldn't miss your granda's funeral. Try an' keep your chin up, pet.'

'Aye, I will. G'night, Mammy.'

'Good night, pet.'

'Aw, Dilly, I'm so sorry. I know how much yer loved that man. He were like a dad to yer, weren't he?'

Bessie placed her arm about Dilly's shaking shoulders

and Dilly leaned into her. Images were flashing in front of her eyes. Daniel standing uncomfortably in his Sunday-best suit at her wedding to his son. The tears of joy in his eyes when he'd visited their first-born child. The kindness he'd shown to the children that terrible time so long ago when she had been forced to take all the children to Ireland and leave them with him and Maeve. There had been so many kindnesses shown with nothing expected in return, and now he was gone and she knew that he would leave a huge hole in her heart. And yet deep down she wasn't surprised. The last time she had seen him she had sensed that he had been trying to say goodbye to her. Daniel had never been the same since the day he had lost his beloved Maeve, and now Dilly could only pray that if there was a heaven, they were together again.

Chapter Nineteen

Dilly arrived at the farmhouse in Ireland late the following evening after hitching a lift on a farmer's cart from Dublin. Despite the reason she was there and the sadness that hung over the farmhouse like a cloud, she enjoyed seeing the family again.

Roddy was growing like a weed and seemed well-adjusted and happy, which should have pleased Dilly, but instead it left her feeling somewhat worried. Bessie had hinted on the night they learned of Daniel's death that she would like to accompany Dilly to Ireland to see him, but Dilly had managed to put her off, saying that she didn't think the timing was appropriate. Was Bessie having second thoughts about letting her son go to live with Roisin and Declan? They clearly adored the child and treated him as their own. There didn't seem to be the same desperation to have their own child since Roddy had gone to live with them, although Dilly knew that they hadn't given up hope of it happening for them one day. She pushed thoughts of that aside. For now she would just concentrate on getting through the next few days.

Friday dawned grey and dismal, much like the mood of the mourners who were preparing to say their goodbyes to Daniel.

By mutual agreement it had been decided that the children would stay at the farmhouse under the watchful eye of a neighbouring farmer's wife. Dilly felt that funerals were no place for children to be so they would stay at home helping the woman to prepare a tea for any of the mourners who wished to come back when the service was over.

The wind was cutting as they followed the hearse to the little church perched high on the hill. Once the hymns had been sung and the funeral service was over they then all trooped into the churchyard to watch Daniel be interred in the same grave as his wife.

The priest solemnly began to recite the last part of the service, 'Earth to earth, ashes to ashes . . .'

A tear trickled down Dilly's pale cheek as Daniel's coffin was slowly lowered into the grave. It was the end of an era but she felt grateful for all the years she had known him. As they were standing there, the first drops of rain began to fall and soon it was as if the heavens had opened; the rain came down in torrents, soaking them all through to the skin in seconds. The mud on the coffin lid slid off the sides of it and the priest began to chant more quickly, keen to get back to the warm fire in the rectory and the nice hot cup of tea he knew his housekeeper would have waiting for him. At last it was over, and after shaking the hands of the family and offering his condolences, he strode away, his sodden vestments slapping against his cold legs.

'It was a nice service, wasn't it?' Roisin sighed as they

made their way back through the churchyard, leaving the gravediggers to finish their job.

'Aye, it was,' Declan answered in a wobbly voice. He had doted on his granda and would miss him sorely.

They arrived back at the house looking like drowned rats and Mrs O'Leary, the kindly woman who had stayed to care for the children, ushered them all towards the fire.

'The solicitor is in the parlour,' she told them, handing out towels. 'Once you're warm and dry, you can all go through if you've a mind to. I'll see to getting everyone a drink and the food is all ready.'

Shelagh gave her a grateful smile as they all moved towards the parlour that had housed Daniel's coffin until a very short while ago. They were all keen to get it over with now.

Just as Liam had prophesised, the will held no surprises – until the end when the solicitor cleared his throat and read, '"And to Dilly Carey who has been like a daughter to me, I bequeath my beloved Maeve's wedding ring".'

The breath caught in Dilly's throat as her hand rushed to her mouth and tears dripped from her eyes.

The solicitor fumbled in his pocket and handed her a small box containing the said ring and Dilly clutched it to her heart. To her it was priceless and she would treasure it for ever. There was nothing that Daniel could have left her that would have meant more.

Hugging her cape about her, Olivia hastened along Manor Court Road, intent on getting out of the biting wind. She'd just done a long day's shift at the hospital and if she hurried, she'd be in time to bath Jessica before tucking her into bed. It was dark, and as she turned into Earls Road she almost collided with someone standing on the corner.

'Oh, I'm so sorry, I wasn't looking where I was going,'

she said then stopped abruptly when she looked up into Roger Bannerman's eyes.

'It's quite all right, I've been waiting for you,' he told her as she made to walk past him.

'What for?' she asked. 'I don't think we have anything to say to each other.'

'Oh, but I think we do.'

Something about his tone of voice made her blood run cold.

'I'd like to talk about when Jessica's birthday is, for a start-off,' he went on. 'Because I've been doing my sums and I have every reason to believe that Jessica is my child. She *is*, isn't she, Olivia?'

'Don't be so ridiculous,' she blustered, not quite knowing what else to say. 'Of course she isn't – and even if she was, what could you do about it?'

'Oh, quite a lot, I believe.' Taking her elbow he drew her into the shadow of a high hedge surrounding one of the gardens. 'As you know, my wife Miranda hasn't presented me with a child as yet, so if Jessica is mine I think you should be honest with me. I want to be part of her life and see her grow up. She deserves to have a father figure in her life. I could take her out and get to know her.'

'Jessica is mine!' Olivia spat. 'And that little girl is adored by the whole household, so don't even *think* of trying to take her from me. I'd fight you every step of the way!'

'I didn't say I wanted to take her away from you, did I?' Roger snapped. 'Not unless you refuse to let me see her, that is!'

Olivia's face set. 'I'd beware of going down that road,' she warned him. 'First of all, you would have to prove that she was yours – and how would you do that if I were to say that you weren't the only man I was sleeping with

154

at the time? Secondly, you forget who my father is. Do you really think that Max Farthing would sit back and let you take his granddaughter from me without a fight? Why, he'd hire the finest solicitor in the land and you'd stand no chance. My father could buy and sell you, so don't you forget it, because if you start your threats a few well-chosen words in the right ears would ensure that you'd be finished in this town – and then you'd have put your poor wife through all that heartache for nothing!'

'Quite a little spitfire when you get going, aren't you?' he said with amusement and Olivia bristled as he tried to place his arm about her waist. 'I do admire a woman with spirit and I've missed you. Perhaps we should pick up where we left off?'

She furiously slapped his hand away. 'Don't you *dare* touch me! You're disgusting and I rue the day I ever met you! I just wonder what your wife would have to say if I were to pay her a visit and tell her what you've just suggested!'

He took a step back and Olivia felt that for now at least she might have the upper hand.

'You wouldn't dare.'

'Try me,' she goaded.

He took another step back. 'Look, this is getting silly,' he sputtered. 'I merely wanted to discuss our daughter's future with you. I never set out to upset you.'

'She is not *our* daughter – she's *my* daughter,' Olivia growled. 'And I warn you, if you *ever* approach me again I shall go and visit your wife and tell her everything! She won't want anything more to do with you when I've finished speaking to her. Now – get out of my way!'

He stepped aside with what dignity he could muster as Olivia swept past him, her heart beating furiously. Just as she had feared, Roger had clearly put two and two together and now he saw Jessica as a way of proving his manhood to himself.

'He'll have access to her over my dead body!' Olivia muttered to the empty street but inside she felt sick and she had a terrible feeling that despite her spirited defence, she hadn't seen the last of Roger yet, not by a long shot. She would have to tell everyone to be extra vigilant from now on when they took Jessica out, and pretend she'd heard rumours of a man hanging around small children. If Roger took it into his head to try and take her, and succeeded, Olivia knew she would lose the will to live because that child was her whole life.

For now, she hoped that she had averted the crisis – but for how long? asked the niggling little voice inside her head.

Chapter Twenty

'So how was Roddy?' Bessie asked eagerly.

Dilly had barely set foot through the door of the house in St Edward's Road but she smiled wearily as she answered, 'He's turning into a fine strong little boy. I swear he's grown at least an inch every time I see him.'

'And did he ask about me?'

Dilly glanced at Nell uneasily before saying, 'Well . . . we did talk about you. I told him you were back from London, but then he already knew that from your letters.'

Bessie's face fell. 'But he didn't say that he'd like to see me, did he? Don't bother lying, Dilly. I can read you like a book. In fairness I can't blame the poor little scrap. I've been a poor apology for a mother, haven't I?'

Dilly felt sorry for her as Bessie's shoulders sagged. 'At least you know he's happy and thriving where he is,' she said quietly, then keen to swerve the conversation away from Roddy, she asked Nell, 'Is there any tea in that pot?'

'Not unless yer like it stewed but we can soon remedy

that,' Nell said cheerfully as she filled the kettle. 'Now tell us how the funeral went.'

Dilly shrugged. 'As well as a funeral could go, I suppose. Liam and Shelagh are moving into the farmhouse now and they're talking about taking on a farmhand who'll be able to live in their cottage. The farm is getting a bit too big for Declan and Liam to manage on their own now. But how is everything here?'

'Fine an' dandy,' Nell responded. 'Your Seamus an' Mary keep them shops runnin' smoothly atween 'em now. Ain't it about time you gave him a promotion to manager or sommat?'

Dilly stared thoughtfully into the flickering flames before answering, 'Do you know what, Nell? I think that's a very good idea. Seamus deserves some recognition for how hard he works – so does Mary if it comes to that, although of course she'll have to finish soon. It's not long now until the baby is due. I'll speak to them both tomorrow. After all, I rarely have to even visit the shops now. I stick to working on new designs to try and keep them all busy.'

Bessie was impatiently tapping her foot and clearly keen to get back to their former conversation.

'So how is Roddy doing at school?' she persisted. 'And has he made many friends there?'

'He's doing fine and is very popular as far as I know,' Dilly answered, stretching her feet towards the brass fender. It was so shiny she could see her face in it but then Nell took a great pride in the whole of the place and everywhere was as neat as a new pin.

'I was thinking – seeing as I'll be finishing work for a while early in December – that I might go over to Ireland to visit him.'

Dilly sighed. She'd seen this coming and knew that she wasn't going to be able to put Bessie off for ever. Roddy

158

was still her son, after all, although she doubted that Roisin and Declan would be very pleased to see her.

'I'll put it to them the next time I speak to them,' she promised. 'But are you sure you're doing the right thing? Roddy is so settled, it would be a shame to spoil that.'

Bessie guiltily wrung her hands together. 'I know he is and I'm more than grateful fer all your Declan an' Roisin have done fer him. But the thing is, I had a lot o' time to think while I were doin' me trainin' in London an' I'm ashamed at what a rotten mam I've been to him. After all, he didn't choose who his dad was, did he? So I decided that per'aps it's time I tried again. I could get us a little house somewhere an' bring him back; be the sort o' mam he deserves.'

Dilly's heart sank as she imagined what effect this would have on the child and on Declan and Roisin too, for that matter. They would be heartbroken to lose him and she couldn't imagine Roddy being any too happy to have to leave them either. Even so, she knew that she couldn't interfere so she told Bessie resignedly, 'Why don't you just go and feel the ground first before you make any decisions? You'll be pleased and surprised to see how happy he is there, I'm sure. I'll tell you what I'll do, if you do wait till December I'll come with you. I can take them all their Christmas presents then.' She smiled gratefully as Nell pressed a steaming cup of tea into her hand and Bessie seemed satisfied as she flitted away upstairs.

'I reckon she's dead set on fetchin' him back,' Nell commented worriedly. 'She's never stopped talkin' about him since yer left. I fear for the poor little chap, I really do, 'specially as he's so settled over there.'

'I do too,' Dilly said. 'But there's not much we can do about it, is there, if that's her decision. He is her son, after all.'

The door opened then and Max strode in with a wide smile on his face. 'Hello, Nell. Evening, Dilly. I called in on the offchance to see if you were back yet.'

'Well, as you can see I am,' Dilly answered.

He surprised her then when he said, 'Why don't you let me take you out to dinner tomorrow evening?'

Normally Dilly would have refused his offer but she heard herself saying, 'Why not? It would be nice to relax for a few hours. I feel as if I've been travelling for ever. But now come and sit down and tell me all that's been going on here.'

Nell slid a cup of tea into his hand then discreetly sidled from the room to leave them to it. The way she saw it, it was a damn shame that they couldn't come together. They clearly thought the world of each other but were too honourable to become lovers whilst Camilla was still alive – if you could call her existence in the asylum being alive, that was. From what she'd gathered the poor woman was nothing but a slobbering wreck now. Still, she couldn't live for much longer, surely? Nell made her way to her own comfortable bedroom, thinking how very lucky she was.

Max was humming to himself the following evening as he straightened his tie in his bedroom mirror. Another ten minutes and it would be time to go and pick Dilly up, and he was looking forward to their meal together. It wasn't often she agreed to be seen out with him. Dilly was a great one for fretting about what people might think.

'Mr Farthing – I think you'd best come.'

Gwen's voice outside his bedroom door startled him and he opened it to find the young woman wringing her hands together.

'What is it, my dear? Is something wrong?' She was clearly very agitated.

'There's someone to see you downstairs,' she said nervously, then took to her heels before he had a chance to ask another thing.

With a sigh Max clicked his bedroom light off. Whoever it was that wanted to see him could wait until tomorrow. He had no intention of being late for Dilly. He descended the stairs and glanced up and down the hallway before heading for the drawing-room door, which was standing open. Gwen would probably have shown the visitor, whoever it was, into there.

A tall figure stood with its back to him in front of the roaring fire and as Max asked politely, 'Hello, may I help you? I'm afraid I'm rather pushed for time at—' He halted abruptly as the figure turned to him and he came face to face with his son.

'Samuel!' The word came out as a gasp as different emotions flooded through him.

'Hello, Father.'

Max frowned. The chap looked absolutely dreadful. He was as pale as a ghost and he'd lost a tremendous amount of weight. One arm was strapped to his side in a makeshift sling and he didn't look any too clean either.

'Do you mind if I sit down?' Samuel dropped heavily on to one of the fireside chairs and the shock that the first sight of his son had evoked in him began to drain away as Max stared at him.

'Look,' Samuel said pathetically, 'I know you probably hoped you'd never set eyes on me again after some of the dastardly things I've done, but I had nowhere else to go. I'm at rock bottom and if you turn me out I don't know what I'm going to do.'

Max felt a rush of anger. 'What – like trying to sell the house I bought for you and Niamh right from under our noses?'

161

Samuel had the good grace to look ashamed. 'I realise how rotten I've been and all I can say is I'm sorry,' he muttered. Then, 'You said *trying* to sell the house. Do you mean that you still own the house and that Niamh is still there?' This was the last thing he had expected. He'd hoped that Niamh would have been long gone by now.

'Sorry doesn't quite cut it this time.' Max joined his hands behind his back, ignoring his son's question. 'Didn't you give a thought to what might happen to your wife? Were you really happy to see her turned out on to the streets? Thankfully I found out what you had done in time, but it cost me dearly. I had to pay back the money to the man who had bought it off you – a full five hundred pounds! And I bet it didn't last you more than a few months or even weeks, did it? Money runs through your hands like water, it always did.'

'I know.' Samuel suddenly grimaced and despite the fact that Max wanted to throw him out on his ear he found himself asking, 'Are you in pain?' Samuel was still his son, after all.

Samuel gritted his teeth. 'Yes. It's my arm – I got set upon by some thugs months ago and they broke my arm. I couldn't afford a decent doctor and the quack who saw me didn't make a very good job of setting it. That's why I haven't been able to work.'

Max was aware of Mrs Pegs standing in the doorway and turning to her now he asked, 'Would you mind rustling up something to eat and a hot drink for Samuel, Mrs Pegs, and ask Olivia if she'd come in, please?'

'Right y'are.' She shuffled away and luckily almost bumped into Olivia who was just going to take Jessica up to bed.

'Your dad's in the drawin' room an' he wants to see yer right away,' she hissed as she hurried towards the kitchen.

Olivia nodded as she looked down at Jessica who was holding her hand. He probably wants to kiss her good night before he goes out, she thought as she steered the child towards the drawing room. Then when she saw who was sitting in the chair, she stopped dead.

'*Samuel!*' It was impossible to keep the shock from her voice.

'Hello, little sis . . . though you're not so little now. You're all grown up, and who is this?'

'This is Jessica, my daughter,' she answered guardedly. Their father didn't look happy at all but then that was understandable when she thought of the way Samuel had disappeared off, leaving Max to clean up his mess the last time.

'I can't believe you're married,' Samuel said and she felt herself flush.

'Olivia, would you telephone the doctor for me and ask him to come at his earliest convenience. Your brother is unwell and his arm needs attending to.'

'Of course.' Olivia was only too glad of a chance to escape and tugged Jessica out of the room.

Max meanwhile began to pace backwards and forwards as his mind worked overtime. He knew that he should turn Samuel out. He *deserved* to be turned out, damn it, but he was still his flesh and blood and he knew that he wouldn't be able to bring himself to do it, not while the lad was in this state anyway. But then a little voice in his head whispered, *But he's not a lad any more. He's a full-grown man and he should be capable of taking care of himself.*

'So when did Olivia get married?'

Samuel's voice sliced into Max's thoughts but he was saved from having to answer when Mrs Pegs bustled back in at that moment with a laden tea trolley. 'There are some cold cuts o' meat left over from dinner an' some crusty

163

bread,' she told Samuel, her voice heavy with disapproval. 'You'll 'ave to make do wi' that fer now.' Then turning her back on him she asked Max, 'Will there be anythin' else?'

'Not for now, Mrs Pegs. Oh actually yes, there is one thing. Could you ask Gwen to light a fire in Samuel's old room and make sure that the bed is aired?'

She sniffed but nodded. He was the boss, after all – though from where she was standing he should chuck the young bugger out on his ear.

Samuel was attacking the food like someone who hadn't eaten for a month so Max took the opportunity to leave the room. There was no alternative now but to telephone Dilly and cancel their evening out. He would need to be present with Samuel when the doctor arrived if he wanted to discover the extent of his son's injuries. He just hoped that Dilly would understand and forgive him.

Chapter Twenty-One

Bathed, shaved and dressed in decent pyjamas for the first time in months, Samuel snuggled down into his comfortable bed. He wasn't at all happy with what the doctor had told him – that he would need to go into hospital to have his arm reset – but then he supposed that he didn't have much choice if he wanted to regain the use of it again. He wasn't looking forward to it though; Samuel was a coward at heart. It hadn't helped being told that even after the operation his arm would probably never be the same again, although he might be able to use that to his advantage. His father couldn't expect him to do a manual job if his arm wasn't strong.

His thoughts turned to Olivia. He hadn't noticed a wedding ring on her finger so what could have gone on there? He couldn't imagine that his father would have been very pleased if she'd presented him with an illegitimate granddaughter. And the house – he'd supposed that the man he had sold it to would have moved in long ago, but his father had informed him otherwise so he'd have to go back to it at some point and live with Niamh again. It would probably be better than living here, he thought. Although he and Niamh had been forced to cohabit they had never lived as man and wife and there was no reason why that should change. He just wished she'd divorce him. At that, his thoughts turned once again to Constance, and guilt lurched inside him again. He didn't care about any of the bad things he'd done in his life apart from the murder of his daughter, but then over time he'd managed to convince himself that he'd only helped her on her way. The kid would have died anyway, wouldn't she?

He turned over and winced as he put pressure on his arm. The doctor had told him that he'd book him into the hospital for his operation the following day if it was possible. The way he saw it, the sooner the better. He might as well get it over and done with and then he'd be able to get on with his life. On that thought, Samuel fell into an exhausted sleep.

'So he's back then?' Dilly said the next morning as she poured out a cup of coffee for Max. He'd called in on the way to one of his factories and she saw at a glance that he was none too happy about it.

'Yes, but then doesn't he always when the chips are down.' Max's eyebrows drew together as he strummed the table with his fingers. He was clearly agitated but Dilly could understand that. 'I'm so sorry I had to cancel our meal,' he said again but she waved his apology aside.

'Don't be so silly. I would have done exactly the same in your position. But does he know about Niamh yet?'

Max shook his head. 'No. He knows that I managed to keep the house. He also knows that Olivia has a little girl,

166

but we haven't really spoken in depth yet. There have been so many changes since he disappeared. To be honest I felt like showing him the door after all the rotten tricks he's pulled but I couldn't do it, not with him being in the state he was.'

'Of course you couldn't. He's still your flesh and blood, isn't he? When is he going into hospital?'

'This morning hopefully. The quack who set his arm made an awful job of it. Samuel can't even bend it so they've got to break it and reset it if he stands any chance of ever using it again.'

Dilly winced. It sounded painful. 'And when will you be telling him about Niamh and Ben?' she asked then. It had always been obvious that Samuel had no love for her daughter – but how would he react when he discovered that she was happily living with someone else in New York and now had another child? Might he try to spoil things for her?

'I see no reason why he needs to know about them,' Max answered. 'Most people think that Niamh is still in Ireland and I certainly shan't be enlightening him other-wise. She deserves a bit of peace now, don't you think?'

Dilly smiled at him gratefully.

'I shall also have to tell him that Mary and Seamus own the house on Abbey Green now, otherwise he may show up there thinking that he can move back in.' The thought had only just occurred to Max but now he realised he needed to tell Samuel sooner rather than later. Mary was getting close to her time now and the last thing he wanted was Samuel going round there upsetting her.

'And how will you explain Jessica?'

Max shrugged. 'There's not much I can say about that, is there? I mean, I know word went round when Olivia first came home that she'd been married and widowed, but I don't think most people believed it for a minute. Samuel is no fool either. He'll soon put two and two together. The only good thing is, Olivia is a strong young woman and she'll give him what for if he dares to say anything derogatory to her. You know what she's like with Jessica – she'll defend her to the death if need be.'

'That's something, I suppose,' Dilly sighed as Max rose from his seat.

'Well, I'd best be off. I have to pop into one of the factories then I'm going home to run Samuel into the hospital – if they can get him in today, that is. He's gone without his breakfast, just in case. What have you got planned?'

'Working as usual,' Dilly told him as she helped him into his coat. 'It's an ongoing challenge, to come up with new designs to keep everyone happy. I just thank God Mary and Seamus are so efficient and such a support.'

She saw Max to the door and waved him off then hurried away to her office to start work.

Samuel had his operation that day and when Max went to visit him the following night his son told him, 'I reckon I'll go back to the house on Abbey Green when they discharge me, Father. It's silly putting on you when Niamh and I have our own home.'

'Ah, but you don't have your own house any more,' Max informed him gravely.

Samuel frowned. 'But I thought you said you'd bought the house back from the buyer I sold it to?'

'So I did, but I then gave it to Mary and Seamus when they got married.'

Angry colour rushed into Samuel's cheeks. '*Seamus* and *Mary* married? And why would you give them our house? And where is Niamh?'

Max patiently answered the questions. 'Yes, Seamus and Mary are married, and happily so, I'm pleased to say. I gave them the house as a wedding gift when they got married because I knew they would value it, unlike you did. And Niamh went to Ireland shortly after you left. There was nothing to keep her here any more after she lost Constance, was there?' As far as Max was concerned, that was all his son needed to know about Niamh.

Samuel was flabbergasted and none too pleased into the bargain, not that there was much he could do about anything.

'So what am I supposed to do now?' he asked sulkily.

'Well, I suggest you come back home and let your arm properly heal then you get yourself a job,' Max said with no trace of sympathy. 'The position you find yourself in is of your own making and I believe it's time for you to grow up. I warn you now, there will be no more handouts from me. When you are discharged I will feed you and give you a roof over your head until you've recovered, but any money you need will have to be earned.'

Samuel stared at him incredulously. 'But you heard what the surgeon said. My arm will never be as strong as it was. What sort of job am I supposed to do?'

'There's office work, or you could drive and do deliveries. I would be happy to employ you in either of those positions.'

Samuel opened his mouth to protest but then quickly clamped it shut again as he tried to get a rein on his temper. He was on sticky ground here. His father clearly hadn't forgiven him even if he had given him shelter, and he couldn't afford to antagonise him at the moment.

'And what about Niamh?' he asked instead. 'Will you inform her that I'm home and will she be coming back? She is still my wife, after all.'

'Oh *please*, Samuel, don't add the title of hypocrite to your list of wrongdoings!' his father sneered. 'We both know that you and Niamh were married in name only. Not that I blame the girl. There is no need for her to know that you're back. She's quite happy where she is and I want it to remain that way. But now I must be going.' He stood up and lifted his coat and hat. 'Think on the options I've given you and decide what you want to do. I realise that you won't be able to work for a few weeks, of course. Five or six, I believe the surgeon said, before your plaster cast comes off. Good evening.'

He strode away down the ward then, leaving Samuel to quietly fume. Office work or making deliveries indeed! Still, it was better than sweeping the factory floors as his father had had him doing once before. And it wasn't as if it would be for ever. Once he was fully recovered he'd be off like a shot, although as yet he had no idea where he might go. He'd exhausted the hospitality and the finances of his schoolfriends. But something would turn up, it always did. And he still had his trump card up his sleeve if all else failed – his knowledge about Olivia's true parentage – and he would use it if necessary. He had never cared about whose life he might ruin.

In a slightly better frame of mind, Samuel Farthing turned over and settled down for a nap before supper was served.

'So how is he?' Mrs Pegs asked as she served Max his meal that evening.

'The operation went well, by all accounts. He'll be coming back here when he's discharged and then in a few weeks' time I shall find him a job.'

'O' course I know it ain't none o' my business, but are yer sure that's wise?' the kindly woman asked. 'Trouble

170

seems to be Samuel's middle name an' things 'ave been goin' so smooth here since he left.' Mrs Pegs felt that she could speak openly to her employer because of the length of time she had worked for him. Why, she looked on him almost as a son now.

'You know the old saying, Mrs Pegs – blood is thicker than water. I'm not quite as soft as I might appear and my first instinct was to send him packing – but I found I couldn't do it. Camilla would never forgive me.'

'But she don't even know the time o' day any more, God bless 'er!' Mrs Pegs pointed out.

'You're quite right, but I do – and I have to live with myself. But if he's any trouble at all to you, you just let me know immediately.'

She briefly placed her hand on his shoulder and gently squeezed it before pottering off back to the kitchen as Olivia and Jessica came into the dining room to join him for dinner.

Samuel was discharged the following day and for the first week he was on his best behaviour. However, boredom soon kicked in and he began to mope about the house. There wasn't much else he could do with not a penny in his pocket.

Oscar and Lawrence didn't seem to be any happier to see him than their father had been, but they were polite even if they were slightly distant.

'So,' Samuel said one Thursday afternoon when Oscar had brought George round for his weekly play with Jessica. 'You're an old married man now, eh?'

Oscar glanced at Olivia and shrugged. 'I suppose you could call me that.'

'Well, I hope you don't mind me saying, old chap, but you don't seem particularly happy about it.'

'Actually, I do mind. The state of my marriage is nothing to do with you so I suggest you keep your opinions to yourself. At least my wife and I still live together, which is more than can be said for you and yours.'

Seeing the angry flush in Oscar's cheeks, Samuel grinned. He'd clearly hit a nerve. Penelope wasn't the most attractive of women if he remembered correctly, and he couldn't imagine why Oscar would have married her in the first place, unless . . . He glanced at Olivia and saw that she too had blushed. Could it be that the suspicions he had always harboured were true – that Oscar and Olivia had feelings for each other, which they had been forced to ignore because they believed that they were related? If they were in love, it could be another string to his bow, for were they to discover that they *weren't* blood-related, there would be nothing to stop Oscar divorcing Penelope and them being together. How much would Oscar pay for such knowledge, he wondered. Samuel smiled benignly as he watched the two youngsters playing, acting out the part of the doting uncle to perfection.

Chapter Twenty-Two

'That's it then, me last day at the hospital – fer now at least, till another vacancy comes up,' Bessie said after returning from her final shift. 'Still, at least I've got the trip to Ireland to look forward to. Just think – this time next week, God willin' we'll be there.'

It was early in December and Bessie was counting the days now until she and Dilly set off.

Nell expertly flipped some sausages over in the frying pan. They were having sausage and mash that night, one of Bessie's favourites, and Nell had made a nice drop of onion gravy to go with it.

'Would yer give Dilly a shout?' Nell asked. 'An' tell her dinner'll be on the table in five minutes. She's been in that bloomin' office since first thing this mornin'.'

'Will do.' Bessie scooted off to tell Dilly and get washed and changed out of her uniform before dinner. It was strange to think that she wouldn't be wearing it for a while but then she'd already agreed to help Seamus temporarily with the running of the shops, so she wouldn't have time to get bored. Mary was only weeks away from giving birth now and moving about like a ship in full sail.

Minutes later, she and Dilly arrived back in the kitchen at the same time just as Nell was serving the meal.

'Just look at that,' Bessie said, appreciatively eyeing the fat juicy sausages. 'Yer can keep all yer fancy fare as far as I'm concerned. There's nothing to beat good old-fashioned plain food.'

Dilly smiled wearily as she pulled out a chair.

'Yer look all in, lass,' Nell remarked and Dilly shrugged.

'It can't be helped. I promised Rosalie in New York that I'd get these designs to her for Christmas so I can't slack.'

'At least you'll get to have a few days' rest next week,' Bessie piped up cheerfully through a mouthful of mash.

'I suppose I will,' Dilly said. 'And I'll get to take over everyone's Christmas presents.'

'I shan't be takin' Roddy's.'

Dilly and Nell looked at each other before Dilly asked, 'Whyever not?'

Bessie swallowed her food, then on a more serious note she confided, ''Cos I've decided it's time I brought him home an' started bein' a proper mam to him. It's what Malcolm would have wanted me to do.'

'But . . . he's so happy there,' Dilly spluttered, horrified. 'And it's been so long since you saw him. He might not want to come back with you.' There – it was out in the open.

'Happen it will take him a while to settle down but he'll soon get used to it,' Bessie said confidently. 'I've still got more than enough o' the money my Malcolm left me to put a good deposit down on a little house for us an' I want to feel I've done right by him. It ain't fair to leave him with your Declan and Roisin any longer.'

174

'But they *adore* him!' Dilly said in a panic. 'It will destroy him if you take him away from them now, Bessie. I beg you to give this a little more thought. Roddy isn't a parcel to be passed about at will. He's a little boy, a very *settled* little boy!'

'An' he's also *my* little boy,' Bessie said stubbornly as Dilly pushed her plate away. She'd lost her appetite, although if she were honest with herself, this wasn't entirely unexpected. She'd made it more than clear that she had had been contemplating this for some time now. Declan and Roisin were going to be devastated but there was nothing they could do about it if Bessie had really made her mind up.

'But how will Roddy feel if he bumps into Samuel and discovers that he's his father?' Dilly was feeling desperate now and was ready to do anything to stop Bessie going through with her plan. 'You know that Samuel never had time for him before, so how is Roddy going to react to find him back here again?'

Bessie scowled. 'I stopped being afraid of Samuel Farthing long ago,' she said with contempt. 'And if he tries to make trouble for us it will be all the worse for him, you just mark my words.' Then, her voice softening, she reached across the table to take Dilly's hand as she pleaded, 'Try an' understand, Dilly, please. I've felt so ashamed 'cos I couldn't love the little chap, but I'm that bit older now an' I'm sure we could get closer.'

Dilly scraped her chair across the quarry tiles as she repeated, 'Just give it some thought, eh.' With that she walked from the room as an awkward silence settled between the two women left there.

Over the next few days, Bessie went to view a few houses. Up to now none of them had been quite right but each time she set off, Dilly's heart sank further. She supposed she should telephone Declan to warn him and Roisin what Bessie was planning, but she couldn't bring herself to do it. She knew that it would break them, and just before Christmas too! So she remained silent, praying that Bessie would have a change of heart.

The day of their departure finally arrived, foggy and dark.

'There's no point in even setting off. The ferry'll never leave the port in this – it's a right pea-souper out there,' Nell muttered sceptically, glancing towards the window.

Dilly was inclined to agree with her but Bessie would not be put off. 'Of course it will. The fog will have cleared by the time we get to the docks,' she insisted, placing her suitcase by the door and putting her coat and hat on.

'Well, if the worst comes to the worst we'll have to stay in a hotel for the night and hope we can go in the morning,' Dilly said wearily. She wasn't looking forward to this trip at all.

Nell kissed them both and handed Dilly a basket packed with food for the journey. 'Give 'em all my love an' have a safe journey,' she told them as they set off. Then with a last sympathetic glance at Dilly, 'An' good luck, lass. Don't you get worryin' about nothin' here.'

The train was on time but the journey was delayed because of the fog so they arrived in the docks with only minutes to spare before the ferry was due to leave. However, as they approached it with a porter in close pursuit pulling a trolley with their luggage on it behind them, a burly, bearded seaman descended the gangway humming merrily.

'She's not sailin' today, I'm afraid, ladies,' he told them. 'The next one to go will be first thing in the mornin' – if the fog clears, that is.'

176

'Oh dear,' Bessie groaned. 'What shall we do now? It's too far to go all the way back home again.'

'We'll just book into a hotel for the evening,' Dilly said patiently.

'There's a decent one just along at the end o' the dock there,' the seaman informed her with a cheeky wink. 'I could keep yer both company, if yer like.'

'No, thank you very much,' Bessie said huffily as Dilly pressed her lips tightly together to stop herself from laughing. Bessie could be such a prude.

'Thank you very much,' Dilly told the man, then turning to the porter she asked, 'Would you mind showing us the way?'

They set off with Bessie still bristling and soon after they were comfortably settled for the night.

When Dilly drew the curtains in her room early the next morning she was relieved to see that the fog had all but cleared, apart from some sea mist, so she went next door to wake Bessie. After a hurried breakfast they headed for the docks again and not too long afterwards were strolling along the decks of the ferry, trying to keep warm as they waited for it to leave.

'I don't know what they'll all think of us turnin' up a day late!' Bessie fretted.

'I rang them from the hotel last night to say we'd been delayed so they know what's happening,' Dilly told her for the third time. Bessie had been on tenterhooks all morning and couldn't seem to stand still for a second.

'So what do you think Roddy will think o' me now?' she asked.

'Well, I shouldn't expect too much too soon. You have to appreciate that he hasn't seen you for years.'

'But I've written to 'im!' Bessie pointed out heatedly.

'It isn't quite the same as seeing him though, is it?'

177

'I suppose not,' Bessie admitted with a sigh as the ferry's engines whirled into life. 'But I want to make it up to 'im before he forgets I'm his mam altogether. Do you know I'm in me late thirties now, so I ain't likely to have another child, am I? Where did the time go?'

'It just has a habit of flying by,' Dilly answered. It started to drizzle then and they both ducked under cover to avoid getting soaked through. The sea was grey as was the sky, but thankfully it wasn't too rough.

By the time the ferry pulled into Dublin, Bessie had worked herself up into a rare old state.

'What if he hates me?' she said in a panic as Dilly tried to get their luggage together and the gangway was hauled into place.

'I'm sure he won't. Now give me a hand with these cases, will you? And keep your eye open for Liam or Declan. One of them should be here to meet us.'

They were almost at the bottom of the gangway when Dilly spotted Liam striding towards them and as always her heart had a little shock. He was so like Fergal had been in his younger days that whenever she saw him she was reminded of her late husband.

He grunted at Bessie and gave Dilly a hug then picked up both their cases as if they weighed nothing and began to lead them across the quay to the waiting horse and cart. Shelagh had been nagging him lately to get a motorcar for when they were coming in to Dublin, but Liam wouldn't hear of it despite the fact that they were becoming so popular.

'What would I want one o' them dirty noisy things for? The old horse an' cart were good enough for me daddy an' they're good enough for me, so they are,' he'd insisted. Liam was still quite old-fashioned in some ways so Shelagh hadn't argued the point.

Dilly could feel the disapproval towards Bessie coming off him in waves as he steered the cart through the town although he didn't say a word. He would know how much Declan and Roisin would be dreading her arrival and Dilly could understand how they must all feel, up to a point. It was a sad situation all round. Roddy had been the result of a vicious rape, so it was no wonder that Bessie had never been able to bond with the child. But then he had never asked to be born. Finally the lonely, frightened little boy had found what it was to be loved with Roisin and Declan. Now, because of a belated attack of guilt, Bessie might snatch him away from them, and the trouble was, there was nothing at all any of them could do about it. Roddy was still legally Bessie Ward's child.

'Is everyone well?' Dilly asked as the silence became uncomfortable.

'Aye they are . . . at the moment,' Liam answered gruffly.

Dilly said no more but merely turned her coat collar up against the bitter cold. The wind had dropped and so had the drizzle, and the sky had turned an eerie grey colour. If it was going to snow she just hoped they could get to the farm before it started.

They were all feeling stiff by the time the cart turned into the farmyard. Liam helped the women down from the high narrow plank seat and told them brusquely, 'Get yourselves inside in the warm. I'm going to stable the horse then I'll bring in your luggage.'

Bessie was staring about, hoping for a sight of Roddy as she followed Dilly across the cobbles. She'd thought he might be waiting for her but then it was very cold so she couldn't really blame him for staying indoors.

'That was good timing, so it was,' Shelagh greeted Dilly as they entered the kitchen. The warmth wrapped itself around them like a blanket and their cheeks started to glow. 'The stew is just about ready to serve up.'

'Well, it smells delicious – in fact, it's making my stomach grumble,' Dilly answered brightly, dropping a kiss on her sister-in-law's rosy cheek. She turned her attention to the children who were scattered about the room. They were usually all over her when she first arrived but today they seemed subdued, and were keeping a wary eye on Bessie.

'Hello, Bessie, would you like to take your coat off and go and sit by the fire?' Shelagh said politely but there was no warmth in her greeting.

Bessie didn't even seem to notice as she peeled her outdoor clothes off. 'Is Roddy not here?' she asked, ignoring the glares of the children.

'No, he's round home – I mean at Roisin and Declan's cottage,' Shelagh answered awkwardly.

'Oh, then perhaps I should go round there an' let 'im know we've arrived.'

'No – don't do that,' Shelagh said a little too quickly. 'They'll be just about to have their meal too, no doubt. I dare say he'll be round in a while.'

'Very well.' Concealing her disappointment as best she could, Bessie took a seat on the settle at the side of the fire and folded her hands primly in her lap. This wasn't the sort of welcome she'd hoped for at all, but then she supposed it was to be expected.

'Dilly, I've made a bed up for you in Bridie's room if you don't mind so that Bessie can have the box room to herself.'

'Of course I don't mind.' Dilly smiled affectionately at Bridie, who seemed to have shot up at least another inch since the last time she'd seen her.

'I really don't mind where I sleep,' Bessie said hastily.

'The sofa will do for me. I don't want to put you to any trouble. I rather thought I'd be sleepin' at Declan's place wi' Roddy.'

'It's quite all right, we have more room,' Shelagh answered with no glimmer of a smile and Bessie fell silent, feeling more out of place by the minute.

Liam returned then, bringing the visitors' luggage with him and once they'd been shown to their rooms and had unpacked their things the two women went downstairs again to join the family for dinner.

The lamb stew and fluffy dumplings that Shelagh had made were delicious but Bessie was so nervous at the prospect of seeing Roddy again that she could barely eat a thing. A large apple pie that melted in the mouth, accompanied by thick, creamy custard followed but Bessie declined her portion and was relieved when the meal was over. It had been a very sombre affair.

She insisted on helping Dilly and Shelagh with clearing the table and washing and drying up then swallowed her impatience as she resumed her seat by the fire.

Dilly and Shelagh were exchanging news about back home, Liam was smoking his pipe and reading the newspaper and the children had all disappeared off upstairs somewhere. Then at last the kitchen door opened, letting in a blast of icy air, and a solemn-faced Declan stepped through it followed by Roisin and Roddy.

Bessie gasped at first sight of her son. He had grown and looked even more like his father if that was possible. She staggered out of the chair on legs that had suddenly turned to jelly and smiled tremulously at him . . . but he studiously avoided her eyes.

'Hello, Bessie,' Roisin said quietly.

'Hello.' Bessie couldn't drag her eyes away from Roddy. He was almost up to Roisin's shoulder now and seemed to be all arms and legs. In fact, he reminded her of a leggy little foal.

'Hello, Roddy.'

He regarded her sullenly for a moment then suddenly, before anyone could stop him, he turned and bolted back the way he had come.

Chapter Twenty-Three

'It's all right, Mrs Pegs, I'll get it,' Olivia shouted down the hall when she heard someone rapping on the front door. Jessica was tucked up in bed, it was Gwen's evening off and Olivia knew Mrs Pegs would be putting her feet up at the side of the kitchen fire, probably with a glass of sherry in her hand – purely for medicinal purposes, as she always told them. Olivia had no idea where Samuel and her father were but they were both out too as far as she knew.

She struggled with the bolt on the door then unlocked it and inched it open – and was confronted by Roger Bannerman standing on the doorstep.

'What the hell do you think you're doing coming here?' she managed to hiss when she was over the initial shock. She made to shut the door in his face but Roger hastily put his foot in and stopped her.

'Please, Olivia, I haven't come here to argue. I just need to talk to you.'

Opening the door wider, she jerked her head towards

the drawing room. 'You'd better come in here,' she told him in a low voice.

'Who is it, luvvie?' Mrs Pegs' voice echoed along the hallway.

'It's all right, it's just someone to see me. Stay where you are,' Olivia called back as she ushered Roger ahead of her.

Once in the drawing room she crossed to the fire and threw some lumps of coal from the brass scuttle on to it before turning to him and asking pointedly, 'Well? What do you want?'

He took off his hat and began to turn the brim through his fingers as he stared at her. 'Look, I know we ended up arguing the last time we spoke, but I think we should discuss Jessica's future now, don't you?'

'I already have my daughter's future planned out, thank you.' Olivia's voice was colder than the hoar frost on the grass outside. 'She'll be starting school after Christmas. She's very much looking forward to it as it happens and then we'll live here happily together until she's older and decides what sort of career she wants to go into.'

'But I should be helping – financially, at least, if she's my daughter.'

'I've told you, she isn't.' Olivia took a cigarette from a packet on a small table; she rarely smoked but she felt an urgent need for one right then. She took a spill and lit it from the fire then turned to look at him. 'What do I have to do to convince you?'

'She's got my eyes,' he said, and her heart began to thump. He'd noticed.

'I think you'll find any number of children have blue eyes,' she bluffed, blowing a plume of smoke into the air.

'Not the exact same colour blue as mine. Oh come on,

Olivia, admit it! I only want to help. It can't be easy bringing her up on your own. I could pay for her to have a private education.'

'I could pay for that myself if that was what I wanted for her,' Olivia said tersely. 'But I want her to go to the school on the green so that she can get to know the children who live hereabouts.' Her stomach was churning, she was painfully aware that her father could arrive home at any minute. How would she explain Roger's presence? Her father had tried gently on a few occasions to find out who Jessica's father was, but she had always managed to stall him. If Roger were to start showing up on a regular basis it wouldn't take long for Max to put two and two together!

'I really think it would be best if you left now,' she told him with her chin in the air. 'You're just wasting your time. You are *not* Jessica's father so stop pestering me or I shall do what I threatened and visit your wife.'

He shrugged as he put his hat back on. 'Go ahead because I've decided that I'm going to speak to Miranda about Jessica – this very evening, as a matter of fact. Oh, I know she'll be upset but I'd rather she heard it from me than you. I shall tell her that it was you who chased me, and that I succumbed in a moment of madness and that I've suffered all manner of guilt at my betrayal ever since. Miranda adores me and I know she'll forgive me – then if you speak to her it will be just your word against mine. Who do you think she will believe?'

'*Get out!*' Olivia spat as her eyes flashed fire.

'Very well, but I warn you, I shall be back – and I'll keep coming back till you allow me to see my daughter.' He turned about and left the room, leaving the door to swing open behind him as Olivia began to tremble. She heard the slam of the front door then dropped on to the nearest chair and sobbed as if her heart would break.

From behind the office door, Samuel listened closely. What a turn-up for the books, he thought smugly. I couldn't have timed coming home better if I'd tried. Though it had been a bit of a rush getting into the office before Roger caught him eavesdropping outside the drawing-room door. Samuel had been aimlessly walking the streets just to get out of the house. There was nothing else to do with no money in his pockets. He rubbed his arm, which was aching now although the cast had been off for a while. It had taken longer to heal than the surgeon had thought it would, and Samuel had taken full advantage of the fact. He couldn't do so for any longer though, and only that day his father had told him to prepare to start work the following week. Driving vans and making deliveries! Samuel's lip curled in disgust then his thoughts returned to the conversation he had just overheard. So, Roger Bannerman was Jessica's father! He'd never believed for a second the concocted story Olivia had told him about being widowed in London. Now he just had to decide how he could turn the knowledge to his advantage.

With a sly smile, Samuel crept from the office as quiet as a mouse and made his way up to his room to give the matter some thought. It would be no good threatening to tell the man's wife. Roger had said that he was going to tell her himself – although he might well have been bluffing . . . And then as he paced up and down it suddenly came to him. Roger might well tell his wife what had happened between him and Olivia – but he wouldn't want it to become common knowledge for Miranda's sake. Nor would Olivia want their father to know, come to that. Max was a man of high morals and should he discover that Roger was Jessica's father, he'd feel obliged to persuade Olivia to allow him some contact with her. Olivia wouldn't

186

like that one little bit. She was fiercely possessive of the child and she cherished her like the Crown Jewels. Olivia wasn't rich but she had her allowance and what she earned at the hospital . . . perhaps it was time he had a little talk to her? His silence must be worth something and there was no time like the present. With a spring in his step he went back downstairs to confront his sister.

'I think I'll turn in if you don't mind,' Bessie said timidly later that evening. There had been a strained atmosphere ever since Roddy had bolted earlier on that night at sight of her, closely followed by Roisin and Declan, and now she just wanted to hide away from everyone.

'Would you like a hot drink before you go up?' Shelagh asked politely but Bessie shook her head.

'No, thank you, I'm fine. Good night, all.'

Dilly watched her go with tears in her eyes. Bessie's pain was so tangible that Dilly could almost feel it – but what more could she have expected? She'd abandoned Roddy years ago and even before that she'd never been a loving mother to him. Surely she hadn't expected him to fly into her arms?

'Actually, I think I might go up too,' she told Shelagh and Liam. She had a feeling that Bessie might need someone to talk to.

'Sleep tight, Mammy,' Declan answered and Shelagh looked up from the socks she was darning to smile.

At the top of the stairs, Dilly tapped on Bessie's bedroom door before opening it to find Bessie sitting on the bed in floods of tears.

'Now come along, that's quite enough of that,' she said gently, crossing to sit beside her and place an arm about her shoulders. 'You and Roddy have a lot of time to make up. It's not going to happen in a day now, is it?'

187

'I . . . suppose not,' Bessie sniffed, mopping at her eyes with a scrap of white lace handkerchief. 'But he looked at me as if he hated me, Dilly!'

'Of course he doesn't hate you, but he doesn't know you very well either, does he? Children have short memories. He probably can only vaguely remember living with you now.'

'But I always wrote to him!'

'Words on paper aren't quite the same as spending time with someone, are they?' Dilly patted her hand. 'Don't try to rush things. Get to know him again, let him get to know you. Show him that you care and let things take their course. It's no good going at this like a bull in a china shop. Perhaps tomorrow you could suggest that you go for a walk together? Ask him to show you his school – some of his favourite places maybe, so that he knows you're interested in him.'

Bessie gave her a watery smile. 'Thanks, Dilly, I will.'

Dilly pecked her gently on the cheek before heading off to tuck into the deep feather mattress with Bridie. She was a weary traveller who longed for her bed.

'I was thinking I might ask Roddy if he fancied going for a walk today,' Bessie told Shelagh at breakfast the next morning. Liam had already gone out with Declan to bring the cows down from the fields and into the barn for the winter because they feared snow was on the way.

'I suppose you could ask him.' Shelagh was doing her best to be a good hostess to Bessie, but knowing how much Declan and Roisin adored Roddy she was finding it very difficult. After all, what gave Bessie the right to just swan back into his life after all this time? The child was quite happy where he was, which was more than he had been when he arrived, and to Shelagh's mind Bessie should leave well alone. She hadn't wanted him then – so why now?

Once again, Bessie insisted on helping with the breakfast pots then putting her warm coat on she headed off to Roisin and Declan's cottage.

Roisin answered the knock on the door and ushered her in without a word. She'd been expecting her. Roddy was sitting at the table reading a comic and he eyed her warily as she smiled at him.

'I was thinking, seeing as it's Saturday and you don't have to go to school today, we might go for a walk together?' Bessie suggested hopefully.

Roddy glanced at Roisin as if for consent and when she gave an imperceptible nod he shrugged. He clearly wasn't overly impressed with the idea.

'Where do you want to walk?' he asked, his voice sullen.

'Wherever you like. You could perhaps show me some of your favourite places?'

He moved away from the table, his shoulders hunched, to get his outdoor clothes and Roisin peeped at Bessie from her position at the sink where she was washing the breakfast pots. She felt that she should hate her. After all, wasn't she capable of taking Roddy, the child she and Declan loved as their own, away from them? And yet she found that she couldn't. Bessie was clearly struggling with her emotions and she obviously wanted to try and make amends to Roddy for the past.

A tense silence stretched between them until Roddy returned in a thick coat and stout boots. As he slouched towards the door Bessie followed him without a word. Roisin chewed on her lip and helplessly watched them go.

Dilly was at the window of the farmhouse and she too watched the pair set off for their walk.

'I don't know who I feel the most sorry for,' she

commented to Shelagh. 'Bessie so wants to feel that she's doing the right thing, but poor Roddy doesn't want to know. How will he react if she suggests he comes back to Nuneaton with her?'

Shelagh joined her in time to see the pair disappear around the side of the barn. 'The wean considers this is his home now. Perhaps Bessie should think of that and put his feelings first,' she answered sensibly.

Dilly agreed with her. 'I think she's just plagued with guilt because she couldn't love him as she felt she should,' she confided. 'And I know she's seriously considering taking him back, but I'm sure she'll have a change of heart when she sees how wrong that would be. Bessie isn't a bad person.'

Shelagh could only hope that she was right.

Bessie and Roddy had walked in silence for some way along the lane when she asked him brightly, 'Where are you taking me?'

Hands thrust deep into his coat pockets and head down, he mumbled, 'Nowhere in partic'lar.'

'Isn't there somewhere special you like to go?'

Another shrug. 'To be sure, but I go to them places wi' Bridie an' me friends.'

He even sounds Irish, Bessie thought as she peeped at him from the corner of her eye. But then he would, after all; he'd been here for almost half his life now.

'I was thinking, when I get home I might look around for a nice little house to live in.' Her comment brought no response from him whatsoever so she went on, 'I'm working for Dilly at present, helping out with her shops, but as soon as another vacancy comes up at the hospital I shall go back to nursing again. You do understand that that's why I let you come here, don't you? So that I could go and do my nurse's training? I thought you'd be more settled here rather than have to leave you with people you didn't know.'

They'd reached the top of a rise now and the view from it was quite breathtaking. The fields fell away in multi-coloured tones of green like a giant patchwork quilt, interspersed with hedgerows and small copses.

'Did you hear me, Roddy?' A few moments had elapsed and he hadn't answered her question. Still he remained silent until suddenly he turned and faced her.

'You sent me here 'cos you didn't want me or love me,' he told her bluntly. 'An' that's just fine, 'cos Roisin an' Declan are my family now an' I'm much happier with them than I ever was with you.' With that he raced away, leaving Bessie gasping with dismay.

Things certainly hadn't got off to a good start between them but then Dilly had said that she'd have to take it slowly. Somehow she was going to have to gain Roddy's confidence and prove to him that she'd changed and really did care about him.

Chapter Twenty-Four

'What a pretty sight, very cosy,' Samuel sneered as he walked into the drawing room the following Thursday afternoon to find Olivia and Oscar down on their knees playing with the children. He'd just made a delivery and had decided to call in for a hot drink before going back to the factory.

The colour instantly rushed to Olivia's cheeks. 'Shouldn't you be at work?' she questioned coldly.

'I am, sister darling. I just popped in to cadge a drink off Mrs Pegs. It's damned cold in the cab of that van.'

Oscar self-consciously rose and dusted his knees, feeling vaguely uncomfortable. Samuel could always make him feel like he'd been caught doing something he shouldn't.

'I might go through to the kitchen and get her to rustle a cup of tea up for us too,' he said, making a hasty exit.

Samuel immediately seized his chance as he sidled up to Olivia. The children had gone back to playing and he didn't want to miss his opportunity.

'Wouldn't happen to have a few bob going spare, would you?' he asked cajolingly.

Olivia blinked. 'But I gave you five shillings yesterday!'

'Huh! And what do you think that will buy? I spent that last night on a few drinks with the chaps.'

'I can't keep doing this, Samuel,' she hissed furiously. 'I'm not made of money, you know! Don't you get paid tomorrow?'

He studied his fingernails. 'I do indeed but there's still tonight to get through – so unless you want me to have a word in Father's ear about . . .'

With an angry toss of her head Olivia crossed to her handbag, which was on the chair by the door and withdrew her purse, her mouth set in a straight line.

'Here.' She dropped two half-crowns and a florin into his hand. 'That should be enough for you to go out tonight – but don't bother coming back again this week.'

At that instant Oscar entered the room again, just in time to see Samuel hastily drop something into his pocket. It didn't take much working out to guess what it was as he then saw Olivia stuff her purse back into her bag.

Samuel strolled away then and Oscar looked at Olivia intently before asking, 'Have you just given him money?'

'Just a little loan.' She forced a smile before suggesting to the children, 'Shall we go through to the kitchen and see if Mrs Pegs has any of her lovely scones made?'

They whooped with delight as she herded them in front of her and once alone, Oscar stroked his chin thoughtfully. Why would Olivia be giving Samuel money? He knew she didn't have any more time for their brother than he did. Come to think of it, she hadn't been herself for a little while now; she'd lost weight and seemed to be very on edge. Something was clearly bothering her and he wondered if it was anything to do with Sam. Suddenly he desperately missed the closeness that had once existed between his sister and himself. They were on good terms now but she never confided in him as she had used to, and he always felt as if she was keeping him at arm's length. Gone were the days when she would perch on the end of his bed and tell him all her secrets and what sort of a day she'd had.

The front-door bell rang then, yanking him out of his reverie, and he heard Gwen scuttle along the hallway to answer it. Seconds later his heart skipped a beat when Penelope swept into the room.

'Ah, I thought I'd find you here.' As she removed her gloves and waddled towards the fire Oscar couldn't help but notice how much weight she'd put on in the last few months. The drab brown outfit she was wearing and the way she'd pulled her lank hair into a tight bun at the nape of her neck didn't do anything to enhance her appearance either. The buttons on her coat were straining across her ample chest. 'I was going to call on Nancy Bennett but when I got there I was told by her maid that she's ill in bed with bronchitis, so I thought I might as well come here and have a lift home with you and George in the car. It really is very thoughtless of her,' she went on. 'She'd invited Merrylin Beddows for afternoon tea too. Surely she could have let us know that she was indisposed?'

Penelope looked around then before asking, 'Where is George?'

'Olivia has just taken him and Jessica along to the kitchen to see if Mrs Pegs has any scones for them.' He saw the look of disapproval flash across her face. She had made it painfully clear that she wasn't at all happy that he brought George along here each week to see his cousin. She had never believed the story about Olivia being widowed and left with a child to bring up whilst she was in London, and she and Oscar had had bitter rows about it.

'I don't want my son mixing with a child who was born out of wedlock!' she'd informed him righteously but on this point, Oscar had stood his ground.

'I'm quite sure that if my father can accept Jessica then we can too,' he'd thundered back and she'd been so shocked that she was rendered temporarily speechless. It hadn't lasted for long though and she still gave him grief from time to time about him bringing the boy here. And now she'd found out that her son was in the kitchen with the servants having afternoon tea. It just wasn't good enough as far as she was concerned.

'I'd rather like some tea myself,' she said stiltedly. 'I've come out in the cold all for nothing and you know what a delicate constitution I have.' She dabbed ineffectually at her nose with a scrap of lace handkerchief. 'I shall probably come down with a wretched cold now. But I'll have my tea in here.'

Oscar almost choked. Delicate constitution? She was built like a brick outhouse!

'I'll go and get some for you,' he offered and again she sighed with frustration.

'Can't you just ring the bell, dear? That's what the servants are for!'

After casting a withering look her way he set off for the kitchen. The afternoon was ruined. The children wouldn't be allowed to play for long now that Penelope had turned up, and he did so enjoy the few short hours he spent with Olivia each week. Still, he supposed he'd have to grin and bear it. There wasn't much else he could do. Penelope was his wife, after all, for better or for worse, although he couldn't help but feel he'd only ever had the worst of her!

Just as he'd feared, as soon as the children returned to the room, Penelope began to nag at them.

'Don't *shout*, darling, it's *so* common,' she scolded

195

George as he started a game of Snakes and Ladders with Jessica on the hearthrug. 'And *do* get up off your knees. Those trousers came from London and were dreadfully expensive. You don't want to ruin them, do you?'

Oscar looked towards Olivia with an exasperated expression on his face and eager to avoid an argument she carried a small side table over to the children, telling them patiently, 'There you are. You can play on this.'

Penelope sniffed and cast a scathing glance in Olivia's direction. She detested her sister-in-law, although she always tried to conceal the fact. Olivia was everything she would have liked to be – slim and pretty – and sometimes when she saw her and Oscar together she seethed with jealousy. He never smiled at her the way he smiled at his sister, and they always seemed so at ease with each other, whereas with her she always felt that Oscar was choosing his words carefully.

Now as she took a sip of the scalding tea she wondered how long she could bear to wait before suggesting they should leave. Every minute spent in Mill House was a minute too long as far as she was concerned. The trouble was that George was clearly enjoying himself – and again the jealousy kicked in. At home he was very quiet and polite but here he seemed to become a different being, laughing and giggling and letting his hair down. It never occurred to her that at home he wasn't allowed to do these things. His nanny was kind but firm and like Penelope believed that children should be seen and not heard.

'I win!' Jessica suddenly piped up and Penelope shuddered as George started to giggle. The child was just like her mother – as common as muck – and to Penelope's mind the sooner the two children got to school and away from each other the better. She and Oscar were still fighting over which school their son should attend. She wanted him to go to a private prep school or be educated at home, but Oscar was being stubborn and insisting that he should attend a local school. There had been no sighting of another baby yet either, despite the fact that she occasionally demanded her conjugal rights. Her eyes rested on Oscar. He was still remarkably good-looking but he'd turned out to be a huge disappointment as a husband. Settling back in her seat she eyed the minute hands on the clock on the mantelpiece, willing them to whiz round quickly so that she could escape this madhouse. It was no wonder that Camilla, her mother-in-law, had gone insane if her children had been as unruly as these two were when they got together.

An hour later, Oscar drove them home in silence. George was as quiet as a little mouse in the back seat and Oscar found that he had nothing to say to Penelope. They didn't seem to have anything in common apart from their son and they even argued about him. Penelope and he had completely different ideas about how he should be brought up and it constantly caused friction between them. In many other things, Oscar tended to let her have her own way but he'd be damned if he'd let her spoil his son's childhood. To his mind children should be allowed to play and have fun, not sit like little stuffed dummies.

Only the weekend before, Oscar had suggested getting George his first pony and Penelope had been horrified at the very thought of it.

'But riding is so *dangerous!*' she'd gasped. 'He could break his neck if he fell off!'

'Oh, don't be so bloody ridiculous!' Oscar had snapped before he could stop himself. He'd never sworn at her before and she'd been startled and disgusted.

'If you are going to use foul language then I suggest you

see less of George,' she'd sniffed and Oscar had been repentant.

'I'm sorry, but George should be allowed to do the things other children do. It's not as if he has anyone to play with, is it?'

'And whose fault is *that*?' Penelope had snapped as ugly red colour crept up her thick neck. 'If you'd share our marital bed more often instead of me having to *beg you* to join me, he'd probably have brothers and sisters by now!'

Oscar had strode away at that point with a guilty expression on his face because he knew that she was right. Sometimes he just longed to run away but he knew that he never would. There was George to think of now and at least he still got to spend a few stolen hours with Olivia each week. Thoughts of Olivia brought him back to the present and he frowned, his eyes tight on the road ahead. There had been a chap hovering about outside the house when he'd arrived earlier that afternoon; it was the second time Oscar had spotted him there in as many weeks and it had just come to him who he was. Roger Bannerman. He'd met him a few times at the gentleman's club he and his father sometimes frequented in town. But why would *he* be hanging about outside Mill House? And then it came to him: the fellow had belonged to the same Amateur Dramatic Society Olivia had used to go to before she went away to London. Could it be that he was waiting about for her? No, surely not. Roger was a married man. It was strange all the same though, and disquiet niggled away at Oscar like a sore tooth.

Chapter Twenty-Five

'I can't believe how quickly the time has flown,' Shelagh said for want of something to break the silence that had settled like a cloud over the farmhouse kitchen. 'Just two more nights and you'll be away home again.'

Dilly raised a smile and nodded as she glanced at Bessie, who was watching Roddy like a hawk. He'd be going back to Roisin and Declan's cottage any time now to get ready for bed and he clearly couldn't wait to leave. They'd all had supper together but it hadn't been a success. In fact, the atmosphere had been strained and by now, Dilly's nerves were stretched to breaking point. All Bessie's attempts to get close to her son had failed dismally, despite her best efforts, and Dilly could sense that she was getting desperate now as the time for them to leave drew near.

'Ah, here it comes,' Declan suddenly announced, and as they all followed his glance towards the window they saw the first flakes of snow start to flutter down. 'Thank goodness I've got all the animals down from the fields and into the barn. I'm only surprised it's held off for as long as it has – I've been expecting it for days, to be sure.' Then turning to Roisin he suggested, 'Shall we be away then, lass? The time is running on and I for one am ready for me bed.'

Roisin rose from her seat and Roddy jumped up too, but Bessie halted them when she said, 'Could I just have a word before you go?' She tugged at the neckline of her dress and licked her lips nervously before going on, 'As you know, me an' Dilly will be goin' home the day after tomorrow an' . . .' She took a deep breath and ploughed on, 'The thing is, I shall be wantin' to take Roddy with me, back to where he belongs. I shall never be able to thank you an' Declan enough, Roisin, for all that you've done for him, but now I feel it's time he came home. I am his mother, after all.'

Roisin gasped and clung to the back of the nearest chair for support as Declan sucked his breath in. But it was Roddy to whom everyone's eyes turned when he roared, 'Oh no you ain't me mother! *She* is!' He stabbed a trembling finger towards Roisin as tears flooded into his eyes.

Bessie felt as if she was being torn apart but what could she do? She'd tried befriending him, bribing him with treats even, but nothing had worked so now she felt she just had to come straight out with it. 'But she isn't, pet.' She held a tentative hand out to him but he slapped it away furiously, swiping the tears from his cheeks with the back of his hand.

'You're just a wicked witch who wants to spoil me life,' he accused. 'But I won't come back with you. I won't! *This* is me home now an' I'm stayin' put. You never wanted me and I *hate* you!'

Bessie's hand flew to her throat. She so wanted to deny what he was saying but the trouble was, he was stating the truth. She had never wanted him, and his words only hammered it home to her.

'I . . . I know I've not done right by you,' she told him chokily. 'But I'm goin' to try harder from now on, I promise.'

His head wagged from side to side as his fists clenched and unclenched with rage. 'You won't get the chance 'cos I ain't comin' back with you an' you can't make me!' With that he flung himself at the door and once he'd swung it open he disappeared into the swirling snowflakes. The draught made the fire roar up the chimney as they all stared at each other in horrified silence. Then Bridie's gentle sobs broke the spell and Declan raced out into the night after the boy.

'I'm so sorry,' Bessie sobbed. 'But I had to come out wi' it an' let him know I'm takin' him home so as he can get used to the idea.'

Roisin lowered her head, feeling as if she was caught in the grip of a nightmare. The thought of losing Roddy was almost more than she could bear. And the worst thing about it was there wasn't anything she could do to prevent it. As Bessie had stated she was his legal mother.

'I'd better get round home and check that he's all right,' she said quietly as she shuffled towards the door, and once she'd gone through it, Liam quietly closed it behind her before turning to the children, who were all watching wide-eyed.

'Get yourselves to bed now, there's good weans,' he encouraged and without a word they all rose and did as they were told. Once they'd gone he turned his attention to Bessie to ask, 'Are you quite sure you're doing the right thing? The lad is happy here, as you can well see, missus.'

Bessie detected a note of loathing in his voice and deep down she knew that she deserved it. She'd abandoned

Roddy here years ago without a second thought and now she'd turned up out of the blue to drag him away from everyone and everything he'd come to love. And he *did* love them, he'd made that more than clear.

'I'm sorry,' she muttered shamefaced. 'But he is my son and he's coming back with me. I've made my mind up.'

'Then if there's nothing more I can say to make you reconsider, I'll bid you good night.' Liam stamped from the room as Dilly wrung her hands together in despair. Poor Roddy – and poor Bessie too, if it came to that. For wasn't she just finally trying to do what she felt was right?

'Shall I make us all a fresh pot of tea?' she suggested, much as Nell would have done had she been there. Nell was a great believer that tea was a cure for all ills.

Shelagh shook her head, looking worn and tired. 'Not for me, lass. I reckon I'll go up and join Liam if you don't mind.' She left the room without another word and now that they were alone Bessie looked at Dilly imploringly.

'I *am* doin' the right thing, ain't I?' she whispered in a shaky voice.

'I can't answer that,' Dilly answered truthfully. 'But let's get turned off down here, shall we, and get ourselves to bed? Things might look better in the morning.'

Upstairs, sleep eluded Bessie and she stood at the tiny bedroom window gazing out into the fast-falling snow. It was bitterly cold and she was shivering, but she barely noticed as she stood there wondering what Roddy was doing right then. He had looked at her as if he hated her, and truthfully she couldn't blame him. *But I'll make it up to him*, she promised herself. *From this day on I'll be a proper mam to him.*

Shelagh was stirring a pan of porridge on the top of the stove the next morning whilst the children got ready for school upstairs, when the kitchen door slammed open and Roisin exploded into the kitchen to ask breathlessly, 'Is Roddy here?'

Shelagh started and almost dropped the wooden spoon she was holding before she answered, 'No, of course he isn't.'

Dilly, who had been in the process of laying the cutlery out on the table, felt a ripple of fear run up and down her spine like an icy finger but it was Bessie who rushed forward to ask, 'Why? Ain't he round at your place?'

Roisin shook her head distractedly as she gazed towards the window where the snow was coming down like a solid sheet. 'No. Declan went out to help Liam with the milking and I got on with making the breakfast, but when it was ready I called him but he didn't come downstairs. I went up to see what was keeping him, only to find he'd not been to bed.' She started to cry then, deep shuddering sobs that shook her frame.

'Has he taken anything with him?' Shelagh questioned in an effort to take control of the situation.

'No, not even his coat from what I can see. Me and Declan talked to him when we first got back last night and then we went to bed. He must have crept out soon after that – and look at the weather.' Her anxious glance strayed to the window. 'He'll not last long out in that,' she said dully.

Bessie felt as if someone had punched her in the stomach as her legs gave way and she sank heavily on to the chair. The poor lad, he must *really* hate her to take such desperate measures. Hadn't he told her so? It was all her fault.

'Right, Dilly, will you run over to the cowshed and tell Declan and Liam what's happened. We need to start looking for him straight away. If the poor little mite's been out in this all night . . .' Roisin's voice trailed away. It was

203

just too awful to think about what might have happened but Dilly was already racing towards the door and soon after she came back with Liam and Declan in tow.

'Keep the children off school today,' Liam ordered Shelagh. 'I doubt the school bus will be running anyway. I need to know that they're safe and in the warm at least. Now me and Declan are going out to start looking for him. There's no time to lose.'

'I'll come with you,' Roisin said, heading for the door but Liam held his hand up. 'No, you won't. It's best you stay here in case he shows up, so it is. We'll round some of the men from the neighbouring farms together and they'll help us. Now get us his coat and a blanket for when we find him. He'll be frozen stiff, poor little wean.'

Roisin hastened away to do as she was told as the women looked helplessly on, for the same thoughts were in all their minds. How would Roddy have survived in such appalling weather conditions if he hadn't managed to find shelter?

Bessie was quietly crying and Dilly crossed to her to lay a comforting arm about her shaking shoulders. 'Don't fret, they'll find him,' she said soothingly, but a little part of her mind asked, *Will it be in time?*

But Bessie shook her off and went to stand just outside the door to watch the men depart. Her mind was in turmoil as she recalled the terrible things Roddy had said to her the night before, and she was forced to examine her reasons for wanting to take him back with her. Deep down she knew that they were purely selfish, and the knowledge made her feel ashamed. She hadn't wanted Roddy back because she loved him. She'd wanted him back because of guilt, because she felt that it was the right thing to do. But not once had she considered *his* feelings – and now it might be too late to tell him how sorry she was.

'Come on in, lass. There's nothing to be gained by you standing out here.' Dilly's voice sliced into her whirling thoughts.

'No. I'll come in in a while.'

Aware that it would be useless to argue, Dilly hurried back into the comforting warmth of the kitchen where, seeing how distressed she was, Shelagh was instantly at her side.

'Oh poor Dilly. You always seem to land in the thick of any family trouble, don't you?' she sighed. 'Even when it's not your fault you get dragged right into it.'

'But it *is* my fault.' Dilly's eyes were dull as she stared out at the worsening weather. 'I brought Bessie here suspecting what she had in mind, and Declan is my *son*! I should have realised how this would affect him and Roisin. And above all, poor young Roddy.'

'But if Bessie had a mind to come and take Roddy away, you couldn't have stopped her,' Shelagh pointed out.

'What's done is done now, and all we can do is pray that they find the lad safe and sound.'

The two women fell silent then. It was hard to believe that an animal could survive in such atrocious conditions, let alone a child.

Nearly a whole hour had gone by before they managed to coax Bessie back into the kitchen, and by then she was trembling from head to foot with cold.

'Go and get changed into some dry clothes,' Shelagh urged. 'Else you'll be ill and we'll have you to worry about you too.'

But Bessie refused, her mouth set in a grim line as she stood on watch at the window. The rest of the children crept about the house like mice as the minutes turned to hours and the hours ticked away. Shelagh had a large pan of rabbit stew bubbling away on the fire but no one wanted

205

any as the vigil continued. Mid-afternoon the light began to fade but still there was no sign of the men returning and Dilly began to fear the worst as the snow continued to fall steadily. At one point, Patrick went out to get a shovel and clear a path through the snow to the barn so that he could feed the animals. And then at last they heard the faint sound of voices and Liam, Declan and a number of men appeared in the yard.

'Well?' Shelagh asked hopefully as they spilled into the kitchen.

Liam shook his head. 'No sign of him yet. We've come back for something warm to eat and drink and to get some oil lamps. It's too dark for us to see further than the ends of our noses now. I reckon we'll have to stop the search in another couple of hours or so till it gets light again.'

Shelagh hastily served them all with mugs of tea and dishes full of stew as the men vied to get close to the fire. Within twenty minutes they were ready to go out again, but hope was fading fast now. If they didn't find him soon, Roddy would be facing his second night outdoors and they all understood that they might then be searching for a corpse.

Once the men had gone again it was Dilly who suggested tentatively to Bessie, 'Do you think you should be letting Samuel know what's happened? He is Roddy's father, after all.'

Bessie came out of her trance-like state to glare at her. 'Why should I let *him* know?' she demanded. 'He's never even looked at Roddy.'

'I'm aware of that,' Dilly said soothingly. 'But I shall have to telephone Max this evening to let him know we won't be home as soon as he expected us to be. With the weather like this we could be trapped here for days. I'll tell him what's happened with Roddy too and then leave it up to him whether or not he tells Samuel, shall I?' she ended tactfully.

Bessie's shoulders sagged. What difference would it make if Samuel knew that Roddy was missing anyway? He wouldn't care.

'Very well.' And after exchanging a worried glance with Shelagh, Dilly made her way to the telephone in the hallway. She ought to ring Nell too, she realised; otherwise she'd be worried when they didn't arrive home when expected.

Chapter Twenty-Six

'So the long and the short of it is, the men are still out looking for the child now.'

'I see,' Samuel replied as he stood in front of his father an hour later in the drawing room of Mill House. If he were honest, he didn't give a hoot where Roddy was, but seeing that his father expected some sort of reaction he tried to look concerned. 'In that case all we can do now is hope that they find him safe and well.'

'Hmm, quite.' Max turned around to gaze into the fire as Samuel quietly slipped from the room. Despite his words, Max knew his son didn't give a damn about the child's whereabouts. He'd given up hoping that Samuel would acknowledge Roddy as his son years ago, but he'd still felt duty-bound to tell him that he was missing and why. He'd half-heartedly hoped that Samuel would say he'd go to Ireland at the first opportunity to join in the search if need be, but he knew now that there was more chance of hell freezing over than of that happening. He screwed his eyes tight shut as he thought of Dilly, once again stuck in the middle of everything. Poor soul, she'd be frantic. Max knew how fond she was of Roddy. He looked towards the clock. It was already half past eight at night. Now all he could do was pray that the search party would find his grandson before they were forced to call the search off.

Outside Mill House, Samuel turned the collar of his coat up and set off down Manor Court Road. The pavements were icy but thankfully the snow had held off until now. He'd been paid his first wage today, pittance that it was, and was keen to get to the back room of the pub where he knew there would be a card game going on. He snorted then as he thought back to the conversation he'd had with his father. Roddy was missing – so what? As far as he was concerned, the kid should never have been born in the first place.

It was then that a rather smart motor car pulled up beside him. Samuel's mouth fell open when he saw Lilian King smiling at him from the back seat. She had a travelling rug tucked around her legs and she looked much older than the last time he'd seen her, when she'd sent him packing with a flea in his ear.

'Ah, Samuel, I thought it was you, which was why I had my chauffeur pull up. I heard you were back in town.' Her brightly painted lips stretched into a smile as she asked, 'Would you like a lift somewhere, darling?'

Darling? Samuel was confused. Could it be that the wheel had come off with her young lover and she wanted him back? He hesitated for the briefest of seconds before fixing a smile on his face and scrambling into the car to sit beside her. Then grasping her hand he said, 'You're looking quite radiant, Lilian. You seem to get younger every time I see you.' He was lying, of course. There were more lines on her face now than on a map of England, but she was disgustingly rich and not afraid to spend her wealth on anyone who was in favour.

She gave a coy, girlish giggle. 'Why, you little flatterer you. Now where would you like to go?'

'Actually, I wasn't going anywhere in particular,' he lied as he gazed at her adoringly.

'In that case you must come home with me and have some supper.' She rapped on the glass that divided the back of the car from the driver and told him curtly, 'Home, Henry, if you please.'

'Yes, ma'am!' The driver instantly steered the car into the road with a little smirk on his face.

Roddy blinked and narrowed his eyes as he peered through the swirling snow. He thought he'd glimpsed a light through the darkness but couldn't be sure. He'd been stumbling along for hours now, having lost all sense of direction. Everywhere looked so different when coated with snow and he had no idea whatsoever where he was any more. It didn't really matter, he just wanted to lie down and sleep now. His eyes were heavy and his vision was blurred; the only thing he had to be thankful for was the fact that his hands and feet had long since lost all feeling and no longer hurt him.

He wished he could say the same for his stomach. It was grumbling ominously and visions of great piping hot dishes of Roisin's delicious stew kept popping into his head. He'd had nothing to eat or drink since early that morning when he'd let himself quietly into someone's cowshed and had drunk his fill of milk fresh from a cow. He'd then managed to find a couple of fresh laid eggs in the nearby barn, despite the fact that chickens didn't lay so well in the winter, and he'd swallowed them raw from the shells. That seemed an awful long time ago now. But more than anything he needed to sleep so he continued to stumble on in the direction where he thought he'd seen the light. If there was a farmhouse there would likely be a barn nearby and at least he could get out of the snow for a while and rest.

His theory was proved to be correct and seconds later he found himself on the outskirts of a large farmhouse. A huge dog on a long chain emerged from a large wooden kennel and began to bark ferociously so Roddy hastily darted into the shadows, keeping a safe distance. Then sure enough, a barn loomed out of the snow and hurrying towards the high wooden doors he slid one partly open as quietly as he could, and slipped inside. It was pitch black within and he stood for a second trying to steady his breathing and work out what it was he could hear. Then it came to him: the barn was full of sheep snuffling amongst the hay that was strewn across the floor.

Keeping close to the sides, he skirted his way around until he came to a ladder that he guessed must lead up to a hayloft. Climbing the ladder was harder than he'd thought it would be, for his fingers wouldn't obey his commands and twice he toppled back down the stairs to land in a heap on the hay. His teeth were chattering now and his clothes, wet with snow, clung to him. He wished again that he'd thought to wrap up warmly when he'd run away but it was too late for wishing now, so with a last concerted effort he tackled the ladder again. Thankfully this time he made it to the top just as some life began to return to his numb limbs. The pains in his hands and feet were excruciating, and tears began to chase down his pale cheeks. He wished Roisin was there. She'd know what to do to make the pain go away and she'd hold him close and he'd breathe in the sweet scent that belonged only to her. But he couldn't go home, much as he yearned to, even if he'd known the way, until he was sure that Bessie was gone – or she'd make him leave everything he held dear.

Dropping into a pile of fresh-smelling hay he pulled some of it around him to act like a blanket. He'd seen Declan do the same thing with injured sheep he brought down from the fields, and it had always worked.

Shivering uncontrollably, he welcomed the tears that slid down his cheeks. At least they were warm . . . then finally he fell into an exhausted sleep.

'I reckon we're going to have to stop for tonight,' Liam said sadly as they skirted the hedge surrounding Mick McMahon's farm on the outskirts of Enniskerry. The men were frozen through and tired, and much as they hated the thought of having to abandon the search they were also wise enough to know that there wasn't much more they could do in the dark.

They drew together, a miserable little crowd holding their oil lights aloft.

'I fear you're right,' Declan agreed, stamping his booted feet to try and get some feeling back into them. 'Shall we all assemble back at my place at first light to start again?'

The men had no time to answer for at that moment one of them exclaimed, 'Isn't that footsteps in the snow there! Yes, it is! Look, the trail leads to McMahon's farm. The prints aren't very big either – they could easily belong to a boy. Should we follow them before we give in?'

But his words hung on the air, for the men were already striding towards the farmyard. Thankfully the snow had finally stopped falling and the sky was ablaze with stars.

'Look – they go towards the barn here,' Liam said a few

minutes later, and they all turned in that direction. Liam was there first, and he swung one barn door open and held his lamp higher to peer about, disturbing the sheep and making them skittish.

'The footsteps definitely led into here,' he muttered.

'Aye, they did. Why don't we try up in the hayloft?' one of the men suggested as he made his way through the sheep towards the ladder.

'I'll go up,' Declan said with authority. He was desperate for a glimpse of Roddy, and if the lad was up there, he wanted to be the one to find him. Gripping the lamp with one hand and the rough wooden rungs of the ladder with the other, he slowly made his way up to the loft – but at first sight it appeared to be empty. Then suddenly he noticed a pile of hay in one corner and cautiously approached it. Bending down, he gently pushed some of it aside – then a cry of joy escaped him. *'He's here!'*

A cheer went up amongst the men assembled at the bottom of the ladder until one shouted, 'Is the wean all right, Declan man?'

'He's breathing but he doesn't seem to be conscious,' Declan shouted back. 'Throw that blanket up here and I'll pass him down to you. We need to get him into the warm as soon as we can.'

Tenderly transferring Roddy on to the blanket and gathering the corners together, he then lay on his stomach and carefully lowered the child down to the waiting arms below.

'We'll take him into the McMahon place,' someone suggested, and much as Declan longed to take him home he had to admit that it made sense. It was a long walk back home and Roddy needed to get inside by a fire as fast as humanly possible.

Within no time at all, Roddy was carried into the

farmhouse kitchen and Mrs McMahon fussed over him as the men crowded around the fire.

'Brendon, fetch me a bowl of hot water and go and get me a pair of your pyjamas and your dressing gown,' she told her son bossily. 'And you Breeda, make some tea, lots of it and give these men a cup each.' Then addressing her husband, 'Father, push the sofa closer to the fire. This little 'un is like a block of ice, so he is.'

In the blink of an eye, Cathleen McMahon had stripped Roddy out of his wet clothes and after washing him all over in warm water had him dried and cosy in a pair of her son's thick pyjamas and socks as Declan looked anxiously on. She then began to rub his hands and feet and gradually a tiny spot of colour appeared in each of his cheeks and he gave a low moan.

'That's it, meladdo,' she told him encouragingly. 'You come back to the land o' the living now, eh?'

When Roddy's eyelids slowly fluttered open, the first person he saw was Declan leaning over the back of the sofa staring down at him and he gave him a weak smile.

Declan's throat was full as he offered up a silent prayer of thanks, then turning back to the men he asked Liam, 'Would you run back to the farm and let them know that we've found him and that he's all right, thanks be to God!'

'Aye, and tell them that he'll be staying here tonight,' Cathleen McMahon said firmly. 'He doesn't need to be venturing out in the cold again till we're sure he's properly on the mend. And you men, get yourselves away home. You've all done well, so you have.'

Liam and the men slipped away but Declan stayed on. He didn't want to leave until he was quite sure that Roddy really was all right. Roisin would never forgive him if he did. Hunkering down, he took one of Roddy's hands in his as he asked, 'So how are you feeling now?'

'Hot!' Roddy declared in a thin voice. 'And me hands an' feet have pins an' needles in 'em.'

'That's 'cos you've come in out of the cold,' Declan explained. 'And your hands and feet hurt 'cos they're thawing out. Just keep them under the blankets and they'll be back to normal in no time.' He turned to Mrs McMahon then and asked in a low voice, 'Do you think we should be sending for the doctor?'

She shook her head. 'I doubt the doctor would get through, but if need be we'll send for him in the morning. Roddy's a tough, healthy little lad and once he's warmed up hopefully he'll have nothing worse than a nasty cold to contend with. But let's wait till the morning and see, eh? Now why don't you get yourself off home an' all? You look fit to drop, so you do. You're welcome to stay here but no doubt Roisin will only fret if she doesn't hear from your own good self that the lad's all right. He'll be fine here with us and we'll take good care of him, I promise. I shall sleep in the chair over there to keep an eye on him through the night, so you've no need to worry. Then if he's better in the morning, Father there will bring him home in the cart for you – if he can get along the lanes, that is.'

Declan nodded. He would have preferred to stay with Roddy but he knew that what the kindly farmer's wife had said about Roisin was true. Why, she'd probably set off through the snow to come here herself if he didn't go back to reassure her.

'Very well . . . and thank you.' He bent and self-consciously ruffled Roddy's hair, then once again he turned and set off into the bitterly cold night.

In the early hours of the next morning it started to rain. Roisin and Declan had had very little sleep and when they came down to the kitchen they looked weary.

'I'll make us all a brew,' Roisin said, crossing to the deep stone sink to pump water into the soot-blackened kettle. Then glancing across at the main farmhouse she commented, 'Looks like we're not the only ones up early. The light's on in Liam's kitchen too. Seems they couldn't sleep either.'

Across the yard, Bessie sat huddled over the dying fire. She hadn't bothered going to bed – she knew that she wouldn't have been able to sleep – and during the night she'd done a lot of soul-searching. Roddy might have died because of her, and she knew that for as long as she lived she would never be able to forgive herself for upsetting him so badly. But what was done was done – and now somehow she had to make it up to him. If he survived unscathed, that was. She shuddered as her imagination ran riot. What if the time spent out in the cold had repercussions? He might develop pneumonia or . . . No. She stopped her thoughts from going along that route. There was no point in torturing herself further.

Hearing a noise behind her she saw Shelagh emerge through the stairs door.

'Why, Bessie, you're up early!' the woman said in surprise. Then as a thought occurred to her, 'Or have you not been to bed at all?'

Bessie shrugged. 'There would have been no point.' Shelagh saw the pain in her eyes and couldn't help but feel sorry for her. She'd so wanted to hate her. After all, they all looked upon Roddy as part of the Carey family now, and Bessie was threatening to take him away from them all.

'You must all really hate me!'

Shelagh was shocked. It was as if Bessie had been able to read her mind.

'Well, I don't,' she answered honestly. 'I wanted to, but after getting to know you I think you're just doing what

216

you feel is right – and no one should hold that against you.'

'But if I was anything at all of a mother I would have put Roddy's feelings above my own,' Bessie miserably screwed the scrap of handkerchief into a ball in her restless hands.

The conversation was stopped from going any further when Liam suddenly appeared, his hair tousled and his eyes still heavy with sleep. Then seconds later, Roisin and Declan rushed through the kitchen door.

'Doesn't look like anyone got much rest last night,' Liam commented wryly.

'We were wondering if it's too early to set off for the McMahon farm,' Declan said. 'Luckily the rain that's fallen in the night has softened the snow so we should be able to get a cart through to them now. I know Mick offered to bring Roddy home if he's well enough, but we'd rather fetch him ourselves. We just have to hope that it doesn't freeze now else the lanes will be like skating rinks.'

'I could perhaps come with you?' Bessie suggested hopefully, but one withering look from Roisin silenced her.

'I think you've done quite enough, don't you?' Roisin said and her voice was colder than the slush that lay on the ground outside. 'Besides, I doubt very much that Roddy would want to see you just yet. Come along, Declan. It's time we were off.' And with that she flounced from the room as tears trickled down Bessie's pale cheeks. She'd been well and truly put in her place – and she knew that she deserved it.

Chapter Twenty-Seven

'Well, I suppose I should be going. My father is a stickler for punctuality,' Samuel said regretfully as he swung his legs over the edge of the deep feather bed, a martyred expression on his face.

'Oh, darling, *must* you go?' Lilian's wrinkled hands stroked down his bare back. 'I can't believe that your father would allow you to do such a menial job. Stay here with me.'

Samuel looked over his shoulder at her. Without her paint and powder she looked positively ancient in the light of day, but she *was* ridiculously wealthy.

'I have to live,' he said pathetically, and instantly she began to draw him back towards the pillows.

'Of course you do, but from now on I shall keep you in the manner you should be kept,' she promised.

'Well, in that case shall I ring the maid and tell her to serve us breakfast in bed?' Samuel certainly hadn't taken much persuading.

'Yes – but not yet . . .' Lilian drew him towards her and he went unprotestingly. This certainly beat sitting in a draughty old van all day, even if Lilian was past her prime!

Over in the Farthing household, Max glanced at his watch in annoyance. The breakfast would be cold if Samuel didn't get a move on. For two pins he'd start without him. Olivia was on an early shift at the hospital and had left over an hour ago so there was only Samuel to come down now.

'Would you mind very much just popping up and asking my son how long he's going to be?' he asked Gwen as she came in with a dish full of devilled kidneys. They were one of Mr Farthing's favourites and Mrs Pegs had cooked them especially for him.

'O' course I will,' she chirped brightly as she scooted towards the door. 'I shan't be two ticks now!' Almost immediately, she was back to tell him, 'Mr Samuel ain't in his room, sir. It don't look like his bed's been slept in.'

'Oh, very well, thank you, Gwen, I'll start without him.'

Max concealed his annoyance until Gwen had left the room then his hands balled into fists. Damn it, it appeared that Samuel was up to his old tricks again. He'd thought his behaviour was too good to last, and there were deliveries waiting to go out today too. He'd have to get to the factory in Attleborough first thing now to make sure someone else got on to it. He'd give him a roasting for sure when he did decide to turn up! *But not too much of a roasting*, a little voice whispered. Max lived in daily fear of Samuel telling Olivia about the secret he'd stumbled upon, so he'd have to tread carefully with him.

Suddenly losing his appetite, Max pushed his plate away and rose from the table. One way or another it had been a distressing couple of days and he'd not slept properly since Dilly had rung him from Ireland to tell him that Roddy had gone missing. Thank goodness he was safe now though. Dilly had rung again late the previous evening, to share the good tidings. Max had intended to pass the information on to Samuel this morning, not that he'd seemed overly concerned when Max had told him of Roddy's disappearance. In fact, he hadn't turned a hair.

Max supposed he shouldn't have expected any other reaction. Samuel had shed no tears over Constance when she died either and he sometimes wondered if his son had a heart. With a sigh he set off to start his day's work. Samuel would show up when he was good and ready – that was his way.

'They're here!' Shelagh shouted excitedly as she glimpsed the trap pulling into the yard mid-morning. She'd been rolling pastry on the kitchen table but she clapped her hands together, sending a cloud of flour into the air, and after swiping her hands down the front of her apron she shot to the door. Bessie instantly rose to join her and together they watched Declan walk to the back of the trap and lift Roddy down. He and Roisin had travelled back curled beneath a tarpaulin with Roddy swaddled in blankets and with a stone hot-water bottle that Cathleen McMahon had insisted he should have at his feet. The weather had taken an unexpected turn. It was raining quite heavily and the fierce wind that had blown up made the trees appear as if they were involved in some macabre dance as it whipped through the leafless branches.

'How is he?' Shelagh asked as Declan strode towards his cottage with his precious bundle gripped tight in his arms.

'He seems to be fine.' Shelagh could hear the relief in his voice and Roisin was grinning from ear to ear with relief too. 'I'll pop round and see you in a minute but I want to get meladdo here into the warm first. We'll need to keep a close eye on him for a few days.'

'Of course.' Shelagh stepped back and closed the door against the appalling weather, almost tripping over Bessie who was standing right behind her.

'Do you think they'd mind if I went round to see him?' Bessie asked, and Dilly and Shelagh exchanged a look before Shelagh answered cautiously, 'I shouldn't just yet. Let them get him settled back in first.'

'What you mean is, he won't *want* to see me,' Bessie said dully. 'And who could blame him?'

Patrick, who was now a sturdy thirteen-year-old, glanced uncomfortably at Dilly before escaping into the yard to help his father again. None of the children were at ease around Bessie and she could sense it, which only added to the strained atmosphere.

Dilly began to wash some pots in the sink whilst Shelagh went back to her pastry-making and Bessie sat hunched at the side of the fire.

An hour passed before Roisin appeared to tell them all, 'He's settled by the fire now, and apart from a runny nose and a heavy cold he seems none the worse for his adventure, thank goodness.'

'May I go and see him?' Bessie persisted boldly.

Roisin nodded slowly. She supposed that the meeting couldn't be postponed for ever. 'Yes – but you won't get upsetting him again, will you?' she warned her.

Bessie shook her head and left the room without another word.

'Do you think I should follow her?' Roisin asked anxiously.

'No, I think you'd best leave them to have a talk,' Dilly advised. 'I don't think Roddy will be doing anything daft like running off again in a hurry.'

221

Roisin secretly agreed with her but it didn't stop her stomach from churning. 'I'll give her ten minutes then – but after that I'm going round there whether she likes it or not.'

Dilly sighed, wondering where it was all going to end.

Meanwhile Bessie was picking her way across the yard with her heart in her mouth. She knew that Roddy wouldn't be pleased to see her but there were things that needed to be said. The rain had turned what remained of the snow to thick slush and she felt it creep across the top of her shoes. She didn't mind; at least the rain had made the lanes passable for the horse and trap.

Outside Roisin's door, Bessie took a deep breath. She knew that what she was about to say would change both her life and Roddy's for ever, but she was determined to go through with it. She owed her son that much at least.

She tapped lightly on the thick wooden door then without waiting for an answer she stepped into Roisin's cosy kitchen. A fire was roaring up the chimney in the inglenook and the brass pans that were suspended from the beam above it sparkled like gems in the light. Two sofas were positioned on either side of the fire with plump cushions scattered across them and the tempting smell of roasting pork hung in the air. Bessie could see why Roddy loved the place so much; it was neat as a new pin and warm and inviting.

When she entered, Roddy glanced up from one of the sofas but as soon as he saw who it was, he quickly looked back towards the fire as a flush crept into his cheeks.

'It's all right, I haven't come to upset you again,' Bessie assured him as she moved to the other sofa and took a seat opposite him. 'I've come to say I'm sorry.'

Roddy met her eyes cautiously. 'What do you mean?'

'I mean I've been very selfish,' Bessie admitted, folding

222

her hands in her lap. 'I didn't give a thought to how you might feel about leaving Ireland and Roisin and Declan. I just thought that it was time I tried to become a proper mother to you, and the only way I could see of doing that was to take you home with me. But I've left it too late, ain't I, Roddy? And I'm so very, very sorry!'

He was still staring at her warily and she felt tears prick sharp as needles at the back of her eyes.

'So . . . what will happen now?' Roddy held his breath as he waited for Bessie's answer.

'I shall be going home with Dilly just as soon as the weather permits. And I shall be leaving you here – where you belong.'

His face suddenly lit up brighter than a summer sky and she realised with a little start that this was the first time he had smiled at her properly since she had arrived.

'Do you really mean it?' he asked.

When Bessie nodded, he let out a whoop of joy. 'An' can I stay here for always?'

Again she nodded as she rose to her feet. 'Yes, for always – but there is one thing I'll ask of you: will you write to me from time to time, just to let me know how you're going on?'

He nodded eagerly, 'Yes, I can do that. I might even see you sometimes when I come back to Nuneaton to see Grandfather.'

'That will be nice,' she croaked as she turned to leave. She'd said what she'd come to say and now she couldn't get away quickly enough. It wouldn't do for Roddy to see her break down and she was in grave danger of doing that at any minute.

She was almost at the door when Roddy suddenly said, 'Thanks, Bessie.'

She nodded and shot through the door then leaned

223

heavily against the outside of it as the rain lashed down on her, quickly plastering her hair to her head. 'Thanks, Bessie,' he had said. *Bessie*, not Mother.

Eventually she made her way back to Shelagh's kitchen and when she stepped inside, the women looked anxiously towards her.

'It's all right, he's fine,' she told them, then addressing Roisin she said: 'I went to say sorry to him – for attemptin' to take him away, I mean. An' as I was leaving he called me "Bessie". That says it all, don't it? I'm Bessie, you're Mammy.'

Roisin's hand flew to her mouth but Bessie wasn't done yet. 'I also went to tell him that I wouldn't be takin' him away from you. He loves you an' Declan like you're his own mam an' dad. So if it's what you want, I'm prepared to let you keep him. For always.'

'You are?' Roisin mouthed incredulously as a large smile spread across Shelagh's face.

Bessie nodded. 'Yes. If you want me to put it in writin' I'm prepared to sign it.'

Roisin shook her head. 'I don't think there'll be any need to do that. Your word is good enough . . . and thank you.'

In a voice that trembled, Bessie turned to Dilly and Bessie asked, 'When can we go home?'

'Oh, I should think the ferries will be crossing again by now. We could go tomorrow if you like? To be honest I'm a bit nervous about being away any longer now that we know Roddy is safe. Mary is very near her time and I want to be there for her and Seamus when the baby does decide to put in an appearance.'

Bessie disappeared through the stairs door to start her packing without another word.

'Poor lass,' Shelagh said with compassion. 'At least she put Roddy's feelings afore her own in the end.'

The following morning, when Declan had piled Dilly and Bessie's luggage into the back of the trap, everyone assembled in the farmyard to wish them goodbye. The rain had stopped falling for now but the sky above them was a canopy of scudding black clouds and the wind was cruel.

'Well, goodbye, everyone. Have a wonderful Christmas.' Dilly kissed them all and climbed up to sit on the high wooden seat beside Liam who would be taking them back to the ferry in Dublin.

Bessie paused before climbing aboard to glance at Roddy who stood between Roisin and Declan. His face was solemn and he was holding tight to Roisin's hand, but suddenly he shocked everyone when he stepped forward and said quietly, 'Goodbye, Bessie.'

His mother gulped to swallow the lump that had formed in her throat.

'You just take care now,' she said tremulously, 'an' don't forget, write to me now an' then to let me know what you've been up to. An' if you should ever need anythin', you know where I am.'

He nodded then further shocked her when he leaned forward and rising on tiptoe planted a gentle kiss on her cheek. It was the first time in the whole of his short life he had voluntarily kissed her.

Declan handed her up into the trap then and soon they were rattling down the drive. Bessie turned once to wave and Roddy waved back, then she turned her eyes to the front, certain in the knowledge that she'd done the right thing.

Chapter Twenty-Eight

'For goodness sake, woman! Ain't it time you stopped work fer the day now? You've been shut in here since the crack of dawn,' Nell scolded as she slapped a cup of tea down on the table at the side of Dilly.

Dilly grinned as she put down her pencil and stretched. 'I promised Philip and Hayden I'd have these designs to them by the end of the week. They're for the new spring collection next year so they need time to get them made up,' she said. 'But don't get fretting. They should all be done and ready to go into the post by tomorrow evening and I can relax a little more then – till the New Year, at least. I'm rather pleased with them even if I do say so myself. What do you think?'

Nell peered over her shoulder at the sketches spread across the table. 'I'd say they're some o' the best you've ever come up wi',' she admitted grudgingly. 'An' I reckon they'll run out of the shops, but I'd still like yer to call it a day. There's no sense in overdoin' it. Anyway, Max said he'd be round this evenin'. Why don't yer go an' freshen up while I warm yer dinner up?'

'I think I just might.' Dilly stifled a yawn as she rubbed her aching back. Her head was aching too but she hadn't noticed it till Nell had stopped her working. Max had been on at her for ages to go and get her eyes tested at the opticians. She'd been suffering for a while with headaches now and he'd pointed out that she might need spectacles. She'd put it off; needing spectacles was like an admittance that she was getting older but she supposed she should go really. Half her life seemed to be spent sketching nowadays and it had put a lot of strain on her eyes.

As Nell left her in peace, Dilly took a last glance at the sketches. She'd been working on these particular ones for the past week – ever since she'd got back from Ireland, in fact – and now Christmas was racing towards them. She realised that she hadn't even been Christmas present shopping yet – apart from the gifts that she'd bought early to take to Ireland, that was. It would be a relief when she did put the drawings in the post, then she could afford to spend a little more time with Olivia and Jessica – and Mary, of course. The poor girl was really struggling now with the birth so imminent. She waddled rather than walked and the day before, she'd complained that she'd forgotten what her feet looked like. Seamus was spending as much time with her as he could, which thankfully was possible now that Bessie was working in the shops for them.

Since coming back from Ireland, Bessie had thrown herself into work to try and forget what had happened over there. Dilly felt infinitely sorry for her although she still thought that Bessie had made the right decision in allowing Roddy to stay with Roisin and Declan. Bessie herself knew it too, but it didn't take away the hurt of knowing that she'd given up the rights to the only child she was ever likely to have. Yet there was also a measure of relief now that the decision had been made. At least now when she thought of him she knew that he was happy and had forgiven her for her earlier neglect of him. She'd even confided in Dilly that she hoped perhaps in years to come they might be able to build a relationship, even if it was only as friends. Dilly hoped it would come about. Bessie deserved that at least.

Fifteen minutes later, after washing her hands and face and tidying her hair, Dilly joined Nell in the cosy kitchen. The smell of the steak and kidney pie Nell had baked that afternoon made Dilly's stomach grumble with anticipation as she took a seat at the table. The room really did look very festive. A Christmas tree stood in pride of place in a sturdy bucket of earth next to the large dresser, and Nell had taken Jessica for a walk in the woods to collect some holly. It was dotted about the room in vases and empty jars now, the bright green leaves and the red berries shining in the light from the fire.

'I must say, everywhere looks very Christmassy,' Dilly told her approvingly and Nell's chest puffed with pride. When she wasn't working in the shop she spent every minute cleaning and polishing, and the whole house gleamed from top to bottom.

'It would be a crime not to look after a lovely house like this,' she said as she placed Dilly's meal in front of her. She had never been so happy as she was now, and there was nothing she wouldn't have done for her friend.

'So what's your plans for tonight?' Nell asked as Dilly tucked into her dinner.

'Nothing much,' Dilly answered through a mouthful of pastry. 'Me and Max will probably just have a chat and a drink when he arrives and then I might get myself off to bed so that I can make an early start tomorrow.'

The words had barely left her lips when there was a tap on the door and Max appeared.

'Well,' Nell chuckled. 'Talk o' the devil an' he's bound to appear.' The smile slid from her face as she saw that Max looked agitated.

'Is something wrong?' Dilly laid her knife and fork down as she saw that Max wasn't his usual cheerful self.

'I just passed Seamus coming out of their house on my way here. He was going for the doctor.'

'Why? Is it Mary? Is the baby coming?' Dilly was on her feet in a second, her dinner forgotten.

'It appears so. Apparently she's got a severe backache and he says she looks awful. He's gone for the doctor just to be on the safe side. Do you want me to run you round there? The car is outside.'

'Please.' Dilly was already tugging her coat on.

'Do you want me to come an' all?' Nell offered but Dilly shook her head.

'No, you stay here, Nell. Bessie will be home for her dinner soon. It might just be a false alarm.'

'Eeh, but won't it be lovely if it ain't?' Nell grinned. 'It's only a week away from Christmas an' Mary will be able to enjoy it if she's got the birthin' out o' the way.'

Dilly raised a smile then followed Max out to the car and within minutes they were on their way.

Seamus wasn't back when they arrived at the neat little house on Abbey Green but the second Dilly set eyes on Mary she knew that this was no false alarm. Mary was walking up and down the living room with her hands in the small of her back and the minute she saw her mother-in-law she whispered shamefacedly, 'I think I might have just wet meself, Dilly. I ain't done that since I was a very little girl.'

'And you haven't done it now,' Dilly promised her, throwing her coat over the back of a chair. 'I think your waters may have broken. Have you had any pains yet?'

'A few,' Mary said.

'How far apart are they?'

Mary grimaced. 'About every ten minutes or so, I should think.'

'Right then, young lady, let's get you up to bed. The doctor will want to examine you when he arrives so we need to get you out of those clothes.' Then turning to Max, who was looking extremely flummoxed, she asked, 'Will you go and get some water on the boil please. As much as you can.'

'Of course.' Max gladly shot off in the direction of the kitchen as Dilly led Mary gently up the stairs. The poor girl was as white as a sheet and her lips had a strange bluish tinge to them that Dilly didn't like the look of at all. She helped her out of her clothes and into a nightdress, then after placing a wad of towels on the bed she helped her to lie down.

'Right now – is everything ready?' she asked.

Mary nodded. 'The crib is over in the corner all made up ready, an' the baby clothes are inside it. We should warm them by the fire.' Then suddenly placing her hand on Dilly's arm she told her, 'You've been better than me own mam to me, Dilly, an' I just want you to know how much I appreciate it.'

'Get away with you,' Dilly blushed. 'Now just lie quietly and save your energy and focus on bringing this little one into the world. I can hardly wait to meet him or her. What would you like?'

Mary shrugged and winced all at the same time. 'I'm not much bothered, to be honest, so long as it's healthy, although I think Seamus would quite like a little lass.

Funny that, ain't it? Most men hanker after a son.'

Dilly smiled as she rolled her sleeves up and wondered why it was that babies usually decided to put in an appearance at night-time. And then Mary let out a low throaty groan as she clutched her stomach.

'Crikey,' she gasped when the pain had passed. 'That were a strong 'un.'

Dilly dragged the crib to the side of the bed. 'Don't get fretting. Just think – soon you'll have a lovely baby to put in here,' she said encouragingly, although she didn't at all like Mary's colour. Her face was as pale as dough and her lips seemed to be even bluer than they had been when she arrived. Sweat was standing out on Mary's brow now and Dilly rushed away to fetch a bowl of cool water to sponge her with. It looked set to be a long night. From her experience first babies always took their time in coming and she wanted to make her daughter-in-law as comfortable as she possibly could.

Max was in the kitchen when she got downstairs and she was amused and touched to see that he had a variety of pans as well as the kettle heating water.

'I don't think we'll be needing all that just yet,' she told him gently. 'Mary could be hours yet.'

'Better to be safe than sorry,' Max blustered and Dilly grinned to herself. Men always flew into such a panic during childbirth. She collected a tin bowl and a clean cloth, and as she was approaching the stairs the front door opened and Seamus flew in like a whirlwind, clearly in a panic.

'I've left a message with the doctor's wife. He's out on a call at the minute but she'll send him round the second he gets back. The midwife is on her way too. Is Mary all right?'

'Of course she is, pet.' Dilly gave him a reassuring smile.

231

'Now why don't you go into the kitchen with Max and make us all a nice cup of tea. You look more in need of one than Mary does.'

He shocked her then when he said, 'I'm scared, Mammy. Mary wouldn't let me tell you before, but she's not been too good lately – breathless and tired all the time.'

'But that's quite normal during the last part of a pregnancy,' Dilly told him. 'Think of all the extra weight she's been having to cart about.'

'Aye, happen you're right,' he conceded doubtfully and as Dilly went upstairs he hurried off to put the kettle on.

Mary was in the grip of another fierce contraction when Dilly entered the bedroom. It couldn't have been more than a few minutes since she'd had the last one. Perhaps this baby was going to prove her wrong about taking its time. It appeared to be in a hurry to be born. After crossing to the bed she let Mary squeeze her hand until the pain had passed then told her, 'Don't worry, lass. Seamus is back downstairs and the doctor and the midwife are on their way. They shouldn't be long now.'

'Dilly . . .' Mary held tight on to her hand. 'If it's a little lad it's to be called David, then Seamus after his daddy . . . and if it's a little lass I want her to be named Primrose, then Dilly after you.'

'Oh, lass.' Dilly's throat was full at the honour Mary was bestowing on her. 'That's a lovely gesture.'

'I . . . I love the name Primrose,' Mary said weakly. 'It makes me think of the spring when everything is just coming to life – like she is . . .'

'It's a beautiful name,' Dilly agreed as she mopped Mary's forehead. The curtains were drawn tight against the bitterly cold night and she was pleased to see that her son had lit a fire in the little grate. Everywhere was warm and cosy; now all they had to do was wait.

It wasn't long before footsteps sounded on the stairs and the midwife appeared, huffing and puffing. Nurse Meldrew was a huge woman with a heart to match, and she beamed as she slipped her coat off and undid her large black bag.

'Right,' she said authoritatively to Dilly. 'If you'd be kind enough to fetch me some hot water so I can wash my hands, we'll have a look at this young lady here. A cup of tea wouldn't come amiss either. I've just come straight from delivering a bonny baby boy over in Weddington and my mouth is as dry as a bone.'

Dilly flitted away to do as she was told. Downstairs, Seamus was already preparing a number of cups and saucers on a tray. He followed Dilly upstairs with it as she carried the water, but as soon as he set foot through the bedroom door the nurse told him harshly, 'Downstairs, if you please, sir. A birthing room is no place for a man.'

He placed the tray of tea down on the bedside table and looked helplessly at Mary before slouching out of the room looking like a whipped dog.

'B-but I want him to stay,' Mary whispered.

The nurse shook her head. 'It would only distress him, dear. Men have no stomach for childbirth. He'd probably end up in a heap on the floor and I want to concentrate all my efforts on you. Now, let's have a look at you, eh pet?'

She listened to Mary's heart then felt her pulse and Dilly couldn't help but notice that she was frowning as she then prodded about Mary's swollen stomach making the girl gasp with pain. When she was done she beckoned Dilly out of earshot to ask, 'Has the doctor been sent for?'

'Yes, he'll be here shortly. But is everything all right?' Dilly asked anxiously.

'Of course,' the nurse said. The last thing she wanted was anyone panicking while she was trying to do her job.

'But this baby seems to be in a hurry. Have you everything ready – towels and plenty more hot water?'

Dilly nodded but then their attention was drawn back to the bed as Mary writhed in the grip of another contraction.

The nurse efficiently began to prepare for the birth, strapping a huge white apron across her navy uniform and rolling her sleeves up.

'I – I think I'll just pop down and check on my son if you don't mind.' Dilly's voice came out as a croak. For some reason she felt dreadfully uneasy and she knew that Seamus did too.

'Off you go then, dear. Just send the doctor up as soon as he gets here, please.'

When Dilly entered the living room she was surprised to see that Nell and Bessie were there too, fussing over Seamus like mother hens.

'I couldn't stay at home frettin',' Nell said apologetically. 'An' I was just comin' out the door when Bessie got home from work so she decided she'd come too. Eeh, ain't it excitin', Dilly. You'll be meetin' your brand new grandchild soon!'

The sound of the bell on the front door prevented Dilly from answering and Seamus leaped up and rushed off to answer it without a word. He loved Mary with every fibre of his being and couldn't bear to think of her being in pain.

'It's the doctor,' he announced as a tired-looking gentleman toting a big black leather bag followed him into the room.

'I'll take you up to Mary,' Dilly volunteered and the doctor nodded politely to the people assembled in the room before following her upstairs.

The minute he entered the bedroom, Mary looked towards him and gave him an apprehensive smile.

'Now then, young lady, what's all this, eh? I thought I'd told you that I wanted this baby to be born in hospital.'

'Sorry, Dr Greaves,' Mary mumbled as he slipped his greatcoat and his jacket off.

'But why should the baby need to be born in hospital?' Dilly asked.

The doctor and midwife exchanged a glance and suddenly Dilly could hear the music of her own heart beating a tune in her chest.

Dr Greaves had already lifted the sheet and bent to examine Mary and her question went unanswered but then he straightened to tell Mary, 'It's too late to get you there now, I'm afraid. If you do exactly as Nurse Meldrew and I tell you, I reckon you'll be meeting your son or daughter within a couple of hours. Do you think you can do that for me?'

Mary gulped and nodded as sweat ran down her cheeks to soak into the pillows beneath her head.

'I want Seamus to be . . .' Whatever she had been about to say was forgotten as another mighty pain ripped through her, but Mary bit down on her lip and bore it without screaming.

'You're being so brave, pet,' Dilly said admiringly.

Once the pain had subsided, Mary managed a weak smile. 'That's 'cos I want this little 'un to be born healthy,' she panted.

'Of course it will be.' Dilly squeezed her hand, wishing she could rid herself of the sense of foreboding that had settled on her like a darkness.

When the next contraction began to build, the doctor prompted, 'That's it, Mary. You should feel the need to push on this one. Now just remember to breathe slowly . . . and put all your efforts into it. You're doing brilliantly! I wish all my first-time mothers were as good as you.'

Sure enough, as the pain intensified, Mary lifted her head and pushed with all her might, making the veins in her face stand out and her lips turn an even more frightening shade of blue.

'That's it, well done, rest now,' he told her as the pain wore off and Mary sagged back against the pillows.

'Why don't you go down now and talk to the father-to-be?' the doctor suggested tactfully to Dilly. 'I'm sure Nurse and I can handle the next bit.'

Dilly rose from her seat at the side of the bed. She desperately wished to stay, but it was clear that she wasn't wanted.

'Very well, but please call if there's anything you need.' She left the room and the second she entered the sitting room Seamus almost pounced on her.

'Is it here yet? Is she all right?'

'It should be any time now.' Dilly forced herself to sound cheerful. 'She's been as good as gold, hardly a whimper out of her. But now who's for a cup of tea? I know I'm ready for another one.' She hurried off to the kitchen to put the kettle on as Seamus resumed his pacing up and down the room, his eyes straying every few seconds to the ceiling above.

Finally, an hour later a little cry pierced the silence. There was no mistaking it – it was the sound of a newborn child.

'Me lass has done it!' Seamus cried triumphantly and before anyone could stop him he'd hared off up the stairs.

'You have a beautiful baby girl,' Nurse Meldrew told him and his mouth fell open with astonishment as he gazed towards the bed where the still-unwashed child lay cradled in a towel in her mother's arms. He'd imagined this moment since the day Mary had informed him he was

236

to have a baby, but never in his wildest dreams had he imagined such a perfect little being. She had a shock of dark hair and a tiny rosebud mouth, and for Seamus it was love at first sight.

'Let's get this little one washed now,' the midwife said then, gently taking the baby from Mary's arms. 'The doctor needs to look at your wife, Mr Carey. This is highly irregular. Fathers aren't usually allowed to see their new-born until both mother and baby have been washed.'

However, the doctor surprised her then when he told her, 'I think we could allow Father to stay this time while you go and see to the baby, Nurse.'

She looked at him, ready to object but something in his face made her clamp her mouth shut and silently leave the room with the precious little bundle clutched in her arms.

Seamus couldn't help but notice that the doctor was watching Mary closely as he prepared an injection.

'You've done really well, lass,' he told Mary, turning his attention back to her. Seamus could see that she looked absolutely exhausted but then he supposed that was normal for someone who had just given birth.

'Seamus,' Mary gasped. 'I want you to promise me that you'll take good care of our baby.'

Seamus frowned. 'But of course I'll take good care of her – that goes without saying. We'll *both* take good care of her!'

He moved slightly to one side then as the doctor leaned over and administered the injection but he kept a tight grip on Mary's hand. There was something wrong but as yet he couldn't put his finger on what it was.

'I want you to know . . . that I've had the best years of my life with you and I wouldn't have missed them fer anything, I love you *so* much,' Mary whispered.

Bewildered, Seamus looked towards the doctor. 'Why is

she talking like this?' he asked, then started as Mary suddenly groaned and clutched at her chest.

'Mr Carey, I must ask you to leave immediately.' The doctor grasped Seamus's elbow and practically frogmarched him out of the room before closing the door and hurrying back to Mary.

Seamus bit his lip before rushing downstairs to cry out, 'Something's wrong with Mary! The doctor won't let me stay with her!'

The midwife, who had been in the process of washing the baby in a tin bowl full of warm water that Dilly had ready, instantly passed her tiny charge to Dilly before pounding off upstairs without a word.

'What's going on?' Seamus was almost beside himself with fear.

'I don't know, lad,' Nell answered sombrely as she patted his hand. 'But if anything *is* wrong, at least Mary is in the best hands.'

Dilly finished drying the baby then tenderly dressed her, marvelling at how beautiful she was. She then pressed her into her father's waiting arms and he gazed at her in awe as they waited for some word from the nurse or the doctor.

What seemed like a lifetime later, Dr Greaves appeared looking gaunt and downhearted. They turned expectant faces towards him and he gulped deep in his throat before telling Seamus, 'I'm so very sorry, Mr Carey. We did all we could, but I'm afraid your wife . . . she's gone.'

Chapter Twenty-Nine

'I don't understand. What do you mean, she's gone?' Seamus was clearly in shock as he stared at the doctor in disbelief. So too was Dilly. This had started off as such a happy evening with everyone excited at the prospect of meeting a brand new member of the family – and now it had turned into a nightmare.

'Here, let me take the bairn.' Nell lifted the child from its father's arms. She would take her into the kitchen and warm her some milk up to keep her satisfied. The family needed some privacy. Bessie and Max quietly followed her, and now that he was alone with Dilly and Seamus the doctor sagged as he wiped his bloodshot eyes.

'Mary came to see me some months ago when she started to get breathless,' he explained as gently as he could. 'So of course I gave her a thorough examination and made her have some tests done at the hospital.'

'But she didn't tell me about any of this,' Seamus objected.

The doctor held his hand up to silence him before going on, 'Sadly, the results of the tests confirmed what I had suspected. Mary had a severe heart defect. I really cannot understand how it had gone undetected for so long. Anyway, I was forced to inform her how serious this could be. Had I known of her heart condition before she became pregnant I would have seriously advised her against it.' He cleared his throat. 'I also told her that she needed to speak to you about it, Mr Carey – Seamus – but she was adamant that you shouldn't know and of course I couldn't go against her wishes, I would have been breaching patient confidentiality. She didn't want you to worry you see. Eventually she did agree that she would at least go into hospital for the birth, but unfortunately the labour started unexpectedly early, and there was not enough time.'

Seamus was chalk-white as he struggled to come to terms with what the doctor had said.

'I can't believe that she didn't tell me,' he choked as Dilly gripped his shoulder with tears streaming down her cheeks.

'She wanted this baby more than anything in the world. You would do well to remember that and take comfort from her,' the doctor advised. 'But now if you are ready and you wish to, you may go up and spend a few minutes with your wife. The nurse has already left to tell the undertaker that you have need of him. I'm so sorry, my dear fellow. Mary was a truly lovely person.'

'Yes, she was,' Seamus answered shakily yet still his cheeks were dry.

'Go on up to her, pet,' Dilly whispered. 'The little one will be fine down here with us. Mary told me that she wanted to call her Primrose if it was a little girl. Are you happy with that?'

He nodded. 'Yes, we spent hours coming to a decision,

and she was supposed to have lots of little sisters all named after flowers: Violet, Rose, Heather, Daisy . . .' His voice trailed away and he rose shakily on legs that felt as if they had turned to jelly and quietly left the room.

The doctor meanwhile slid his arms into his coatsleeves and prepared to depart. 'I'm going to leave these two tablets here for him in case he can't sleep,' he told Dilly after rummaging about in his bag. 'And once again I'm so sorry, Mrs Carey. Please do get in touch if there's anything else at all I can do.'

'Thank you, Doctor.' Dilly saw him to the door and once she'd closed it behind him she leaned heavily against it and screwed her eyes tight shut. What was this going to do to Seamus? she wondered fearfully. Mary had brought him back from the dark place he'd been in after returning from the war and he'd been like a different person. And now for this to happen . . .

Upstairs, Seamus opened the door leading to the bedroom he had shared with Mary and gazed across at the bed. The nurse had washed and changed her before leaving and now his wife lay with her arms crossed across her chest and her thick hair spread across the pillow like a fan. She looked so peaceful that he could almost believe she was merely sleeping; any minute she would open her eyes and give him that smile that could always make his blood turn to water.

He crossed to her and sat on the side of the bed with his head bowed for a moment then said brokenly, 'Oh Mary, my love, *why* didn't you tell me how ill you were?'

When only silence greeted him, it struck him that he would never hear her voice again – and at last the tears that he had held back came in a torrent that threatened to choke him. Climbing on to the bed, he took her into his

241

arms for the very last time. She was still warm and he breathed in the special scent that belonged only to her.

Downstairs, the mood was equally sombre. Baby Primrose had finished all the milk that Nell had warmed up and now lay contentedly in her arms fast asleep.

'Let me hold her, would you?' Dilly asked and once the infant was pressed to her she nuzzled her neck. 'Don't worry, little one. You may have lost your precious mammy but there are still a lot of people here to love you.'

'That's as maybe,' Bessie said practically. 'But who is goin' to look after her on a daily basis? Seamus can't – he has to work.'

Dilly's mind was too fuddled with grief to think straight at present and she shrugged as Bessie came over to peer down at the sleeping babe.

'She's just perfect, ain't she?' she whispered. 'Can I have a little hold of her?'

'Of course.' Dilly held the slumbering infant out to her and as Bessie held her against her chest the most amazing thing happened, for she suddenly felt such a rush of love and tenderness that it almost took her breath away. This is how I should 'ave felt the first time I held Roddy, she thought. Making a decision, she said, 'I'll stop 'ere tonight to look after the baby. Seamus won't be in no fit state, God bless 'im.'

'Are you sure?' Dilly asked uncertainly. She'd had every intention of staying there herself.

'Quite sure,' Bessie answered, her eyes never leaving the tiny little face and so it was decided.

Mary was buried the day before Christmas Eve and they all knew that Christmas would never be quite the same again for any of them. The ground in the churchyard was frozen solid and it had taken the gravediggers the whole of the preceding day to prepare the grave. Now as the coffin was lowered, Seamus stood straight-faced but dignified as he silently said his goodbyes to the young wife he had adored. Bessie had stayed with him since the night of Mary's death and was still at home now looking after baby Primrose, who stole the hearts of all who met her.

Seamus supposed that he should be crying, as many of the female mourners were, but the pain he felt went beyond tears and he knew that he would shed them for years to come in private. And then as he looked up, he saw her, his Mary, standing at the head of the open grave.

Take care, my love, she whispered, and after glancing around he realised that he must be the only one who could see or hear her. *I'll always be with you, every time you look at Primrose, and I'll live on in your heart.* And then just as suddenly as she had appeared she was gone, leaving him feeling strangely comforted. She wasn't so very far away from him, after all, and she would live on in their daughter.

As soon as they got back to the little house on Abbey Green, Seamus lifted Primrose from her crib and buried his face in her downy hair.

'We'll get by somehow, little one,' he murmured and Bessie, who was standing close by, then spoke up.

'Aye, you will,' she told him. ''Cos I've decided I'm stayin' on to help you with her. You have to work and she needs a mother figure in her life – till she's a bit older, at any rate,' she ended hastily. She didn't want Seamus to get the impression that she was trying to take Mary's place but the thought of being parted from the baby was painful now. She had bonded with her as she never had with Roddy, and although this caused her to suffer all manner of guilty regrets, she couldn't help it.

'Are you sure about this, Bessie?' Dilly couldn't keep

243

the note of relief from her voice. She'd worried constantly about how Seamus was going to manage once he went back to work after Christmas.

Bessie nodded with conviction. 'Absolutely sure. But now you go an' see that all the mourners are helpin' themselves to food an' drink, Dilly. This little madam is due fer a bottle an' she'll raise the roof if it ain't on time.'

She, Nell and Dilly had spent the whole morning preparing a cold spread for the mourners who wished to return after the funeral, and now Dilly bustled away to ensure they were all being served. Bessie looked at Seamus and asked, 'How did it go?'

He shrugged, his eyes tight on his little daughter. He was as besotted with her as Bessie was and never tired of sitting just drinking in the sight of her as she slept in his arms. He even bathed and changed her although he was the first to admit that he was nowhere near as good at it as Bessie was.

'If you really meant what you said just now, I'd be more than happy to pay you,' he told her. 'It would take a great weight off my mind to know that she's with someone who'll take good care of her. The only problem I can foresee is, what will people say with you moving in here so soon after Mary's . . .' His voice trailed away. It was still too raw to acknowledge.

'They can say what they want as far as I'm concerned,' Bessie replied with a defiant toss of her head – then her voice softened as she saw how hard it was for him to hold himself together. He was hurting – badly – and it showed.

'Have a good cry if you've a mind to,' she murmured. 'I of all people know just how yer feelin'. When I lost my Malcolm I wished that I could die too.'

Seamus shook his head. 'I don't want to die. I have Primrose to live for and I promised Mary that she'd be

244

well looked after. Today . . .' He hesitated. Would Bessie think he was mad if he told her what he'd seen at the churchyard? 'At the end of the service I saw Mary standing at the head of her grave.'

'I can well believe it.' Bessie's eyes grew misty. 'I saw my Malcolm more than once in the days after he passed away. I reckon he came back to let me know he was still about and to check that I was all right. That's the sort of man he was and why I loved him so much. An' that's somethin' you an' I have in common. We've both lost people who can never be replaced 'cos they were the love of our lives.'

Seamus nodded in agreement. 'You're right. Do you know what, Bessie? Despite what's happened I count meself lucky 'cos I'd rather have had the short time I had wi' my Mary than a whole lifetime wi' someone else.' And then came the pent-up tears, hot and scalding, and crossing to him, Bessie let him bury his head on her shoulder as the pain poured out of him.

Chapter Thirty

July 1927

'I insist you stop right this minute,' Max said sternly. 'You'll work yourself into the ground at this rate. Now go and titivate and I'll take you for a ride out into the country. It's a beautiful evening – we could stop for a drink somewhere.'

Dilly looked up from her sketches. Max was right, it was time she stopped – but working seemed to be the only way she was able to stop worrying about the family. It had been seven months since Mary had died and her heart broke afresh every time she laid eyes on Seamus. It was as if a light had gone out inside her son, although he was still working as hard as ever. The only time he ever seemed to be remotely happy was when he was with Primrose, whom he clearly adored. She looked like a miniature version of Mary with her bright sparkling eyes and springing dark curls, and Dilly guessed that every time he looked at her, he saw her mother. It was heartbreaking but there wasn't a thing she could do about it. She thanked

God for Bessie though. She absolutely doted on the baby and was still staying with Seamus at Abbey Green. She'd shown no inclination to return to nursing although the hospital had recently been in touch with her to offer her a permanent position. True, the local gossips had had a field day immediately after Mary's death, but Bessie didn't care.

'He didn't wait long till he moved someone else into the poor lass's shoes, did he? His poor wife can hardly be cold in her grave yet!' Nell had overheard one woman say one day in January while she had been queuing to get some postage stamps for Dilly.

Nell being Nell had let rip. 'Why, you wicked dirt-mouthed bitch,' she'd roared for all to hear. 'Have yer no compassion in yer whatsoever? Would yer rather that helpless little babby be left wi' no one to care fer her? Bessie looks after that child from the good of her heart. She's no designs on Seamus whatsoever. Why, she's a good ten years older than 'im fer a start-off! Yer should be ashamed o' yourself, an' I just hope the Good Lord will forgive yer.'

The woman had looked shame faced and thankfully after that, the gossip had died down a little, much to Dilly's relief. And then there was Olivia. She had lost so much weight now that she looked almost skeletal, and she jumped at her own shadow. Both Dilly and Max had begged her to go to the doctor's but Olivia simply shook her head each time they asked and told them that she was fine. Something was worrying her, Dilly was sure of it, but until Olivia confided to her what it was, Dilly was unable to help her. Sometimes she felt that she was destined to always be worrying about one or another of her children even though they were now all adults.

'Actually, that offer sounds very tempting,' she told

Max now, and she meant it. 'I'll just pop through and tell Nell that I won't be here for supper, then I'll go and get ready.'

When Dilly darted out of the room, Max leaned across her table to study the sketches she'd been working on. They really were remarkably good and when made up, the items were selling as fast as she could create them. It was no wonder she was now a very wealthy woman in her own right. She deserved it, but he still worried that she worked too hard, especially now that she had no need to. He wandered through to the kitchen to Nell who was humming merrily as she scrubbed the large oak table that took up the centre of the room.

'I don't know who is the worst – you or Dilly. You're both always working,' he teased.

She grinned. 'Well, I do like to have everywhere ship-shape,' she admitted, looking around the gleaming kitchen with a measure of satisfaction. She knew that if she lived to be a hundred she would never get bored of living in such a beautiful house. Recently Dilly had given her money to buy some new furniture for it and had even left the choosing of it to Nell, who'd had a field day. Until now she'd never had anything brand new and she treasured each piece as if it was the Crown Jewels.

'So where are you plannin' on takin' her tonight then?' Nell asked.

'I thought about the Dog and Hedgehog out Dadlington way. The countryside is very nice around there.'

'It'll do her good to get out,' Nell answered, then glancing towards the door to make sure that Dilly wasn't coming yet she confided, 'I do worry about her. I thought when Seamus took over managing all the shops fer her she'd have more time on her hands, but she seems obsessed with workin' on those dratted sketches.' She sighed. 'I know they earn her a lot o' money an' it ain't my place to tell her what she should or shouldn't do, but like I told her, "There ain't no pockets in shrouds. Yer can't take it wi' yer, pet."'

'I agree with you, she does work far too hard,' Max agreed. 'And when she isn't working she's running around looking after Jessica or Primrose. Mind you, I think she finds that a pleasure. I just thank God for Bessie. She's doing an amazing job with that baby.'

Dilly appeared then, looking fresh in a cotton dress she had designed herself. It was cream covered with tiny sprigs of lavender, and ideally suited to a warm summer's evening.

'Yer look fresh as a daisy,' Nell commented admiringly, but then as far as she was concerned, Dilly always looked fresh as a daisy. It was hard to believe that she was now over fifty, especially considering how hard she worked – not that she ever complained. Dilly just seemed to take everything that life threw at her and make the best of things.

'Right, we'd better be off then.' Dilly smiled at Max and happy to oblige he offered his arm and they left Nell to it.

Back at the Farthing residence, Olivia was reading Jessica a story before tucking her into bed. It was her favourite time of the day and she always looked forward to it.

'I made a new friend at school today, Mummy,' Jessica interrupted when her mother was nearly halfway through the tale of *Goldilocks and the Three Bears*.

'Did you, sweetheart? That was nice,' Olivia replied affectionately.

'Yes, it was,' Jessica agreed solemnly. 'Her name is Martha Mundy. We played together during the breaks in the playground and after school her mummy and daddy

249

came to take her home. Why haven't I got a daddy, Mummy?'

Olivia felt herself break out in a sweat and her heart began to pound uncomfortably fast. She had always known this question would come one day but she hadn't expected it quite so soon.

'Well, the thing is . . .' She licked her dry lips and forced herself to go on. 'Your daddy and I lived in London for a time and sadly he died shortly after you were born.'

'How did he die? Was he poorly?' Jessica asked innocently.

'Look, why don't we talk about this another day when you're not so tired?' Olivia pulled the blankets up under Jessica's chin and planted a hasty kiss on her forehead. Suddenly she couldn't wait to get away. She so hated lying to her.

'All right, Mummy.' Jessica yawned and snuggled down and Olivia quietly crept from the room. Once out on the landing she clamped her hand across her mouth and ran for the bathroom where she was violently sick. Samuel was still taking money from her even though he hadn't been near the house in months. He was happily living with his elderly lover again by all accounts but it hadn't stopped him from waylaying Olivia on her way home from work each week. The only good thing was that she'd seen neither hide nor hair of Roger for at least the last three weeks now. It was very strange, as up until then he too had lain in wait for her, trying to get access to Jessica. *Perhaps he's just given up?* she mused, although she couldn't quite let herself dare to believe it. He'd been so insistent until then, determined that he should have some part in her daughter's life – so why had he suddenly disappeared off the scene? His unexpected absence was playing havoc on her nerves as much as his harassment had, and sometimes Olivia felt as if she might snap under the strain. With a sigh she cleaned up her mess and prepared for bed.

At that moment in the gentleman's club in town that Max frequented, Samuel was just entering the bar. Most of the members preferred the quiet rooms where they were served and where they could sit and enjoy a drink and a read of the newspaper in peace, but tonight Samuel felt in need of some male company. Lilian's frumpy married daughter, Elspeth, who thoroughly disapproved of him and made it more than obvious, was visiting her mother this evening so Samuel had decided to make himself scarce. A group of men were standing at the bar drinking a toast if he wasn't very much mistaken, and as Samuel approached, one of them said, 'Hello there, Samuel. Long time no see eh, old chap? Come and join us, why don't you. We're just raising our glasses to Roger's good news.'

Samuel's eyes rested on Roger Bannerman. 'Oh yes – and what's the good news then?'

'Roger's just had it confirmed that he's going to be a father, haven't you, old man!' Monty Brett slapped Roger on the back so resoundingly that he almost knocked him off his feet.

Roger gave a wonky smile. He'd clearly drunk more than his share of champagne already. 'Yesh, I have,' he slurred with a silly grin on his face. 'Me an' the little wifey had almost given up hope – and then out of the blue it finally happensh!'

'Congratulations.' Samuel shook his hand and accepted a glass of champagne. His mind was racing. Would this mean that he'd no longer want Jessica? If so, then that would be an end to him being able to blackmail Olivia.

He sipped his drink, blinking as the fizz made his eyes water. And then another idea occurred to him. The tables might just be reversed now. If Roger's wife, Miranda, was expecting a baby of their own she'd be none too pleased to find out that Roger already had a child by someone else, surely?

He drained his glass and clapped Roger on the shoulder. 'Well, thanks for the drink, but I'm afraid I have to go now. I only popped in for the one. I hope all goes well for you.'

Roger was laughing uproariously at something one of the other chaps had said and barely acknowledged him as Samuel left.

Once outside, Samuel pushed his hands into his pockets and grinned broadly. This might all turn out for the best, after all. Whistling merrily he went on his way. He'd perhaps call in to the Salutation for a pint next. It was far too early to go back to Lilian's yet. He passed through Abbey Green and was heading for Abbey Street when he saw a group of children playing on the pavement. Some were playing hopscotch, others were rolling hoops across the cobbles but one of them in particular stood out from the rest. It was a little girl with copper-coloured hair, exactly the same colour as his daughter Constance's had been. She had her back to him, but he saw that she was the same build as Connie too. His heart started to pound, and unbidden, a picture flashed in front of his eyes. He was standing over the bed the second before he had placed the pillow across her face and she was looking up at him from those glorious trusting eyes. Commonsense told him that this little girl couldn't possibly be her. Constance was dead and buried, and yet . . . his footsteps faltered and dizziness overcame him as he groped for a wall to support himself. And then the child turned and looked at him. Her face was nothing like Connie's and her eyes were blue. Badly shaken, he lurched into the nearest pub.

Wading through the sawdust that was scattered across

the floor and a fug of foul-smelling cigarette smoke, he went towards the bar. 'A whisky, and make it a double,' he told the surly-looking landlord, ignoring the glances of the many working-class men who were drinking there. He knew that he must look totally out of place in his fancy clothes but he didn't care. He needed a drink.

The landlord slammed it down in front of him and after pushing some money across the bar Samuel downed it in one go and told him, 'Another!'

Half an hour later, he wobbled back out into the street feeling tipsy and also very nauseous. The children had disappeared, no doubt dragged into their homes by their mothers long since, and Samuel breathed a sigh of relief. The encounter with the copper-haired child had unnerved him more than he cared to admit, and he wondered if he was going soft in the head. For most of the time he was able to push away the image of what he'd done to his own flesh and blood, but lately he'd been having bad dreams and they usually included Constance. One particular nightmare had been so bad that Lilian had been forced to shake him awake and he'd found himself lying in a tangle of bedclothes wet through with sweat. The dream had been so vivid that he hadn't dared sleep again that night in case it returned.

Samuel wondered if this was his punishment for killing his own child. And, ironically it had all been for nothing, for he'd really thought that with no child to tie them together, Niamh would divorce him and he would be free again. Now, as far as he knew, she was happily living in Ireland but they were still bound together. It was very frustrating because he had an idea that Lilian might be ready to marry him now if he were free. She was getting older, and if they were married, all her wealth would come to him when she died. That might happen sooner than she anticipated, he thought viciously, once he had a ring on her wrinkled finger . . . but as it was he could only be her fancy man. As things stood, he knew that Lilian's daughter would have him out of the house quicker than he could say Jack Robinson. She thoroughly disliked him and didn't try to hide it – and the feeling was mutual. Until Niamh had a change of heart therefore, about granting him his freedom, he would just have to make the best of things. Feeling sorry for himself, Samuel Farthing went on his drunken way.

Chapter Thirty-One

It was a beautiful Saturday evening in mid-August as Dilly finished reading the letter she had just received from Niamh. It seemed that James was coming along in leaps and bounds since Dilly had bought him his puppy, and he was even stringing words together now. Niamh wrote that boy and dog were inseparable; Charlie the golden cocker spaniel even slept on James's bed at night now. Dilly's thoughts were far away in New York with her daughter and her family. Niamh wrote regularly and her letters always made Dilly miss her more and wish that she was closer so that Niamh could see her grandson growing up. She adored Jessica and Primrose and spent as much time as she possibly could with them, but nothing made up for the loss of her daughter's presence, and she felt resentful towards Samuel. Were he and Niamh not still legally married, Dilly suspected that Niamh and Ben would have returned to their roots, but there was little chance of that ever happening.

Niamh would never grant him a divorce because of her religious beliefs, nor would she and Ben willingly have another child.

Then there was Declan, over in Ireland. She could still feel the pain as sharp as a knife when she recalled the time he had chosen to live in Ireland with Maeve and Daniel rather than with her and Fergal when he'd been no more than a little lad in short trousers. She had missed seeing him grow up too. And Olivia, the beautiful daughter she had been forced to give away at birth. She also still grieved after Kian, and suffered all manner of guilt because she hadn't as yet visited his grave in France to say her final goodbyes. So much loss. The family was truly scattered now. *The trouble is, I never seem to find the time to travel*, she told herself, but deep down she knew that she was lying. Once she saw Kian's grave it would come home to her with a terrible finality that he really was gone for ever, and as yet she hadn't been brave enough to face it. *But I will one day*, she vowed as Nell pottered in with a glass of lemonade for her.

'Why don't you come an' sit out in the garden, lass?' Nell said. 'It's lookin' a treat since you took Archie on. I could never get it lookin' like he did.'

Dilly had employed Archie Kemp, a recently retired miner who lived just along the street, to work on the garden part-time, and he'd completely transformed it. Archie was blessed with green fingers; everything he touched seemed to burst into blossom and thrive, and he and Nell were getting along like a house on fire. Archie had lost his wife some years ago and now Nell had taken to cooking for him on the days he visited.

'Well, while I'm cookin' fer us it's no trouble to do a bit extra,' she'd pointed out to Dilly, and had then blushed furiously. Nell always made sure that she looked her best when Archie was due and Dilly had a feeling that he had a soft spot for Nell too.

'I think I will come and join you.' Dilly laid Niamh's letter aside and stretched. She'd been sketching all day and was tired now.

Max had gone to pay his weekly visit to Camilla in Hatter's Hall so she knew there would be little chance of him calling in that evening. He still went religiously, even though it had been some time since Camilla had been able to recognise him. It was so sad, Dilly thought, when she remembered the vibrant attractive woman Max's wife had once been – but then that was life.

Taking her glass, she followed Nell out into the garden where she had two chairs placed ready for them. The old friends settled down side by side and when Nell lifted her knitting, Dilly asked, 'So what are you knitting now then?' Whatever it was, it looked far too big to be anything for any of the children.

'Oh . . . it's just a pullover fer Archie. I thought I'd do it 'im fer Christmas.' Nell kept her head bent as her needles clicked furiously and Dilly grinned as she relaxed back into the chair. It really was a beautiful evening and she watched fascinated as the bees and the butterflies buzzed amongst the flowers that Archie had planted.

'I like those tall flowers over there,' she commented and Nell's eyes followed her gaze.

'They're hollyhocks,' she told her. 'An' them in front of 'em are Michaelmas daisies. Them climbin' up the wall are sweet peas, an' them in that bed over there are dahlias. Pretty, ain't they? Archie always tells me what they're called when he plants 'em. I'm gettin' to be quite an expert on flowers now.'

'It's a good job one of us is,' Dilly said. She'd always been far too busy working to have time for planting things, unless it was vegetables when the children were younger, of course. As her mind slipped back in time she could remember when the vegetables she managed to grow were sometimes all they had to eat. It seemed a million years ago now and she still had to pinch herself when she looked at her bank balance.

She was so engrossed in her memories and enjoying the garden that when after a while Nell's knitting needles became still, she didn't notice.

'So . . . when are you goin' to slow down, lass?' Nell suddenly asked in her usual forthright manner.

Dilly frowned. 'What do you mean?'

'Exactly what I say,' Nell said in a no-nonsense sort of voice. 'You can't be working all the hours you do 'cos you need the money now?'

'Well, no that's true,' Dilly admitted. 'But what would I do with myself if I didn't work?'

Nell sighed. 'You could enjoy yourself more. Go on holidays, spend more time wi' the grandkids. Visit France, go an' see Niamh an' Declan again.'

Dilly wondered if Nell was a mindreader. 'I don't think I'm quite ready to retire just yet,' she said, wondering if it was true.

'Then it's more the pity. None of us knows what's just around the corner, do we? In fact, there was somethin' I've been meanin' to ask yer.' She looked so flustered that Dilly wondered what was coming. It wasn't often that the cat got Nell's tongue.

Nell licked her dry lips nervously. 'The thing is, Archie has asked me to go to the picture house wi' him on Monday evenin', an' I wondered . . . should I go? I ain't never been to a picture house in me entire life!'

'Of *course* you should go,' Dilly said immediately. 'And you can choose a new outfit from the shop to go in as well

258

– my treat. A night out will do you the world of good.'

'Hark at the pot callin' the kettle black,' Nell said sarkily and they grinned at each other. 'In that case, I'll tell 'im yes, an' I don't need a new outfit. I've got more than enough clothes since I've been livin' 'ere wi' you,' she said coyly and for now the subject was dropped.

Soon after, Dilly went inside and ran herself a bath. She and Nell never tired of having the luxury of an inside bath, and never forgot the days when they'd had to drag the tin one from a nail in the wall outside into the kitchen and fill it painstakingly. And then empty it!

It was as she lay soaking in the hot water that Dilly thought of Nell's forthcoming date with Archie. She was pleased that Nell had met someone nice and hoped that the two might find happiness together – but if they did, it would mean that Dilly would be rattling round this huge house like a pea in a pod, all alone again. *Goodness me, they've not even been out alone together yet and I'm marrying them off*, she told herself, then turned her thoughts to the winter designs she was working on as she forced herself to relax.

'So where's Nell then?' Max asked when he called into Dilly's on Monday evening.

Dilly grinned at him. 'Gone to the picture house with Archie Kemp.'

'The gardener?' When Max raised an eyebrow, Dilly tittered.

'Yes, and between you and me I think they're quite enamoured of each other. I've seen this coming for a while.'

'Well, good luck to them.' Max lifted a thin towel and began to dry the dinner pots Dilly was washing. 'You have to take every chance of happiness you can get in this life, from what I can see of it.'

'Hmm,' Dilly agreed, then filling the kettle she asked, 'How was Camilla this week?'

He shrugged. 'Much the same. They tend to keep her sedated now to stop her harming herself. She badly scratched all her arms with her hairclips last week while the nurse was gone getting her dinner tray. They've removed them all now and keep her hair in a plait instead.'

'I see.' Dilly sighed. 'And any word from Samuel?'

'Nothing, although I believe he's still living with his rich widow. She's not been too well, from what I'm hearing.'

'Oh dear.' Dilly secretly hoped he would stay where he was. Things ran so much more smoothly without Samuel about causing trouble.

She made a pot of tea and carried it to the table where Max joined her. 'I was wondering if perhaps you wouldn't like to go to the cinema?' he suggested hopefully. 'You haven't had a proper night out in ages.'

'You know as well as I do that if we did that, it would only cause more gossip,' she answered quietly. She was painfully aware that a lot of people still thought she was Max's mistress and she had no intention of fuelling the fire.

Max looked disappointed but he didn't push the subject. He knew Dilly too well by now to do that.

'Actually, I don't know if I should tell you this, but Olivia was saying at dinner this evening that there's a lot of gossip going around about Seamus and Bessie too.'

Dilly nodded as she poured the tea into the cups. 'I know. It started shortly after Mary died when Bessie stayed over at Abbey Green. I can't believe that people don't have better things to do! Bessie is doing a wonderful job of caring for Primrose. In fact, I don't know how we'd manage without her.'

'It's funny, isn't it? That Bessie can love Primrose as she does and yet she couldn't bond with her own child. Speaking of which, I had a letter from Roddy today. He's coming to stay with me for a few days next week before he goes back to school. I intend to take some time off so that I can take him out sightseeing.'

'How lovely.' Dilly was truly pleased for him. 'But isn't it a long way for a young lad to travel on his own?'

'Oh, he won't be,' Max assured her. 'Declan is putting him on the ferry in Dublin and I'm meeting him off it, so he'll only be on his own for the sea passage, and Declan is going to get someone to keep an eye on him for that distance.'

'Well, that's wonderful. Bessie might get to see him too then?'

'I shall make sure she does,' Max said kindly, and the conversation went on to other things.

The following week, Max arrived at his home late in the afternoon with Roddy who as promised, he had met off the ferry. It was a Thursday, so Dilly was there and so were Oscar and George.

'Well, look at you, lad!' Oscar exclaimed when Roddy entered the room. 'I swear you've shot up at least another foot since the last time I saw you. If you keep growing like this, you'll be a nuisance to the aeroplanes.'

Roddy smiled back as he told him proudly, 'I'm the tallest in me class, so I am.'

'I don't doubt it,' Oscar replied as the two young ones ran forward to greet him.

'You can come and play with my train set if you like,' George offered and Roddy blushed. He considered himself far too grown up to play with six-year-olds now.

'Perhaps when he's had something to eat,' Max told

George as he affectionately ruffled his hair. 'I'm sure Roddy must be starving after his long journey and Mrs Pegs promised to have something ready for us. But first Roddy has something rather exciting to tell you all, don't you?'

Roddy nodded as he looked directly at Dilly. 'Me mammy – that is Roisin – was goin' to write to you and tell you, but she only found out for sure yesterday, an' seeing as I was coming she told me it would be all right if I told you. She's having a baby.'

Roddy was clearly delighted at the prospect but Dilly's heart turned over. Roisin had never managed to carry a child to full term so the chances were that she wouldn't carry this one either. She'd thought that she and Declan had given up trying for a wean of their own now but even so she plastered a smile on her face as she answered, 'Why, isn't that wonderful news! You must all be very excited.'

'We are.' Roddy looked like a miniature version of Samuel as he beamed from ear to ear. 'I've told them I'd like a little brother – I mean, a boy.' He flushed guiltily. He obviously thought of Declan and Roisin as his parents now but didn't want to hurt anyone's feelings.

'Right, well I don't know about you, old chap, but I could eat a horse,' Max said, which made the children laugh. 'Let's go and see what Mrs Pegs has got lined up for us, shall we?'

He left the room with Roddy and Dilly following behind. Once alone with Oscar, and when the two little ones had gone back to their play, Olivia commented, 'I do hope all goes well for them this time. They've lost so many babies in the past.'

'So I believe.' Oscar chewed on his lip for a moment then confided, 'Actually, I have some news too. Penelope is expecting another baby as well. She told me yesterday morning.'

Olivia reeled in shock but somehow managed not to show it, as she kept her eyes firmly fixed on the children.

'I see. Then I suppose I should say congratulations.' The pain she was feeling was immense. Lately Roger had stopped harassing her and her relationship with Oscar was better than it had been for some long time, but now . . .

'Thank you,' Oscar responded quietly. He certainly didn't seem too excited about the prospect of becoming a father again. 'Anyway, I suppose I should be getting George home now that we've seen Roddy. The cook will have his meal ready and you know what Penelope can be like if we're late . . .' His voice trailed away as he began to collect George's things together.

'Of course. We mustn't keep Penelope waiting, must we?' Olivia couldn't keep the note of sarcasm from her voice and Oscar flushed as he bundled a loudly protesting George into his coat. Once they were gone, she sat and stared miserably into the empty fireplace.

Chapter Thirty-Two

Bright and early the next morning, Max tapped on the door of Seamus's house in Abbey Green. Bessie answered, and her eyes immediately flew to Roddy. She'd been expecting them with mixed emotions and now as she looked at her son, her heart beat faster as it always did as she saw his father smiling up at her.

'Why, look at you – you'll be as tall as me soon,' she said, forcing a smile. 'Come on in.'

Max ushered Roddy ahead of him into the living room where Primrose was sitting happily chewing on a peg doll in the middle of a blanket Bessie had laid on the floor for her. Roddy instantly relaxed as he crossed to her. He loved babies and the sight of Primrose reminded him of the wonderful news that spewed out of him before he could stop himself.

'Me mammy is going to have a baby,' he gushed, then remembering who he was talking to his face flooded with colour. 'I mean . . . Roisin is,' he ended lamely.

Bessie's heart was full of sympathy and guilt as she caught his hand in hers and drew him down on to the sofa at the side of her. 'Why, that's wonderful news. And Roddy . . . Roisin *is* your mammy to all intents and purposes and you shouldn't worry about calling her so. I'm just Bessie. Perhaps you'd be more comfortable calling me that, and perhaps we could be . . . friends?'

She was heartened when he didn't immediately withdraw his hand from hers and even more so when he looked at her uncertainly before bestowing a beaming smile on her.

'I . . . I'd like that,' he answered shyly and somehow Bessie felt as if they had taken a massive step forward in their hitherto rocky relationship.

'And what would you like? A little brother or a little sister?'

'Oh, a brother, though Mammy and Daddy say they don't care what it is so long as it's healthy.'

'Well, happen they're right there,' she agreed. 'After all, Primrose here is a girl and she's not so bad, is she?'

'No, she's grand so she is,' Roddy responded easily and with that he crossed to drop beside her, making her coo with delight.

'Shall we go through to the kitchen and leave these two to it for a while?' Bessie suggested and Max, who had listened to their conversation with a huge lump in his throat, could only nod.

'It was touching to see a spark finally between them. I think they'll get on better from now on,' he told Dilly that evening after leaving Olivia to put Jessica and Roddy to bed. 'I just wish Samuel could have had the same nature as his son. Roddy is a grand little chap and I can see why Roisin and Declan love him so much.'

265

'So can I,' Dilly agreed. 'And I hear you're going to be a grandpa again too. Olivia called in on her way home from the hospital and told me Oscar's news.'

Max nodded. 'So I believe, although I doubt Oscar will be thrilled about it. I hate to see him so unhappy, Dilly. Who would have thought that the agreement we made all those years ago would still be having consequences now?'

Dilly bowed her head, for there was nothing she could say to that.

The following morning, as Dilly was working on her sketches, she heard someone knock on the front door. Nell was at the shop so with a sigh she took off her hated spectacles and went to answer it. She was shocked to find Samuel standing on the front step and stared at him blankly.

'Good morning, Mrs Carey,' he said politely. 'I'm sorry to call on you unannounced but I have something of importance to discuss with you. Could you spare me a few moments of your time?' Deep down he couldn't believe that he was kowtowing to a former maid but he wanted to get her on side and didn't have much choice.

'Er . . . I suppose so.' Dilly held the door wider and ushered him into the hallway. She then led him towards the drawing room which was rarely used and his eyes were almost on stalks as he looked about at the tasteful furniture and drapes. She must be doing better for herself than he had thought.

'Well, what can I do for you?' Her voice was icily polite and not lost on Samuel, but he kept his false smile firmly in place as he took off his hat.

'It's about Niamh I want to speak to you actually,' he told her.

'I see. Go on.'

266

'Well, this is rather delicate, I'm afraid. You see I now find myself in another relationship.'

'I think we are all aware of your widow friend,' Dilly replied, determined not to give him an inch.

He felt his temper rising but managed to control it with an effort. Just who did this guttersnipe think she was talking to?

'Then you'll probably also know that my . . . friend is somewhat older than me and she hasn't been in the best of health for a while.'

'And what could that possibly have to do with Niamh?'

'The truth of the matter is, my friend and I wish to get married and so I wondered if you would get in touch with Niamh for me and see if she's had a change of heart yet about releasing me from our marriage. Or perhaps you could give me her address in Ireland and I could contact her myself?'

'That won't be necessary,' Dilly said a little too hastily. 'I can tell you without speaking to her again that she'll never agree to a divorce. It goes against her religion and Niamh has morals.'

Samuel's temper was simmering now and getting harder to control by the second. 'But perhaps if you were to talk to her and tell her how stupid this is? We don't love one another, we never did. If she would just agree to a divorce, we could both get on with our lives. We only got married in the first place because—'

'Because you raped her and left her with child!' Dilly spat, her eyes flashing fire.

Samuel ground his teeth together, a habit he often adopted when he was very angry.

'But that child is out of the way now, so why should we remain married?'

Dilly looked stunned. '*That child* had a name, in case

you'd forgotten. It was Constance. And what do you mean, *she's out of the way*? You almost sound as if you wanted it.'

'I mean . . . she died,' he blustered, but a terrible seed was sown in Dilly's mind as she recalled the look on Constance's face when Samuel had called them all on the night she died. The doctor had seemed fairly confident that she had turned the corner, that she would make a full recovery – but then they had allowed her father to have a few minutes alone with her and . . .

'Oh, this is getting us nowhere,' Samuel roared as cold sweat stood out on his forehead. Dilly also noticed that his hands were shaking but before she could say any more he turned and stamped out of the house, leaving the front door to swing open behind him.

Badly shaken, Dilly stood there and waited for her heart to return to a more normal rhythm.

That evening, she confided to Nell that Samuel had called, and told her the reason why.

'Yer don't think he'll go to Ireland to try an' find her, do yer?' Nell asked. 'I wouldn't put it past the rotten bugger! An' what a shock he'd get if he were to find out that she's livin' happily in New York wi' Ben an' a fine little lad, eh?'

'I'd rather he didn't find out. He'd only try to make more trouble for her.'

Nell scowled as she looked at her. Dilly was as white as a ghost and jumpy as a newborn kitten tonight.

'He didn't threaten yer, did he?' she asked angrily. ''Cos if he did he'll feel the length o' me—'

'No, no he didn't threaten me,' Dilly assured her hastily. 'It was just a bit of a shock to find him standing on my doorstep after not seeing him for so long, that's all.'

'That's all right then,' Nell said grumpily. 'But if yer not feelin' yerself I could allus stay in tonight. Archie wouldn't mind. We weren't goin' anywhere special.'

'No, you go,' Dilly urged. 'I'm fine and Max will probably be calling in anyway.'

'Well, all right then – if yer sure.' Nell then pottered away to start getting ready. *I'm turnin' into a right little gadabout*, she told herself, *an' long may it last. I ain't enjoyed meself so much fer years!*

When Max arrived later on he too noticed that Dilly didn't seem to be herself.

'Is everything all right?' he asked.

Dilly flashed him a smile. As much as she loved Max's company, tonight she just wanted to be on her own. Samuel's visit had shaken her to the core.

'Fine except for an awful headache,' she lied. 'I think I might get myself an early night if you don't mind?'

'Of course I don't mind. But is there anything I can get you before I go?'

'Nothing at all,' she told him. 'You get off and spend some time with Roddy. He'll be going home in a couple of days. The time seems to have raced by, doesn't it?'

'It certainly has,' Max sighed. 'I have to say, he's a lovely lad. Your Declan and Roisin are doing a marvellous job of raising him. His manners are such that you could take him anywhere. I'm proud to call him my grandson and it's lovely seeing him and Bessie getting along at last. But hark at me, I'll get off now and let you get some rest. I'll call round tomorrow evening, shall I?'

'That would be nice. And by the way, I've decided that I'll take Roddy back to Ireland. Now that we've had the good news about the new baby I want to check how Roisin is, so if you'll just take us to the railway station I'll accompany him on from there.'

'Are you sure?'

Dilly smiled and nodded, then saw him to the door, and

once he was gone she sank on to a chair, buried her face in her hands and sobbed as if her heart would break as she thought of her beloved little Connie.

In the widow's luxurious house, Samuel was knocking back brandy as if it was going out of fashion.

'Is something wrong, my love?' Lilian asked from her seat at the side of a roaring fire. She had a large woollen rug tucked around her legs. That was something Samuel had noticed lately: older people seemed to always feel the cold and sometimes he felt as if he might melt in the stifling heat.

'Not really, my darling.' He sighed dramatically. 'It's just that I *so* want to make an honest woman of you. I hate to think about people gossiping about us. And Elspeth – I know she disapproves of me.'

'Now don't start on about my darling girl,' Lilian scolded gently. 'And as for people gossiping . . . let them. While they're talking about us they're leaving someone else alone. You know the old saying, dearest: "sticks and stones may break my bones but words can never hurt me"!'

The last of the daylight was struggling through the window, highlighting the deep wrinkles on Lilian's face, clogged with face powder. The colour she'd applied in thick layers to her thin lips was bleeding into the myriad lines surrounding her mouth and suddenly Samuel felt bile rise in his throat. He swallowed it. He badly needed some time alone. He still wanted to marry her, since Lilian was security – for life if he could only manage to put a ring on her finger.

'I think I might pay a visit to the gentleman's club in town,' he said in a shaky voice.

Lilian was no fool. She knew why Samuel stayed with

270

her but she could afford the luxury of having a handsome young man swinging on her arm. She also understood that sometimes he needed to be with people his own age.

'Take the new car, darling,' she told him indulgently. 'I shall be waiting for you when you get home.'

He pictured her sitting up in bed, stripped of all her paint and powder, a frail old woman, eager for his lovemaking, and dredged up a fake smile. 'I shan't be late, precious.'

Hurrying away, glad of the fresh air, he thought of the first visit he would make to the whorehouse, then he might try his hand at a game of cards. But he'd avoid Abbey Street. He didn't think he could risk seeing the child with the copper-coloured hair today. He thought of Dilly again then and silently cursed as he made for the garage that Lilian had had built especially at the back of the property. He'd spotted something in Dilly's eyes when they'd been talking about Constance. She'd seen what he'd done, written all over his face – he was sure of it. But then suspecting it was one thing – proving it, another. Even so, he was feeling sick at heart as he picked up the starting handle and made his way to the front of the new toy Lilian had bought for him.

Chapter Thirty-Three

Gwen was busily packing Roddy's clothes. He would be going back to Ireland the following morning and she was missing him already. She and Mrs Pegs, the whole family, in fact – had loved having him to stay and hoped it wouldn't be too long before he came to see them again. Mr Farthing had taken him to say goodbye to Bessie and once she'd finished this job Gwen was looking forward to putting her feet up by the kitchen fire with Mrs Pegs and listening to the wireless.

Leaving Roddy's pyjamas neatly folded on the end of the bed – they could be packed in the morning – she ran downstairs. She had just reached the hallway when someone rapped on the door and hurrying to answer it, she found the same man who had come to see Olivia a few months ago.

'Was it Miss Olivia you were wantin'?' she asked. 'She's just puttin' Jessica to bed but I can tell her you're here. Would you like to wait in the drawing room?'

'Yes, thank you.' He removed his hat and once she'd shown him into the drawing room she scampered off to tell Olivia she had a visitor.

When Olivia entered the room and saw who it was, her stomach did a somersault. He had left her alone for weeks; she might have known it was too good to last.

'What on earth do you want, Roger?' she asked wearily. 'I still feel the same about you not having any involvement in Jessica's life, if that's what you've come about.'

'Actually, it's quite the opposite,' he said quietly.

Olivia raised her eyebrows. 'What do you mean?'

'Well . . . the thing is, everything has changed.'

'I don't understand. Explain yourself?'

Avoiding her eyes, he told her awkwardly, 'Miranda is going to have a baby.'

'Oh I *see*,' Olivia answered shrewdly, as comprehension dawned. 'And now suddenly it's imperative that she *doesn't* find out about Jessica. Is that what you're saying?'

Shamefaced, he nodded.

'Well, well! How things change.' Olivia was actually enjoying his discomfort. Suddenly the shoe was on the other foot. 'Does that mean that you'll be leaving us alone in future and not harassing us any more?'

'Absolutely,' he promised. 'As you know, we'd just about given up hope of ever having a child, but now . . . Well, I don't think Miranda would take very kindly to discovering that I already have a child.'

'I've never said that Jessica *was* yours,' Olivia pointed out coldly. 'It was you who wouldn't leave us alone.'

'Yes, I know. Look, I'm sorry if I've upset you but I was desperate. I suppose it was male pride. I needed to know that I could father a child, and now that Miranda is expecting I know that I can.'

'Male pride indeed!' Olivia snapped as her eyes flashed

273

fire. 'You would have upset my child just for that! But now let this be the end of it, because if you harass me one more time I shall tell your wife about our affair personally and she can form her own conclusions about who Jessica's father was!'

Roger nodded before shuffling towards the door then he was gone – and Olivia let out a huge sigh of relief. At last, all the months of fretting and worrying were over. With luck, things could now return to normal and she would be able to take her daughter out and about again without fear of bumping into Roger.

Once outside, Roger put his hat back on and headed for the club. He felt in need of a stiff drink and he usually called in there on a Thursday. He took his favourite seat at the side of the fire, gave the steward his order and picked up a newspaper – but he'd barely had a chance to open it when someone sat down beside him.

'Oh, evening, Samuel.' He'd hoped to have a few moments to himself. His confrontation with Olivia had left a sour taste in his mouth but he didn't wish to appear rude.

Samuel took a long drag of the cigar he was smoking as he settled back in his seat and blew a plume of blue smoke into the air before saying, 'I think it's time you and I had a little chat, don't you, old chap?'

Roger frowned. 'What about?'

'About my sister – and your daughter.'

Roger felt his chest constrict. Surely Olivia hadn't told Samuel about their affair? She'd seemed so keen to keep it secret.

'I don't know what you're talking about,' he bluffed, tugging at the collar of his shirt. He'd broken out in a sweat.

Samuel concentrated on tapping the ash from his cigar into a large cut-glass ashtray before answering, 'Oh, but I think you do. You see, I've been making a few enquiries and according to the grapevine you're in for a promotion now that you're finally making Miranda's father a grandfather. Word has it that he's over the moon. Well, of course he would be, wouldn't he? First grandchild and all that. I'm told that he set you on in his firm when you married his only daughter – but that's where the problem lies, isn't it? You see, this baby *won't* be his first grandchild, will it? And how would he react if he were to find out that you'd been cheating on his precious daughter? Tut-tut! I don't think he'd be very pleased at all, do you? In fact, I think you could well and truly find yourself chucked out on your smug little arse!'

Roger had paled alarmingly but Samuel wasn't done with him yet.

'I happen to know that you've been harassing and threatening my sister for months, but you never did anything about it, did you? What were you afraid of – your wife's reaction to your adultery or your father-in-law's?'

Roger swiped the sweat from his forehead with the back of his hand. Much as he hated to admit it, Samuel had hit the nail on the head. He was convinced that Jessica was his and had told Olivia so, had even told her that he wanted to be involved in her life, but he'd never had the guts to go through with it and now his cowardice was coming back to bite him, just when he was well and truly in his father-in-law's good books.

'So what do you intend to do?' Roger asked him with a quiver in his voice. He'd had nothing until he'd married Miranda and been accepted into her father's firm, and he'd have nothing again if this were to come out. Not a penny piece to call his own.

'Hmmm . . . well now, let me think.' Samuel tapped some more ash into the ashtray. 'I suppose silence can be bought but it doesn't come cheap.'

'How much do you want?'

'Are we talking of a one-off payment or a monthly thing?'

Roger paled even further, if that were possible. 'I suppose a monthly payment,' he gasped.

'I dare say I could keep my mouth shut for regular payments of twenty pounds.'

'*Twenty pounds!*' Roger was horrified. 'But I'm not a rich man,' he blustered.

'Not my problem, I'm afraid. Now what's it to be? Do we shake on it or do I go and pay your father-in-law a little visit?'

'You'll have it,' Roger ground out as Samuel rose from his seat.

'Excellent. What about we start now?'

'I haven't got that much cash on me!' Roger felt as if he'd been backed into a corner and was having to control the urge to thump Samuel on the nose.

'Then shall we say the same time here tomorrow?'

Roger ignored the outstretched hand and scowled as Samuel laughed. 'Till tomorrow then.' With that he sauntered away as Roger sat silently fuming. Twenty pounds a month! How the hell was he going to explain that amount of money going missing on a regular basis to his wife?

'Right then, young man,' Max said the next morning as he stood on the station platform with Dilly and Roddy. 'You take care of yourself and come and see us again soon, do you hear me? Oh, and here's a little spending money for you. Put it away safely now.'

Roddy stared down at the two half-crowns Max had slipped into his hand. 'I will,' he said breathlessly, 'and thank you, sir.'

Max then lifted their bags aboard, asking Dilly, 'How long will you be gone?'

'Three or four days probably. I'll ring you,' she promised, then she was ushering Roddy aboard and as the train pulled out of the station they both waved at Max from the carriage window.

Roddy loved the train ride and the voyage on the ferry even more, but by the time it steamed into Dublin they were both tired and glad that the journey was over. Declan was waiting for them at the docks and after kissing Dilly he swung Roddy into the air as if he were a five-year-old.

'We've missed you, laddie, so we have,' he told him and Dilly was touched to see the deep affection between them.

Once Roddy and the bags were settled in the back of the cart Declan shooed the horse into a trot and they headed for the farm. 'So how did the visit go?' he asked.

'Really well, and at last Bessie and Roddy seemed to have reached an agreement. They got on really well and Bessie told him that it's fine to call you and Roisin Mammy and Daddy if he wishes to.'

'That's grand then,' Declan smiled just as the cart jolted as they went down a rut in the road.

'When *are* you going to treat yourself to a motor car?' Dilly asked as she clung to the edge of the narrow plank seat for dear life. 'Surely you can afford one now with the farm doing so well? If not, I'll buy you one.'

'You will not!' he answered swiftly. 'I could afford one if I'd a yen fer one but the horse an' cart were always good enough fer me granda and they're good enough fer me.'

'Oh, you're so like your daddy for being stubborn,' Dilly scolded but she was proud of him really. 'And what

277

wonderful news about the baby. Roddy is so excited about it.'

The smile slid from Declan's face. 'Aye, it is good news but to be honest we had no intention of Roddy finding out about it yet awhile,' he confided after glancing in the back of the cart to make sure that Roddy had dozed off.

'Whyever not?'

Declan raised his eyebrows. ' 'Cos it's still early days an' we'd no wish to raise his hopes. You know Roisin's history for carrying weans well enough. She usually loses them round about her third or fourth month. Trouble was, he heard Roisin telling Shelagh about it and there was no stopping him then. He'll be right upset so he will if this little soul goes the way o' the others.'

'When will it be due?' Dilly asked, solemn-faced now. Sad as it was, she knew that Declan was right.

'Early in February.'

'So she's over three months already? Surely that's a good sign?'

'Aye, it is,' he said slowly. 'But still too early to raise our hopes too high just yet. Funny thing is, Roisin's been completely different this time. Usually she slows down and takes things easy but this time she's just gone on as usual.'

Dilly worried her bottom lip with her teeth. The poor girl had clearly convinced herself from day one that she wouldn't carry the baby to full-term. Perhaps it was just as well. If anything did go wrong again then it wouldn't be such a bitter disappointment to her.

It was dark by the time they reached the farm but refreshed from his nap Roddy flew into the farmhouse and flung his arms about Roisin, who seemed just as pleased to see him.

'Why, it's been so quiet here without you,' she laughed, hugging him tightly. 'Did you have a good time?'

'Yes, I did. I went to see Bessie and Primrose – we call her Primmy for short – and Granpa gave me this – look.' He dug deep into his pocket and showed her the two shiny silver half-crowns and Roisin was impressed.

'It's rich you are,' she told him affectionately. 'You'll be able to spoil yourself, won't you will when we next go in to Enniskerry.'

'No, I shan't,' Roddy responded. 'I shall save it till the new baby comes then I'll buy it something really nice. But now I must go and check on me new calf. Is he all right?'

'Right as ninepence,' Roisin beamed, and Roddy didn't see the way her face had fallen at his mention of the baby as he raced across the farmyard.

'Don't write the baby off just yet, pet,' Dilly said tenderly as she gave her a hug. 'The little soul is still growing inside you.'

'Aye, it is – but for how much longer?' Roisin answered pessimistically, then raising a smile she said, 'But hark at me feeling sorry for meself. You must be parched. I'll away and put the kettle on.'

While she was gone, Dilly glanced around the neat and cosy little room. There was no evidence of a baby anywhere as yet, whereas with the others Roisin had been busily knitting tiny matinee coats and sewing little nightgowns by now. She offered up a silent prayer that this time things might be different and Roisin and Declan might finally be granted the one thing in the world they longed for, a child of their own. Not that they didn't adore Roddy, of course, but this one would be the icing on the cake.

The following day, Roisin drove them into Enniskerry on the horse and cart and they spent a pleasant couple of hours shopping. Roisin absolutely refused to look at baby things but Dilly did manage to buy a couple of hand-embroidered little nightgowns while Roisin was in the greengrocers. She would leave them with Shelagh just in case all went well. Before they set off for home, Dilly treated them both to a cream tea in the tiny tea shop in the marketplace. She could feel herself beginning to wind down and was suddenly glad that she'd come.

When they got back, Dilly helped Roisin to put the shopping away, then after borrowing a pair of stout shoes she set off for a walk leaving Roisin to begin preparing the evening meal. She wandered through a copse perched on the side of a hill and some time later came out the other side of it to find herself high on a hilltop with a view spread before her that seemed to stretch for miles. With a sigh of contentment she sat down and wrapped her arms about her knees. They were almost into September but the day was warm with a gentle breeze and Dilly felt as if she could have sat there for ever. Life was so different here to the life she led in the Midlands. Here, there was nothing but the sound of cattle lowing in the fields, birds singing and the sigh of the breeze through the trees. She watched a wily old fox break from cover of the copse and slouch along the hedgerow, his nose sniffing the air for a scent of the rabbits that were playing in and out of their burrows, and suddenly wondered what it would have been like if she had done as Maeve had begged her all those years ago and moved the family here to live. Their lives might all have turned out so very differently. Fergal's health might have improved in the clean country air. Niamh might never have been raped by Samuel. Seamus might have decided to stay and work the land rather than go to war and return with shell shock. Kian might have decided to do the same and could still be alive. But then she would not have been there to see Olivia grow up, and Dilly knew that she couldn't have borne that.

It was strange to think that on the faraway night when

she had handed her newborn daughter over to the Farthing family she had changed so many people's lives for ever. It was a sobering thought and after a time she rose and slowly made her way back to the farm.

The rest of Dilly's visit passed in a blur and before she knew it Declan was loading her bag into the back of the cart for the trip to the ferry.

'Just slow down a little bit, pet,' Dilly urged Roisin as they said their affectionate goodbyes. 'There's no sense in tempting fate.'

Roisin shrugged; she hadn't mentioned her pregnancy once since Dilly had arrived. It was as if she had blanked it from her mind and had already accepted that she would not carry the baby to full term. 'What will be will be, and at least we have Roddy now,' she replied.

Dilly didn't press it any further. This was something Roisin would have to handle in her own way. God knew it was understandable. Her daughter-in-law had had far too many disappointments in the past to raise her hopes this time.

Declan was quiet on the drive to the ferry and eventually she asked him, 'Are you happy, son?'

'Aye I am, Mammy.' He turned his dazzling smile on her, the one so like Fergal's in his younger days. 'We don't ask for a lot out here, just enough to live comfortably and keep the wolf from the door. Most of what we earn is ploughed back into the farm for more stock but we're content – and that's worth far more than any amount of money.'

Dilly suddenly felt guilty as she thought of her growing bank account. Even if she were to stop working there and then, she probably had enough put by to last her the rest of her days if she lived sensibly.

'If ever you need any money I could—' she began, but Declan silenced her with a shake of his head.

'We have all we need, so we do, and we have each other. Admittedly the baby would be a great blessing, but Roisin hasn't been so obsessed about having our own child since Roddy arrived. He is ours to all intents and purposes, though I'm glad to hear he's getting on better with Bessie now. I'd not want him growing up with a chip on his shoulder thinking that she hadn't wanted him because of something he'd done. Perhaps one day when he's older she'll sit him down and explain why she wasn't able to bond with him, but till then he's happy where he is.'

Dilly felt a rush of pride. When had this son of hers grown to be so wise?

She'd forgotten to telephone Max or Nell the evening before to let them know that she'd be coming home, so that evening when the train pulled into the station at Nuneaton she strode briskly along the platform and headed for home. It was no more than a ten-minute walk and she was looking forward to a nice hot cup of tea and a chat with Nell. However, as she approached the house in St Edward's Road she saw that it was in darkness. Inserting her key in the lock, she let herself into the back door.

'Nell!' Her voice echoed around the empty room but the fire was burning brightly which could only mean that Nell couldn't have been gone very long. She'd probably popped out to visit Archie.

Clicking on the light, Dilly wearily stripped her coat off, remembering the sound of laughter that had filled Declan's and Liam's homes, and suddenly she felt profoundly lonely.

Chapter Thirty-Four

As the summer gave way to autumn, Lilian took to her bed and Samuel was gravely worried. He'd visited Dilly again in September to find out if she'd asked Niamh about giving him a divorce, but she'd sent him away with a flea in his ear. Admittedly he was still sitting pretty at the present time. Lilian was a generous woman, and then of course he had the twenty pounds he was blackmailing Roger for each month, but now Samuel wanted to get a ring on to Lilian's finger before anything happened to her. It appeared that the only way he might possibly do it was if he tracked Niamh down and asked her for a divorce himself. He couldn't remember the exact address of where her Irish family lived but he knew it was fairly close to Enniskerry – and how many farms could there be in that back-of-beyond place?

Late in October he made a hasty decision and after getting Lilian's maid to pack him a bag he told his mistress that he would be away for a few days on business for his father and set off in his latest motor car for the docks. He would leave the car at a hotel close by and catch the ferry that same day hopefully. The journey there was uneventful and late that afternoon he stood at the ship's rails and watched the coast of Ireland appear through a sea mist that had appeared out of nowhere.

Once he was on dry land again he hailed a cab to take him to Enniskerry. The driver had no idea where the Careys' farm was but Samuel was sure that someone there would know. The scenery was lost on Samuel as the cab driver drove him through the lush green fields. He could think of nothing worse than being stuck in this out-of-the-way place. He far preferred gambling casinos, dance halls and jazz music. Samuel was a great fan of the Prince of Wales, who was reputed to run around the grounds of Buckingham Palace every morning for at least an hour before breakfast for the sake of his health and who loved playing golf at Sandwich. The Prince was also an adept Polo player and one of the most eligible bachelors in the country. Samuel envied him his lifestyle and stared about at the rolling fields glumly. The sooner he had done what he had come to do and got out of this Godforsaken place the better, as far as he was concerned.

'So where do you want droppin', sir?' the driver enquired as they finally drove into Enniskerry.

'The nearest hotel, if you please, and wait for me – I'll make it worth your while.'

The driver touched his cap and nodded after pulling up outside the only hotel in town. 'Right you are, sir.' He was only too glad of a chance to pull his cap over his eyes and settle for a quick kip – especially if he was getting paid for it.

Once inside the hotel, a poor establishment compared to the ones he was used to, Samuel narrowed his eyes and stared about. A large log fire was roaring in the grate and tables and chairs were set higgledy-piggledy about the room. The place was almost empty apart from a few very old men who sat drinking and puffing on their pipes, and they eyed him curiously as he crossed to the bar.

The landlady, an enormous woman with flame-red hair, eyed him suspiciously before asking, 'What can I be getting for you, sir?' It wasn't often they saw a toff in these parts.

Samuel gave her his most charming smile. 'A brandy, if you please, my dear.'

Reaching beneath the bar for a bottle she poured some amber liquid into a glass and shoved it across the bar to him, saying 'That'll be one shillin', if you please.'

'I was wondering,' he bestowed another smile on her, 'if you'd happen to know where I'd find the Carey farm?'

'What would you be wanting with the Careys?'

'Oh, they're very good friends of mine. I haven't seen them for some long time and as I was passing through I thought it was time I paid them a visit. Unfortunately, I seem to have mislaid their address and I don't know this area.'

It sounded plausible enough so she gave him directions. He was pleased to hear that the farm wasn't more than a couple of miles away. With any luck he'd have time to see Niamh and be back on the ferry heading for home that same evening. He didn't want to spend a moment more than he had to in this dull backwater.

After draining his glass he thanked the landlady and went back out to the cab where he found the driver snoozing. He gave him directions to the farm and in no time at all they were off again. As they jolted along on the rutted lanes, Samuel cursed beneath his breath. This really was hell as far as he was concerned and he could hardly wait to get back to the hustle and bustle of civilisation.

'I'll wait here for you if you don't mind,' the cab driver told him at the end of the lane leading to the farm. 'There's only the rust holding this old jalopy of mine together, and that lane looks even worse than the ones we've been driving on.'

'Oh, very well,' Samuel snapped irritably. He'd never been one for exercise but the driver was clearly not prepared to go any further. Getting out of the cab he set off down the winding drive. At least he had no fear of the cabbie driving off without him – he probably owed the little fellow a considerable amount of money by now.

By the time the chimneytops of the farmhouse came into view, Samuel was in a foul mood. Twice he'd stepped into muddy puddles and now his shoes were filthy and the bottoms of his trousers were covered in splashes. *But then it will all be worthwhile if I can make Niamh see sense and get her to agree to a divorce,* he consoled himself. No doubt their meeting would be fairly uncomfortable. After all, they hadn't seen each other for years, but he'd turn on the old charm and perhaps then she would see that what he was suggesting made sense for both of them. At last he came to the farmyard where he saw a woman with a mouthful of wooden clothes pegs clipping wet washing to a line that was strung across the yard. He headed towards her, keeping his smile firmly in place.

'Mrs Carey?'

At the sound of his voice she started and almost dropped the sheet she'd lifted from the clothes basket. She obviously hadn't seen him coming. She spat out the pegs but before she could answer him a tall, powerful-looking man appeared out of a large building on the other side of the yard and stared at the newcomer curiously. Samuel knew that he certainly wouldn't like to upset him and he stuck out his hand. Liam was sturdy and thickset with hands like hams, and as he guessed who the visitor was, his face set into a frown. Ignoring the proffered hand, he asked curtly, 'What are you doing here? You're not welcome.'

Samuel swallowed before fixing a smile to his face. 'I haven't come to cause any trouble,' he said faintly. 'I just wish to see my wife.'

He saw Liam and the woman exchange a worried glance and guessed that this must be Liam's wife, Shelagh.

'Why would you want to see her now after all this time?'

Samuel kept his smile firmly in place. 'Well, I rather think that's between Niamh and me, but I promise I haven't come to upset her. If I may just talk to her I'll be on my way again. I've no wish to stay.'

'Well, you got that right at least,' Liam growled in an uncharacteristically vicious tone. 'You're not wanted here so clear off now – or do I have to help you go with my toe up your arse?'

'Liam, please!' The woman hurried across to him and took his arm but he gently shook her off.

'Leave this to me, lass,' he told her. 'If this piece of scum thinks he can turn up here out of the blue to upset me niece he can think again.'

'I told you – I haven't come to upset her.' Samuel began to lose his temper. 'But it is important that I see her, if you please, and I have no intention of leaving here until I do!'

Liam shook his head and stood his ground between Samuel and the farmhouse door. 'Then you'll have a long wait, laddie. Niamh don't live here any more. Hasn't for a long time.'

Samuel's mouth gaped open. 'What do you mean, she doesn't live here? Where is she then?'

'Far enough away for you never to be able to find her, so sling your hook or I'll help you leave, so I will!'

Sensing that he would get no more out of Liam, Samuel turned to the man's wife. 'Will *you* tell me where she is?' he asked in a more reasonable tone. Normally his charm and good looks never failed to work on the ladies but it was having no effect whatsoever on her. If anything, she was looking at him as if he was something disgusting that she had stepped on in the farmyard.

'Like Liam said, she's gone as far away from you as she can get. And can you blame her, after the way you treated the poor lass?'

Another man appeared from the cow sheds then and Samuel recognised Dilly Carey's son, Declan. He came to stand at Liam's side and glowered at him.

'What's he want?' he asked shortly as his hands clenched into fists.

Liam snorted. 'He wants Niamh,' he answered.

'He'll see me sister again over my dead body.' Declan took a step towards him, his whole demeanour threatening, and Samuel realised then that he was on a fruitless mission. He'd get nothing out of any of these, which meant he'd come all this way for nothing. Turning about, he cast a scathing glance over his shoulder and strode away gathering together what pride he could. He'd be damned if he'd beg them for information; it would have fallen on deaf ears anyway.

Again he found the cab driver snoozing at the top of the lane and after climbing into the back seat and slamming the door, Samuel roused him and said, 'Hey, you! Get me back to the ferry in Dublin and as quickly as you can.'

Bad-tempered young divil! the cabbie thought. It was about time someone taught him some manners, but he didn't reply, he merely jammed the old jalopy into gear and rattled on his way.

*

Samuel arrived back in Nuneaton in a thoroughly bad humour. He'd had a lot of time to think on the way home. If Niamh had moved away, the Carey woman must have known about it, and so must his father – so why hadn't they told him? She was still his wife, after all, even if it was in name only.

He set off for Dilly's house at a brisk pace, his temper adding speed to his steps. She'd damn well tell him where Niamh was tonight, even if he had to shake it out of her. Outside her residence he stood for a moment and stared up at it. It was a very imposing house – not bad at all for a former maid!

After pounding on the front door he fumed as he waited for it to be answered.

'Yes, can I 'elp yer, lad?' Nell asked.

Pushing her aside, he strode along the hallway to a room at the far end of it where light showed from beneath a door. He pushed it so hard that it banged back against the wall and danced on its hinges – and there was Dilly, sitting at the side of the fire as if she hadn't a care in the world whilst he had just returned from a fool's errand.

'Where is she?' he growled.

'Wh-where is who?' Dilly looked startled and well she might after the way he had barged in.

'Your bitch of a daughter!' Samuel's eyes were sparking fire. 'I've just been all the way to Ireland only to be told she doesn't live there any more. So where is she?'

Dilly's chin rose in defiance although he noted that her hands were trembling. 'Where Niamh chooses to live is no concern of yours.'

'Oh yes, it bloody well is – until I can get her to agree to a divorce. Now tell me, woman, or I swear I'll shake it out of you if I have to.'

He'd only advanced one step towards her when a

warning voice told him, 'I don't think you will, laddie. Has no one ever taught you that it's wrong to bully women?'

Samuel swung about to be confronted by a tall grey-haired chap standing across the other side of the room by the table. Nell had gone to stand beside him and he could feel her resentment towards him coming off her in waves. The chap was elderly, but still strong and more than capable of handling himself by the looks of him.

'Now I suggest you leave straight away else I might have to chuck you out on your arse on the pavement – an' you wouldn't like that, now would you? Furthermore I'll warn you that if I see you anywhere near here again, I shall teach you a lesson you won't forget in a hurry.'

Samuel's hands balled into fists of frustration as he turned and stamped back the way he'd come, his cheeks flaming with humiliation.

All in all, it had been a bad day from start to finish and he was no nearer to getting his divorce than he had been – further away if anything because he didn't even know where Niamh was living now.

Inside, Archie patted Dilly's arm. She was clearly shaken.

'Who the hell was that nasty piece o' work, lass?' he asked, and dreaded to think what might have happened to Dilly had he not been there.

'It was Max's son, Samuel Farthing,' she said with a catch in her voice.

'Ah, Nell's told me all about him.' Archie shook his head. 'He's the black sheep o' the family ain't he?'

'You could say that.' Dilly swallowed hard as she tried to regain her composure. 'A long time ago he raped my daughter . . .' Tears sprang to her eyes. She had just witnessed the vicious side of Samuel and could only imagine how terrifying it must have been for her dear girl on the night he had attacked her. 'After the rape she discovered she was pregnant,' she went on in a wobbly voice. 'And Max made him do what he thought was the right thing and marry her. At the time we both thought it would be for the best . . .' Tears rained down her cheeks. 'If only I'd known what a beast he really was I would never have let her marry him. He made Niamh's life hell on earth, and after Connie, their little daughter, died Niamh went to live in Ireland with my in-laws.'

'I see,' Archie said gravely.

Nell nodded at Dilly and she went on, 'Before Samuel raped Niamh she had an understanding with Ben, a young man my in-laws had adopted. Now she's living with him in New York and they have a little son. But it appears that Samuel wants to track her down now. I think he's going to try and bully her into giving him a divorce.'

'Well, rest assured he'll not learn where she is from me,' Archie said stoically. 'An' if he shows his face round here again I'll knock his bloody block off – oh, sorry for swearin' in front of a lady.'

'Oh Archie, I'm no lady. I used to scrub and clean and wait on tables for the Farthings before I opened my first little shop.'

'Pardon me fer sayin', but as far as I'm concerned, you're more of a lady than some o' them that were born wi' a silver spoon in their mouths,' Archie said. 'My Nell's told me what a true friend you've been to her over the years an' I'm grateful to you for that.'

'It worked both ways,' Dilly informed him. 'There have been times when I really don't know how I would have coped without Nell, especially when my children were all younger.'

As Archie and Nell exchanged a loving glance, Dilly felt

a lump form in her throat. She had a feeling that she might not have Nell for much longer and the thought of being completely alone again saddened her, not that she begrudged Nell her happiness.

'Well, let's try an' forget him for now, eh?' Archie suggested then with a wink at Nell. 'How about a nice milky cup o' cocoa, eh, gel? There's nowt like it to make yer feel better.'

With a last concerned glance at Dilly, Nell nodded before bustling away to warm some milk.

'Archie, can I ask you a favour?' Dilly said then.

'Of course, anythin', lass.'

'Would you mind very much not mentioning Samuel's visit this evening? I wouldn't want it to get back to Max. Samuel has caused him enough heartache over the years as it is and he'd be so angry if he knew he'd been here upsetting me.'

'Mum's the word,' Archie promised, tapping the side of his nose, and once again Dilly thought what a thoroughly nice man he was.

Chapter Thirty-Five

'Are you sure she's all right?' Seamus asked Bessie as they stood at the side of Primrose's cot on a blustery October evening. Outside, the wind was blowing a gale but inside the nursery, all was warm and cosy.

'The doctor assured me it's nothin' more than a cold,' Bessie told him in a whisper. 'I've just put that bowl o' steamin' water on the floor by the cot to get some moisture into the air so she can breathe easier.'

'You really are marvellous with her,' Seamus said as he gazed tenderly down on his little daughter. Every time he looked at her he saw Mary, and he thanked God for her every single day. As long as he had Primrose, his Mary would never be truly gone from him. 'I don't know what I'd have done without you these last months,' he admitted and Bessie chuckled softly.

'It's been my pleasure carin' for this little one, I can promise you. I think I love her almost as much as you do.

Carin' fer her beats nursin' any day o' the week an' I never thought I'd hear meself say that.'

In actual fact, Bessie loved living with Seamus full stop. He was easy to get along with and she was relaxed in his company. He worked long hours now. Dilly had promoted him to manager and although she now had a huge team of seamstresses who kept her shops stocked with her designs, as well as a number of drivers to deliver them, Seamus was still kept on his toes travelling from one establishment to the next, overseeing everything and checking that none of the staff were off sick. When this occurred he'd been known to step into their shoes if need be, and strangely the women clients didn't seem to mind a man serving them. It just went to show how times were changing. Dilly was now a very well-known designer and Seamus was understandably proud of his mother, although he sometimes wished that she wouldn't drive herself so hard. When she wasn't working she spent as much time as she possibly could with Jessica and Primrose and she spoiled them shamelessly. She even designed their clothes and had her seamstresses run them up, and people often commented on how lovely the little girls always looked. Seamus paid Bessie a modest salary, which he often offered to raise but she wouldn't hear of it.

'What do I need any more for?' she'd ask with raised eyebrows. 'I've got me board and keep as well as the money my Malcolm left me safely tucked away in the bank. No, if you've any cash goin' spare, put it away for Primrose when she's older. I've more than enough for my needs.'

So eventually Seamus gave up offering and accepted that she was happy as she was.

Now as they tiptoed from the room she told him, 'I've got your dinner keepin' warm in the oven. I wasn't sure what time you'd be home.'

He sighed happily. Bessie was a very good cook. 'How many times must I tell you that you don't have to worry about cooking for me?' he asked.

She shrugged. 'While I'm cookin' fer me an' the little 'un it's no trouble to do a bit extra. A man should have a hot dinner waitin' for him when he gets home after a hard day's work.'

Once he'd sat down, she presented him with a plateful of lamb chops, mashed potatoes and mushrooms, and despite what he'd said he cleared the plate in minutes and was looking around for some pudding.

'I was thinkin' we ought to decide what we're goin' to get Primmy for Christmas,' Bessie remarked as she put down a bowl of her home-cooked apple pie and a jug of thick yellow custard.

At mention of Christmas, Seamus frowned. It would be his first without Mary and he was dreading it. Had he been alone he would have locked himself away and cancelled everything, but he knew he couldn't do that for his daughter's sake. He wanted her to remember Christmases as happy times.

'I know what yer thinkin', lad.' Bessie laid a gentle hand on his arm. 'It's hard fer me too at this time o' the year when I think back to the too few Christmases I spent wi' my Malcolm. He used to spoil me rotten, God bless his soul.'

She sat down next to him and for a few moments they were both lost in their memories. They had both lost the loves of their lives, which was what made them so easy with each other. They knew how the other was feeling and understood.

'Perhaps we should invite yer mammy round fer Christmas dinner?' Bessie said thoughtfully. 'I've a feelin' Nell will spend the day with Archie an' I wouldn't like to think of Dilly all alone.' She chuckled then. 'Atween you an' me I wouldn't be surprised if we heard weddin' bells before too much longer. Nell an' Archie are gettin' on like Darby and Joan accordin' to Dilly.'

'Well, good luck to them, that's what I say,' Seamus responded, then becoming serious he added tentatively, 'Does it bother you, Bessie – the rumours that are still going around about you and me living together?'

'Does it hell as like!' she snorted. 'You an' I know the truth of it. You loved your Mary an' I loved my Malcolm. Ain't nobody could take their places fer either of us. You've got your bedroom an' I've got mine an' it's as simple as that – so let 'em get on with their gossipin', that's what I say!'

He looked relieved. Sometimes he felt guilty because Bessie centred her whole life around his little daughter. He'd often told her that she was welcome to come and go as she pleased when he was at home, but she seemed quite content to stay in.

'Where would I be gallivantin' off to at my age?' she'd replied. 'No, thanks very much but I'm quite happy at the side o' the fire knittin' and listenin' to the wireless. I do enjoy me Thursday afternoons round at Mr Farthing's though. Primmy loves playin wi' George an' Jessica when they get home from school, an' they're ever so good with her, gentle as lambs. I called in to see Mrs Pegs today as it happens, after I'd taken Primmy to the doctor's, and she gave me some bad news. It seems that Oscar's wife Penelope has lost the baby she was carryin'.'

'Really? Then I'm very sorry to hear that,' Seamus said genuinely. It would be God help poor Oscar now though, if he knew anything about it. Penelope had really wanted that child and no doubt she'd take the loss out on her husband. Poor bloke, he couldn't seem to do right for doing wrong.

'Anyway, enough sad talk. Any suggestions on what we should get Primmy for Christmas?' Bessie reminded him, and for the next half an hour or so they tossed ideas at each other.

'There won't be enough room in Santa's sleigh for all that lot,' Bessie joked eventually. 'An' she ain't even a year old yet so perhaps we'd better narrow it down a bit, eh?'

At that moment, Primmy woke up and began to wail and they almost collided with each other in the stairs doorway as they rushed to tend to her.

At that precise moment, Samuel was standing outside in the marketplace in the howling wind with his hands pushed deep into his coat pockets and his hat pulled low over his eyes waiting for Roger Bannerman to appear. It was payday and Roger knew better than to be late.

Before long, Samuel saw Roger hurrying towards him, glancing nervously to either side of him to make sure no one was watching.

'Here.' He grudgingly thrust a note into Samuel's hand and made to turn away. As far as Roger was concerned, they had nothing to say to each other.

'Just wait a minute,' Samuel snapped. He didn't like Roger's attitude one little bit.

Roger paused and knowing he had the upper hand, Samuel grinned as he thrust the money into his pocket. 'I was thinking that I'm letting you off too lightly,' he said, peering at Roger's face in the glow of the street lamp. 'I reckon next month we should make it twenty-five pounds.'

Roger visibly paled. 'Now hold on a minute,' he objected. 'I'm not rich, you know. It's hard enough trying to account to my wife where the twenty has gone. I reckon she thinks I've suddenly developed a gambling addiction.'

Samuel shrugged. 'Not my problem, old chap,' he

responded affably. 'See you the same time next month. And don't forget, it'll be a fiver extra next time.'

He sauntered away then, whistling merrily as Roger stood there fuming. It was true – he was not a rich man – comfortably off, admittedly, because he worked for his father-in-law, but Miranda's father only owned a printing works in Corporation Street. He was nowhere near as wealthy as Samuel's father who seemed to have his finger in all sorts of pies. Stepping into the shadows, Roger sagged against the wall. What was he to do? The extra money would have to come from somewhere. And then it occurred to him. On certain days of the week he was on the counter serving the customers. He would have to steal some of the cash flow, just a little at a time so it wouldn't be missed. Roger was all too aware that he had his faults, but stealing wasn't one of them and the idea was abhorrent to him – but then how else was he to raise the money? He had no doubt at all that Samuel would carry out his threat of telling Miranda about his affair with Olivia if he didn't meet his demands. The chap was rotten to the core. Feeling thoroughly dejected, he set off for home.

'I'm so sorry, Oscar,' Olivia told him sincerely when she came in from her shift at the hospital to find her brother sitting with their father in the drawing room. She was still in her nurse's uniform and she slid her cape from her shoulders and looked at him with concern.

Oscar had called in earlier in the day and left a message with Mrs Pegs but he'd wanted to come and tell his father personally.

'It was just one of those things, the doctor said. Probably just nature's way of getting rid of something that wasn't quite right. Penelope doesn't think that though. As usual it's all my fault, although I don't quite know what I've done that might have caused it.'

'You didn't do anything,' Max told him as he tipped another shot of brandy into Oscar's glass. His son looked like he could do with it. 'But you have to remember that Penelope will be grieving and she'll lash out at anyone. Just try to be patient with her.'

'Huh! That's easier said than done,' Oscar scoffed. 'Another maid walked out today because my wife threw a glass of water at her. That's the third in as many months.'

Olivia stared at him sympathetically. She hated the thought of Penelope carrying Oscar's child but she would never have wished for this to happen.

'It's ironic, isn't it?' Oscar sighed. 'There's Penelope who gave birth to George as if she was shelling peas and then loses this one. Then Dilly told me the other day that her daughter-in-law in Ireland who has never managed to carry a child to term is still going strong. Not that I'd want her to come to any harm,' he added hastily.

'Yes, I'm aware of that,' Max responded, pouring a small sherry for Olivia. 'Roddy is really excited about the new addition by all accounts, bless him. And now that Roisin is over five months things are looking more hopeful, although Dilly says Roisin and Declan are still trying not to raise their hopes.'

As if talk of her had conjured her up from thin air, Dilly breezed in at that moment. She was clearly very pleased about something, if her smile was anything to go by, but the instant she saw Oscar it vanished. 'I'm so sorry about the baby, Oscar,' she said immediately. 'Please give my condolences to Penelope.'

'Thank you, Dilly. I will.'

'All right, that's enough sad talk for now,' Max said then, hoping to take his son's mind off things. 'What were you looking so happy about when you came in, Dilly? You were beaming like a Cheshire cat.'

'Well, as it happens something quite exciting has happened,' she admitted, failing to keep the delight from her voice. 'I heard from Rosalie Crosby a while back – you know, the woman who handles and sells my designs in New York? She asked me to design a new collection of ladies' nightwear for her some time ago so I posted twenty designs on to her and today I heard that the factory delivered them to her stores as a completely new line, and they are selling as fast as they go on the shelves. It was a new departure for me too, and I've had to learn a lot in a very short time, but it's been very rewarding. I spoke to Philip on the telephone this evening and he wants to try something similar in London now. Of course it will mean burning the midnight oil to design a completely different collection, but it's wonderful news, isn't it?'

'It's just brilliant, well done,' Olivia said, planting a gentle kiss on her cheek.

'And that's not all,' Dilly rushed on breathlessly. 'Rosalie also informed me that Florian Lefèvre, who owns a number of well-known fashion houses in Paris, visited one of her stores in New York recently and he wishes to meet me to discuss the possibility of me doing some designs for him!'

The others congratulated her too but Dilly couldn't help but notice that Max didn't look overly thrilled at the news.

Some time later, Oscar left and Olivia went upstairs for a bath, and now that they were alone Dilly asked Max, 'Aren't you happy with my good news?'

'Well . . . of course I'm pleased for you,' he answered cagily. 'But are you sure you want to take on all this new work? I would have thought you were doing too much already.'

Dilly straightened her back in the way he'd come to

know so well. 'I appreciate your concern for my well-being but I'm not quite in my dotage just yet,' she informed him primly. 'If I didn't know you better I might suspect that you were jealous!'

'Don't be so ridiculous,' he said, far more sharply than he had intended to. 'You know damn well I only worry about you overdoing it. After all you're working flat out to fulfil the orders you already have. New York, London – and now possibly Paris!'

Dilly was instantly contrite. 'I'm sorry,' she said. 'But you should know what I'm like by now and I'm too old to change. What's the saying? A leopard can't change its spots. I just seem unable to resist a challenge.'

He gave her a rueful grin then sighed, 'Whatever am I going to do with you, eh? I reckon you'll still be turning out new designs when you're a hundred!'

'I doubt I'll still be around then,' she responded, but the awkward moment was gone and they were easy with each other again.

'Even so, should you have to go to Paris to meet this Florian Lefèvre chappie I won't let you go alone,' Max said adamantly.

Dilly giggled. 'But I went to New York on my own,' she pointed out.

'Yes, you did, but the difference there was you had Niamh and Ben waiting to meet you.'

Dilly shook her head, highly amused. 'I don't think I need a chaperone at my age. I'm hardly a flighty young girl any more, and think of the gossip it would cause if you were to come with me. Why, they'd have a field day. Isn't Paris supposed to be the city of lovers?'

'Even so, I insist you allow me to accompany you. What do we care about what people say after all these years, Dilly?'

'Well, we'll see,' she said, reluctant to commit herself just yet. 'Rosalie gave me a contact number so I'll get in touch and see what exactly he has in mind. She seemed to think that Mr Lefèvre was most interested in the bridal designs and a lingerie collection . . .'

Already her head was full of possibilities and Max watched her ruefully. There really was no stopping Dilly Carey!

Chapter Thirty-Six

Early in December as Nell and Dilly sat at breakfast one morning, Nell announced sheepishly, 'I've somethin' to tell you, pet.'

'Oh yes, and what would that be?' Dilly was only half-listening as she spread some toast with marmalade. She and Max would be sailing to Paris the following week to meet Florian Lefèvre and she was feeling excited and nervous about it all at the same time. Max had wanted to take a passenger flight but Dilly had refused. She wasn't quite brave enough to fly yet.

'Well, the thing is . . .'

Something about the tone of Nell's voice caught Dilly's attention then. Her old friend seemed very nervy and on edge, and she was fiddling with the fringes on the tablecloth.

'Spit it out then,' Dilly urged with a smile.

Nell gulped deeply before blurting out, 'Archie's asked me to marry 'im. We ain't getttin' any younger, see, so he

303

thought, Why not? We get on well an' he treats me like a queen. What do yer think, Dilly? Am I too old for all this lovey-dovey stuff?'

'Why, that's wonderful!' Dilly exclaimed with genuine pleasure. 'You and Archie are perfect together and of course you're not too old. You go ahead and tell him yes as soon as you can. Archie is a lovely man and I'm thrilled for you both.'

'He is lovely,' Nell blushed. 'But . . . well what will *you* do? What I mean is, if I marry Archie he'll no doubt want me to move into his house with him, although it's only rented. I worry about you being alone.'

'I'd be perfectly all right . . . although there is another option,' Dilly said thoughtfully. 'How would Archie feel about moving in with us? He's here half the time anyway doing the garden and odd jobs about the place, and I know how much you love this house. You've done far more to it than I have and we all rub along together, don't we? It's not as if you'd see much of me anyway. I'm locked away in my studio half the time.'

Nell was touched by Dilly's thoughtfulness. She did love the house. That was the only disadvantage to marrying Archie that she could see: the fact that she would have to leave it – and Dilly, of course.

'I could put the idea to him and see how he feels about it,' she said slowly.

Dilly grinned. It seemed that love was in the air. Only the day before, she'd received an invitation to Philip Maddison and Deborah March's wedding in the spring. He'd clearly taken Dilly's advice when she'd told him that Deborah would be perfect for him and now they were going to be married. Dilly couldn't have been more pleased about it.

'Well, this won't get the work done, will it?' Dilly said

as she rose from the table. 'You speak to Archie about my suggestion. It would be wonderful if I could keep you here, but of course I'll completely understand if Archie prefers you to live under his own roof. Just know that I couldn't be happier for you.'

With that, Dilly headed for her workroom and Nell set off for the shop. She was only working part-time now as Seamus had recently set on a young lady to help her. The lass, who was in her early twenties, had taken to the work like a duck to water, and she and Nell got along famously. The customers liked her too, which was a huge bonus, so all in all things were working out for Nell. And not before time, Dilly thought joyously.

Dilly spent all day in her workroom not even coming out for a cup of tea. She wanted the designs she was working on for Florian Lefèvre to be perfect.

Eventually a grumbling stomach sent her to the kitchen, where she found Archie, all attired in his best bib and tucker, waiting for her.

Hand-in-hand with Nell, who stood beside him, he said self-consciously, 'I thought I'd get this out o' the way an' come an' have a word. Nell says she's told you as I've asked her to marry me. Is that all right, Dilly?'

Dilly burst out laughing. 'Why, of course it is, Archie! And I think it's the best news ever. You don't need my permission – I'm not Nell's mother, you know.'

'Even so, you've put a roof over her head an' been real good to 'er,' he said. 'She also told me about your kind offer of comin' to live 'ere.' He looked really uncomfortable now. 'An' lovely as the offer is, I'm afraid I'll have to turn it down.'

'Oh, I see.' Dilly couldn't keep the disappointment from her voice.

'The thing is, I wouldn't feel right,' he tried to explain.

'I've allus prided meself on payin' me own way in life, see? Unless o' course you'd agree to me payin' rent for me an' Nell, an' then that'd be different.'

'But there'd be no need for that,' Dilly told him, and before he could open his mouth to argue she rushed on: 'I think it's time I was honest with you. Firstly, I was being rather selfish when I made the offer. For one, I'd hate to lose Nell – she does just everything for me about the house which gives me time to work. And for two, I was thinking how useful it would be to have a live-in handyman – someone to do the odd jobs, the gardening, bring in the coal in the winter and things like that. If Nell goes, I'll have to do all that myself.' She put on her most miserable face. 'Finally, I know how much Nell loves this house. Look at it – she's chosen almost every single thing you see. I know it would hurt her to leave it but I also know she loves you to bits. Still, you have a right to do as you please, of course.'

Archie glanced at Nell, who was watching him hopefully. 'Well, I have to admit I hadn't thought of it like that,' he said slowly. 'And perhaps we could chip in, in other ways as well, perhaps by gettin' a few groceries or a bit o' coal in?'

'Oh, that would be perfect,' Dilly said, and meant it. 'This is such a big house. I'd be nervous if I was all alone in it. Having a big strapping man like you here would make me feel so much safer too. Look at the way you handled Samuel that evening. What would I have done if I'd been here all by myself?' She gave a dramatic little shudder and Archie was won over.

Nell meantime was smothering a grin with her hand. Nervous on her own indeed! Dilly was one of the strongest women she knew.

Archie's chest puffed with importance as he replied. 'In that case, I'd be happy to accept your very kind offer,' and

Nell yelped with joy. It would truly have broken her heart to leave this house that she had made into a home, although if she'd had to make the choice between the house and Archie, he would, of course, have come first.

'It's a deal then,' Dilly said happily. 'So when is the wedding to be?'

'How about early in March?' Nell suggested. 'That will give us plenty of time to get rid of your things.'

Archie's face dropped. He and his late wife had lived in their home since they'd been married, and the furniture and the knick-knacks they'd acquired over the years held sentimental value for him.

'I think I have a solution to that too,' Dilly piped up, seeing his expression. 'There are still empty rooms here. Why don't you bring everything with you, Archie, and make those rooms into yours and Nell's? We could each have our own sitting rooms and bedrooms then, and that would give us all a little more privacy. We'd have to share the kitchen, of course.'

'What a crackin' idea.' Nell's face was alight with excitement. 'We've always used the kitchen as our dinin' room,' she told Archie, 'so we could use the empty dinin' room as our lounge fer a start-off.'

Dilly looked on indulgently as Nell rattled off her plans to Archie, then as her stomach rumbled ominously again she went to help herself to a portion of the delicious home-made fish and potato pie that Nell had been keeping warm for her. There was little chance of Max calling in that evening. He'd informed her the night before that he was going to visit Lawrence and his family this evening so after a slice of Nell's lemon meringue pie she'd treat herself to a leisurely soak in the bath and have an early night. That way, the lovebirds could have some time to themselves to make their plans.

On the eve of their trip to Paris, Dilly flew into a panic.

'What if Florian doesn't like my designs?' she fretted to Max.

'Of course he will. Everyone likes your designs. That's why he's invited you to Paris,' he pointed out sensibly.

The clothes that Dilly planned to take with her were laid out across the back of a chair all ready to pack into the suitcase Nell had placed ready. She'd insisted that Dilly shouldn't pack them until the eleventh hour so that they wouldn't get too creased.

'And what if my clothes aren't right? I've heard the women in Paris are very chic!' Dilly wailed.

Nell, who was busily ironing a silk blouse that the seamstresses had made for Dilly especially for the trip, rolled her eyes. 'Will you just hark at yourself!' she scolded. 'You could wear a paper bag an' still look smart. Fer goodness sake stop your worritin' – everythin' will be fine.'

'Yes, yes – of course it will,' Dilly agreed, getting a grip on herself. She was acting like a silly girl about to embark on her first date and suddenly felt foolish.

There was a tap on the door then and Archie appeared. 'By heck! It's enough to freeze the hairs off a brass monkey out there,' he told them, stamping his feet. 'I wouldn't be surprised if we didn't 'ave some snow afore much longer.' Then, looking towards Dilly: 'All ready to go are yer, lass?'

'She won't be goin' anywhere if she don't calm herself down,' Nell grumbled as she swiped the iron up and down the sleeve of the blouse. 'She'll be givin' 'erself a blooming heart attack at this rate.'

Archie chuckled. He knew how much Nell thought of Dilly and that she'd miss her while she was away.

'I think I'll just go and check on the samples again,'

Dilly said suddenly and disappeared off into her workroom before any of them could say a word.

Dilly had had the seamstresses make up some of the designs she would be taking to Paris so that she could show Monsieur Lefèvre the finished products. They were absolutely perfect as far as Nell could see but still Dilly was panicking that they wouldn't be good enough.

'Eeh, I'm so relieved that you're goin' with her,' she confided to Max. 'She's got herself worked up into a right old state an' no mistake.'

'She'll be fine with me,' Max promised. He was actually quite looking forward to the trip, if truth be known. Lawrence and Oscar would manage his businesses for him while he was gone and it would be nice to spend some time alone with Dilly without all the family commitments they each had.

Glancing at his watch, he rose and started to put his coat on. 'Well, I'm off,' he told Nell and Archie. 'We've a very early start in the morning. Try to make Dilly get some sleep, would you?'

'Huh! I'll do me best,' Nell said darkly. 'But I might have to resort to knockin' her on the head wi' a hammer to calm her down tonight.'

The journey had been enjoyable, the crossing on the ship calm, and now as Dilly stared from the cab window on the way to the hotel Max had booked for them she was gripped by excitement.

'I can't believe we're in Paris!' she told him, as excited as a child, and Max grinned. He loved to see her like this.

'So where are we staying?' she asked, still gazing from the window. She didn't want to miss a thing.

'The Hotel d'Angleterre on the rue Jacob,' he told her as he fished in his overcoat pocket for their reservations booking form. 'It was built in the eighteenth century according to the research I did, and writers and royalty have stayed there over the years.'

'Fancy that.' Dilly was in awe. Paris was a hive of activity with little cafés dotted all along the main roads. Tables and chairs were placed outside them for sightseers, but none of them were taken at present. People preferred to go inside at this time of the year, out of the cold. Dilly was enjoying herself immensely. She was also very pleased that she'd agreed to Max coming with her and had been more than impressed when he'd given the cab driver the address of their hotel in French.

'I wasn't aware that you could speak French,' she'd commented, astounded, and Max had laughed and tapped the side of his nose.

'Ah well, there's still a lot you don't know about me,' he'd informed her with a gleam in his eye. And now here they were cruising through the streets of Gay Paree: it was like a dream come true.

'What time is Monsieur Lefèvre coming to collect you in the morning?' Max asked and Dilly had to drag her eyes away from the sight of the River Seine. She was shocked at the width of it.

'About ten o'clock.'

'Ah, then we'll have a leisurely meal this evening and then go for a stroll if you won't be too cold?' Max offered solicitously.

'I can wrap up and I'd love it,' Dilly told him. They were only going to be here for a couple of days and she wanted to see as much of the city as she could.

The hotel impressed Dilly no end. She gazed around, drinking it all in. The foyer was enormous, and a large, highly polished staircase rose from one end up to a huge galleried landing. The carpet underfoot was so thick that she felt as if she was sinking into it, and expensive flocked wallpaper covered the walls.

Max collected their keys from the desk, again addressing the receptionist in perfect French, and then a porter with their luggage on a long trolley directed them to the lift. It was late afternoon by then and Max thought Dilly might be tired after the long journey but she was as excited as a child on a Sunday-school outing.

'Perhaps you'd like a short rest before we go down to dinner?' he suggested but Dilly shook her head.

'Oh no, really – I'm fine.'

They were following the porter along a labyrinth of corridors but at last he stopped and bowed.

'Madame.' He opened the door and Dilly stepped into a room that made her gasp with pleasure. It was decorated in shades of cream and lilac, and a huge bowl of fresh-cut flowers stood on a small table, filling the room with their scent.

Max grinned. 'Glad you came?'

'I certainly am, and this is only the beginning.'

'Good. Well, I'll go and get changed and then I'll come and collect you for dinner.'

The second he was gone Dilly unpacked the precious samples of her designs and hung them in the huge yew-wood wardrobe. Nell had gone to so much trouble to make sure that they were pressed perfectly that Dilly didn't want to let her down. In just a few hours now she would be showing them to Monsieur Lefèvre. She did a little skip of pure joy before heading for the luxurious marble en-suite bathroom to prepare for dinner.

An hour later, looking very smart in a new pin-striped suit bought especially for the trip, Max tapped at Dilly's door. There was no answer so he knocked again, a little louder this time. Still no answer, so he gingerly tried the door. It was unlocked so he stepped into the room and saw Dilly, sprawled across the bed in her dressing robe, snoring softly.

He crept over to her and gazed down at her slumbering face, thinking he had never seen her look so beautiful and wondering as he had many times before, what it would be like to wake up beside her each morning. Then with a sigh he gentled a strand of copper hair from her flushed cheek, pulled the satin eiderdown over her and backed out of the room. She was tired out from the journey and all the anticipation; it would be wise to let her rest. He knew she would want to look her best for tomorrow.

Tonight, Max Farthing would be dining alone.

Chapter Thirty-Seven

When Dilly answered Max's knock on the door the next morning she flushed guiltily. 'I'm so sorry about last night,' she began. 'I didn't realise I was so—'

'You don't have to apologise.' He smiled tenderly at her. 'You were worn out and I didn't like to disturb you.'

She was looking positively radiant today so he assumed that the sleep had done her a power of good. He held out his arm and she tucked hers into it, then after locking her door they went downstairs for breakfast. Dilly thought she would be starving after missing dinner the evening before but she was so nervous the food seemed to stick in her throat, although Max ate enough for both of them.

'Now would you prefer it if I stayed here while you go off to visit Monsieur Lefèvre's shops?'

Dilly looked horrified at the very idea. 'Oh no! What if he talks to me in French? I won't understand what he's saying. *Please* come with me, Max.'

'Of course.' Max patted her hand and told her sternly, 'Now eat something, or you'll make yourself ill.'

Dilly frowned down at the pancake on her plate and whispered, 'I've never heard of having pancakes for breakfast.'

Max chuckled. 'This is a continental breakfast, my dear, and quite delicious if you'd only try it. And by the way, that dress you're wearing is perfectly lovely. One of your own designs, I assume?'

She nodded self-consciously. The dress was in a deep burgundy colour in a very fine woollen material with a cream draped neckline and cream cuffs on the long sleeves. It had a dropped waistline, which was also decorated with a cream sash, and one of the straighter skirts that were so popular at the moment.

'Thank you. It's one of the designs I've brought to show Monsieur Lefèvre. This style is selling really well in London.'

In her local shops she tended to stock the budget-priced clothes that the hardworking Midlands folk could afford, but for Monsieur Lefèvre she had used only the very finest of materials for her samples.

'He'll be here in three-quarters of an hour,' she said suddenly, glancing at the clock on the dining-room wall.

'Then we have plenty of time for another cup of coffee,' Max answered calmly. He was determined not to let her get flustered.

Eventually they made their way upstairs again and Dilly collected her coat and the cloche hat she'd had made especially for the journey. Staring into the mirror, she positioned it at a jaunty angle, then after collecting the case containing her samples and sketches she went back down to the foyer to wait for Monsieur Lefèvre. Max was already there, lounging on one of the comfortable leather sofas reading a French newspaper.

314

'How will we know him? How will he know us, if it comes to that?' she asked suddenly as panic started to build again.

With a sigh Max placed the paper down. 'He will go to the reception desk and I've told them where we're sitting,' he said. 'And now what I want you to do is just enjoy the experience. What's the worst that can happen? If he doesn't like your designs you're no worse off than you were yesterday, but I'm sure he will, so just be yourself.'

She nodded and straightened her back just as a fat balding man who was impeccably dressed swept into the foyer. He was quite short for a man and not at all what Dilly had expected. Dilly had always imagined Frenchmen to be tall, dark and handsome – but somehow she just knew that this was Monsieur Lefèvre. She was proved to be right when after a word with the beautiful girl on reception he turned and walked towards them. He smiled, making his waxed handlebar moustache go all of a quiver. He was very plump and older than she'd expected too, but his smile seemed to stretch from ear to ear.

'Madame Carey?' he asked in a strong French accent when he came to a halt in front of them.

Max was proud of her as Dilly rose gracefully from her seat and extended her hand. She had her professional head on now and there was not a single sign of nerves in sight.

Monsieur Lefèvre took the proffered hand and bowing dramatically, he kissed it soundly. Then turning to Max he held out his hand and said, 'Bonjour, Monsieur Carey.'

'Oh, but Max isn't—' Dilly tried to explain.

But Monsieur Lefèvre was already ushering them towards the door. He clearly thought that Max was her husband, much to the latter's obvious amusement.

'You must call me Florian,' he told Dilly, gripping her

elbow tightly. 'And may I call you Dilly? It eez such a pretty name, *non*? My driver is outside waiting to take us to my fashion 'ouse.'

Max trotted along behind them carrying the case containing the samples. Dilly glanced helplessly at him over her shoulder. Monsieur Lefèvre might not be very big in stature but he was clearly used to getting his own way. Once in the car, the Frenchman pointed out places of interest to them as they sped along before asking Dilly, 'How long are you staying? You will be doing some sightseeing before returning – yes?'

'I'm afraid not. We're going home tomorrow.'

'Oh, zat is too bad.' He shook his head. 'Paris is the citee for lovers – you should 'ave stayed longer and enjoyed yourselves.' Dilly felt herself blush as Florian Lefèvre gave Max a cheeky wink.

Soon they were travelling through the centre with luxurious shops lining the streets either side of them.

'Ah, here we are!' Florian stepped out of the car once the driver had pulled into the kerb and gallantly helped Dilly get out too.

Her mouth gaped open as she gazed at his establishment. This was no mere shop, it was more like an emporium and was at least three floors high. Expensive-looking clothes on mannequins were displayed in the windows either side of huge double doors that had *Maison Lefèvre* emblazoned above them in gold lettering.

For the life of her, Dilly couldn't think of a single thing to say. She was speechless. Even the shops in New York could not compare to this. Counters were dotted about with immaculately dressed young women standing behind them, selling perfumes, cosmetics, hats and scarves all the colours of the rainbow and all made of the sheerest chiffon or real silk.

'Why – it's out of this world,' she finally managed to squeak.

His chest puffed with pride, Florian led them towards a lift where a smart young man in a braided uniform waited, his hands behind his back and his legs apart as if he was standing to attention.

'Which floor, monsieur Lefèvre?' he asked his employer in French as they all got inside. And suddenly they were rising swiftly, leaving Dilly's stomach on the ground floor. When a bell tinkled and the lift stopped she was relieved to step out of it. On this floor, day dresses and coats were displayed along one side and ladies' lingerie on the other.

'The third floor eez for my bridal gowns and what you say . . . ballgowns and ze cocktail dresses. But come, we will go up there later. First I wish to see your designs, madame.' Florian escorted his visitors through a door hidden behind a thick velvet curtain and into what proved to be a rather magnificent office.

It's a far cry from my workroom, Dilly said to herself as she thought of the old table back at home that was always covered in sketches. This room contained a splendid desk that took up the whole of the centre of the space. It was so highly polished Dilly could see her face in it, and in front of it was an enormous leather chair.

'Theez is my sanctuary,' Florian informed them airily. 'Come. See the *magnifique* view from my window.'

Dilly peered out, her eyes stretched wide. She could even glimpse the Eiffel Tower in the distance and the city of Paris lay sprawled far beneath her. It was a sight she would never forget.

'But now . . . eez 'ow you say? Time to get down to ze business? *Oui?* But first we must 'ave a leetle apéritif.'

He crossed to a mahogany drinks cabinet and took out a carafe of red wine and three sparkling cut-glass goblets.

317

It was a little early in the day for Dilly to be drinking, but not wishing to appear rude she took the proffered glass.

'*Sauté!* It is good, *oui*? The grapes were grown in the vineyard of my estate. But come, I am impatient to see what you have brought for me.'

Placing her glass down carefully, Dilly began to take out the samples of clothes she had brought to show him and laid them out across the huge desk. He fingered each one thoughtfully as his other hand stroked his moustaches whilst Dilly held her breath and waited for his reaction.

'You 'ave also brought me some sketches to look at?'

Dilly nodded and laid them out on the desk beside the samples. The little Frenchman examined each one carefully. His face gave nothing away, and Dilly began to feel anxious. Happy to stay in the background, Max gave her an encouraging wink.

Eventually, their host laid the last of the sketches down and took a great swallow of his wine before turning to her and telling her gravely, 'They are *superbes*!'

Dilly could almost feel the relief throbbing through her veins.

'Now we must talk money,' he said, tipping yet more wine into her glass. 'For this one, made up, I would charge the equivalent of eleven of your Eenglish pounds in my shop.' He pointed to one of the dress designs that was made up in a flat crepe. 'And for this silk one the cost would be equivalent to fifteen of your pounds. Each of your designs would have your name on the label,' he went on as her heart began to race with excitement.

'So now,' he concluded, 'we will come to an agreement on price – *oui*? And when our business is done I insist that you both let me take you out to lunch to seal ze deal.'

'That would be wonderful,' Dilly agreed and as the bartering began she was once again pleased that she'd taken Max along. Converting the French currency into pounds was quite beyond her but Max had everything in hand.

An hour later, they had worked out an agreement that suited all parties and Florian Lefèvre and Dilly shook hands.

'The designs are fresh,' he told her approvingly. 'Fashions are changing but then so is the world. Why, this year, Charles Lindbergh flew his plane, *The Spirit of St Louis*, non-stop between Paris and New York. And in just thirty-three and a half hours! And then there's the *téléphone*. The first transatlantic call from New York to London has occurred. Imagine just lifting the receiver and being able to speak in person to someone thousands of miles away. *Incroyable, non?* Unbelievable. Were my dear *maman* still alive she would not accept such things were possible. But come, now we shall go and see ze goods on ze top floor while my secretary writes up our agreement. And then I shall take you both for a meal, the like of which you have never tasted. Mmmw!' He kissed his fingertips and Dilly grinned secretly to herself.

Dilly was totally enchanted by the outfits on offer in Florian's shop. Max was particularly interested in the Maison Lefèvre millinery department, where a huge selection of hats were displayed to their best advantage. The only department that made Dilly shudder was the furs section. Instead of beautiful fur coats, all she could see was dead animals when she looked at them – although Monsieur Lefèvre assured her that furs were big business in Paris. Rather than offend him she hid the revulsion that the sight of them evoked in her and plastered a smile on her face as he explained that ladies of fashion should never be without one. I'll never be fashionable then, Dilly thought as they moved to another section of the store. Max knew her views on this so well that he could read what she was thinking.

'And now for my *pièce de résistance*,' Monsierr Lefèvre said proudly, leading them towards large double doors on the top floor. He threw them open with a flourish, setting his double chins all aquiver. 'Theez is my viewing salon where my clients may choose their gowns at their leisure.'

Dilly found herself in a large room with enormous windows set into every wall that gave more incredible views of Paris. A raised platform ran the length of the room; it was covered in a rich red carpet. Velvet drapes at the end were like the curtains on a stage, and even as Dilly looked, they parted and a beautiful young woman swaggered through them in an exquisitely elegant evening gown. Gilt-legged chairs were dotted about on either side of the runway, and chic ladies sipping tiny cups of hot chocolate sat watching the models as they displayed Monsieur Lefèvre's most expensive creations.

'In ze spring when my seamstresses have worked their magic, zis is where your designs will be shown for my customers to choose from,' he told Dilly, and she felt a little thrill ripple all through her at the thought of it. The girl on the platform disappeared back the way she had come, to be followed mere seconds later by another model who, hand on hip, sashayed up and down as the customers watched her avidly.

'The ladies in 'ere are ze very elite of our society,' the little man explained in a whisper. 'Once they see a creation they like, they will be measured and ze creation will be made by my most experienced workers to fit zem exactly.'

Eventually they wended their way back to Florian's office and after reading the contract, which had been prepared in English, Dilly was happy to sign it.

'I feel this is just the beginning of a long and lucrative arrangement for both of us,' Monsieur Lefèvre beamed. 'I especially love ze lace basques you 'ave designed – my ladies will love them. They are so much less restricting than ze whalebone corsets our mothers once wore, and they will appeal to ze younger clientèle. But come now we must 'ave a leetle drink before we go to lunch, *oui*?' A Dubonnet, ice and lemon was produced, and Dilly began to feel a little tipsy. She'd eaten precious little since the day before and knew that it wasn't wise to drink on an empty stomach but the French seemed to drink wine like she drank tea.

The meeting with Monsieur Lefèvre had gone far better than she had hoped and when he led her and Max out to his car where the chauffeur was waiting to drive them to a restaurant, she was in a very euphoric mood. As they passed by the perfumery counter, Florian Lefèvre selected a bottle of his most expensive French perfume and insisted that Dilly should have it. She accepted it graciously. However, she knew that she would only ever wear it for special occasions; it was far too precious for everyday use.

The restaurant he took them to almost made Dilly's eyes pop out. It was the height of luxury, and the jewels and diamonds of the beautiful women who were eating there sparkled in the opulent setting.

The head waiter, who clearly knew Monsieur Lefèvre very well, immediately led them to one of the very best tables and presented Dilly with a menu written all in French.

'Please, Florian, you and Max must choose,' she implored him, hoping to avoid any embarrassment. 'I'm afraid my talents don't extend to understanding French.'

Florian chuckled and rattled off what he wanted and

the waiter disappeared, returning a few minutes later with a bottle of champagne in a silver wine bucket full of ice. He deftly opened the bottle – with a satisfying pop! – then poured them each a glass.

'To success!' their host declared, raising his glass into the air. They echoed his cry and all drank a toast. Dilly laughed as the bubbles went up her nose.

'But now Monsieur Carey, tell me a leetle about yourself,' Monsieur Lefèvre said politely when they had ordered and were eating the meal. 'I feel your wife and I 'ave neglected you during our negotiations.'

'Not at all,' Max assured him, 'But I should point out that Dilly and I aren't married. However, we have been friends for many years, which is why I persuaded her to let me come with her.'

'Not married?' Florian raised a bushy eyebrow. 'You surprise me, monsieur. You make such a lovely couple.'

Dilly blushed to the roots of her hair and almost choked on a mouthful of asparagus. 'Max has a wife,' she explained when she had got her breath back. 'But unfortunately Mrs Farthing is very ill and has been in a nursing home for some years now.' She didn't feel it was her place to tell him that Camilla was actually in a lunatic asylum.

'How very sad.' Monsieur Lefèvre regarded them both closely before shrugging his shoulders and turning the conversation skilfully to other things. 'What a great shame it is that you have to go home so quickly. There are so many wonderful sights to see in this fine city.'

'Ah well, I intend to address that this afternoon,' Max told him with a smile. 'It will have to be a whirlwind tour but we shall do our best.'

'Then be sure to visit ze Eiffel Tower and ze Notre-Dame Cathedral – and of course you must take a cruise along ze

River Seine. *Malheureusement* you don't 'ave time to see a show at ze Moulin Rouge.' He gave a cheeky wink. 'It is 'ow you say quite "risque" but per'aps next time. First let us enjoy our lunch.'

And that was exactly what they did.

After the meal, Monsieur Lefèvre insisted that his chauffeur should deliver them back to the door of the hotel, where he jumped out, caught Dilly in a bear hug, plonked a sloppy kiss on each of her cheeks and told her, 'It has been a great pleasure to meet you, madame, and I look forward to ze next time.' He then vigorously shook Max's hand.

'*Au revoir, mes chers amis* – until we meet again,' he called as he jumped back in, and highly amused, Max and Dilly waved goodbye.

'I think he is what you might term a larger-than-life character,' Max commented dryly and Dilly chuckled in agreement.

'I think you're right and that's not just referring to his girth. But come on – let's get changed into more comfortable clothes and then we'll have time to visit some of the places he recommended before it gets dark.'

Now that her business had been satisfactorily concluded, Dilly was in a frivolous mood and Max was only too happy to oblige her.

'So,' he said later as they stood gazing in awe up at the colossal Eiffel Tower, 'your designs will now be sold in New York, London and now Paris. Where do you go from here?'

Dilly said airily, 'Today Gay Paree, tomorrow the moon. Nothing is impossible if you work hard enough to achieve it.' And he suddenly saw her in his mind's eye scrubbing the hall floor on her hands and knees back in Mill House when she had worked as a maid there. She had come a

323

long, long way . . . and he was more proud of her than he could say. Dilly Carey truly was a most remarkable woman in every way.

Chapter Thirty-Eight

It was yet another Christmas morning and as Nell basted the turkey and prepared the vegetables for their dinner, Dilly sat and read through the letter she had received from Declan the day before.

We hardly dare to believe that Roisin is now over seven months pregnant. And thankfully she is finally taking things a little easier. She doesn't have much choice as she is the size of a house now and the baby keeps her awake, kicking constantly. We both pray that this is a sign that the wean is healthy, but we are still not raising our hopes too much. They have been dashed so many times before.

Unconsciously Dilly crossed her fingers and added her prayers to those of her son. She knew how much this baby would mean to them – and to Roddy too, if it came to that – but no doubt they were right to be cautious. They'd suffered so much heartache in the past.

'It's grand news, ain't it?' Nell commented as she saw Dilly rereading the letter. 'Let's just hope as nothin' goes wrong this time. God knows they deserve a bit o' happiness, God bless 'em, an' they'll make wonderful parents. Just look at young Roddy. He's been like a different child since they took him under their wings.'

'Yes, he has,' Dilly agreed. 'I'd like to have been over there for the birth, but I'm busy working on the spring collection for Monsieur Lefèvre and I daren't get behind.'

'Some things are more important than work,' Nell said sternly, as she had often done before trying to make her oldest and dearest friend see sense. 'Work'll still be here when we're pushin' up the daisies. There ain't no pockets in shrouds, yer know, pet. Yer can't take it with you.'

'I know,' Dilly agreed good-humouredly, folding the letter. 'But now let me help you. I'll do the Brussel sprouts, shall I? I know you hate that job.'

The two women worked in a compatible silence until the meal was well under way, then Nell announced, 'I reckon I'll shoot off an' get changed now, Archie will be here in a minute an' I don't want him to see me lookin' like this.'

Nell had taken a real pride in her appearance since she had met Archie and there was a spring in her step and a sparkle in her eye now. It just went to show that love could strike at any age. Dilly's thoughts turned to Max then as she fingered the gold locket he had bought her for Christmas. He had given it to her the night before, since he would be spending today with Olivia and Jessica. Dilly felt vaguely jealous. She'd been invited to join them but as always she'd been concerned about how it might look. Instead she would be having dinner with Nell and Archie, then Seamus and Bessie would be bringing Primrose round for tea. Dilly was looking forward to that. Nell had

had the Christmas pudding and the cake soaking in brandy for weeks before baking them and there was a large trifle standing all ready in the pantry.

As always at Christmas, her thoughts turned to Fergal, and then to Kian, and a lump formed in her throat as she thought of her husband lying in the churchyard in Riversley Road and their beloved son in his lonely grave in France.

Next year I will make the time to visit you, she promised Kian – and then she set about laying the table with their finest cutlery kept for special occasions.

'Oh lordy, I couldn't eat another thing,' Archie groaned as they finished Nell's delicious pudding. 'I reckon I shall be the size of a house once we're married, pet.' He winked at her affectionately. 'You're a damned fine cook.'

Dilly smiled as she watched them. They were perfect together and she knew that they were going to be happy. She felt almost envious. It had been a long time since she'd had a man to come home and cuddle up to and share her worries with. She had Max admittedly, and he was her closest friend and confidant, but it wasn't quite the same. He went home to his lonely bed each night and she stayed in her own. Still, she was very grateful for what she did have – a very healthy bank balance for a start-off. As she began to clear the dirty pots from the table after insisting that Nell and Archie should relax together by the fire, she began to ponder how she might possibly spare the time to visit Ireland and be there for the birth of Roisin and Declan's baby. If all went well, it would be a momentous time for them and she longed to share it, but the trouble was her workload was even heavier now. With a sigh she set the kettle on to boil. Somehow she would have to find a way to be there, but she couldn't worry about it today.

'A very Happy New Year, Dilly,' Max said as the chimes of Big Ben rang in the New Year on the wireless.

'Happy New Year to you too,' Dilly answered. They were standing in Dilly's lounge, opened especially for the small party Nell had persuaded her to have. Seamus was there, although Bessie had refused to leave Primrose. She was at home watching over her. Patty and Lawrence were there too, as well as Olivia and Mrs Pegs. Gwen had stayed behind to care for Jessica. Oscar had called in earlier, but had left after an hour in fear of upsetting Penelope. She was still being very temperamental, although that was nothing new. They were all used to her now and sympathised with Oscar. Nell had also invited the new young assistant who helped out in the Nuneaton shop as she'd taken her under her wing, and they were all having a very pleasant time. Dilly had half hoped that Seamus might show an interest in the girl, Cora Winters. She was a lovely lass, very attractive and in her early twenties, but apart from a polite greeting he had barely looked at her. Dilly supposed that it was far too soon after losing Mary but prayed that someone else would take his eye one day. Her son was far too nice to be alone for the rest of his life.

'So it's 1928.' Max sighed. 'Where do the years go, Dilly? It only seems like yesterday when we were young.' He shocked her when he asked, 'May I give you a New Year's kiss?'

Dilly blushed before glancing about the lounge to make sure that no one was watching them. Everyone seemed to have headed off to the kitchen so she nodded. After all, what harm could there be in a kiss? Everyone kissed everyone else on New Year's Eve to see in the New Year, didn't they?

Max lowered his head and as his lips very gently

pressed on to hers, Dilly felt as if she had fire running through her veins. Every nerve ending tingled and she wished that it could go on for ever as his arms tightened about her. But then she suddenly thought of Camilla lying all alone in her suite of rooms at Hatter's Hall and hastily drew away from him.

'I . . . er . . . had better go and make sure that everyone has a drink,' she told him, feeling ridiculously embarrassed. And then she shot from the room as if she'd been fired from a gun. Max looked on with amusement. Dilly was such a stickler for protocol – not that he would have changed a hair on her head. It was one of the many things he loved about her, although sometimes . . . just sometimes he wished that she would relax her morals a little.

In the kitchen Dilly found them all in high spirits. Now that he'd seen the New Year in, Seamus was putting his coat on ready to leave, and after seeing him on his way Dilly hastily replenished everyone's glasses, apart from Archie's, since he was now glassy-eyed.

'No more fer me, pet,' he said, staggering slightly. 'Else I'll never get meself home an' you'll wind up wi' me stayin' on yer sofa fer the night.'

Dilly chuckled but then Nell pulled her to one side to whisper, 'Dilly, askin' Cora here tonight weren't just 'cos I like the lass, although I do o' course. She's got somethin' I want yer to look at.'

'Oh?' Dilly was intrigued as she looked up to see Cora flushing prettily.

'They're nothing really,' the young woman said modestly. 'Nell spotted them in the staffroom at the shop one day and made me promise I'd show them to you, but I'm sure you won't be interested.'

'I'll be the judge of that,' Dilly answered kindly. 'But what am I supposed to look at?'

329

Cora glanced at Nell as if for support before fumbling in her bag and withdrawing a wad of paper.

'She's been workin' on some designs,' Nell piped up as Dilly took them and began to spread them out on the table, which had been scrubbed clean. 'An' I reckoned they were good enough fer you to take a look at.'

Cora cringed, looking as if she wanted to curl up and die or sink through a gap in the floor. 'They're nowhere near as good as yours but I just enjoy doing them,' she explained in a shaky voice.

'They're actually *very* good,' Dilly replied as she studied the sketches closely. 'I particularly like this one.' She pointed to a sketch of a day dress. 'And that one there is nice too.'

The girl's face broke into a smile. 'Do you really think so?' she asked incredulously.

'Yes, I do.' Dilly noted that some of the proportions weren't quite right, but the girl definitely had a flair. 'Would you mind leaving these with me so that I can have a proper look at them in the morning?'

'I'd love to,' Cora spluttered. Dilly Carey was her idol and the thought that she would spare time to look at some of her work was more than she'd ever dreamed of.

'Right, well, go and enjoy the rest of the party,' Dilly told her kindly, 'and I'll call into the shop to talk to you the day after tomorrow.'

'Oh, thank you. But I really ought to be going now. My parents will start to get worried if I don't show my face soon.'

'Then I'll walk you there,' Archie volunteered gallantly. 'I ain't havin' a young lass like you walkin' the streets all alone at this time o' the mornin' on New Year's Eve – or should I say Day now? The fresh air'll do me good.'

Nell scooted off to get their coats for them and one by

330

one the rest of the party departed with kisses and good wishes for the new year ahead.

'He's such a gentleman, ain't he, my Archie?' she sighed happily when she and Dilly were finally alone again, tidying up in the lounge. 'An' I'm right glad you agreed to look at those sketches o' Cora's. I think the girl's got somethin' there an' I wondered if you couldn't take her on as sort of an assistant to help wi' yer workload. All the big-name designers have people workin' fer 'em, don't they?'

'Yes, they do,' Dilly nodded. It was something she'd never considered before but Nell might just have hit on a very good idea. She knew for a fact that Monsieur Lefèvre had a whole team of people working on designs for his shops.

Stifling a yawn, she looked around at the empty plates and glasses strewn about the room and said ruefully, 'Let's leave all this until tomorrow, eh? I don't know about you, Nell, but I'm so tired I could sleep on a clothes horse now. And I shall certainly have a good look at that young lady's work in the morning, I promise.'

Nell yawned hugely, then clapped a hand over her mouth. 'Let's turn in then, lass. I popped a hot-water bottle into your bed earlier on so you should soon be warm an' cosy.' Glancing towards the ice on the window she shuddered and after pecking Dilly on the cheek she pottered off to bed.

Despite her late night, Nell was up with the lark the next morning and by the time Dilly arrived downstairs in her dressing robe the room was almost back to rights again.

'I told you we'd do the tidying up together,' Dilly scolded, feeling guilty. It was gone nine o'clock and she'd slept like a top.

'A lie-in don't hurt anyone now an' again, an' it didn't

331

take long. Now come an' sit down. I've just made a fresh pot o' tea.'

The two women breakfasted together then Dilly went off to get washed and changed before heading for her workroom. Once she'd studied Cora's designs properly, she was more than a little impressed – and told Nell so.

The old friends spent the day quietly at home. Nell once again cooked Dilly and Archie a wonderful meal and Dilly thanked God that Nell wouldn't be leaving her. She just couldn't manage without her now.

The following morning, Dilly set off for the shop bright and early, armed with the sketches Cora Winters had left with her. Cora was tidying up when Dilly arrived as it was a little early for customers just yet, and she looked at Dilly anxiously before asking, 'What did you think of them? My sketches, I mean.'

'I loved them.' Dilly watched the girl's face light up brighter than a ray of sunshine. 'I particularly like the flapper dresses you drew. You got the dress lengths just right. Just below the knee is very popular at present. Young women like to dance, particularly the Charleston, and they have more freedom of movement in this length. That's why coloured silk stockings to match the dresses are so popular right now – and of course, the new synthetic fabrics are so much lighter and move so much better when women walk. I'm very pleased indeed with your work – so much so that I have a proposition to put to you. How would you like me to train you? You could still work in the shop part-time when Nell isn't here, but for the rest of the time I can tell you what I want and you could perhaps come up with some ideas? It would mean a raise in salary, naturally.'

Cora clapped her hands in pure delight, setting her short blonde curls bobbing and her sapphire-blue eyes shining. 'Oh thank you, I'd *love* it,' she gushed and so it was arranged that that very afternoon when Nell arrived to take over serving in the shop, Cora would join Dilly in her workroom back at the house.

Nell herself was pleased as Punch with the way things had turned out. 'Why that's, grand, lass. An' o' course yer know what this means, don't yer?' When Dilly stared at her blankly she chuckled. 'It means that if young Cora comes up to scratch, yer can tell her what yer want her to do, an' you can go to Ireland to be there fer the birth o' yer new grandchild. Then when yer get back yer'll only need to put the finishin' touches to what the lass has done, hopefully.'

Dilly hadn't thought of that – but Nell was right. Now she would be able to go to Ireland to be there with Declan and Roisin at this critical time.

'Oh Nell, whatever would I do without you?' she laughed, enveloping the older woman in a bear hug.

Nell sniffed. 'Get off, yer daft bugger,' she cussed to belie her pleasure, but her pink cheeks gave her away.

Chapter Thirty-Nine

'So just concentrate on the new Spring collection for now. Do you feel comfortable with that? I have enough designs for day dresses so it's just half-a-dozen evening gowns and four different designs for the matching night-dress and negligée sets in peach and cream – I'll let you choose one other colour and we'll see how you get on.'

'That should be fine, Mrs Carey,' Cora said as they stood together gazing down at the designs they'd already been working on spread across Dilly's work table.

In the brief couple of weeks they'd been working together, Cora had come on in leaps and bounds. Her confidence was growing by the day and Dilly had great plans for her. She already hoped that one day, Cora might be able to become a designer in her own right. True, her sketches were a little rough around the edges but her ideas were wonderful – and once Dilly had put the finishing touches to them she felt sure that they'd be popular. The girl had an instinct for what young people wanted to wear and to Dilly, she was like a

334

breath of fresh air. Added to that, she was a very nice person too, always cheerful and eager to please, so all in all things were working out famously.

'Yer cab's here, pet.'

Dilly looked at Nell, who had come to stand in the doorway of the workroom.

'Come on,' the older woman ordered bossily. 'If yer keep flappin' about yer goin' to miss yer train.'

'I'm coming.' Dilly pecked Cora on the cheek and followed Nell to where two large bags were packed ready by the kitchen door.

'Phew – what've you got in here?' Nell puffed as she carted one of the bags down the path. Dilly followed on with the second one.

'It's nearly all baby clothes,' Dilly said, adding quietly, 'I just pray that they'll be used this time.'

'Now that's no way to be thinkin',' Nell said, wagging her finger sternly. 'You've got to stay positive. Roisin's gone this far wi'out any trouble this time so happen it'll all be plain sailin' now.'

The cab driver had loaded the bags into the boot so Nell gave Dilly a hasty hug and almost pushed her into the back seat.

'I'll be back just as soon as I can,' Dilly promised, winding down the window but Nell shooed her away.

'Just go an' stop worryin', will you. I'll make sure all's well this end. Bye, pet.'

And then the cab was on the move and Dilly waved from the back window until Nell was out of sight.

The train journey was uneventful but the ferry crossing was another thing entirely. The sea was grey and choppy, merging with the grey sky on the horizon, and it was so cold that soon Dilly's teeth were chattering. She stood at the rail for as long as she could bear it, her breath fanning

335

out in front of her on the bitter air like steam from a kettle, but then after a time she hurried into the slightly warmer confines of the passenger cabin where she perched on the hard wooden bench-seat with her arms wrapped tightly about her. It was far too cold to relax, so by the time the Irish coast was sighted, Dilly's muscles ached with holding herself rigid, and there was still the journey to the farm to face yet. However, the sight of Declan standing on the quay, banging his arms against his sides and stamping his feet to keep warm, cheered her considerably. Thankfully he had thought to pile some warm blankets in the back of the cart and he caringly tucked one across her knees and another round her shoulders once he'd handed her up on to yet another uncomfortable seat.

'Oh, my backside is so numb I doubt I'll ever regain the feeling in it,' Dilly groaned as he took up the reins and urged the horse forward.

Declan grinned but she noticed that there were lines about her son's eyes that hadn't been there before.

'So how is Roisin?' she asked.

'Waddling about, carrying all before her.' He shook his head. 'I tell you, Mammy, she's absolutely enormous, so she is. I reckon if she don't have this wean soon she'll burst.'

Dilly patted his arm comfortingly. She could sense how nervous and strained he was. 'There's not much longer to go now, son. Less than three weeks, isn't it?' And when he nodded, she went on, 'Well, just to let you know, bar any emergencies at home I shall be staying until the baby is safely delivered now.'

'Really?' His face lit up. 'Then that'll be grand. I know Roisin will appreciate that.' They fell silent then and as the horse trotted surefootedly along, Dilly huddled as far into her blankets as she could get.

Despite the bitter cold, Roddy came pounding out of

336

the farmhouse to meet them the second the cart turned into the yard.

'You've grown again, young man,' Dilly told him as he helped her to climb stiffly down. 'But now let's get into the warm, shall we? I swear I shall turn into a block of ice if I have to stay outside for much longer.'

The heat in the kitchen was such that she felt like she was walking into a blast furnace and within seconds everyone was laughing as every part of Dilly that was on show began to glow.

'Look at me. You could use me as a lantern,' she joked as Shelagh pressed a piping hot mug of cocoa into her hands and ushered her towards the fire.

'Kian, fill a stone hot-water bottle and bring it here for Dilly's feet,' Shelagh ordered, and the youngster jumped to do as he was told.

It was dark and now the wind was hurling itself against the windows as if it was trying to gain entry but at last, Dilly felt some warmth start to creep into her bones. 'That's better,' she sighed, and as she looked around at all the beloved faces she was glad that she'd come.

Despite what Declan had told her, Dilly's first sight of Roisin shocked her to the core. She really was enormous and Dilly felt sorry for her.

'I have to sleep on my back now,' Roisin complained, patting the huge mound that was her stomach. 'And even then I wake up with cramp and poor Declan has to rub my feet. And if it's not cramp it's heartburn!'

'The things we women have to go through. Men just don't know they're born,' Dilly teased and Liam and Declan grinned sheepishly.

The first week of Dilly's stay flew past. She was quite happy to potter between the farmhouse and Declan's cottage – it was too bitterly cold to venture further unless it was really necessary. And all the time she kept a very close eye on Roisin. The young woman appeared to be a little on edge but then that was to be expected after all the heartbreak she had been through in the past.

Max telephoned regularly, promising Dilly that all was well at home as the wait went on.

'The doctor's on standby and so is Mrs Rafferty, two farms away. She does a lot of birthing for women in these parts,' Declan told her at least a dozen times and Dilly's heart went out to him. The poor chap was in a permanent state of nerves.

It was late one Saturday evening the third week in January as they were all just thinking of going to bed that Declan burst into the farmhouse looking like he'd seen a ghost. Thankfully, all the young people had retired earlier so jumping up from her seat Shelagh asked, 'Whatever is wrong, man?'

'I think the baby is coming!' Declan declared, clearly in a panic.

'Right you are, we're on our way,' Shelagh told him.

'But it's too soon,' Declan wrung his hands together. 'It's all going to go wrong again, isn't it?'

'No, it is not. Now pull yourself together,' Shelagh told him sternly. The last thing they needed was a hysterical father-to-be to deal with. Then she began to bark out orders. 'Liam, would you ride for the doctor and Mrs Rafferty? And Dilly, you come with me.'

The two women found Roisin sitting in a chair in the kitchen of her cottage ashen-faced with her arms wrapped about her swollen stomach.

'So this is it then,' Dilly chirped brightly. 'You're about to meet the new addition to the family very soon now.'

Roisin merely stared at her strangely before saying, 'I just want to get it over with.'

'You make it sound like a trip to the dentist's.' Dilly kept up her cheerful chatter as she took Roisin's elbow and led her towards the stairs. 'Let's get you upstairs and into your nightdress, eh? Liam has gone for the doctor and Mrs Rafferty, though they could be some time. The lanes are thick with frost but then I dare say this little one will be some time yet, so there's no need to panic.'

In actual fact Roisin was far from panicking. She'd promised herself long ago that she wouldn't build her hopes up this time and there was no reason to change her mind now. It would have been just opening herself up to yet more heartache.

Once in the bedroom, Dilly looked approvingly towards the grate where a fine fire was blazing, bathing the room in its golden glow. After padding the mattress with towels that Roisin had placed ready she helped the woman into her nightdress and into bed. Roisin had barely settled back against the pillows when a gush of liquid spurted from between her legs.

'That's your waters gone, pet.' Dilly replaced the soiled towels and smoothed back the stray black curls from Roisin's brow. 'It looks like this little one is in a rush to meet its mammy!'

Rosin turned her head away as if she was completely detached from what was going on. And then the dull ache that she had experienced all day in the small of her back moved round to the front and her first contraction gripped her.

'Squeeze my hand,' Dilly urged, wishing she could take the pain away but Roisin didn't even murmur.

Seconds later Shelagh barged in with a bowl of hot water and every other towel that she could lay her hands on. After glancing at Roisin she crossed to the window, flicked the curtain aside and frowned as she looked out at the frosty landscape. This would slow the horses down somewhat, she feared, but then the baby was probably a good few hours away from being born.

'Now where is the crib?' she asked Roisin, surprised to see that it wasn't in the room all aired and ready.

'It's in the room next to Roddy's.' Roisin stared at her solemnly. 'And I want it left there.'

Shelagh opened her mouth to protest but a stern glance from Dilly made her clamp it shut again. *Poor girl is probably thinking it won't be needed, like all the other times,* Shelagh said to herself and she could have cried. But then another contraction gripped Roisin and all their attention centred on the young mother-to-be.

They heard someone enter the cottage downstairs – Declan, no doubt – and then the sound of someone pacing up and down on the quarry tiles in the kitchen like a caged animal.

'Go down to him,' Shelagh whispered to Dilly. 'And make us all a nice hot drink, eh?'

With a swift glimpse at her daughter-in-law, Dilly nodded and hurried away to do as she was told. Anything was preferable to having to stay there and see that look of resignation on Roisin's face.

Declan was seated in the fireside chair when Dilly got downstairs; his head was in his hands and his elbows resting on his knees.

'Oh for goodness sake!' Dilly felt that desperate measures were called for. 'Whatever is wrong with you two? Don't you want this baby?'

Declan looked up at her from red-rimmed eyes and her heart bled at the despair she saw there.

'Oh aye, we want the wean all right, Mammy. But after all the disappointments . . .'

'But that's not to say that it will be the same this time,'

340

Dilly pointed out, her tone softening. 'Now get yourself away up those stairs and put a smile on your face. That girl needs your support right now.'

He went to do as he was told while Dilly hovered by the window waiting for the kettle to boil and for the doctor and Mrs Rafferty to arrive. Thankfully, Roddy was sound asleep in his bedroom at the end of the landing, completely oblivious to what was going on and Dilly fervently prayed that he would stay that way until the birthing was over.

It was another hour before Liam returned with Mrs Rafferty and the doctor, and Dilly sighed with relief.

'Upstairs, is she?' Mrs Rafferty asked as she began to peel off her layers of outdoor clothes. Beneath them all she was stick-thin, and with her hooked nose and beetling eyebrows she was no oil painting, but her reputation for bringing babies safely into the world was second to none.

'Yes, the door facing you at the top of the stairs. Declan and Shelagh are up there with her.'

'Then they can come down now,' Mrs Rafferty said in a voice that brooked no argument. 'We all know that the birthing room is no place for a man.'

The doctor nodded in agreement as he followed the woman up the steep narrow staircase, and seconds later Shelagh and Declan came back down.

'She's cleared me off,' Declan told his mother in an aggrieved tone.

'And quite right too. They know what they're doing.' Dilly winked at Shelagh as she pushed Declan into a chair. 'Now sit there while I get you a cup of tea. I might put a drop of brandy in it to calm your nerves.'

'Huh! It'll take more than a drop of brandy, I'm thinking,' Shelagh remarked, stifling a yawn. She'd been up since the crack of dawn working about the farm and now she was bone tired.

341

'Why don't you go round home and get some rest?' Dilly suggested. 'There's nothing more you can do here and we'll be sure to fetch you when anything happens. I'm thinking of trying to snatch a nap myself in the chair.' She had no intention of doing any such thing but she was hoping to make Declan relax. He looked as taut as a piano string, ready to snap at any moment.

'Well, if you're quite sure,' Shelagh answered uncertainly. 'I'll perhaps go and try to grab a couple of hours and then I'll be back.' Crossing to Declan she planted a gentle kiss on the top of his head then slipped out into the bitterly cold night, letting in a blast of icy air.

The hands of the clock on the mantelpiece ticked away the seconds, the minutes and then the hours as Dilly and Declan sat on, their ears strained for any sounds from upstairs, but there was nothing save the footsteps of the doctor and Mrs Rafferty moving about the room. Roisin was either having a very easy labour or she was being remarkably brave – for they never heard a peep out of her. Then suddenly at three o'clock in the morning Mrs Rafferty appeared in the doorway.

'It's almost time and we need hot water – as much as you can carry,' she rapped out before disappearing back the way she had come.

'Is she all right?'

Declan's question hung unanswered on the air. Mrs Rafferty had already gone.

He and Dilly filled every bowl they had with the hot water they had bubbling away ready, but once they got it to the bedroom door they were shooed away like naughty children.

And then suddenly at three-thirty the sound of a new-born's cry echoed around the cottage and a look of utter incredulity crossed Declan's face.

'Congratulations, son. If I'm not very much mistaken, that's the sound of your new baby son or daughter.' Dilly's smile was so broad she felt in danger of splitting her face in two. The cry came again, louder this time and now Declan was crying as well.

'Well, whatever it is, it certainly seems to have a healthy pair of lungs,' Dilly said, slapping him on the back.

Declan's eyes were almost starting from his head as he kept them trained on the ceiling then at last they heard the sound of the bedroom door opening and after a few seconds Mrs Rafferty appeared with a broad smile on her face.

'You'd best come with me, lad – an' you too, Gran'ma. There's someone waitin' to meet you up there.'

Declan needed no second bidding and sprinted up the stairs ahead of her, only to stop dead in his tracks in the bedroom doorway for the sight that met his eyes made his legs turn to jelly. Roisin was propped against a mound of pillows with a tiny bundle clutched in her arms and a look of utter contentment on her face.

'Come away in and meet your daughter, Daddy,' she told him softly and he stumbled to the side of the bed with a look of wonder on his face.

'Meet Alannah Carey, Daddy.'

'Aye, and then when you've said hello to her, come here and meet her identical twin, Eilish.'

For the first time Declan looked towards the doctor and saw the second bundle in the man's arms.

'Twins!' Declan's voice came out as a squeak and the doctor laughed.

'Aye, lad, and a finer, healthier, bonnier pair I've yet to see. They'll break some hearts one day, I'll warrant.'

Crossing to him, Declan gently took the second precious bundle from the man's arms and stared down at her in awe. Suddenly all the heartache of the previous years was wiped away and he knew that he would never be happier than he was at that moment as Dilly looked proudly on with happy tears raining down her face.

He carried the babe to her mother and leaning over, he planted a tender kiss on his wife's flushed cheek. 'Sure, aren't you the cleverest lass on the planet?'

'Well, I did have a little help.' Roisin was positively glowing with happiness but then Mrs Rafferty broke up the party when she clapped her hands and told Declan and Dilly, 'Take these little ones and get them bathed now while the doctor and I see to the mother. They'll no doubt be yarking for a feed by the time you've done.'

'They can yark whenever they like and as often as they like and I'll never grow tired of the sound of it,' Declan vowed, and Dilly had no doubt that he meant every word of it. She lifted the second of her brand new granddaughters from Roisin's arms and carried her carefully downstairs. Both of the babies were utterly beautiful, with soft black curly hair and tiny rosebud mouths, and Dilly knew that she would always remember this day for as long as she lived as one of the happiest of her life.

Chapter Forty

'That's right – twins! Two beautiful perfect little girls!'
Dilly told Max on the telephone early the next morning.
She still hadn't been to bed as yet, she was far too thrilled
and excited to sleep and Max could hear it in her voice.
'Liam and Declan have been wetting the babies' heads,'
she went on, glancing across at the pair who were sitting
side by side on the sofa. 'In fact, I think they've drunk
enough poteen between them to drown in by now! Even
the doctor joined them before leaving. I just wonder if he'll
make it to his morning surgery in Enniskerry today. He
had a rare old sway on him by the time he left.'

'And why not?' Max chuckled at the other end of the
line. Dilly's laughter was infectious. 'I'd join them myself
if I was there. Please tell them both how thrilled I am for
them. And what about Roddy? What does he think to the
new additions to the family?'

'Actually he's still sleeping and hasn't seen them yet.'
Dilly looked up at the ceiling, willing him to wake up. 'But

345

it's gone eight now, hasn't it, so he should be stirring any time. But anyway I must go and make some breakfast for us all. It's been a very long night. Will you let everyone there know that all is well, especially Seamus and Bessie – oh and Nell, of course.'

'It will be my very great pleasure,' Max promised.

Dilly rushed away to put the kettle on. It was as she was setting the cups out that Roddy appeared knuckling the sleep from his eyes and looking curiously at all the people in the kitchen.

'Why is everyone in here?' he asked blearily, but before he could say any more, Declan raced over to him, grasped his hand and hauled him back towards the stairs door.

'Didn't I say you could sleep through anything?' he laughed. 'Come an' see what the stork brought while you were abed.'

Roddy was instantly wide awake. 'What – you mean the baby's arrived?' But Declan was already dragging him up the stairs.

'Ssh now.' Declan put a finger to his lips. 'The new mammy is having a nap. She's worn out, so she is, bless her soul.'

They stepped into the bedroom where Roisin was dozing and Roddy frowned, puzzled, as he looked towards the two cribs either side of the bed. Liam had had to go and fetch his children's crib from the loft next door.

'Why are there two cots here?'

'Go and peep inside them and see,' Declan invited, looking like the cat that had got the cream.

He heard Roddy's sharp intake of breath just as Roisin opened her eyes and smiled at the boy. This was a moment she had dreamed of for many, many years. 'Why don't you say hello to Eilish and Alannah, your new baby sisters?' she said softly.

Roddy blinked to hold back tears of joy as he stared at them in amazement. 'But . . . there are *two* of 'em!'

'Aye, there are that,' Declan said proudly. 'Twins. Trouble is, I've no idea how we're going to tell them apart. They're as alike as two peas in a pod, to be sure.'

Roddy was too overcome to speak and he fell on Roisin, who cuddled him to her chest and stroked his hair. 'And now I have everything I've ever wanted in the world,' she whispered in his ear with a smile of pure contentment on her face. 'A tall, strapping, handsome son and two beautiful wee girls.'

Dilly, who had carried a tray of breakfast up for Roisin almost choked as she looked on the happy scene from the doorway. Things had turned out just as she prayed they would – better, in fact, for not only had her beloved son and his wife been blessed with one healthy child but two.

Within the next hour the first neighbour had arrived bearing baby gifts. Mrs Rafferty had wasted no time spreading the wonderful news of the girls' arrival and from then on a steady stream of visitors appeared through-out the day. By late afternoon Dilly was so tired she was sure she could have slept standing up but she kept going on pure adrenalin and joy.

Roisin meanwhile lay in bed nursing and feeding her babies with a look of absolute bliss on her face.

By the time Dilly went to bed that night she was utterly exhausted but thrilled that she'd been there to share such a momentous occasion with her son and his wife. Even so, now that the birth was safely over she was looking forward to going home again. She'd missed Jessica and Primrose, and was also keen to get back to work.

I'll stay for another couple of days, she thought drowsily . . . but then sleep claimed her.

*

Max was waiting at the station for her when she returned home. The twins were a week old by then and thriving. Dilly found that she was missing them already, although she was eager to see Jessica and Primrose.

'You're looking grand,' Max commented as he hauled her luggage into the boot of his car. It was a lot lighter coming back than going as more than half of it had been baby clothes. It was just as well, seeing as they'd ended up with two babies! Nothing would go to waste, that was for sure.

'I'm feeling wonderful,' she answered with a broad smile. 'And the little ones are just adorable.'

'What does Roddy think of them?'

Dilly spotted the concern on Max's face and was quick to reassure him. Perhaps he was worried that now Declan and Roisin had babies of their own they wouldn't want his grandson any more?

'He's absolutely besotted with them and nothing is too much trouble. I swear he'd stand at the side of the cribs and just watch them all day long if he could. He's going to make a perfect older brother for the girls.'

Max let out a little sigh of relief as he helped Dilly into the car. It was so good to have her back; he'd missed her more than he could say.

'Is everything all right here?' she asked then, just as he'd known she would.

'Absolutely fine. Jessica is really excited because I told her you were coming home.' Again he felt sad that Dilly couldn't acknowledge Jessica as her granddaughter. But they had lived a lie for far too long to change it now. Too many people would be hurt if the truth were to come out.

'And Nell and Archie? Have you seen them?'

'Once or twice.' He chuckled. 'I called round quite late

348

one evening and Archie was smoking his pipe by the fire. It didn't look much like he was thinking of leaving either.'

'Well, they're quite old enough to know what they're doing,' Dilly answered with a smile. 'And they'll be married soon anyway. But how is my little lass and Olivia?'

'As it happens, I reckon Olivia has a new admirer – a young doctor at the hospital. She's mentioned him a few times and last night she invited him to dinner. Mrs Pegs really went to town, bless her. You could have put the meal she dished up in front of royalty.'

'Really?' Dilly was astounded. She'd never known Olivia show much interest in anyone apart from Oscar before, but then it was no bad thing. She hated to see the girl so unhappy, and if she had met someone she could be fond of, then that was a good thing as far as Dilly was concerned.

'So – tell me all about him then,' she urged, and Max shrugged.

'I've only met him the once but he seems a nice enough chap and he was wonderful with Jessica. Apparently he was engaged to be married a few years ago but his fiancée died. He's round about thirty I should say, and quite handsome, I suppose.'

'I see.' Dilly's mind was working overtime. If only Olivia could meet someone to make her happy it would go a long way towards easing the constant guilt she felt, but they'd just have to wait and see if anything came of it. Suddenly the excitement of the last weeks and the long journey began to catch up with her.

Max grinned. 'I was going to suggest I take you for a meal but I have a feeling you're ready for your bed.'

Dilly yawned before she could stop herself. 'I am, to be honest, but perhaps we could do it another night,' she said apologetically.

'Of course,' he agreed, as she settled into the cold seat. Within minutes she was fast asleep.

Dilly was very impressed with the work that Cora had done in her absence and was keen to tell her so.

'These designs are fresh and vibrant,' she praised as Cora blushed with pleasure. Admittedly they needed a few tweaks here and there but overall, Dilly was very pleased with them. She had been home for three days by then and was slowly getting back into her old routine.

A tap came at the workroom door and Oscar stuck his head round it. 'Oh sorry, Dilly, I didn't realise you had anyone with you. I just brought a message from Father. He's had to go to London overnight unexpectedly on business and didn't want you worrying. He said to tell you he'll ring you if he gets a chance.'

'Thank you.' Dilly gave him a warm smile. 'Oscar, this is Cora. She's my new assistant designer and she's shaping up beautifully.' She noticed the girl blush again, and hid a grin. It looked like Oscar might have got himself a new admirer too now, if she was any judge. Not that it could ever come to anything while he was tied in a loveless marriage with Penelope.

'How do you do.' Oscar shook her hand and the girl blushed an even deeper shade of red if that was possible.

'H-hello,' she mumbled, and was visibly relieved when Dilly then began to show him some of her sketches.

'You're very talented,' Oscar complimented Cora, but by now the girl was too tongue-tied to utter a sound. Had Oscar but known it, a picture of his face kept flashing in front of her eyes for the rest of the day.

Early in March, Nell and Archie were married quietly at the local register office.

'I'm far too old to be thinkin' of anythin' flash,' Nell said with determination, but she did allow Max to take them all out for a meal afterwards, which everyone thoroughly enjoyed.

Nell looked lovely in a pale-blue two-piece costume that Dilly had designed especially for the occasion, with a matching hat, and Archie looked smart in his new pin-striped suit – the first new one he'd owned since he'd married his first wife many years ago.

They spent their wedding night at Dilly's then the following morning, Max arrived early to drive them to the station where they would catch the train to Blackpool for their honeymoon. Max had generously offered to pay for them to go abroad but Nell had flapped her hand derisively at him.

'Why would we want to go further afield than Blackpool?' she asked. 'Thank you but no, Blackpool will do us just fine.'

And so on a breezy March morning Dilly and Max waved them off, Dilly with a tear in her eye.

'They look so happy, don't they?' she said dreamily, and Max nodded in agreement.

'Yes, they do and long may it last. They're both grand characters and I think they'll be good for each other. If only everyone could have a happy ending, eh?'

Hearing the wistful note in his voice, Dilly glanced at him from the corner of her eye and when the train was out of sight she ushered him towards the exit. For once in her life everything was going to plan and she prayed that nothing would happen to disrupt it.

Chapter Forty-One

January 1930

On a cold and frosty night early in January Samuel was feeling far from happy. Lilian's health had deteriorated over the last few months and now she rarely left her room. It wasn't really a shock; he sometimes wondered how she had managed to keep going for as long as she had. When she was well enough to leave her bed she would spend hours sitting in a chair by the window, waited on hand and foot by her maid. She still insisted that Samuel should share her bed, however, and he was finding it increasingly difficult to stomach. The visits from Elspeth, Lilian's daughter, didn't help matters either. She made no secret of the fact that she couldn't stand Samuel and her feelings were returned tenfold – although he was always very careful to hide it. The way he saw it, there was no point in upsetting the apple cart until he had to.

Lilian's deterioration had brought home to him the urgency of procuring a more solid hold over her worldly goods – and he was prepared to go to any lengths to do that. That very morning, he'd had an appointment with a solicitor in town who'd told him in no uncertain terms that until he could get an address of where Niamh was living there was no chance of him getting a divorce. Even then she would have to be agreeable to it and Samuel knew only too well that she would never co-operate. Hence, at gone three o'clock in the morning, he was pacing up and down Lilian's bedroom whilst she slept on, her mouth hanging slackly open and snoring loudly enough to waken the dead.

Glancing across at her, he shuddered. Without her paint and powder and the wig she had taken to wearing she looked like a corpse already, and suddenly he felt the need to have firmer flesh beneath him. Making a hasty decision, he picked up his clothes and slid off to his dressing room where he quickly got dressed. Lilian had employed a valet to cater to his every need but Peters would be asleep at this time of the morning. Hopefully by the time the chap woke, Samuel would have paid a hasty visit to the brothel in town and be back. They'd recently taken on an exotic beauty there with soft brown skin the colour of cocoa and eyes like warm treacle. Her hair was as black as a raven's wing and Samuel couldn't get enough of her. She wouldn't mind being woken at this ungodly hour so long as he paid her well, so he was in a slightly better frame of mind by the time he sneaked out of the house. The thick stair-carpet muffled the sound of his footsteps, and there was nothing to be heard but the enormous grandfather clock ticking away in the hall.

Samuel fetched his car from the garage and in no time was motoring towards town. He was almost there when he spotted a drinking partner of his emerging from one of the inns in Stockingford.

Drawing the car to a halt, he wound down the window

and called out, 'What are you doing out and about at this hour?'

Richard Treadwell's father owned an abattoir and a rag and bone yard, and Richard was never short of a bob or two. Tonight, however, he looked glum as he turned his pockets out.

'They've got a big card game going on in the back room.' He cocked his head towards it. 'Lousy bastards have cleaned me out. I ain't got a penny left and I've lost me gold watch an' all. Me old man'll go spare in the mornin'. I tell yer, there's big sums changin' hands in there.'

'Really?' Samuel could never resist a challenge and Lilian had been generous that day so his pockets were heavy. The exotic Bianca could always wait until another day. 'I might just go and chance my luck,' he told Richard thoughtfully, and minutes later he was striding round to the back of the inn. The blinds were pulled tight but then Samuel had expected that. It wouldn't do for the police to get wind that the landlord was having a lock-in. Even so, after a couple of light taps to the door a voice hissed, 'Who is it an' wadda yer want?'

'It's Samuel Farthing. I hear there's some money to be made here.'

A soft chuckle reached him as he heard the sound of bolts being slid across the top and bottom of the door.

'Fancy yer chance, do yer?' The landlord sniggered as he yanked Samuel inside and hastily slammed the door shut again. 'You'll find them that's left in there.' He nodded towards a door at the end of the corridor and shuffled away to get more drinks.

Samuel found there were only three men playing cards when he entered the room and they barely glanced up. They were playing for very serious money indeed now and didn't want any distractions. He stood patiently aside and watched. One of them was a well-known magistrate who was often to be found at lock-ins. Another was a factory owner and the third man, Mickey Noon, was a well-known villain, a friend of the late Snowy White. Samuel shuddered as his mind slipped back to the night he had committed Snowy's body to a watery grave. But then the bloke had deserved it, hadn't he? Samuel rarely felt any regret for what he'd done to Snowy. What he'd done to his own daughter, little Constance, was another thing entirely, however, and he still sometimes woke up in a sweat as he recalled what he'd done to her. But not now, he told himself as he reined his feelings in. These chaps were playing for a fortune and he intended to join them just as soon as he could.

Three hours later as the dawn kissed the sky, Samuel sat in shock. He had lost every penny he possessed *and* the brand new car that Lilian had bought him into the bargain. He watched in disbelief as Mickey raked the money piled high on the table along with his car keys towards him and began to ram it into his pockets.

'I'd say that were a good night's work,' Mickey chuckled as the other two men rose and walked away disconsolately. 'An' you, Farthin', 'ad better write me an IOU fer the other two 'undred yer owe me. Don't keep me waitin' fer it too long, mind. I ain't the most patient o' blokes, as yer know.'

Samuel's hand shook with rage as he wrote out the note and shoved it across to Mickey. Unfortunately that night, or morning, he had met his match: someone who could cheat as well as he could.

With his chin down and his hands thrust deep into his coat pockets he started on the long walk back to Lilian's house. It was bitterly cold and slippery underfoot and the further he walked the worse his mood became. The way he saw it, this was all Niamh's fault – hers *and* her bloody mother's. If he hadn't been forced to marry the bitch, none of this would have happened. Only a couple of weeks ago he had seen Dilly and his father driving through town with not a care in the world, laughing together. Anyone seeing her in her fancy hat and posh clothes could have taken her for a lady, but he knew different. Dilly Carey was nothing but scum, a guttersnipe who had once scrubbed floors for his family, and he couldn't understand why Max even gave her the time of day. *She's probably his knock-off, especially now Mother's banged up in Hatter's Hall,* he told himself moodily.

When he arrived back at the house he let himself in and made for Lilian's bedroom. He'd hoped that she'd be asleep but instead she was sitting up in bed looking like a ghostly apparition in the early-morning light that shone through the window.

'Where have you been?' she asked peevishly as he began to undress.

He had the urge to tell her to mind her own business but he knew where his bread was buttered. 'I couldn't sleep for fretting about you, my darling, so I went for a walk,' he muttered instead and she was instantly contrite for snapping at him.

'Oh, my poor darling boy. Come here and show me how much you love me.'

Samuel swallowed his revulsion as he clambered into the bed beside her and felt her stick-like arms wrap around him. He had no idea how he was going to explain away the loss of the car so for now it might be as well to keep her sweet. Plastering a smile on to his face, he began to shower her wrinkled face with kisses as his hands slid beneath her voluminous linen nightgown to explore her sagging breasts and she purred with contentment.

*

356

For the next few days, Samuel barely ventured from Lilian's house. He was too afraid of bumping into Mickey Noon. The time passed interminably slowly until finally on the evening of the fourth day following the card game he could stand it no more. Lilian had been particularly clingy and he felt as if he was being suffocated.

'I think I might go for a stroll,' he said when they'd finished their evening meal in her bedroom. Most of Lilian's meals were served to her on a tray now.

'Oh, darling. Must you leave me?' she pouted.

'I shan't be long. I just need a breath of fresh air, that's all,' he told her with a forced smile.

'Very well, my pet.' She smiled at him cunningly then. 'But don't be too long. I have my solicitor coming tomorrow and I think you'll be pleased about the changes I intend to make to my will.'

Suddenly, Samuel was all ears. 'What changes are they then?' He was trying hard to keep the excitement from his voice.

She gave a rattly laugh as she tapped the side of her nose. 'That will be revealed when I am no longer here,' she said teasingly. 'But let's just say the changes will be to your advantage. You've been so good to me of late.'

In actual fact, Lilian was well aware of Samuel's visits to the whorehouse in town but it suited her to keep him dancing attendance on her. Her body might be failing but her mind was still as bright as a button.

'You are too kind.' He took her wrinkled hand in his and kissed each of her gnarled fingers in turn with a look of total adoration on his face, much to her amusement. She could read Samuel like a book and knew that money was his God.

'Now before you go, do you need any money?'

Samuel's heart skipped a beat. 'Well, I must admit my

357

pockets are empty,' he admitted, feeling like a schoolboy asking his mother for pocket money. This was no time to be proud though.

'Fetch me my bag.'

He quickly did as he was told and after opening it she counted out twenty pounds into his hand.

'There, my sweet, that should tide you over until your allowance is due,' she told him gently.

A mere twenty pounds! He stared down at it trying hard to hide his disappointment. But still it was better than nothing and Mickey Noon might settle for it as a deposit for now.

'Thank you.' He flashed her a smile before striding towards the door and she remained silent as she watched him leave the room. The butler had already informed her that Samuel's new car had not been in the garage for some days and she had a good idea what had happened to it. He'd no doubt lost it in some damned card game but she'd wait till he plucked up the courage to tell her.

Samuel meantime was heading towards town wrapped in his warmest overcoat. A thick hoar frost was already forming on the grass making the blades stand to attention like regimental rows of little soldiers, but tonight the picturesque landscape was lost on him. He was too busy thinking ahead to his confrontation with Mickey.

He thought he knew where he might find him and he wasn't wrong. Mickey was propping up the bar at the Prince and Whistle public house in Church Road in Stockingford, one of his favourite haunts, with an overflowing pint pot in his hand.

'Ah, I was just about to come lookin' fer yer,' Mickey snapped as Samuel made towards him through a haze of blue smoke. 'There's a little matter o' two 'undred pounds yer owe me.'

358

Samuel's eyes shifted about the bar before he hissed, 'Step over here, would you?'

Samuel followed him into a corner away from prying eyes and now Samuel threw down his challenge.

'I want you to play me at cards again,' he said boldly. 'If I win, I get my car back and owe you nothing. If you win, I'll give you double what I owe you.'

'Hmm . . .' Mickey stroked his stubbly chin thoughtfully as he stared back at Samuel from bloodshot eyes. He quite liked travelling in style in Samuel's car and didn't want to lose it – but then he was also fairly certain that he could beat him again.

'Name the place,' he grated out, taking up the challenge.

'The back room here on Friday evening.'

At that moment the landlady appeared, collecting the dirty glasses from the tables, and she was just in time to overhear Mickey say, 'You're on. But I warn you, try any monkey business and I'll kill you with my bare hands. I ain't forgot that the night my mate Snowy was murdered, he was comin' to collect what you owed him.'

Samuel visibly paled as the landlady dashed past them, but then composing himself he retorted, 'I've no idea what you're talking about. I'll see you here in the back room, Friday night at ten.' With that he turned on his heel and left with his cheeks glowing with fear and humiliation. Somehow he had to raise a lot of money before then to get his stake together, and as yet he had no idea how he was going to do it.

The following day, whilst Lilian was ensconced in her bedroom with her solicitor, Samuel stole through to her changing room and raided her jewellery box. It wasn't the first time he'd done it but then there was little chance of the widow realising anything was missing. Since taking to her bed she never wore her jewels any more. He selected a glittering emerald and diamond necklace. Glancing at the clock, he realised that he just had time to get into town and back to see someone who would pay him for the piece before taking it to London to sell it on. It wouldn't do for it to stay locally in case Lilian reported it was missing. He wouldn't get nearly its worth admittedly, but it should be enough to raise a good stake for his card game with Mickey.

Quietly, he collected his coat and crept from the house.

Chapter Forty-Two

Samuel was sulking as he made his way back through the town late that afternoon. The chap had bought the piece from him but Samuel was far from happy with what he'd given him for it. Fifty measly quid when it must be worth two or three hundred at least. But then his back was against the wall, what was he supposed to do?

He could try to tap Roger Bannerman for a bit more – but who else could he turn to? He briefly thought of getting in touch with his father, but that would have to be a last-ditch thing. They hadn't spoken for ages and Samuel had a feeling that he wouldn't be very warmly received. He was so lost in thought that for a moment he didn't spot the woman hurrying towards him holding the hand of a tiny little girl. They were almost level with him before he glanced up, and when he did, the breath caught in his throat. It was Bessie and she looked really well. She'd lost weight and with her fashionable bob haircut and her stylish cloche hat she looked more attractive than he'd ever seen her before.

'Well, well, long time no see, eh?' He eyed her up and down as she stared at him and made to drag the child past him. He sidestepped to stand in front of her and smiled as he saw the colour flood into her cheeks. 'I didn't know you'd had another sprog,' he remarked, and her chin set.

'Actually, Primrose is Seamus Carey's little girl,' she told him coolly. 'I look after her for him whilst he's working.'

'From what I've heard you look after him too,' Samuel insinuated.

Bessie clutched the child's hand. 'Trust you to try and bring everyone down to your level,' she hissed.

'Now, now, there's no need to be like that. I was just thinking how attractive you looked.' It was then that a thought occurred to him. Bessie must be worth a bob or two.

'Actually I've been meaning to come and see you to ask after our son.'

'Huh! Since when have you given him a second thought? Now would you please step out of our way? I need to get Primrose home out of the cold before it gets properly dark.'

'Look, before you go . . . I was wondering, could you see your way clear to lending me a few quid? Just for a while, of course.'

She snorted with derision. 'Me, lend *you* money? Why, you must be stark staring mad! I'd see you starve before I'd give you so much as a crust.' Her eyes were flashing fire now as all the hatred she had always felt for him rose to the surface again. Primrose began to whimper then and jamming her tiny thumb into her mouth she snuggled into the folds of Bessie's cherry-red coat.

Fearful of upsetting the child, Bessie leaned towards him then as a small woman bustled past them.

'I *hate* you,' she choked out. 'And I won't be truly happy

362

until you're *dead,* so *never* – I repeat *never* – come near me again. Do you hear me? Because as God is my witness, if you do, I'll kill you myself!' Then scooping the child up into her arms she shot him one last malignant glance and stepped past, intent on hurrying on her way. The little woman who had heard the whole of the heated exchange glanced fearfully across her shoulder at him then she too scuttled away into the fast-darkening afternoon as Samuel snatched at Bessie's arm. He was really angry now. Just who did this nobody think she was anyway, talking to him like that?

'You wouldn't have the guts to kill anyone,' he sneered, his face so close to hers that she could feel his breath on her face. 'Not like me! I know how to kill – how do you think Constance died? Why, *I* killed her, of course. All for nothing admittedly because that stupid wife of mine still wouldn't divorce me even when there was no child to bind us. And Snowy White? You always had your suspicions there, didn't you?'

Bessie gasped with shock. Connie, poor, darling little Connie.

Realising suddenly that he'd said too much, Samuel gave her arm a vicious twist, making her wince with pain.

'Get out of my sight,' he spat. 'And don't get thinking of telling anyone what I've just told you or it might be *you* I come visiting one dark night. Do you understand me?'

Too appalled to speak, Bessie clutched Primrose more tightly to her. Samuel was clearly mentally unbalanced, just like his mother.

He shoved her and she stumbled away with tears pricking at the back of her eyes. What was she to do? Poor little Connie. And then she thought of Niamh and Dilly and knew that she could never tell them about his confession. It would kill them if they were to find out how that beloved angel had died. Far better for them to continue believing she had passed away through natural causes.

When Bessie had disappeared out of sight, Samuel said to himself, *That didn't go down too well, did it? I must be losing my touch.* He had only two more days to get his stake together before he chanced his luck with Mickey Noon again. Despondently, he trudged on his way.

He arrived back at Lilian's house to scenes of absolute mayhem. The doctor's car was outside the front door, and as Samuel entered the hall, maids were scuttling about up and down the stairs. Raising an eyebrow he asked the butler, 'What's going on, Matthews?'

'It's madam, sir,' the man replied, taking his hat and coat. 'I'm afraid she's had a bad turn so her nurse sent for the doctor. He's in with her now.'

Samuel took the stairs two at a time and barged into Lilian's room to find the doctor leaning over the bed. He stared at the younger man disapprovingly before asking in clipped tones, 'Have you never heard of knocking, my good man?'

Ignoring the question, Samuel barked, 'What's wrong with her?'

The doctor sniffed. He'd heard the rumours about his patient and this young whippersnapper but then it wasn't his business to judge.

'I'm afraid she'd had a very serious seizure.'

'But she'll be all right, won't she?'

The man shrugged. 'I'm afraid it's too soon to say. What I *can* say is that Mrs King is in a very critical condition and must be kept calm and quiet.'

Samuel's mouth gaped open. Lilian had been ill for some time, yet now faced with the fact that she could die he was still shocked.

'Shouldn't you be getting her into hospital or something?' he asked.

The doctor looked down his nose at him. 'Were we to try and move her, I fear she would not even survive the journey.'

'I see.' Samuel sat down heavily on the nearest chair as the doctor felt Lilian's pulse.

'There is nothing more I can do this evening,' he addressed the nurse, snapping his large black leather bag shut and placing a small phial on the bedside table. 'Should she need this through the night, give her only a couple of drops directly on to her tongue. No more, mind – her heart would not withstand a stronger dose.'

'Yes, Doctor,' the nurse agreed solemnly.

'I shall be back first thing in the morning,' he informed her, then with a curt nod at Samuel he strode from the room. Once he'd left, Samuel watched as the nurse straightened the covers over Lilian's frail frame and wiped the dribble from her chin.

'It might be best if you slept in your dressing room this evening, sir,' she suggested tactfully, and Samuel nodded.

'Yes, of course. But would you mind if I had a few moments alone with her first?'

The woman hesitated but then thought, What harm can it do? It was common knowledge amongst the staff that Lilian and Samuel were lovers, so why should she deny him that?

'I'll pop down and get her a fresh jug of water,' she said with a bob of her knee, and seconds later they were alone.

Crossing to stand beside the bed, Samuel stared down at Lilian. She seemed to have aged another twenty years in the short time he had been away from the house. Perhaps it had been the solicitor's visit that had overtaxed her? And then a sudden thought occurred to him: *the solicitor!*

What was it Lilian had said – that she would be changing her will to his advantage!

His heart skipped a beat as realisation dawned. She must have left everything to him rather than her dreadful daughter, Elspeth. He would be rich beyond his wildest dreams . . . if she *did* die, that was. It would be just like her to rally round again. His eyes strayed then to the small phial on the bedside table and a terrible idea was born. The doctor had said her heart would not withstand more than a couple of drops. Hurrying back to the door, he glanced up and down the long landing, but there was no one in sight, so softly closing the door again he rushed back to the bed and pulled the cork stopper from the phial. It was easy to lift her head and tip half of the phial's contents into her slack mouth. She made a gagging sound but once her head was back on the pillow she seemed to be resting again. Quickly then, he refilled the bottle with water from the water glass and sitting beside her he took her hand and adopted the pose of a heartbroken lover just in time before the nurse returned.

When Elspeth arrived an hour or so later, she glared at him. 'I'd be grateful if you would both leave and allow me some time with my mother,' she told him and the nurse in a haughty manner.

'Of course,' Samuel said solicitously, and headed off to the comfortable bed in his dressing room where he instantly fell into a peaceful sleep, convinced that very soon now all his worries would be over.

A tap on the door awoke him in the early hours and he blinked and sat up. 'Yes, what is it?'

'You'd better come, sir,' a tearful maid told him. 'The mistress has had another bad turn an' the doctor's been sent for.'

'Very well.' Samuel slid his arms into a heavy silk

dressing gown – another present from Lilian – and hurried along the landing to her room. He was almost there when the doctor appeared, puffing and panting at the top of the stairs.

'Wait outside, would you, while I examine her?'

'Of course.' Samuel bowed his head and wrung his hands, the picture of a broken-hearted lover.

The minutes ticked away then a sob sounded from within the bedroom. It was Elspeth – and he had to stifle the urge to smile. The doctor helped her from the room whilst she wept into a lace handkerchief, and addressing Samuel, he told him with a grave shake of the head, 'I'm afraid she has gone. I'm not surprised. I did doubt she would last the night.'

'I see,' Samuel said brokenly. 'Then please excuse me. I need to be alone for a time to come to terms with what's happened.' He shot back to his dressing room and once inside he punched the air with glee. He'd done it! The old bag was gone and soon everything would be his. It was a heady feeling. Clambering back into bed, he lay planning his future. Elspeth could deal with sending for the funeral director, then once the funeral was over he'd make sure the miserable cow never darkened his doorstep again – *his doorstep*! Turning over, he sighed with contentment and soon he was once again sleeping like a baby with all his worries behind him.

Early the next morning, a red-eyed maid carried in his tea tray. Tea in bed was a habit he and Lilian had adopted some time ago and Samuel enjoyed being waited on.

'Mrs Carnegie requests you join her in the drawing room as soon as possible, sir.' She laid the tray on the bedside table before moving to the window to swish the curtains open.

Samuel felt a spurt of rage. Just who the hell did Elspeth think she was, ordering him about in what would very soon be his own house? But then he could afford to be nice for now.

'Tell Mrs Carnegie I shall be down presently.'

The maid bobbed her knee and disappeared, leaving Samuel to his thoughts. It was going to be hard to play the part of the broken-hearted lover today, but he'd have to manage it somehow.

He sipped at his tea before dressing then made his way downstairs. All the maids and even the butler were clearly upset and creeping about the house like ghosts. Lilian had been a firm but fair mistress and they were all feeling her loss.

He found Elspeth and her husband, an ugly-looking dwarf of a man, waiting for him stiff-backed in the drawing room.

'Ah, I'm glad you've joined us. Mother's solicitor will be here presently and she wanted you to be present for the reading of the will,' Elspeth told him pompously.

'The solicitor?' Samuel frowned. It was customary for the deceased's will to be read *after* the funeral.

'Yes. Mother requested that it be read the day following her passing,' Elspeth informed him and Samuel nodded. As far as he was concerned, it couldn't happen quickly enough.

'Mother is lying in the day room, should you wish to go and pay your last respects while we wait,' Elspeth added.

Without a word Samuel left the room and walked into the day room. A fine mahogany coffin with heavy solid brass handles was placed on two tables with flickering candles set about it. Funnily enough, he noted that death had been kind to Lilian. Many of the wrinkles had been erased from her face and she almost looked as if she might just be asleep. Samuel's empty stomach growled then as he stared down at her, and he realised that he was hungry. Hopefully the solicitor wouldn't take too long over the reading of the will and then he could have a decent breakfast.

It was the butler who came to advise him that the solicitor had arrived. Samuel followed him back to the drawing room where Mr Watson, an elderly grey-haired man with gold spectacles perched precariously on the end of his nose, was already extracting the will from his briefcase.

'Ah, Mr Carey, now that you have joined us we can begin. The will is very straightforward and this should take no more than a few minutes.'

He solemnly began to read out Lilian's last wishes as Samuel's bored glance strayed to the window. There were quite a few small bequests to the loyal servants and the butler who had been in Lilian's employ for many years. Also a few minor ones to various nieces and nephews. And then came the part he'd been longing for:

And to Samuel Carey, my companion, I leave the new car I recently purchased for him and all of the jewels he has stolen from me over the years.

To my beloved daughter, Elspeth Carnegie, I leave everything else I possess in their entirety, my house, my money, my business shares and all my worldly goods.

'*What!*' Samuel sputtered as Elspeth eyed him with a smug expression on her face. 'B-but there must be some mistake. Lilian told me she was altering the will to my advantage!'

'She has, sir,' Mr Watson told him with a look of disapproval spread across his face. 'She has left you the car, which she strongly suspected you had lost gambling or at cards, and she kindly decided not to report you for the theft of certain pieces of jewellery that have gone missing over the years.'

'And what about my monthly allowance?' Samuel felt as if he were caught in the grip of a nightmare. This couldn't be happening. The widow had tricked him!

'That ceases forthwith,' the small man told him primly. 'She also requested that you leave the property immediately. One of the maids is packing your belongings even as we speak.'

'But this is preposterous,' Samuel said in deep shock. 'Where am I supposed to go?'

'I'm sure you are quite old enough to look after yourself, Mr Carey,' Mr Watson retorted and with a nod towards Elspeth he then began to fold the will and return it to his bag.

Samuel stormed out of the room and headed upstairs where he found a maid busily packing a large trunk with all his clothes, supervised by the butler.

'What the hell do you think you're doing?' he snapped at the girl.

'She is doing as the mistress requested,' the butler informed him. 'Now would you like your car brought round to the front, sir, so that you can take your belongings with you?'

'You know damn well my car isn't here,' Samuel glared. 'In fact, I've no doubt it was you who broke your neck to tell Lilian it was missing.'

'In that case we shall store the trunk in the boot room until you are in a position to collect it.'

Samuel thought he detected a smirk on Matthews' face. The bastard was enjoying this.

'I'll finish my own packing,' he told him petulantly but the butler shook his head.

'Unfortunately we are under strict instructions to do it

for you, so now if there's nothing else, will you please give me your keys and I shall escort you off the premises?'

Samuel stifled the urge to smash his fist into the other man's face but instead turned abruptly and left the room, closely followed by Matthews. At the front door the butler handed him his hat and coat and once Samuel had put them on and handed him the keys, he held the door wide for him to leave.

It was only when the door had closed resoundingly behind him that Samuel realised the true gravity of the situation he found himself in. The card-game with Noon was now only a whisper away and he had nowhere near enough cash as yet to raise his stake. Added to that he now found himself homeless, and as he strode down the drive carried along by despair and anger in equal measure he had no idea at all where he was going to go!

Chapter Forty-Three

The minute that Oscar entered the dining room he detected that something was different. The breakfast was laid out on the sideboard in silver dishes as usual but George was absent from the table and Penelope seemed all of a dither.

'So where's our little man then?' he asked her, injecting some cheer into his voice as he began to help himself to some bacon and sausage.

'I need to speak to you, so I thought it would be best if he breakfasted with his nanny this morning in the nursery,' Penelope replied. He noted that her own plate was loaded with food but surprisingly she hadn't touched it. Usually she could eat for England, hence her ever-expanding girth.

Oscar's spirits dipped and his appetite fled. Since Penelope's miscarriage they had slept in different rooms but could it be that she was about to demand her conjugal rights so they could start trying for another child again? If she did, he didn't know how he was going to face it.

'So what did you need to speak to me about?' He took a

seat at the table and shook out a napkin before placing it across his lap. He had a busy day ahead and didn't have time for his wife's tantrums this morning.

'There is no easy way to say this, so I'll just come out with it.' Penelope licked her dry lips. 'I've decided I want a divorce.'

The forkful of sausage halfway to his mouth paused in mid-air.

'What did you say?' Oscar was sure he must be hearing things.

'I have already spoken to Daddy's solicitor who informs me that it can go ahead on the grounds that our marriage has irretrievably broken down – if you will agree to it.' Her hands were folded primly in her lap but he noted that they were trembling.

'I see.' Oscar laid his fork down and stared at her. He couldn't think of a single thing to say. Deep down he didn't blame her for wanting shut of him. He should never have married her in the first place. But divorce! There was still a great stigma attached to it and he was shocked that Penelope would even consider it.

'But . . . what about George?' he asked lamely.

'He is still your son and I will never stop you spending time with him. We are moving back to Daddy's and the house can be sold. I thought perhaps you might wish to move back to your parents' house or perhaps get somewhere of your own. Daddy did buy us the house as a wedding present, after all.'

'I see,' Oscar repeated. It seemed to be the only thing he could manage to utter. He could see the hurt in her eyes and felt ashamed. She had loved him once, he knew she had, but he had never been able to return it and slowly she had become bitter.

'So . . . will you agree to it?' she asked tentatively. She

had prayed that he would refuse, would argue with her, fight to keep her – but his reaction told her more clearly than words that he had no fondness for her whatsoever. Their marriage was well and truly over – had never really started if she was to be brutally honest with herself.

He sat in stunned silence for some moments before nodding slowly. 'Yes, I agree, if you think it is for the best, but Penelope . . . I'm so sorry I've been such a disappointment to you. I hope we can be friends?'

Tears gathered in her eyes. 'No, I've never looked upon you as a friend – you were always far more than that to me,' she said chokily. 'So once the separation is started I suggest we only see each other when we have to with regards to when you wish to see George.'

'So be it.' Oscar folded his napkin and rose from the table. 'When do you propose to leave?'

'Today,' she told him. 'Daddy is coming to fetch me and George this afternoon and then the maid will see to packing up our possessions before the house is put up for sale. You are more than welcome to stay here until it is sold.'

He shook his head as he reeled with shock. Why hadn't he seen this coming – and why wasn't he upset?

'Perhaps you would like to see George on Sundays?' she suggested then. 'You could collect him from Daddy's house and take him out for a few hours.'

'Yes – yes, I'll do that. In fact, I'll just go and have a few minutes with him now if you don't mind before I go to work.'

'Of course,' she answered, as they stared bleakly at each other. There was nothing else to say and so Oscar slowly left the room and made for the nursery.

'Divorce!' Dilly echoed as she stared at Max, stunned. He had just told her the news and she could barely take it in.

She'd always known that Oscar and Penelope were not happy together, but she'd never expected this.

Max ran his hand through his hair. 'Yes, she wants a divorce. Oscar told me this morning. She was leaving the house today by all accounts and taking George to live with her parents.'

'And what will happen to their house now?'

'It's to be sold. Only fair, I suppose. It was a wedding present from Penelope's parents so Oscar doesn't expect – or want, for that matter – anything out of it. His main concern now is George, although in fairness Penelope has said he can still have regular contact with him.' Max laughed humourlessly then. 'At least it will give the gossips something to talk about again. They had a field day when Olivia came home with Jessica – I don't think they believed for a moment that she was a widow. And now we're to have a divorce in the family!'

'Times are changing,' Dilly told him, feeling his pain. 'Things that were unacceptable before the war are becoming more commonplace now. But if the house is to be sold, where will Oscar go?'

'He'll come home to me, of course. At least until he decides what he wants to do. He's at the house now, packing his clothes up.'

'How sad.' Dilly splashed some brandy into a glass then added some more. Max looked in need of it. Everything had been going so smoothly – she might have known it was too good to last. Bessie had told her about her encounter with Samuel in the street and now Dilly was worried that he might put in an appearance too. He usually did when the chips were down.

'I heard this evening when I called into my club that Samuel's lady love has passed away,' Max said at that moment as if he had been able to read her thoughts.

'Apparently the woman left everything, lock stock and barrel to her daughter, and Sam's out on his ear, so no doubt we'll be having a visit from him as well very soon.'

Dilly chewed on her lip, unsure of what to say. Poor Max, if it wasn't something in her family causing them concern it was something in his. She knew one person, however, who would not be sorry to hear about the divorce and that was Cora. The girl clearly had a huge soft spot for Oscar and Dilly had a funny feeling that he might feel the same about her. It was strange when she came to think of how close Olivia and Oscar had once been. Now Olivia spent every spare minute of her time with her young doctor, and Oscar had become a regular visitor to the house – and Dilly was fairly certain that it wasn't her he was coming to see. Mind you she was aware that she might be letting her imagination run away with her so it would be interesting to see what developed in the future now.

'Where has Samuel gone?' she asked and Max shrugged.

'He's probably holed up somewhere licking his wounds. His lady love was a soft touch and kept him in luxury from what I've heard. Still, he'll survive. His sort usually do.'

He began to absently glance through the sketches spread out on Dilly's work table. Dilly now had three young designers working for her, a factory where the clothes for her own shops were made up, and a team of employees. There was hardly a fashion house in the whole of the country that didn't stock her designs and he was proud of her, although he still fretted that she worked too hard. She was fifty-three years old now although no one would have thought it. There was just the merest hint of grey at her temples, but her face was still relatively unlined and she had kept her youthful figure, no doubt because she rarely sat down. She still insisted on overseeing everything and being heavily involved in her businesses even though she could well have sat back and left it to her staff. But how much longer, he wondered, could she keep it up?

'Do you know, sometimes lately I just feel like getting on a boat or a plane and going far away,' Max said suddenly.

Dilly stared at him in amazement and realised in that moment how tired he must be. He too worked far too hard although he could easily have afforded to retire.

'Then why don't you?' she said. 'Oscar and Penelope are quite old enough to handle their own affairs and it would do you good to get away and have a holiday.'

'If I did, would you come with me?' Dilly's lowered eyes were his answer and he sighed as he drained his glass. Whilst Camilla was alive he knew that she would never agree to anything like that, but time was slipping by far too quickly now. He still visited his wife every week in Hatter's Hall even though the visits depressed him horribly. She was nothing more than a gibbering skeleton, yet still she clung tenaciously to life.

'Here we are then, me lovelies,' Nell said as she bustled in with a tray laden with coffee and cake. 'I made that sponge meself this afternoon an' my Archie reckons it melts in yer mouth.'

Dilly and Max exchanged an amused glance. There were two people who were happy and content with their lot at least. Archie and Nell adored each other and the living arrangements had worked well. In fact, Dilly dreaded them ever saying they wanted a place of their own now. Archie did all the odd jobs and the gardening and Nell kept the house as neat as a new pin, as well as doing almost all of the cooking. She was so good that sometimes Dilly almost felt as if she were living in Nell's house and was surplus to requirements. Not that she would have changed anything; she loved having the couple live with her. It would have been desperately lonely on her own.

'Thanks, Nell, but actually I was just about to leave.' Max placed his empty glass down and Nell stared at it disapprovingly.

'Well, yer've still got time to try a bite o' me cake first,' she said in her usual bossy manner. 'An' a nice hot cup o' coffee will help to keep the cold out.'

Knowing when he was beaten, Max obediently sat down as Nell handed him a cup and began to slice into her sponge cake.

'There now, get that down yer,' she ordered, then glancing at Dilly she told her sternly, 'An' you can have a slice an' all. Yer hardly ate owt at dinnertime.'

'Yes, Nell,' Dilly said meekly as she settled on the seat next to Max. She'd given up trying to get her own way with Nell a long time ago.

At that moment, Samuel was entering the gentleman's club that he knew Roger Bannerman favoured in the hope of catching him. He doubted the chap would be able to increase the amount he gave him each month for his silence, but it was worth a try. He wandered from room to room and then, just as he was about to give up, he spotted Roger standing at one of the bars speaking to a man who worked with him in his father-in-law's printing business. Roger's wife had recently given birth to a second child – a healthy baby boy by all accounts – so he just might be worried enough to help him.

The smile on Roger's face faded the instant he set eyes on Samuel, and stepping away from his colleague he ground out, 'What the hell do *you* want? It's not the end of the month yet.'

'I'm fully aware of that,' Samuel said tetchily. 'But I think we may have to bring this month's payment forward, old chap. I find myself in dire straits, you see. Lilian has passed away and I find myself homeless and almost penniless into the bargain.'

'So? What's that to do with me?'

'It could have everything to do with you if I decided to stop being discreet and paid a visit to your lovely little wife,' Max threatened. 'You might just find yourself in my position as well if that happened.'

As Roger stared at him, the years of hatred he had felt towards him slowly bubbled to the surface. Samuel Carey was scum, the lowest of the low with not a care for anyone in the world but himself. And suddenly he could contain his anger no longer and before he'd even realised what he was doing he'd caught Samuel around the throat and was shaking him as a dog might shake a rat.

'*You bastard!*' he spat, his eyes glowing red with his inner fury. 'Enough is enough – do you hear me, Carey? You'll not get another penny from me, so do your worst. But I warn you, if you do a single thing to hurt my family I'll throttle you myself with my bare hands, you just see if I don't!'

As he shook Samuel to and fro, Samuel's face became an alarming shade of red, and who knew what might have happened if Roger's colleague hadn't rushed forward and dragged Roger off him.

'What on earth do you think you're doing Bannerman?' he shouted as Samuel collapsed across the bar, clutching his throat. 'You could've killed the feller.'

'I wish I bloody well had,' Roger panted not caring who might be able to hear him. He'd come well and truly to the end of his tether. And with that he slammed out of the club, leaving the occupants of the bar to watch him go open-mouthed.

Samuel meanwhile straightened his tie and with what dignity he could muster, slunk out of the room, all too aware of the many pairs of eyes watching his departure. Once outside on the pavement he rubbed at his sore throat as humiliation coursed through him. Damn and blast that bloody Roger Bannerman! Samuel had never realised what a temper he was capable of, but now that he had he'd be sure to give him a wide berth in future. That was another of his little earners out of the window. But now what was he to do – and where was he to go?

His shoulders sagged despondently. There was only one place left open to him – Mill House. The thought of going back to his former home cap in hand yet again was galling, but what choice did he have? It was far too cold to stay outdoors for long. The decision made, he bent his head and trudged reluctantly on his way.

Chapter Forty-Four

Max had just got home and was in the drawing room with Oscar and Olivia when Gwen poked her head round the door to tell him, 'There's someone 'ere to see yer, sir.'

'Then send them in, dear girl,' Max said affably, warming his hands at the fire.

When Samuel stepped into the room, a shocked silence settled.

'So . . . what do you want this time?' Max asked eventually. 'I heard what happened to your ladyfriend and have been half expecting you.'

There was no welcome in his voice and Samuel bristled. 'Well, it's good to see you too, Father,' he said sarcastically.

Max's eyes narrowed. He'd had enough trauma today with Oscar's news and was in no mood for any more trouble. 'Well, what did you expect, son? The red carpet rolling out for you? We've seen hide nor hair of you for the past few years and then you just breeze in as if you've never been away and expect everything to be as it was.'

Samuel adopted an injured air. 'Who else should I turn to in my grief but my family?' he asked pathetically.

'Oh, spare me the bullshit!' Max spluttered, completely uncharacteristically, forgetting there was a lady present. 'That poor woman was nothing more than a meal ticket to you so don't come here pretending to be broken-hearted. Now tell me what it is you want and just go. I don't have time to deal with your problems at the moment!'

Samuel was so taken aback that his mouth momentarily gaped open, but then clamping it shut again he asked, 'Are you telling me that I'm not welcome here?'

'That's exactly what I'm telling you. I've already given you far too many chances. It's time you grew up and became a man.'

Samuel's mouth twisted with spite as he glanced at Olivia. 'So there's no room for me but you'll take her and her bastard in, will you?'

Max's head snapped up. 'Don't you *dare* talk about your sister and my granddaughter like that!'

'Ah, but she isn't my sister, is she? Not really.' There, it was said! There could be no going back now and Samuel was glad. At least he would have his revenge and it would be sweet! He had the pleasure of seeing the colour drain from his father's face as he clutched the back of a chair.

'Whatever do you mean? Of course I'm your sister,' Olivia said quietly.

'Leave it, Olivia,' Max warned her, then to Samuel, 'I suggest you go before you say something you may well live to regret.'

'Don't you mean *you* might regret it,' Samuel asked tauntingly. Then turning to Olivia he asked, 'Why don't you ask him what I'm talking about?'

Olivia glanced from one to the other of them, totally confused. 'Will someone please tell me what's going on?'

Max shuffled forward and grabbed Samuel's arm, ready to drag him from the room, but Samuel shook him off and turning back to the young woman he told her, 'Dilly Carey is your mother. She gave you to my parents on the night you were born. Isn't that true, Father?'

He watched with satisfaction as both Oscar and Olivia gasped, but then Max had him firmly by the arm and with a roar he yanked him towards the front door as if he weighed no more than a feather, his strength fuelled by his anger.

'Get out of my sight!' he bellowed as he threw Samuel on to the front doorstep. 'You are despicable, and from this night on you are dead to me. Now go – and never darken my door again.' He then slammed the door and leaned heavily against it as his heart hammered in his chest. Then drawing himself up to his full height, he went to face Olivia.

'Oh my God,' Dilly fretted as she chewed on her knuckles and paced to and fro later that evening. Max felt he had no choice but to return to Dilly's home and tell her what had happened.

'And you say she took the news badly?' Tears slid down her cheeks unchecked.

'Well, you must accept it came as a grave shock to her. She'll need time to come to terms with it.'

Dilly's head wagged from side to side as Nell placed a comforting arm about her narrow shoulders. This was Dilly's worst nightmare come true. The one thing she had dreaded happening for all those years.

'She'll never forgive me. Why should she?' Dilly sobbed. 'What sort of woman would give her newborn child away? Olivia didn't part with Jessica, did she?'

'No, but she had a home to come back to,' Max pointed

383

out. 'You were struggling to keep your other children alive.'

'And Oscar . . . how did he take the news?'

Again Max shook his head. 'It was a terrible shock to him too, of course, but he'll come round to accepting it – I'm sure he will.'

Dilly suddenly sank on to the nearest chair as her legs threatened to fold beneath her. Despite the fact that she had never been able to acknowledge Olivia as her own flesh and blood, there had always been a special bond between them – but that might be gone for ever now and she didn't know how she would bear it. And what if Olivia decided to stop her seeing Jessica?

'I can't believe Samuel has done this,' she sobbed. But he had done it and now she could only wait helplessly to see what the outcome would be. 'I'll come round to speak to her first thing in the morning and try to explain,' she said with a touch of desperation in her voice but Max advised against it.

'Better to give her a couple of days and let her decide when she feels ready to talk about it,' he suggested sensibly.

Nell nodded in agreement. 'He's right, pet. Give the lass a bit o' time. Her whole world has been turned upside down tonight, thanks to that selfish little . . .' She bit on her tongue and glanced at Max apologetically. Samuel was still his son, after all.

'It's all right, Nell,' he said wearily. 'There's nothing you could say about him that I'd argue with tonight. I don't think he can understand how much heartache this will cause to so many people. I just thank God that Camilla can't understand what's happened. This would have killed her. For all her faults she always adored Olivia. But now I really should be going. Will you be all right, Dilly?'

'She'll be fine,' Nell assured him. 'Me an' Archie will

take care of 'er. We'll stay up all night wi' her if need be, won't we, pet?'

'We will that,' Archie agreed as he puffed furiously on his pipe. He hated crises and to see people upset.

Max opened his mouth to say something else but then clamped it shut and walked quietly from the room. What could he possibly say that would make this terrible mess any better?

It was three whole days before Olivia sent word via Oscar that she would like to speak to Dilly, and during that time Dilly had worked herself up into a rare old state.

'How is she?' Dilly asked him anxiously as Cora hovered in the background.

'Still upset, I'd be a liar to say otherwise, but she's calmer now. Would you like me to give you a lift round there? Then if I may, when we get the chance, I'd like to speak to you, Cora?'

The young woman blushed becomingly as with a nod, Oscar led Dilly out to his car.

Dilly found Olivia standing in front of the fireplace in the drawing room but there was no sign of Jessica. No doubt she was in the kitchen with Mrs Pegs and Gwen.

'Won't you sit down? I've asked Gwen to bring us some tea,' Olivia said politely as if she were addressing a stranger.

Dilly's heart sank. 'Eeh, don't be so formal, lass,' she begged. 'We've always been so easy in each other's company.'

'Quite – and now I know why, don't I?' Ashamed of her outburst, Olivia lowered her head. She'd vowed to conduct herself properly, but the hurt was still raw and she felt like lashing out. Then the words slipped out before she could stop them. 'How could you have done it, Dilly? Just give away your own baby like that as if I was nothing to you.'

'It wasn't like that, I promise you.' Dilly was crying again now. She'd barely stopped since the night Max had gone to tell her what Samuel had done. Slowly, she told Olivia everything. 'And that's why I worked here,' she finished. 'So that I could at least be close to you. I used to wait for your nanny to leave you in the hallway in your pram for a few moments alone just so that I could touch you and talk to you, and I was so proud of you as you grew up. Even though I had given up all rights to you, you always were and always will be my darling girl. And so will Jessica.' A thought occurred to her then and she asked tentatively, 'Does she know about any of this?'

Olivia shook her head. 'No. Robert and I talked about it and he thought it might all be too confusing for her.'

'You and Robert . . . you have a lot in common, don't you?' Dilly said, and for the first time since she'd arrived a small smile hovered on Olivia's lips. Dilly's suspicions were confirmed. Olivia was in love with her doctor boyfriend.

'Rob . . . Dr Male is a very clever man.' She crossed to stare from the window. 'And he's very fond of Jessica.'

'And of you too, if I'm any judge,' Dilly said quietly. A silence stretched between them then until Gwen appeared with a tea tray followed closely by Jessica, who had been told to stay in the kitchen.

'Sorry, Mummy, but I heard Dilly and I wanted to see her,' the child cried, launching herself at Dilly as if she hadn't seen her for a month at least.

Dilly's arms automatically went around her and Olivia couldn't help but feel touched. Dilly had openly adored the child since the first moment she had laid eyes on her, and now she knew why. Dilly was Jessica's grandmother.

'May she stay and have some biscuits with us? Just for a few minutes?' Dilly pleaded.

'I suppose so.'

The atmosphere was a little more relaxed now that the child was present and Dilly was grateful. For the first time in her whole life she felt as if she didn't know what to say to her own daughter. Eventually, however, she rose saying, 'I suppose I should be off. But I hope you'll understand a little more about why I did what I did, now that I've explained the reasons. Please try, Olivia. All I've ever wanted for you was the best.'

When no answer was forthcoming she pecked Jessica on the cheek and left the room. There was nothing more she could do now. The ball was well and truly in Olivia's court.

She was waiting impatiently for Max to visit that evening and when he did, the first thing Dilly asked was, 'How is Olivia?'

'Well, if it's any consolation I think she's equally as angry and confused with me as she is with you.' He rubbed his forehead where a headache was beginning to throb. 'She says she can't understand how I could have kept such a secret from her for so long. At present I truly don't know where this is all going to end.'

'Have you heard any more from Samuel?'

Max shook his head. It had hurt him to send his son away but he didn't see what else he could have done in the circumstances. 'Not a peep. He'll probably go to ground for a time now. Until his money runs out anyway, then he'll be back like a bad smell. But I'll tell you something, Dilly, he'll not get another penny from me. I meant it when I said he has to start being more responsible. He's not a child any more, for Christ's sake, and look at all the damage he's caused. No – enough is enough and I mean it this time. I shall never be able to forgive him for what he's done.'

'Never is a long time,' Dilly said quietly, feeling his pain. 'He is still your flesh and blood and we tend to forgive our children anything eventually.'

'Well, I shan't,' Max said adamantly.

In the Farthing household, Oscar and Olivia were sitting together in the drawing room. Lately they had become close again and it seemed natural to talk about what had happened.

'I was sorry to hear about you and Penelope getting divorced,' she told him sincerely. It was strange now she came to think of it. Not so very long ago she could hardly bear to see them together, yet since she had met Robert all that had changed.

Oscar shrugged. Inside he was quite surprised at how Penelope's decision had affected him too. Once he had done nothing but compare her to Olivia, but since he'd met Cora . . .

'It's probably for the best and I don't blame her for wanting a divorce,' he admitted. 'I should never have married her in the first place.' Then, deciding that he could confide in Olivia, he went on, 'In actual fact I've developed feelings for someone else. She doesn't know about it yet, but if she'd be prepared to wait until the divorce is over . . . well who knows.'

'It wouldn't be that young designer, Cora, who works for Dilly by any chance, would it?' Olivia asked with a smile.

Oscar blushed and nodded. 'I rather think you've got your eyes set on someone too. Robert Male is a nice chap by anyone's standards. Am I right?'

Now it was Olivia's turn to blush. 'We are fond of each other,' she said. 'And we have so much in common. Robert wants to open his own orphanage for children with disabilities and specialise in paediatric care and I'd love to be involved.' Her face clouded then. 'The trouble is, I'm not who I thought I was. Will he think less of me?'

'Not if he really cares about you,' Oscar said sensibly. 'And you could do a lot worse than have Dilly Carey as your mother. I think she's quite remarkable. Look at how hard she's worked to get to where she is. How many other women do you know like that?'

'But she denied me the chance of knowing my real father by giving me away as she did,' Olivia said tearfully.

'From what I can make of it she didn't have much choice. It was either agree to let you go or lose *all* her children. What would you have done in that situation? Think about it – it must have broken her heart.'

'I suppose you're right,' Olivia sighed. She would certainly have a lot of thinking to do over the next few days, that was for sure. And she had to admit that she had always liked Dilly . . . Well, more than liked her really. She couldn't remember a time when Dilly hadn't been there, in fact. Now she knew why.

Chapter Forty-Five

'*Mr Farthing! Mr Farthing!*'

'W-what?' Max snapped awake and blinked blearily in the darkness. He'd been sound asleep. 'What is it?'

'It's me, sir, Gwen – an' I'm sorry to disturb you but there's two policemen at the door askin' to see you.'

Knuckling the sleep from his eyes, Max put the bedside lamp on and peered at the clock. It was 2 a.m. What could the police possibly want with him at this hour?

'All right. Thank you, Gwen. Show them into the drawing room and tell them I'll be down shortly.'

'Right y'are, sir.'

He heard her pad away as he rolled out of bed and into his dressing robe, then after pushing his feet into his slippers he yawned and made his way downstairs. As he passed Olivia's bedroom door she also appeared, having heard the commotion, and asked, 'What's wrong?'

'I've no idea. The police need to speak to me. But you go back to bed, darling. I'll deal with it, whatever it is.'

'Not on your own, you won't.' She fastened the belt on her dressing gown. 'I'm coming down with you. It must be something serious for them to come calling at this hour of the morning.'

Max didn't bother to argue. He knew there would be no point once Olivia had made her mind up about something. They entered the drawing room side by side to find two solemn-faced policemen standing to attention in the centre of the room.

'Right, gentlemen, what can I do for you?' Max asked.

The older of the two, who had sergeant's stripes on the arm of his uniform, removed his helmet and cleared his throat. 'Are you Mr Maxwell Farthing?'

'I am.'

'And are you the father of Mr Samuel Farthing?'

'I am.'

'Then I suggest you might like to sit down, sir. I'm afraid I may have some rather bad news for you.'

The colour drained from Max's face as he felt his way round a chair and sank on to it. He suddenly felt as if his legs didn't belong to him.

'Go on then,' he said hoarsely.

The two policemen exchanged a glance and the older one said gravely, 'A body was found on the rough ground in Tomkinson Road about two hours ago, and we have reason to believe that it may be that of your son, sir. I'm so sorry but I have to ask you if you would accompany me to the morgue to formally identify it.'

Max gasped as Olivia grasped his shoulder. He felt the world tilt and spin but with an enormous effort he managed to hold himself together.

'I . . . yes, of course. If you would just wait here while I go and get dressed?'

'Of course, sir. Take your time, there's no hurry.'

Olivia was quietly crying as Max left the room in a daze. Of course, he reasoned, there must be some mistake. The body couldn't be Samuel's. As long as he made himself believe that, he could face the ordeal ahead.

An hour later, Max stood outside a door within the mortuary plucking up the courage to enter. The older of the policemen patted his arm. He had a son about the same age as the young chap that had been found dead tonight, and he could only imagine what hell this poor man must be going through.

A small balding man in thick bull's-eye lens spectacles and a starched white coat coughed discreetly as Max stood there as if he had been turned to stone.

'Whenever you're ready, sir.'

Max took a deep breath. The sooner he got this over with, the sooner he could go home. There was no possibility that the body through that door could be Samuel's.

'I'm ready.'

The mortician opened the door and ushered Max ahead of him into a cold, soulless room with bare walls and a stone floor. A large table stood in the centre of the room and on it lay a body covered entirely with a crisp white sheet. The mortician took his place at the head of the table and after a nod from Max he turned back the top part of the sheet to reveal the face of the corpse.

Max stared for a moment then closed his eyes as tightly as he could to shut out the sight of his son's lifeless face. He and Samuel had parted on bad terms. Max had told him that he was dead to him – and now he would never be able to tell him otherwise.

'It . . . it is my son,' he said brokenly, and when he swayed the larger of the policemen gripped his elbow and led him quickly from the room. The chap pressed him on to a wooden chair.

'Lean forward and put your head between your knees,' the kindly police officer advised. 'And take deep breaths until you start to feel better.'

Max stifled the urge to laugh. Feel better, he'd never feel better again! But he did as he was told all the same. Eventually, when he had a grip on his emotions once more, he asked, 'How did it happen?'

'It was murder,' the policeman told him bluntly. 'It looks like someone came at him from behind and stabbed him then left him for dead. I'm so sorry. Did your son have any enemies that you know of?'

Max snorted. Where should he begin? Samuel had made enough enemies to write a list of them. But surely none of them would have resorted to murder? He shook his head. Of course they would. And someone had – although at the moment he had no idea who it might be.

'I'm afraid my son was a bit of a gambler so I suppose he had a few enemies but I can't think of anyone who would want to murder him.'

'Very well. When you're ready we'll get you home, but rest assured we will begin investigations immediately.'

Dilly was waiting for him when he got back to Mill House. Gwen had run to fetch her and she and Olivia were sitting stiffly in the drawing room waiting for him.

Dilly rose immediately he entered the room. 'Was it . . .?'

When he nodded, her hand flew to her mouth.

'Someone stabbed him,' Max said woodenly. It still hadn't properly sunk in. Dilly wanted to rush to him and wrap him in her arms but with Olivia looking on she daren't, so instead she crossed to the cut-glass decanter

393

and poured him a stiff whisky. She had hated Samuel for what he had done – but she would never have wished this on him. But someone had, she thought grimly.

Two days later, as Seamus was preparing for work, there was a loud banging on the front door.

'Who would that be at this time of the morning?' Bessie said as she hurried into the hallway to answer it. Primrose skipped behind her as happy as the day was long. Bessie had promised to take her to the park today to feed the ducks if it wasn't too cold. She opened the door to find two policemen standing on the doorstep.

'Mrs Bessie Ward?'

Bessie frowned as she wiped her hands on her apron. 'Yes.'

'We are here to arrest you for the suspected murder of Mr Samuel Farthing. Would you please accompany us to the station.'

'What the hell is going on here?' Seamus blustered as he came to stand behind them and lifted Primrose into his arms. Sensing that something was wrong, the child had started to whimper.

'They're saying that I killed Samuel,' Bessie said in a wobbly voice. The newspapers had been full of his murder the day before.

'But this is preposterous,' Seamus said angrily. 'Bessie wouldn't hurt a fly.'

'We believe otherwise sir,' the officer informed him, flipping open his notebook. 'A witness came forward who saw Mrs Ward and Mr Farthing have a row in the street a while back, and she says that you threatened to kill him.'

'It was just a figure of speech!' Bessie exclaimed. She could remember the incident clearly. 'He was trying to get money off me and I lost my temper.'

'You can tell us all that at the station. Now would you kindly fetch your coat and come with us willingly, please? We don't want to have to use force, now do we?'

As Bessie looked at Seamus helplessly he said, 'Do as they say, pet. But don't worry, I shall be going to see a solicitor first thing, never you fear.'

Bessie untied her apron and white-faced, fetched her coat from the coat rack. Seamus kissed her awkwardly on the cheek and smiled far more confidently than he felt.

'Don't say anything until I get a solicitor to the station to you,' he warned and her lip trembled as she kissed Primrose goodbye. And then Seamus watched as the police led her away, one on either side of her like a common criminal, and loaded her into the back of a police van. Curtains were twitching up and down the street. Some of the neighbours had even come out to openly gawp at what was going on but Seamus saw none of it. He was too busy wrapping Primrose up warmly before setting off to see Max. He would know what to do.

'They've arrested Bessie,' Seamus gasped breathlessly when Gwen showed him into the drawing room at Mill House. Max was sitting in an armchair, too shocked and distressed to even think of going to work, but Seamus's words made his head snap up.

'What?'

'The police – they've taken Bessie on suspicion of murdering your son.'

Max sat upright. 'But that's ridiculous. I know Bessie had good cause to hate him for what he did to her, but I don't for one minute believe she'd do something like that.'

'She wouldn't – and I've come to ask for your help. Can you recommend a good solicitor? I've advised her not to say anything until I can get one to the station to her.'

Galvanised out of his despair, Max rose and hastily

395

fetched his personal address book. 'I'll get my own solicitor, Cummings, on to it straight away. He's the best there is.' Then without another word he hurried away to make a call. Bessie was the mother of his grandson Roderick, and there was no way he believed her capable of murdering her son's father.

When the news of what had happened reached Dilly later that day, she groaned. Nell had heard it from one of the customers in the shop who had almost broken her neck to tell her, and she had instantly closed up and rushed home to tell Dilly.

'Seamus will be worried sick,' Dilly told Nell. 'I must go to him. Perhaps he and Primrose could stay here while this sorry mess is sorted out?'

'O' course they can,' Nell readily agreed. 'I can look after the little 'un while he's off doin' what needs to be done. Cora could allus go back into the shop fer a few days, I'm sure she wouldn't mind.' But Dilly was already heading out of the door. Suddenly keeping the shop open wasn't so important in the greater scheme of things.

She found Seamus with his head in his hands and Primrose running amok. 'What's happening?' she asked the instant she set foot through the door. So Seamus told her as Dilly lifted Primrose into her arms.

'I can't do anything with her,' Seamus wailed. 'She just keeps running around asking where Bessie is. She won't eat or settle down an' she's wet the bed last night.'

'Well, you have to realise that Bessie is the closest to a mother she's ever had,' Dilly pointed out. 'She's cared for Primmy since the day she was born. But don't fret. We'll soon have her out of there. Meantime I'm going to pack some things up, and you and Primmy are coming to stay with me until Bessie is home again.'

Seamus meekly nodded. Without Bessie to organise

396

everything, he felt lost. But it wasn't just that. Now that she was no longer there, he suddenly realised that he missed her.

'In actual fact the police are questioning two suspects, and they're combing the area looking for a third,' Mr Cummings informed them all later that evening in Dilly's home. Nell had taken Primrose off to bed, Archie had gone to the local for a pint, and Max and Oscar had come to Dilly's where they'd agreed to meet the solicitor. Cora was there too. The young lass, who was now considered to be part of the family, had stayed on late to see if there was anything she could do.

'They've also arrested a chap called Roger Bannerman and now they're looking for Mickey Noon, a well-known villain to whom Samuel owed money.'

'Roger Bannerman?' Max narrowed his eyes thoughtfully. 'That name is familiar. I'm sure Olivia used to attend the local Amateur Dramatics Society with him some years ago.'

'Hmm, well, it appears that Samuel was blackmailing him and for some time apparently,' Mr Cummings answered. 'I don't as yet know what for, however.'

'When can I see Bessie?' Seamus asked. He wasn't really interested in the other two suspects.

'I should be able to wangle you a short visit tomorrow after they've done interviewing her,' the elderly man told him. 'But I can't promise it, of course. I'm also trying to negotiate bail for her.'

'I'll stand bail for her regardless of the cost,' Max chipped in, and Mr Cummings made a note.

'How did she seem?' Seamus asked then.

'Confused, upset – but most of all worried about how you and your daughter will manage,' the man said.

Seamus nodded. That was typical of Bessie. She was at risk of being hanged if she was found guilty, yet her one thought was about him and Primmy.

'The problem is, Bessie doesn't have a very good alibi,' Mr Cummings went on. 'On the night of the murder she told the police that she was in alone with Primrose while you were out with a business client, and that she was asleep in bed by the time you came home.'

'That's right,' Seamus agreed, wishing to God that he'd stayed in.

'The police have pointed out quite correctly that in actual fact she could have gone out and done the murder then crept back into the house after you were home and asleep. Unless you could verify that she was in bed when you got home, that is?'

Seamus shook his head in despair. 'Well, of course I can't. I don't make a habit of going into Bessie's room.'

'That's what I thought.' The solicitor sighed and tapped his chin. It had been a very long day and all he wanted was his bed now. 'Anyway, there's no more we can do at this stage so I'll wish you all good night. And never fear, I shall be at the police station first thing in the morning and I'll keep you all informed of events.'

'Thank you, sir.' Max shook his hand and saw him to the door while Cora went off to the kitchen to make a pot of tea. They seemed to be surviving on the stuff at the minute.

'I'll come and help,' Oscar volunteered and the two slipped away.

'I was sorry to hear about you and your wife – getting divorced, I mean,' Cora said awkwardly as she filled the kettle at the sink.

'Don't be.' Oscar took a seat at the kitchen table. 'To be honest we've never been happy together so it's for the best. Penelope is being very reasonable about it under the circumstances, and also very fair about me seeing George, which is my main concern.' He looked embarrassed then as he said, 'The thing is, Cora . . . divorces can be quite long-drawn-out affairs although the solicitor who's handling it said that because neither of us is contesting it, it could all be over in a year or so. Now I know this is probably completely the wrong time to say anything, but . . . well, I've grown very fond of you and I thought – I mean – I wondered if perhaps, if you were prepared to wait until I'm free, we could possibly . . .'

'I would wait for ever for you if need be, Oscar,' she said firmly and he was so shocked that his mouth dropped open.

'You would?'

She nodded. 'Yes, I would.'

'Then I'll say no more for now. It wouldn't be right while I'm still married to someone else, but one day . . .'

Her sweet smile gave Oscar hope and suddenly the future looked brighter – for him at least.

Chapter Forty-Six

'You are allowed to go to the station and see her for one fifteen-minute visit this afternoon,' Mr Cummings informed Seamus the following day. It was lunchtime and the elderly solicitor had been at the police station all day whilst Bessie was being interviewed yet again.

'Will they still not agree to bail?' Seamus asked despairingly.

Mr Cummings shook his head. 'I'm afraid not. They are still holding Mr Bannerman too from what I could gather, but they haven't managed to track down Mickey Noon yet.'

'I see.' Seamus was distraught. Nell and Dilly had been wonderful with Primrose but the little girl was pining badly for Bessie. So was he, he realised with a shock. 'What time can I see her?'

The solicitor glanced at his pocket watch. 'Two o'clock – an hour from now.'

'Nell, would you mind—?'

'If you were goin' to ask would I look after Primrose then the answer is yes,' Nell told him. 'Now you go off an' smarten yerself up a bit. Yer don't want Bessie seein' yer lookin' like that. Yer don't look like you've had a wink o' sleep.'

Once Seamus had left the room, she and Dilly turned their attention back to the solicitor and Dilly asked worriedly, 'How are things looking for Bessie, Mr Cummings?'

He let out a sigh: 'Not good, Mrs Carey. Not good at all, I'm afraid. It seems that Mr Bannerman may be released this afternoon as he has a very good alibi for the evening that Samuel Farthing was murdered. The problem is, whilst Mrs Ward has denied murdering Samuel she openly admits that she is glad he is dead and says that she wishes she'd had the guts to do it.'

'Hardly surprising when you consider that he raped her and left her with child!' Dilly defended her hotly.

'I quite agree, but you must see that it isn't going to look good when she goes in front of the magistrate tomorrow morning.'

'What do you think they will decide?' Dilly asked, fearful again now.

'Well, it's looking like they may well hold her in custody while the investigation continues,' he replied truthfully. 'The only good thing is, I don't think they'll officially charge her with murder until they've tracked down Mickey Noon.'

'But he could be anywhere,' Dilly answered, appalled. 'What will happen if they don't find him?'

'Let's cross that bridge when we come to it, shall we? There's no point in getting yourself all upset,' the man said kindly.

Dilly began to pace up and down like a caged animal. It

was all so unfair from where she was standing. What if Bessie were to hang for something she didn't do? Just the thought of it made Dilly break out in a sweat but she knew that she must hold herself together for Seamus and Primmy's sake. Even Max didn't believe that Bessie was capable of such a thing – and it was his own son who had been murdered!

Seamus was at the police station fifteen minutes early. The desk sergeant led him downstairs to the cells and eventually he unlocked one of them and told him, 'Fifteen minutes, sir.'

As Seamus entered, the cell door clanged shut behind him and the sound echoed hollowly around the restricted space. He found himself in a tiny room with nothing but a narrow bed and a small barred window high up on the far wall. All he could see through it was a patch of leaden grey sky, and he wondered how Bessie could endure it. The floor was stone, the walls were bare and the smell of stale urine hung in the air.

Bessie was sitting straight-backed on the bed; there was nowhere else for her to sit and when she raised her eyes to him he was struck by how ill she looked. Her eyes seemed to have sunk back into their sockets and she had shrunk.

'Oh, Bessie.' He sat down beside her and took one of her cold hands in his. 'How are you bearing up, lass? Please know we are doing all we possibly can to get you out of here. Are they treating you all right?'

She lowered her head before saying quietly, 'They've been very kind to me actually but I didn't do it, Seamus, I swear I didn't – although I wanted to when I said those words to him. As God is my witness, I am innocent.'

'You don't have to tell me that. We all know you are innocent, even Mr Farthing,' Seamus assured her.

She licked her lips then and confided, 'The day we had the row – when we were overheard, me an' Samuel – he . . . he told me something terrible.'

'What was it?'

She gulped. She had kept the terrible secret for so long that it would be a relief to finally confide in someone now. 'He . . . he told me it was him who had killed little Constance so that Niamh would give him a divorce.'

When Seamus gasped she went on, 'An' that bloke that were murdered – Snowy White, it were plastered all across the newspapers for a while, if you remember? – Samuel told me that he killed him too. I'd always had my suspicions because Snowy had come to the house on the day he was murdered and I heard him shouting at Samuel.'

'My God, have you told the police this?'

Tears rained down her face. 'No, I was too afraid of what it would do to Niamh and Dilly. Even the doctor was surprised on the night the poor little lamb died. We all thought she'd turned the corner an' was goin' to get better, but then Samuel came round an' we gave him a few minutes alone with her – an' she died then. He must have suffocated her with the pillow or somethin', God rest her angelic soul. I've had nightmares about it ever since but I kept quiet. So you see, I did have a motive for killin' him. The police will never believe that I didn't when this comes out.'

'I disagree,' Seamus told her. 'If anything, it will show them what a thoroughly bad lot Samuel was. You *have* to tell them, Bessie, for mine and Primmy's sake at least. We can't do without you!'

She saw that there were tears on his cheeks too and stared at him open-mouthed.

'The thing is,' he bumbled on, 'I've developed feelin's for you . . .'

'Don't be so daft,' she hissed. 'I'm over nine years older than you an' you loved your Mary!'

'Age doesn't matter,' Seamus told her matter-of-factly. 'And yes – I did love my Mary with all my heart and soul. But the love I feel for you is different. It feels right to have you living with us and I'm very fond of you, Bessie, far more than I'd realised till all this happened. I look forward to coming home to you each evening after work. I love the way you care for Primmy and I've no need to tell you that she adores you. Sadly, she never knew her real mother but you've taken her place in her heart. Do you think you could ever feel anything for me?'

'Well,' she answered cautiously, 'I do love being with you and Primmy. I've been happy with you both and can't imagine life without either of you now . . . but you see, my Malcolm was the love of my life. There's no one could ever take his place.'

'I wouldn't want to,' Seamus assured her sincerely. 'We've both loved and lost, but surely we could find peace again with each other?'

She blinked and sniffed before telling him shyly, 'Do yer know, I rather think we could – if I get out o' this mess, that is. If not, we both know where I'm headed – fer the hangman's noose.'

'Over my dead body!' Seamus said grimly. 'And that's why I'm going to send Mr Cummings in and you're going to tell him what you've just told me. Please, for any future that we might have together, will you do that for me, Bessie?'

She nodded slowly.

Dilly was heartbroken when Seamus told her of what Samuel had done that evening. Max was horrified too and they sobbed on each other's shoulders for their tiny

404

granddaughter's stolen life. And then suddenly, something occurred to Dilly.

'My God – I've just realised! Now that Samuel is gone, Niamh and Ben will be free to get wed.'

'You're right. We must get in touch with them straight away. But Dilly, let's not tell them about what Samuel did to Constance just yet. I don't want to cause Niamh any more grief. Do you agree?'

'Yes,' she answered solemnly. 'Shall we just go and send them a telegram and tell them that Samuel is no longer alive and so they're free to marry?'

'Max nodded. 'Yes – and then at least something good will have come of this whole tragic mess.' Thank God Camilla is beyond understanding that her son is dead.'

Bessie appeared before the magistrate the following morning and as Mr Cummings had expected she was remanded in custody pending further investigations. Seamus's spirits were as low as they could get, but then late that afternoon as they all sat brooding at Dilly's house, a constable arrived to tell them that Mickey Noon had been arrested in Bedworth.

'He was holed up with one of his gambling chums and he put up a rare old fight when we found him,' he told them. Then, shuffling from foot to foot, he confided, 'Strictly speaking, I shouldn't be here telling you this, but none of the chaps down at the station have liked having to hold Mrs Ward. She's a good lass an' none of us believe she's guilty. There's something else as well. Noon had Mr Farthing's wallet on him and there were bloodstains on his clothes.'

Seamus's heart leaped with hope. 'So what will happen now?'

'They're interviewing him right now but between you

and me I reckon they've got him dead to rights. Samuel Farthing didn't turn up for a card game they'd arranged by all accounts and he owed Noon a lot of money so Noon must have gone looking for him. He was also in possession of Samuel Farthing's car.'

'Thank God,' Seamus murmured, then extending his hand he said to the constable, 'Thank you for telling us this. Will you keep us informed?'

'It'll be my pleasure, sir.' And with that the constable replaced his helmet and quietly went back on his beat, leaving them all on tenterhooks. Surely the nightmare would be over soon now?

The nightmare ended at three o'clock the next day when Mickey Noon was formally charged with the murder of Mr Samuel Farthing and Bessie was released without charge.

Seamus was waiting as she was led up from the cells and she fell into his arms, sobbing her heart out.

'It's all right,' he soothed, stroking the damp hair from her brow. 'It's all over. Now come along, I'm taking you home.' And that was exactly what he did.

Chapter Forty-Seven

July 1930

Nell and Dilly were in the kitchen in St Edwards's Road when word reached them that Bessie had been released without charge. The waiting had been unbearable, but now at last it was over.

'Thank you so much for coming to tell me, Max,' Dilly said quietly as he stared at her in concern. She was as white as a sheet and looked extremely unwell and completely exhausted. All that had happened over the last few months had clearly caught up with her.

'Seamus must be so relieved . . .' Dilly began, then to everyone's horror she suddenly gave a little gasp, clutched at her chest and crumpled into a heap on the floor.

Max was at her side in an instant, snapping, 'Nell, ask Archie to run for the doctor.'

All of a fluster, Nell ran outside to find Archie as Max sat on the floor holding Dilly in his arms. She was completely unconscious and as tears ran down his face he rocked her gently to and fro and prayed as he had never prayed before, 'Please, dear God, don't take her from me now.'

'She's had a slight stroke,' the doctor informed them an hour later. 'Mrs Carey is going to need complete rest for at least a month, and she should take this as a warning. This time she's been lucky, but if she carries on as she is doing there's no saying what will happen next time.'

'I'll make sure as she don't lift a finger, doctor,' Nell vowed. 'I tell you, I've been expectin' somethin' like this fer ages. She pushes herself too hard – she allus has.'

Max was heartily grateful that Nell was there to take charge of things. Nell could be quite formidable when she wanted to be and he had no doubt she'd take Dilly in hand. Not before time, as far as he was concerned.

As Nell and Archie sat in the garden with Dilly late in July listening to the birds and enjoying the afternoon sun, Dilly suddenly said, 'Do you know what, Nell? I think I'm ready to go and say my goodbyes to Kian now.'

'Huh! An' about time too,' Nell replied approvingly. She knew how hard it would be for Dilly, but she also knew that her old friend would never know real peace until it was done. The last few months had been difficult for all of them, but Nell thought that it was perfect timing. A break away would do her the world of good. In the weeks since she had suffered her stroke Nell had fussed over her like a mother hen and refused to let her do a thing, but now at last, Dilly was looking more like her old self again. It had been a difficult time for Dilly, having to sit back and be waited on, and she had been forced to do a lot of soul-searching. Her head told her that she was still a young woman, but now her body was telling her that it truly was time to slow down.

One of the few bright spots of the last few months was the news from New York that Niamh and Ben were now legally wed and expecting a little brother or sister for James. The other had been the very quiet register office wedding of Seamus and Bessie. The pair had married early in March with only the family present and Primrose acting as their tiny flower girl. They had refused any kind of celebrations to follow the marriage but thankfully they seemed happy enough and Dilly could only pray that it would last. They had all known enough heartache to last for their entire lifetimes. Now, as if thoughts of them had conjured them up from thin air, the couple walked through the garden gate with Primmy skipping ahead of them.

'Mammy and Daddy have some nice news,' she told Dilly, scrambling on to her lap. She'd started to call Bessie 'Mammy' soon after the wedding and Dilly thought it was no bad thing.

'Oh yes – and what would that be then?' she asked, tickling her grandchild under her chin.

'I is goin' to have a baby brother or sister,' Primrose declared importantly. 'But not for a long time 'cos Mammy has to wait for the stork to bring it.'

Dilly's shocked eyes flew to Bessie, and she coloured becomingly.

'I know – it's mad, isn't it, another baby at my age – but there it is. If it's a girl we're goin' to call it Rose – for Mary. She always wanted her girls named after flowers, didn't she, pet?'

Seamus smiled affectionately at his wife and Dilly's heart soared with joy. At long last, all was finally going well for all her children.

'That's wonderful news, I couldn't be more thrilled for you,' she told the happy couple with a catch in her voice.

'It is that,' Nell joined in, handing Primrose one of the

jam tarts she'd made that afternoon. 'Archie, go an' fetch the sherry out here, this calls fer a celebration.' And her husband good-humouredly plodded away to do as he was told.

'I've got some news as well,' Dilly said then, 'though nowhere near as exciting as yours, of course. I've decided to go to France and visit Kian's grave.'

Seamus frowned. 'Are you sure you're well enough, and are you ready for it, Mammy?' he asked worriedly.

Dilly nodded. 'I don't know if anyone is ever ready for something like that, but I'm as ready as I'll ever be and thanks to Nell I'm feeling much better. I certainly won't be missed here so I might make a little holiday of it while I'm at it. Cora has the design team well and truly in order, and you lot are so efficient that you really don't need me to oversee the businesses any more. The past few weeks have proved that, and I'm beginning to feel somewhat surplus to requirements.'

'Well, I don't know about that, but a holiday would certainly do you good,' Seamus said, his voice tender. 'You've been really poorly, Mammy. In fact, you gave us all quite a scare.'

She patted his arm. 'Bless you for caring, pet. I'm fine now, it's just that we've all been through so much . . . Anyway, we won't think of that now. Only happy thoughts, eh? I might go off and book the holiday tomorrow while the weather is still fine.'

'I could come with you, if you like?' Seamus offered. He didn't like the idea of his mother going off all alone just yet.

Dilly chuckled. 'You'll do no such thing. You'll stay here and keep my businesses running smoothly for me and look after your wife and family, my lad.'

'Yes, ma'am!' He gave her a mock salute, which Primrose

410

promptly copied and soon they were all laughing, and the joyful sound echoed around the garden.

'I might pop round and see Max,' Dilly said a little later when everyone had gone. It was a beautiful evening and she was feeling rather restless. She and Olivia were once again on speaking terms, although the ease that had once existed between them was no longer there. It was sad, but Dilly was wise enough to know that it was all in Olivia's hands now. At least she had come to see her while she'd been confined to bed, which Dilly hoped was a good sign. Hopefully one day Olivia would forgive her. If only, she thought and then stopped herself. There was one more secret that she had carried for many years that made her wake at night in a cold sweat. A secret she had never shared with anyone, not even Nell, her most trusted friend. *But perhaps one day I shall be able to share it*, she told herself . . .

She found Max in his study poring over his ledgers, but he closed them when she appeared and asked, 'Hello, Dilly. I wasn't expecting you. Should you be out on your own yet?'

'Stop fussing,' she told him. 'I'm fine now and actually I've made a decision. I'm going to France just as soon as I can to visit Kian's grave. I think it's time, don't you?'

'Would you like me to come with you?' he offered. He knew how long she had been bracing herself to do this, and he knew that it wasn't going to be easy for her.

'Thank you, but no. You should be here, especially as Camilla is so ill.'

'She'll pull through, she always does,' he answered, splashing brandy into two glasses. Then handing one to her he asked, 'Is there anything else on your mind?'

411

She hesitated before shaking her head. 'No, nothing. Is Olivia not in?'

'No. She and Robert have gone to look at an old house in Henry Street that he thinks would be perfect for a children's home. Between you and me, I think they'll be making an announcement any time now. They seem completely compatible.'

'Are things any better between you?' she asked then, and he sighed.

'Not really. Oh, she's always polite but I don't think she can get past the fact that I'm not her real father. I doubt she'll ever truly forgive me for the deception.'

Dilly knew then that it was time for the truth, and taking a deep breath she steeled herself to tell him, 'But . . . you are!'

His head snapped up as he stared at her and she told him gently, 'That one night we shared so long ago . . . we both felt so guilty afterwards so I blocked it from my mind. Do you remember it, or have you blocked it too?'

Guilty colour crawled up his neck as he whispered, 'No, Dilly, I haven't blocked it or forgotten a single second. How could I?'

'I've lived with the guilt of what we did for too long,' she told him. 'But just remember, we were both at such a low ebb . . . it would never have happened otherwise. You loved your wife and I loved my husband. We were just comforting each other and things got out of hand.'

Unbidden, both their minds wandered back to the night when Max had entered his library to find Dilly making up the fire just before she finished work for the day. She'd been requested to come and wait on table at a dinner party at Mill House, but Camilla had called it off at the eleventh hour, so Dilly had done a few odd jobs for Mrs Pegs instead. She'd been crying when Max found her, worried

412

sick about how she was going to make ends meet now that Fergal had been crippled, and Max himself had been heartsore at the death of his little daughter Violet. It had seemed so natural when he placed his arm about her shoulders to offer her solace and then suddenly he was crying too and they had comforted each other and one thing had led to another. Before they knew it, they had made love there on the rug in front of a roaring fire, and at the time it had seemed the most beautiful thing in the world.

When it was over they were both horrified at what they had done and had never mentioned the incident since, but looking back now, Max knew that that was when his feelings for Dilly had begun to grow.

'But . . . how can you know be sure Olivia is mine?' he asked incredulously and Dilly smiled sadly.

'Women have a way of knowing. My body told me within days of us lying together – there were signs – and long before Fergal and I lay together again, I knew I was carrying your child. Anyway, then when Camilla wanted to take Olivia I felt that I wasn't being completely heartless to let her go because she would be being brought up by her natural father.'

'But – whyever didn't you tell me this before?' he asked with a look of amazement on his face.

'Because you didn't need to know. You felt guilty enough about what we'd done as it was. But now . . . well, I think you should explain the truth to Olivia. I doubt she'll ever fully forgive me, but I'd like her to know that you are her natural father, and then perhaps your relationship can go back to the way it was.'

Max hugged her unexpectedly. 'Thank you,' he said chokily. 'You have just given me the most precious gift imaginable. But what if Olivia despises us both even more

413

when she discovers that we were unfaithful to our partners?'

'I can't answer that,' Dilly said truthfully. 'And it's up to you whether you tell her or not. But I'm going to go now, I have packing to do. Good night, Max.'

She wept freely on the way home, oblivious to passers-by who glanced at her curiously. All her secrets were out in the open now and there need be no more lies. She just had to do one more thing now – and then at last she might find the peace she craved.

'You're going *when*?' Nell asked the next morning.

'Tomorrow,' Dilly told her. 'I have to do it now, Nell, while I have the courage – otherwise it could be years again before I feel able to.'

'Then I'd best help you wi' your packing,' Nell said stoically. 'I'll get Archie to fetch some suitcases down from the attic. But how long are you goin' for?'

Dilly shrugged. 'I have no idea, to be honest. It could be for a week or a month or even longer. I'm just going to wait and see how I feel when I get there.'

Nell chewed on her lip worriedly. 'But you'll be so far away, an' all on yer own. How will we know yer safe?'

Dilly chuckled. 'There are telephones. Don't worry, I shall keep in touch.'

Nell knew there was no more to be said and bustled away to get Archie to fetch the suitcases.

'Tomorrow!' Max too was horrified when she told him her plans that evening. 'But it's so soon. Are you sure you'll be all right, travelling all that way all on your own?'

'Of course. I've gone much farther than France before on my own, if you recall.'

'Yes, of course you have. I'm sorry. I suppose I'm just surprised at the speed of things.'

'Well, you should know by now what I'm like when I make my mind up about something.' Avoiding his eyes, she asked, 'Have you spoken to Olivia yet?'

'Only to tell her about your proposed trip. She told me to pass on the message that she hopes it all goes well.'

Dilly's heart ached. Once, Olivia would have come round to tell her herself, but there was nothing she could do about that.

'So shall I come and take you to the station?' Max offered then. 'Or I could even drive you to the ship, if you like.'

'I already have a cab booked,' Dilly told him, although she appreciated the offer.

'Then I shall wish you a safe journey and Godspeed.'

'Thank you.' They stared at each other for a moment with all the things they longed to say hanging in the air between them unsaid . . . then Max turned and left abruptly. He didn't want to prolong their goodbye. Dilly had changed lately and he wasn't even at all sure that she'd come home.

Chapter Forty-Eight

The journey to France was pleasant and uneventful, and once there Dilly travelled by bus and train to the small village of Pozières. The village was six kilometres north-east of the town of Albert and Dilly fell in love with it immediately. It had a relaxed atmosphere about it and the small hotel she had booked into was delightful, with views of rolling fields from her bedroom window.

'How long will Madame be staying, pleez?' the tiny hotel owner asked and Dilly shrugged.

'I haven't decided yet. Will that be a problem?'

'No problem at all, madame. Now come, you must see your room.'

Madame Paschal was a small homely woman with a ready smile and a tight grey bun perched high on the top of her head. It was hard to distinguish her age but Dilly guessed she must at least be in her late sixties.

'It eez a family 'otel,' the woman explained to Dilly as she showed her up the stairs. 'We are not what you English say "posh", but we are cosy, *oui*? Now 'ave you any *préférence* for your evening meal?'

'I'm sure anything you serve will be delicious,' Dilly told her, and she was equally pleased with her room, with its floral wallpaper and French provincial décor.

Once she had unpacked, Dilly strolled about the village in the late-afternoon sunshine. A flower seller stood on one corner and Dilly bought a bunch of lavender for her bedroom. Tiny cafés with tables and chairs outside them were dotted along the high street and she stopped to enjoy a coffee as she sat and watched the world go by. It felt strange to be idle and not constantly on the go, rushing from one place to another, or bent across her work table, but she found that she was enjoying herself. Elderly men sat outside their houses with berets on their heads contentedly puffing on their pipes as children played in the streets, and slowly Dilly felt herself begin to relax. She had already found out that the cemetery where Kian was interred was to the south of the village, but she wasn't quite ready to think about going there, not just yet. It was enough for her to know that she was close to her son.

Three whole weeks passed before she suddenly felt the urge to do what she had come for. The time had passed in a blur of days filled with sunshine the colour of melted butter and cloudless blue skies, but today the sky was overcast. Large stormclouds were rolling across the sky but Dilly knew that the time was right.

'Today you go to visit ze grave of your loved one, yes?' Madame Paschal asked at breakfast as if she was a mind reader. She had many visitors from foreign shores stay at her hotel so that they could visit the graves in the war cemetery. Dilly had asked directions early on in her stay and despite her beautifully cut clothes and her quiet

417

dignity, Madame Paschal had sensed a great loneliness in her.

'I think so,' Dilly answered as Madame Paschal poured more coffee into her cup.

She then pointed towards the sky. 'Do not worry about ze weather. We shall have ze downpour then *pouff*! – ze sun will be out again,' she promised. 'But until then you must borrow an umbrella. I shall fetch you one.'

Dilly smiled as she drained her cup and went to get her bag. It was time.

When she arrived back in the foyer, Madame Paschal was waiting for her with the promised umbrella. 'It eez your husband?' she asked gently.

Dilly shook her head. 'No, my son.'

'Ah, how sad.' The woman shook her head sympathetically. 'It eez a terrible thing to lose a child but you will feel better when you see zat he eez at peace.'

Dilly smiled her thanks and set off. She had decided she would walk. It was not so very far as the crow flew and here she had all the time in the world. But first she stopped at the flower stall and left bearing an armful of pure white lilies.

When she arrived at the cemetery, she stared. It was nothing like she had expected. All along the frontage were tall stone arches broken in the middle by the entrance, which consisted of two enormous wrought-iron gates. Along the sides and the back of the cemetery were large stone tablets fixed into the stone rubble walls bearing the names of the war dead grouped into regiments. But it was the row upon row of white headstones that took her breath away. So very many of them and each someone's son, lover, husband, brother. It seemed such a terrible waste of young lives. The letter bearing the number of Kian's grave had been destroyed many years ago in the fire above

418

Dilly's shop, but even now it was engraved on her heart and she stumbled forward. It was then that the heavens suddenly opened and rain spattered on to her face to mix with her tears. She managed to open the umbrella Madame Paschal had insisted she should take, and moved on. And then at last she came to the row and after walking along it for a while she saw his name. *Kian Carey.*

Blinded by tears and heedless of the rain, she sank to her knees and reverently touched his grave.

'I am here, my darling boy,' she muttered brokenly and just for a moment she sensed him near her and the ache in her heart eased slightly. She had no idea how long she knelt there with the rain pouring down on her. She told him of everything that had happened over the years, and of the nieces and nephews that he had never had the privilege to meet. And then suddenly the rain stopped as abruptly as it had started and within seconds the sun was blazing in the sky again and the dark clouds disappeared as if by magic. Within no time at all the wet grass began to steam gently in the heat from the sun, covering the cemetery in a thin mist.

Dilly gently laid the lilies on Kian's grave and rose from her knees feeling strangely comforted. It was then from the corner of her eye that she saw someone striding towards her, and when she looked in that direction she was convinced that she must be seeing things.

'Max!' she gasped as he drew nearer.

He came to stand beside her and took his hat off respectfully as he stared down at Kian's grave.

'But . . . what are you doing here? And how did you know where I was?'

'I've been here for a few days, as it happens, but I had a few things I needed to do before I came to see you. Madame Paschal told me that I would find you here – remember

419

that you told me before you left what hotel you would be staying at.' Then, very gently: 'Do you feel a bit better now that you've finally come?'

'I do,' she told him, her eyes tight on Kian's gravestone. 'And I've had a lot of time to think while I've been here, and I've come to some decisions. I'm going to sign the businesses over to the children, Max. I'm tired and somehow I don't have the same interest in them as I once did.'

'That's strange, because I've decided to do exactly the same.'

'Really?'

He nodded. 'Yes. I've already handed my businesses over to Lawrence and Oscar. But I'm here for a reason, Dilly. Well, a number of reasons really. Firstly, before you retire there is one more little job I think you might enjoy doing. You see, Olivia and Robert have named the day and she asked me to ask you if you would design her wedding dress for her. She thinks it would be nice to wear one of her mother's designs. And of course, I shall give the bride away.'

'*You told her!*' Dilly breathed.

'Yes, I did. There have been enough lies. I want everything to be out in the open from now on. And Dilly, she forgives us – both of us. When she and Robert are married they'll continue living at Mill House, with Gwen to help out with Jessica. Mrs Pegs has decided to retire, God bless her, and she's going to live with her widowed brother in Yorkshire.'

Happy tears sprang to Dilly's eyes.

'Another reason I am here is to tell you that Camilla passed away the day after you left. Her funeral was last week.'

'Oh, Max. I'm *so* sorry.'

'Don't be,' he said. 'I'm not sorry at all. I did my grieving for Camilla many years ago and her passing was a blessed relief for the poor soul. Even the children are glad that her suffering is over. The funeral was a very quiet affair with only very close family members present. But finally I'm here because . . .' He took a deep breath. 'Because I've been looking around for a nice cottage where I could retire and I found just the right one nestled in the hills over there, just a breath away from the village but so quiet and tranquil that all you can hear there is birdsong and the sigh of the wind in the trees.'

'You're coming to live in *France*?' she gasped.

'Why not?' He grinned at her. 'It's not so very far away if I want to go home regularly to see the children and grandchildren, and they'll enjoy coming to stay here too. I think I've finally earned some time to myself, don't you?'

She nodded. 'I suppose you have.'

'Of course, the cottage will need a woman's touch but I shall leave that side of things to you when we're married.'

'*Married!*'

His laughter rang about the cemetery. 'Well, you didn't think I'd want to live here alone, did you? You could always leave Nell and Archie in your house so that we have somewhere to stay when we want to go home and visit and I rather think it's time I made an honest woman of you – so what do you say? Will you marry me, darling Dilly and help me turn the cottage into a proper home for us?'

She stared at him for a moment with happy tears in her eyes, then linking her arm through his she replied nonchalantly, 'I suppose I shall have to, shan't I, if you put it like that? You always did have appalling taste when it came to interior design. Now come and show me that cottage.' As they walked away, a beautiful rainbow

421

suddenly appeared in the sky right above them, forming a perfect arc. As Dilly looked up at it, and the message of hope it contained, she smiled with all her heart.

Max's eyes followed hers and he squeezed her hand. 'I think that's a sign of good things to come isn't it,' he said quietly, and as the peace she had always craved crept into her soul, Dilly had the strangest feeling that he just might be right.

Epilogue

26th July 1963
Obituary

Mrs Dilly Farthing, the internationally renowned fashion designer, died peacefully in her sleep yesterday at the age of eighty-six in Pozières in France, surrounded by her loving family. She will be buried next week at a private service in France with her beloved husband, Maxwell Farthing, who died late in June.

Mr and Mrs Farthing retired to a cottage in the hills surrounding Pozières following their marriage thirty-three years ago. As well as being a household name in the fashion industry, Mrs Farthing was also known for her charitable deeds. Following her retirement, she set up homes for war veterans and was heavily involved in raising funds for children's charities. She also founded an orphanage, run by her daughter, Olivia, and Olivia's husband, Dr Robert Male, in her home town in the

Midlands. Mr and Mrs Farthing leave behind a number of children, grandchildren and great grandchildren.

Mrs Farthing's son Declan said, 'We would appreciate it if the funeral could be a quiet family affair as my mother would have wished. She was a truly remarkable woman and will be sadly missed by everyone who knew and loved her. Our Dilly was that rarity . . . a true lady.'